Praise for Isabel Ashdown

'Beautifully crafted and satisfying'
MARI HANNAH

'Original and compelling'
HOWARD LINSKEY

'A dark unrelenting psychological thrill ride'
PUBLISHERS WEEKLY

'A brilliant story of friendship and lies with
a twist I never saw coming'
CLAIRE DOUGLAS

'Draws you in, right from the first page'
SAM CARRINGTON

'A taut thriller'
PRIMA MAGAZINE

'A tense and claustrophobic read'
Lesley Thomson

'Twisty, gripping, and utterly unpredictable'
WILL DEAN

'Gripping, clever and beautifully writter'
PHOEBE MORGAN

'Carefully observed, unexpected and mesmerizingly beautiful'
EASY LIVING

'Kept me up three nights in a row'
HOLLY SEDDON

ISABEL ASHDOWN

ONE GIRL, ONE SUMMER

Isabel Ashdown is the author of ten novels. She is also a writing coach, a Royal Literary Fund mentor and host of the 'Get Writing' Facebook group. Her 2009 debut *Glasshopper* was twice named among the Best Books of the Year, and today, her books continue to attract international readers and rave reviews. Isabel lives with her carpenter husband, with whom she has two grown-up children and a pair of ageing dogs. Her happy place is anywhere with a coastal view.

www.isabelashdown.com

You can also find Isabel on:
X @IsabelAshdown
@isabelashdown_writer
IsabelAshdownBooks

Also by Isabel Ashdown

Homecoming
33 Women
Lake Child
Beautiful Liars
Little Sister
Flight
Summer of '76
Hurry Up and Wait
Glasshopper

ISABEL ASHDOWN

ONE GIRL, ONE SUMMER

ORION

First published in Great Britain in 2024 by Orion Fiction
an imprint of The Orion Publishing Group Ltd
Carmelite House, 50 Victoria Embankment
London EC4Y oDZ

An Hachette UK Company

The authorised representative in the EEA is Hachette Ireland,
8 Castlecourt Centre, Dublin 15, D15 XTP3, Ireland (email: info@hbgi.ie)

3 5 7 9 10 8 6 4 2

A CIP catalogue record for this book is
available from the British Library.

ISBN (Mass Market Paperback) 978 1 3987 0392 6
ISBN (eBook) 978 1 3987 0393 3
ISBN (Audio) 978 1 3987 0394 0

Typeset by Born Group
Printed and bound in Great Britain by Clays Ltd, Elcograf S.p.A.

MIX
Paper | Supporting
responsible forestry
FSC
www.fsc.org   FSC® C104740

www.orionbooks.co.uk

For Kate Shaw, my agent and friend

'I wish I were a girl again, half savage and hardy, and free; and laughing at injuries, not maddening under them! Why am I so changed?'

Emily Brontë, *Wuthering Heights*

PART ONE

PART ONE

1. Nell

Saturday

Flashbulb memory. This was the topic, a half-remembered chapter from some psychology textbook, snaking through Nell Gale's mind as she finally reached the dawn-bright summit of Highcap after the long trek from town. A random recollection of facts and revision unlikely ever to be used again, now her studies were over. She leant against the stone marker, her gaze fixed on the shimmering line of the ocean as she zoned out all feeling, mastering her breathing, her thoughts.

Her recollection of the night before, indistinct as it was, seemed to Nell as vague and unsettling as a hazy nightmare half-vanished the morning after, and she prayed that that might be the case. Because memory was a strange thing, an unreliable thing, wasn't it? And, if she worked hard enough at reshaping the small parts she *did* recall, perhaps she might convince herself that last night never happened at all.

That she'd never been there, off her face on vodka, stumbling down that foul-smelling alleyway, *out of control*.

3

She checked her watch, her stomach turning at the sight of its scratched glass face and the unmistakable strands of dark hair caught in the strap. *Not hers.*

Almost without thought, she tore the watch from her wrist, digging her fingers deep into the soil at the edge of the marker, to bury both it and the night before beneath the dry earth of Highcap summit. With a rush of cold nausea, she bent over her knees and vomited at the edge of a gorse bush, grateful that, in this moment at least, there was no one around to witness her shame.

Sliding down against the stone, Nell wept a little, and rested awhile. Far below, the main road meandered like a faultline along one side of the campsite, while, to the other, the glistening sea swept the Dorset coastline, a wild blue brushstroke. At this early hour, only a few tiny washbag-clutching figures moved about the grassy plain below, which, from Nell's vantage point, appeared strangely 2-D, made all the more surreal by the recent addition of a giant gold rabbit, positioned on the main path to welcome newcomers to the campsite. Auntie Suzie had officially unveiled 'Goldie' at the start of the season, and Mum, happy enough to drink her sister-in-law's prosecco, had nudged Nell and sniggered and whispered that she thought a better name might be 'Auntie Suzie's Child-Scaring Rabbit'. Why did her mum always have to be such a bitch?

Nell tried to push away thoughts of her mother and rose to her feet again, taking in the rolling green landscape that stretched for miles. This was the one thing she would miss, if she ever got away from this place. This view; this air.

If she ever got away? Because that had always been the plan, hadn't it? To get away. She shook her head at the stupidity of the idea, an idea encouraged by the adults in her life, right up until the moment when her mother had pulled the rug from under her. *Why?* Nell had demanded when they'd argued again yesterday. With A levels and the endless incarceration of school finally behind her, this was meant to be the summer to beat all others, a summer of adventure and independence. Why would her mum, who herself had travelled and experienced all the things Nell wanted for herself, deny her this? Who was she to withhold the money Grandad had gifted *her*?

Down in the campsite, a few more early risers emerged from their mobile homes to potter about like Playmobil people. Despite her desperation to escape the place, Nell could never completely shake her feeling of pride – or perhaps it was belonging – at being part of the Gale family, regardless of the occasional local resentments the name invoked. Theirs was one of the oldest names in Highcap's graveyard, and the Golden Rabbit campsite was built on land owned by their family going back generations, land that was once worthless, turned into a goldmine by her grandfather's father.

It was still one of the prettiest sites around Highcap – one of the smallest, with fewer static homes and a large expanse of grassland given over to hikers' tents and passing tourers. Right now, the on-site farm shop, with its cheery bunting and candy-stripe awning, had not yet opened its doors for the day, and with at least twenty plots still unoccupied, you'd be forgiven for thinking the summer season hadn't yet got underway.

As Nell contemplated her descent, the wind rose, whipping through her red curls and causing her oversized shirt to flap like a sail. She grew aware of a small aeroplane approaching from out over the water, the distant burr of its engine like the pleasing hum of a lawnmower on a lazy Sunday morning. How ordinary she must appear to the approaching pilot, she thought, high overhead in the cloudless sky. How carefree. Ha, if they only knew the half of it.

In a sudden change of direction, the plane swooped away again, veering off along the coast and further out above the shimmering water. Nell wished she were in that small plane; she wished she were anywhere but here, nearly nineteen and still at home, while the best of her friends headed off to uni and the worst of them stuck around, seemingly happy enough to stay in Highcap forever, having babies and marrying the boy next door.

She checked the time on her phone. It wasn't yet 7 a.m., and, other than that circling plane, all was still. The main road below had been empty for at least the past ten minutes. But now, a vehicle appeared, and, as it turned in through the campsite gates below, she recognised it as her mother's battered orange Citroën. Nell traced its journey along the well-tended path, past Goldie and the farm shop and the various communal blocks, until it stopped near the children's playground in a parking bay reserved for staff.

'*Shit.*' At once, Nell remembered she was meant to be home with Albie for Mum's early cleaning shift, a concession she'd grudgingly agreed to last night before she'd slammed the front door on their argument.

'Just get him to tennis practice at eight,' Mum had called after her with a dismissive flap of her fag hand, one foot inside the kitchen, one out the back door. 'Then you can do whatever you like.'

Ha! 'Anything except go travelling?' Nell had yelled back, shrill with rage. But she knew her brother had his under-fourteen championships coming up next month, and she knew he couldn't afford to miss his training, and so, for Albie's sake alone, she'd agreed.

'*Shit-shit-shit,*' she repeated in a low murmur, setting off towards the coastal path with greater purpose now, one eye on the scene below. If she hurried, she could drive Albie to tennis in Mum's car and still get it back in time for the end of her shift.

Nell's distant view was clear enough to see the passenger door of the car fly open and Albie tumble out in his yellow beach-camp sweatshirt, already in a run, board wedged beneath his arm as he headed for the skate ramps. Mum gave a hasty little wave in his direction and turned away. With chaotic red hair bursting like springs from her headscarf, she hurried off to the showers with her cleaning trolley, mobile phone pressed to her ear. Simultaneously, Nell's phone rang in the palm of her hand, and she muted it with a tut and shoved it into the back pocket of her baggy trousers.

Across the camp lawns, a bare-chested young man emerged from a small blue tent, his white sneakers brightly contrasting with the faded red of his cap and scruffy cut-off denim shorts. He pushed his elbows back in a leisurely stretch and slung a towel over his tanned shoulder. Nell wished he'd look up in her direction, and she wondered how old he was, whether he was a good person.

Without turning, he sauntered over the grass, making for the shower block, and Nell continued downwards, picking up pace as an uneasy feeling settled in the pit of her stomach. She was now entirely visible to anyone who might glance up from the campsite below, but she had the strongest sense that if they did, they wouldn't see her; that she had somehow become invisible to all the world. She felt like a ghost, as though the events of the night before had in fact killed her, banished her to the outside.

Overhead, the hum of the aircraft repeated, shaking her back to the present. This time it felt closer, and Nell's hair whipped wilder as the circling plane cast a slow-moving shadow over the rolling hills.

In the distant play area, Albie scaled the highest skate ramp, and Nell, desperate to be seen by her brother, raised her arms high in a double wave, like a stranded explorer sending out an SOS. Albie halted; legs planted wide in a familiar stance of concentration. Her heart lifted. It was how he stood on the tennis court: alert, bouncing the racket head off the palm of his hand, waiting for the serve. After just a beat, he waved back, madly, beckoning her down, his little dancing hop conveying how happy he was to spot his big sister high up on the hill.

Again Nell's phone rang, insistent, and, weakened by the sight of Albie's daisy-bright dance, she brought the ringing phone to her ear.

'Mum?' she answered, raising her voice against the intensi-fying roar of the plane. The ground beneath her grew dark and her own shadow disappeared.

Over on the main road, Auntie Suzie's white Land Rover was now turning in through the gate, with Uncle Elliot's head craning from the open window, his face turned skyward. Nell's heart pounded as the shadow of the plane grew wider and darker and the deep thrum of its engine drowned out all other sound. At the shower blocks, Mum stepped out onto the path and squinted into the sky overhead.

'Mum?' Nell spoke into the phone, but her voice was muffled beneath the roar.

Albie was still balanced at the top of the skate ramp, waiting for his sister, or perhaps transfixed by the spectacle himself, and for long seconds, Nell could not move. Inert, she was gripped by the strongest sensation of drifting high above herself, high above them all, helpless with certainty that another bad thing was about to happen.

'Nell?' Mum's voice echoed through the handset, but later Nell wouldn't be sure whether she'd imagined it, because the next thing she heard was the bone-crunching explosion of metal and glass, as the campsite below her disappeared behind a vast cloud of billowing grey dust. Caravans and tents and a child's bright red skateboard toppled toy-like across the green coastal plain, and Auntie Suzie's Land Rover ploughed headlong into the giant golden rabbit.

Apart from her own ragged breathing, all on the coastal path was silent.

For a second or two, Nell could only look on blankly, shock preventing her imagination from forging too far ahead. Alone on the hill, she surveyed the scene. To the north side, Auntie Suzie's crumpled Land Rover stood motionless beside the toppled mascot, blocking the passage for an early-morning campervan arriving on the entrance path behind them.

The intact section of the campsite was suddenly populated with adults and children rushing from their tents and caravans, gathering on the grass in clusters to gaze on at the cloud of dust and smoke, which slowly cleared, revealing the children's playground to be in ruins. Impossibly, the crashed plane appeared to be sitting directly on top of the skate ramp.

Where Albie had just been.

Cold fear rushed at Nell. *Where was Albie? Where was Mum? Why hadn't they come out yet?* With rigid fingers, she fumbled to get a grip on her phone and dialled 999. This, Nell would recognise later, would be her flashbulb moment, the memory she would recall for ever more, a vivid technicolour showreel of where-she-was-when-it-happened, in the seconds that separated the before from the after.

'Ambulance!' she cried when the operator connected at the other end. 'There's been a plane crash at the Golden Rabbit Holiday Park – on the Port Regis-to-Mere road, at the foot of Highcap Hill! I'm there now – I'm on the hill. I can see everything!' Information spewed from her, startlingly articulate and clear.

'OK, give me your name, love.' Patiently the call handler extracted the details she needed while Nell began the breathless race downhill, stumbling on mossy mounds and slippery stone, skidding to a halt as she realised the operator was cutting out, her words drifting through in a disjointed jumble. 'What – see now?' the woman wanted to know. 'Is – hurt? – smoke? 'ell?'

Nell screamed in frustration. 'I can't hear you! I can't hear what you're saying!'

At last, the line cleared. 'All right, love. It's just a poor signal your end. Nell, can you see if the main road is obstructed in any way?'

Nell glanced down towards the road, which was getting busier now with morning commuters. As her coastal path dipped into a shallow valley, she lost sight of the holiday camp altogether, and for several minutes she could tell the woman nothing at all.

'The road's clear,' she replied in a sprinting gasp as she crested the next upward slope.

Uncle Elliot was now out of his vehicle, but slightly stooped over and being assisted by the couple from the campervan stuck behind them.

'My uncle just got out of the Land Rover – I think he's hurt. But he's walking!' she shouted down the line.

'Your uncle?'

'Yes – on the main path. At the campsite – but I still can't see my—' A whimper escaped Nell as the words refused to come, and shocked by the sound of it, she bit down on her lip, tasting blood. 'OK, OK, OK,' she murmured, forgetting momentarily that the operator was still on the line.

'All right, Nell,' the woman said, 'I'm still here. What's your uncle's name?'

'Elliot Gale. He runs the campsite with my Auntie Suzie.'

'OK. How close are you to the scene now?'

'Maybe ten minutes, if I run!'

The line cut out.

Stuffing the phone into her back pocket, Nell used the time to pick up pace on her next sweeping downward descent. She knew her estimate was ambitious; on a good day, at a regular hiking pace, it took at least thirty minutes to descend from Highcap summit to the campsite below. If she put her all into it, maybe she could do it in fifteen?

When she reached the boundary to the birdwatching platform of Kite View, she paused for breath, wincing at the stitch radiating beneath her ribs and the hangover that pooled in her stomach. Below, an untidy line of twenty or thirty campers was now crossing the grassland away from the main site, heading towards the foot of the coastal path. Directing them from the grass clearing at the centre of the tents and caravans, seemingly unscathed, was Auntie Suzie, instantly recognisable in her khaki waistcoat, scruffy pale hair beneath her peak cap.

Nell scanned the line of campers, desperate to spot her mum and Albie among them, but they weren't there. Sweat ran down the centre of her back and her head pounded, but she swallowed hard, pushing off again at speed just as her phone sprang back to life.

'Signal's bad,' Nell told the operator, panting as she forged on, her boot skidding on the stony slope. 'We'll probably cut out again in the next dip.'

'OK, understood. The emergency vehicles are already—'

But Nell had stopped listening, and she had stopped moving.

Through the smog of the shower block, the small figure of her mother was emerging with yellow gloves dangling from one hand. *She looks like a bomb victim*, Nell thought, taking in the image in a single appalled gulp. The garish mint green of her cleaning tabard flashed feebly beneath a wash of black dust, and her red hair, usually bundled up in an African scarf, fell over her shoulders in dirty coils.

Unsteadily, Mum paused for a moment, turning this way and that, before throwing down her cleaning gloves and breaking into a run. Tearing off along the footpath, she sprinted, cutting past the farm shop and its fallen awning, heading with purpose in the direction of the children's playground. For long moments, she disappeared, and Nell watched, breath held.

Across the site, smoke and dust drifted, slowly revealing the true extent of the damage. The aircraft's tail end lay crumpled flat against the turf of the playground, its nose tilted skyward, its wings snapped clear, one of them now speared through the collapsed roof of the shower block.

'Nell?' the operator persisted. 'Hello, Nell? Are you still there?'

But Nell's attention was on the children's playground, just beyond the plane, where something was going on. Mum was back in view.

'Hang on,' she barked, impatiently.

To Nell, it looked, bizarrely, as though her mother was shaking a rug, her small frame moving in and out of view, up and down, as she cast aside debris and discharged fresh plumes of dust into the air.

'My mum's right by the wreckage,' she whispered into the phone, as though to raise her voice would risk the worst.

'Your mum's there too?' the operator repeated.

'Uh-huh,' Nell replied, flatly. She couldn't allow herself to feel the relief she ought to about Mum, not until she saw Albie was OK too. 'It's . . . it's the family business. She cleans. She just came out of the shower block. She's . . . I think she's looking for my brother.'

Fresh adrenaline surged through Nell's veins, and she pressed on, closing the gap, bringing the scene into clearer focus. Uncle Elliot was now lying on his side a little way from his vehicle, with a blanket over his shoulders, while the campervan woman sat in a folding chair beside him and spoke into a phone. The campsite had completely vacated, and Auntie Suzie's campers were all assembled at the base of the coastal path below Nell.

She glanced back towards the horror scene of the playground, just as Mum re-emerged. Stooped low and with the power of someone much larger, she dragged Albie, corpse-like, away from the playground and out onto the deserted grass plain. As Nell watched, immobilised by the terrible sight, one of Albie's bright tennis trainers detached from his foot. He would be furious at the grass stains he was undoubtedly scuffing up on the heel of that exposed white sports sock, and it was this small detail that almost undid Nell altogether.

Numbly, she watched as her mother gently lowered Albie's head to the ground and shrugged off her tabard to make a pillow beneath his neck. With urgent movements, she stepped out of her skirt and began tearing strips from it to wind around his arm, tugging hard at the ties before finally dropping to her knees.

Even from here, Nell could see that the yellow of Albie's favourite sweatshirt was almost entirely stained with blood. *With Albie's blood.*

Mum seemed so small as to be childlike, now wearing just her white knickers and tank top as she stooped over her boy, who had matched her in height since his twelfth birthday.

'Mum!' Nell called out, waving her arms, her pitch rising. '*Mum!*'

'*Nell?*' Mum jumped to her feet in response, spinning full circle, a frantic catch in her voice, but her eyes never landed on her daughter, reinforcing in Nell that sense of having entirely vanished.

'I've got to go,' Nell cried into the phone. 'I can't—' She heard the call handler's protests, but already she was running full pelt, because her little brother was down there, bleeding into the Dorset soil, and she had to tell him she was sorry. To tell him she'd never let him down again.

Breathlessly, she negotiated the craggy downward paths that separated her from Albie, twice tripping on the flapping hems of those damned trousers, grazing her wrists and slicing her elbow on a shard of flint. But the pain barely registered; she was focused only on getting to him, and on batting away the fear that crept coldly at the base of her neck. *She was to blame.* If she'd just gone home – if she'd never gone out in the first place – none of this would have happened. How could she possibly live with the guilt if her brother didn't make it? With sudden clarity, she knew that what had happened to *her* last night was irrelevant, compared with the thought of losing Albie. If she lost Albie, she'd have nothing to live for. Nothing at all.

At the final boundary, Nell leant heavily on the sheep fence, to press her forehead against the cool resistance of the wooden post, steadying herself for the last stretch. When she raised her head, the view below seemed changed. Not so far away now on the coastal path stood the campers, backlit by the bright white of the sun-struck sea, while in the campsite, Mum remained huddled over Albie, and on the entrance path, Auntie Suzie crouched beside Elliot. All, to Nell, seemed disturbingly still – until, directly ahead of her, in the children's playground, she spotted movement from the smashed aircraft, as the head and shoulders of the pilot rose from the cockpit, his movements cautious as a spaceman fallen to earth.

Aghast, Nell tumbled over the next stile, her gaze never leaving the impossible scene. As she reached the top of the manmade steps that would lead her to the grassland below, the pilot clambered stiffly from the plane and balanced precariously on what little was left of the demolished skate ramp.

Even from this distance, Nell could sense the man's desolation, in the way his shoulders slumped, his head hung darkly beneath blooded features. He reached down into the smoking hollow of the cockpit and hefted something awkward from the space below. A rucksack? A parachute?—

'*No*,' Nell whispered, feeling her knees buckle as she started down the final stepped decline. '*No*—'

The wailing harmony of emergency vehicles sang through the air as two blue-lit ambulances appeared on the main road up ahead, and, briefly, Nell's hope soared. But then, before relief even had a chance to take hold, the aircraft in the playground, pilot and all, exploded into flames.

2. Cathy

Saturday

The big digital clock on the wall of the hospital family room displayed 18.47; almost exactly twelve hours since the plane landed in the playground of the Golden Rabbit holiday camp. Half a day.

Cathy had been watching the numbers tick slowly upwards since she'd arrived with Albie in the ambulance just after eight that morning, each turn of the hour prompting her to head out into the bleachy blue corridors in search of an update. In search of some hope. Throughout the day, the answers had shifted in small increments: 'He's being closely monitored . . . He's lost a lot of blood . . . He's in good hands . . . The injuries he's sustained are concerning . . . He's scheduled for surgery . . . He's going into theatre at seven.'

When the time arrived, a nurse led her through glaring strip-lit hallways to the pre-op suite, and Cathy kissed his forehead and told him she loved him, all the while knowing that he couldn't hear her. That he couldn't speak to tell her, *Don't worry, Mum,*

I'm gonna be fine. Now, the clock turned 19.00 and Cathy fired off a text to her sister-in-law.

Albie has gone into surgery. They need to see how bad the damage is before they can say more. What news on Ells?

Suzie returned a typically formal reply. *We are still in A&E. Elliot is concussed and they haven't yet stitched up the gash in his head. They say we're next. I hope so. Suzie*

She always signed off with her name, Cathy noticed, as though it were an email, not a text. They didn't actually text each other all that often, she supposed. Sometimes it felt to Cathy as though the fifteen-year gap between them was more like a whole genera-tion. She often wondered how her brother and Suzie had stayed together all these decades; Elliot was the same age as his wife but way less uptight. Like chalk and cheese, Dad always said. More like paper and scissors, Cathy would reply with a smirk, and Dad would ignore her, because the quip was well-worn and he didn't understand why his daughter couldn't make more of an effort to bury the hatchet.

Does Dad know yet? Cathy texted back, thinking of Nell back home, taking her grandad his dinner next door, under strict instructions not to let on about the crash until they had more news on Albie's condition.

We haven't told him, Suzie answered. *But I completely disagree with you and Elliot about keeping it from him. The campsite is still his business. The crash was all over the local news at six – national too. Dad won't be happy if he finds out from someone else. Suzie*

Oh, fuck off. He's my dad, not yours, Cathy wanted to reply. The air crash had taken out landlines in the immediate area, so there was no risk of anyone calling him, and Dad didn't even own a TV, as her sister-in-law well knew. Suzie was such a know-it-all, and Cathy had been listening to this kind of I'm-older-than-you lecture from her since she was a child, for God's sake.

Of course, gallingly, on this matter, Suzie was absolutely right. Dad's fury at being kept out of the loop might well put his heart under more stress than the shock of the news itself, and Cathy really didn't want another critically ill family member on her hands right now.

I'll phone Nell, she replied. *Get her to drive him in.*

She allowed her eyes to return to the clock. Albie had been in surgery for eighteen minutes now. How long did these things take? These *investigations*. 'We'll know when we know,' one particularly unhelpful auxiliary had told her as they'd wheeled Albie's bed away less than half an hour ago. What kind of answer was that?

Cathy stared at the phone in her hand and wondered what she should say to her daughter. Earlier, when Nell had arrived with a fresh set of clothes for her, they'd sat silently like two strangers at a bus stop for almost an hour, before Cathy couldn't take it any longer and sent her home to check in on her grandad. She knew Nell was feeling guilty, and she knew all the girl wanted was for her mother to say it wasn't her fault, that these things were out of our control, that Albie was going to be fine. But, in the gaping horror of the aftershock, Cathy just couldn't. She couldn't tell Nell that she shouldn't feel guilty, because, God forgive her, she should.

She tapped out a message to her daughter. *When Grandad's had his dinner, bring him to the hospital please.*

Why? How's Albie? came Nell's swift reply.

He's in surgery.

Is he OK?

I don't know, Nell. They'll tell us when they bring him out. Can you bring my toothbrush and some toothpaste? I'll be staying overnight.

What do I tell Grandad?

Cathy stared at her daughter's question and knew her next reply was punishing even as she typed it. *Tell him what happened. No point in trying to keep it from him.*

When Nell didn't immediately reply, Cathy felt tears prick her eyes for the first time since they'd arrived in the hospital all those hours earlier. What if Albie didn't make it? What if Nell never got to see her brother again?

She tapped out a follow-up text and pressed send: *X*

While Cathy waited, time passed slowly without news, and stealthily her dread deepened. Still that wall clock ticked forward. Still no news.

Her mind kept drifting back to the scene of the disaster, her stomach tightening every time she lingered on the moments in the immediate aftermath when, stunned, she'd stumbled from the shower block and first witnessed the devastation.

She couldn't stop thinking about the young man who had smiled and said good morning to her just seconds earlier, before heading into the furthest shower booth. She couldn't stop thinking about the way in which the ceiling had come down between them with a strangely muffled thud – the well-worn roof split in two, she would later learn, by the severed wing of the plane. And she couldn't stop thinking about Albie's crimson-soaked sweatshirt, and the way his wound had just bled and bled, no matter how much pressure she applied . . .

'Come here, my girl.'

Cathy looked up to see her father standing in the doorway to the family room, with a pale-faced Nell beside him, looking tiny in her oversized hoodie.

'Oh, Dad.' She stepped into his broad arms and pressed her face into the comfort of his scratchy wool sweater, worn year-round, whatever the weather. *You can bury me in this,* he'd once told her when she'd had to wrestle it off him to put it through the wash. She'd slapped his arm at the time and replied that he'd easily outlive the rest of them – and the jumper, for that matter.

For long minutes, she leant into him, allowing her tears at last to fall, safely concealed within her father's silent embrace, her two small feet planted childlike between his great boots, weighty hands steadying on her back. *Like a tree*, she thought; *he's like an ancient oak.*

When she felt the light touch of Nell's hand on her shoulder, Cathy pulled away from her father and dried her eyes with a shake of her head, embarrassed. Briefly, she cupped Nell's face in her hands. Wide fear was radiating from her daughter's eyes. 'You OK?' she asked her, briskly.

Nell nodded, her chin crumpling.

'He'll be fine,' Cathy said, turning back to her dad, taking his hand and looking from one to the other, gathering her strength. 'We have to believe he's going to be fine.'

'He's a Gale,' John Gale said with a slow, certain nod. 'Of course he'll be fine.'

He drew them both in, his daughter and granddaughter, and held them, uniting them as only he seemed able to do. In Cathy's pocket, a text sounded out on her mobile and she rushed to check it, her shoulders dropping when she saw it was just her sister-in-law.

Elliot is with the doctors now, getting stitches and an MRI scan to check his head. They said to go and get a coffee. Can you meet me in the canteen? I need to talk to you. Suzie

Cathy puffed out her cheeks. 'It's Suzie. She says to go and meet her in the canteen – Elliot's being seen to now.'

'What about Albie?' Nell asked, close to tears.

'The nurses have my mobile number, and they promised they'd message me the minute he gets out of surgery. OK?'

Nell didn't look convinced, her fingers working restlessly at the cuffs of her sleeves, and Cathy knew nothing she said would soothe the girl's fears. She smiled flatly. 'They'll be in touch soon enough. Have you got any cash, Dad? I left my bag in the car at the site . . .'

Dad patted his breast pocket where he kept his wallet and nodded towards the door. 'Think we could all do with a cuppa.'

The three headed out along the corridor and took the lift to the canteen on the ground level, where the overhead lighting and bright linoleum floor gave off an otherworldly glow against the dimming sky outside. All around the vast space, hospital staff took their evening breaks in clusters of easy chatter, while the concerned friends and relatives of patients dined sedately, as though library-quiet rules applied here in this serious place of medicine.

Suzie was sitting alone at a large table beside the window, drinking coffee.

'Do you want something to eat?' Cathy asked her by way of a greeting.

Suzie looked startled to see the family *en masse*. 'No, I'm fine,' she said, and she rose to give her father-in-law a quick hug. 'Cathy didn't mention you were all here.'

Already, Cathy could feel her hackles rising, just at being in Suzie's presence for thirty seconds, and without response she turned her attention to taking the drinks order and bringing her irritation to heel. 'Dad? Do you want something?'

Dad pulled a twenty-pound note from his wallet and handed it straight to Nell, granting her the job instead. 'I'll have a cup of tea, love, and get whatever you and your mum want. Oh, and see if they've got a slice of cake – the kind of thing your mother doesn't let me eat at home.' He gave his granddaughter a sly wink, and eased himself slowly into the chair beside Suzie, forcing Cathy to take the seat opposite.

'What's the news on Elliot, Suze?' Dad asked, folding his arms on the table. His wide, flat fingernails were stained with the earth of his allotment, his knuckles thickened with age.

Suzie placed her paper cup down and blinked. She looked uncharacteristically shaken, her pale frizzy hair let loose from its usual constraining cap. 'I think he'll be fine. I'm sure he'll be fine. He wasn't wearing a seat belt – you know how I'm always going on at him about that – and, well, he smashed his head on the window frame when we crashed the truck.'

'And how's Goldie?' Cathy asked before she could stop herself.

'Goldie?' Dad asked.

'The *rabbit*.' Suzie sighed, with exaggerated patience.

Dad sent a warning shot across at Cathy, and Suzie, ever the grown-up, continued without further acknowledgement.

'The police have already been round asking questions. While we were waiting in A&E,' she said, her eyes downcast. 'Have they been to see you yet, Cathy?'

Suzie glanced up and, at once, Cathy detected something furtive in her expression. She shook her head. 'I talked to a couple of PCs down at the campsite, but it was chaos, and I was too busy worrying about Albie to be much help. I was inside the shower block when it happened.' Cathy thought again of that smiling young man, disappearing as the ceiling caved in. The terrible way it seemed to suck the air from the space. 'Did anyone else get hurt?' she asked. 'I mean, other than the pilot?'

Suzie's fingers worried at the knots at the back of her neck. 'I got most of the campers off the grounds straight away. There were a handful of adults unaccounted for at that point. No children. But you know what holidaymakers are like: they often move on without signing out, don't they? Anyway, the police took copies of the register, said they needed to work out . . .' She hesitated, looking suddenly appalled. 'To work out if anyone might be trapped. They're still down there now, clearing through the rubble.'

Dad ran a hand through his thick white hair, and Cathy felt guilty that he was only hearing these details now. 'I just thank God no other kids came to harm,' he said.

The table fell quiet as the three eyed each other, none of them expressing the true horror they felt at the prospect of someone being trapped under the fallen walls of their happy holiday park. Of someone being *dead*.

It was Nell who broke the silence, as she set down the canteen tray with a clatter of teaspoons and slid into the seat beside Cathy, her eyes darting between them. 'What?' she said in a small voice.

'We were just talking about the crash,' Cathy said, feeling her stomach tip as she snatched a sideways glance and saw the desolate expression on her daughter's face. 'Hoping no one else got hurt.' She leant down to reach inside her bag for her cigarettes, and stood to leave.

Sombrely, Nell pushed a large slice of chocolate cake over the table to her grandad. 'The pilot . . .?' she ventured.

'Well, I don't think *he* stood a chance,' Cathy replied, her tone harsher than she'd intended. Of course it was a tragedy that anyone should die, but, so far, she'd been unable to feel anything for the man responsible for Albie's injuries. She cast around the table, to a general murmur of agreement.

Nell shook her head, her lips parted, her brow furrowed in the way it did when she was building up to say something.

Cathy dropped back into her seat and pushed her cigarettes to one side. 'Come on, then. Spit it out,' she said, irritably.

Dad glowered. 'Steady,' he cautioned.

Cathy raised a conciliatory hand. 'Sorry. *Sorry*. I'm stressed out and I'm dying for a fag. I didn't mean to bite your head off. I meant, what's on your mind, Nell?'

'I was wondering about the kid, that's all,' Nell said, in little more than a whisper.

Dad frowned, his eyes turning back to his daughter, fork hovering between his plate and his mouth.

'Kid?' Cathy repeated. Her heart hammered anew as her fears for Albie merged with this fresh fear, this new image, of a different, faceless child in the playground, one she had failed to see or save.

All attention was on Nell now, as a new tension worked its way through the family.

'What do you mean, "the kid", Nell?' Suzie pressed when her niece didn't immediately answer.

Nell's shocked expression looked almost like guilt. 'There was a child,' she finally replied, in a tone that suggested they ought to already know about it. She swiped away a tear. 'I thought . . . I thought, they must've found them by now – I thought . . . I mean, I spoke to them, the police, down at the campsite . . .'

Cathy thought about Albie laid out upstairs in the operating theatre. If another child had come to harm, they'd know by now, wouldn't they?

'Nobody's mentioned a child, love. They must be talking about Albie.'

Nell swallowed hard. 'I didn't *hear* about another kid, Mum – I *saw* him!' Allowing a brief pause for the information to land, Nell continued, 'Afterwards, after the crash, I was running down the hill, just watching and praying Albie would come out OK – I barely looked away for a second. I could see everything from up there, even through the dust and smoke – I could see how the plane's wings had come away, and its tail all bent funny, and then . . . and then the pilot just kind of appeared. He was climbing out of the plane's . . . you know, what is it? The cockpit? He climbed out, onto the skate ramp.'

24

She hesitated, her focus anchored on the mug in her hands as she described the recollection. 'That's when I saw the kid.' Now she looked up, at three expectant faces. 'He was so small . . . he was . . . I mean, maybe they haven't found him 'cause he was fine after all? He could've, you know, got thrown to safety? By the explosion. And then maybe, I dunno, just wandered off . . .?'

Nell's eyes searched the faces of her assembled relatives, but no words of comfort followed. Each family member waited for another to speak. With a gasp, Nell clasped a hand over her mouth, muffling a loud sob, and awkwardly Cathy patted her daughter's other hand, not knowing what to do or say.

Suzie was the first to speak, with a shake of her head. 'Maybe you've got it wrong? I mean, you *were* a very long way off, Nell. And there have been no kids reported missing. You couldn't be certain of what you saw from that distance.'

'I could see *Mum* just fine, and *Albie*, when they drove up . . .' Nell's words tumbled out in a rush, as tears streaked her cheeks.

'Yes, but you could easily have been mistaken, Nell – the smoke – the shock – I think you must've got it wrong, or we'd know about it by now.'

In a burst of fury, Cathy rapped her knuckles hard on the table. 'If my daughter says she saw it, Suzie, then she saw it. OK?'

'Enough,' Dad growled, and the two women shrank back.

On the other side of the canteen, a uniformed officer appeared, heading for the drinks machine, together with the detective Cathy had seen talking to her sister-in-law at the campsite earlier. She knew it was wrong to be stoking the flames of her feud with Suzie at a time like this, but somehow it helped, deflecting her energy away from thoughts of the possible terrifying new shape of their future.

Pushing back her chair with a noisy scrape, she strode across the room, and returned seconds later with the pair at her side.

'Oh, hello again,' the detective addressed Suzie. 'Mrs Gale?'

Suzie nodded, her demeanour distinctly unwelcoming.

'I'm DS Ali Samson,' the officer introduced herself to the rest of the family. 'This is DC Garner.' She turned back to Suzie. 'How's your husband doing, Mrs Gale?'

'He's in A&E,' Suzie replied, with a curt nod.

What was up with her? Cathy wondered. Why was she suddenly so tight-lipped?

'You were down at the crash site this morning?' Cathy asked the detective. 'At the Golden Rabbit?'

DS Samson gestured towards Suzie. 'Yes, we took Mrs Gale's statement earlier. You say you were also on the scene?'

'My son was the one injured by the—' For some reason, Cathy couldn't quite say the words straight. 'He's in surgery right now.'

DS Samson's eyes widened in sympathy. 'Oh, yes – you're the cleaner – is that right?'

The cleaner. Typical that Suzie should have described her as an employee, rather than family. 'I'm Cathy Gale. This is my dad, John,' she said, laying a proprietorial hand on his shoulder and casting a pointed glance at Suzie. 'Dad owns the campsite. Suzie and my brother just run it.'

'OK,' the detective replied, jotting Cathy's name in her notebook. 'We'll want to get a full witness statement from you too, Cathy, perhaps tomorrow morning, once your boy is out of surgery?'

Glancing at the clock at the far end of the canteen, Cathy turned distractedly back to the officers. 'I spoke to your guys down there this morning – but, yes . . . well, I gave them my number.' She gestured towards Nell, hunched over her mug of tea, her hoodie now pulled up over her head so that she looked like some delinquent. 'This is my daughter. She was also there, but way up on the hill, so she saw the whole thing as it happened. Nell?'

26

Straightening up a little, Nell wiped her wet cheeks with a balled-up sleeve cuff.

'Nell, is it?' DC Garner spoke gently to the girl, and Cathy was grateful to him for it. God knew, it was more than she had managed herself. 'You must've had a good view from up on the hill?'

Nell nodded, encouraged. 'It was clear this morning,' she said. 'No mist, just really clear. I was heading down from the top, a bit before seven.'

'Where were you coming from?' DS Samson asked; the very question on Cathy's lips.

Nell paled further. 'Why? I mean, I stayed at a friend's place last night—'.

'Sorry, that's not important,' the detective said, waving the question away. 'Carry on.'

Nell nodded. 'So, I saw Mum and Albie drive in, up to the playground, and then a couple of minutes later I saw Uncle Elliot driving in with Auntie Suzie in the Land Rover—'

'Not Elliot,' Suzie corrected. 'It was me driving.'

A puzzled frown settled over Nell's face. 'Erm, OK.' She looked back at the officers. 'Um, and then, well, you know – the crash. The plane went down.'

As the officer took a few notes, DS Samson dropped to her haunches to be level with Nell. 'We'll definitely want a full statement from you too, Nell. It'll be most likely one of the special air investigators overseeing the case. You could well be our best witness to what actually happened and when. How old are you?'

'Eighteen.'

'OK. Are you able to give us a mobile phone number we can get you on?'

Nell fiddled with her phone and held up the screen for DC Garner to take note, while Cathy eyed her sister-in-law, taking in her scowl, her distracted air. Suzie had barely asked after Albie, and here she was more worried about who'd been driving her precious Landie. Elliot must have been over the limit, the bloody idiot. This was Suzie exercising damage limitation, without a doubt.

Cathy glanced at her daughter, who now silently looked back, willing her mother to ask the question for her.

Cathy cleared her throat. 'Nell says – well, we were just wondering if . . . if anyone else was brought in?' She flushed as she stumbled over the words and felt the grim chill of sweat forming on her upper lip. Some part of her felt inexplicably responsible – not for the disaster, of course, but for not protecting Albie, perhaps? For not seeing it coming. Either way, she couldn't shake the dark feeling that she'd somehow brought this horror upon them all, the family and the community alike. That it was all her fault.

'Brought in?' DC Garner asked.

'I mean, was anyone else hurt? Apart from Albie. And the pilot.'

DS Samson eyed Cathy steadily, as though mentally weighing her up. 'Well, you'll hear about it in the morning news, so I might as well tell you now, as it happened on your property. The recovery crew have completed their initial investigation, and the hospital confirm we have three dead, and a few casualties.'

'*Three*?' John Gale murmured, resting his forehead on the steeple of his fingers. His broad shoulders sagged, as though the air had been let out of him.

Three. The pilot, the young man and the child, Cathy thought, dispassionate with shock. Suzie appeared expressionless, frozen; Nell hid her face behind her hands and wept.

'I'm sorry,' the detective said. 'I know it's hard to hear.'

'My daughter saw a child, right before the explosion . . .?' Cathy replied, an unspoken question hovering.

A silent communication passed between the two officers, before DS Samson replied. 'We *have* just heard that there was a child recovered from the play area,' she said with a solemn nod.

'*Recovered*?' Nell echoed, almost a whisper.

'He didn't make it, I'm afraid.'

A hush descended, dampening the flames of Cathy's earlier fury. Now, all she felt was the sickening churn of anxiety, as the surreal events of the day grew suddenly more tangible. *Albie might die too*, a dark voice inside her whispered, and she brought her hand to her throat as she tried to hold it all in.

'But we don't yet have an identity for the little boy,' DC Garner added. 'All the children on your site register have been accounted for, Mrs Gale, and no parents have come forward to report their child missing. Do you get many local kids coming to your holiday park, to use the playground?'

'No,' Nell murmured. She was shaking her head, and it occurred to Cathy that maybe her daughter really was in shock. She should comfort her; she should tell her everything was going to be all right, that she wasn't to blame for what had happened to Albie. That she loved her. She *should*.

'No,' Suzie replied firmly, breaking into Cathy's thoughts. 'Teenagers sometimes, but certainly not little ones. We're a bit far from town for that.'

'No. *No*,' Nell said, more insistent now. 'He definitely wasn't a local kid.'

All eyes turned her way. 'How can you be so certain?' DS Samson asked.

Cathy stared at her daughter, trying to make sense of her words. Nell returned a darkly hooded expression of sadness, before speaking directly to the detective standing at their table.

'Because he arrived in the plane. I saw the pilot reach in and lift him out, right before the explosion. He was *with* the pilot.'

3. Nell

Sunday

The following morning, Nell was roused by the sound of a taxi idling below her window, and her stomach lurched at the vivid waking recall of yesterday's events.

Feeling queasy – from hunger or nerves, she wasn't sure – she pulled her old hoodie over her pyjamas and headed for the bathroom, suddenly aware of the silence of the house. Last night, when they'd learnt that Albie was finally out of surgery, the doctor had only been able to reiterate that he'd lost a lot of blood and that he was now stable, but, as for the injury, they would have to monitor it over the next twenty-four hours. Satisfied there was nothing more any of them could do, Mum had instructed Nell to take Grandad home, and Auntie Suzie had headed off to collect Uncle Elliot from A&E. Just like that, they had all parted; no hugs, no words of support, no warmth.

Why couldn't they come together at a time like this, Nell wondered, the way other families did? Why did her family have to deal with the pain of this trauma, not together, but very much apart?

Staring into the cracked bowl of the sink, she splashed water over her face, before sprinting downstairs at the sound of a key in the front door. God, was that the time already?

'Grandad – sorry, I slept in!' she called ahead, but halfway down she realised it wasn't him at all. Instead of Grandad's dirt-caked gardening shoes, she saw the flip-flopped toes and lean legs of a middle-aged man – Kip.

'Dad!' she cried out, rushing down the last few steps and into his arms before he even had a chance to drop his patch-work bag.

'Nelly-belly!' He smiled, releasing her from a bear hug to take a proper look at her. Then he sighed heavily, and Nell took in the exhausted expression on his deeply tanned face. 'You look like you've just woken up, sweetie. Look at your bonkers hair.'

He gave a warm laugh, and Nell snatched a glance in the hallway mirror, seeing just how deranged she looked in her *Animal Crossing* pyjama bottoms and XL hoodie, her hair a mass of tangled red curls. She rolled her eyes.

'You've got your mum to thank for that,' he said, reaching out a hand to muss her head as she led them through to the little kitchen at the back, where her phone was charging.

As her dad used the bathroom, Nell checked her messages, but found nothing new from either Mum or Auntie Suzie. *Kip's here*, she tapped out to her mother. *What's the latest? Is Albie ready for visitors yet?*

'Let's get that kettle on,' her dad said, pulling out a chair at the small wooden table as Nell laid her phone down on the worktop. 'You can fill me in on everything.'

She lifted the kettle and turned to the sink. 'So, what's Mum told you?'

'Almost nothing,' he replied with a gravity that betrayed the depth of his concern. 'That's why I took the first flight back.'

After breakfast, Grandad insisted on driving them to the hospital, despite Nell's urging that she should take the wheel.

'He's not insured if he has an accident,' she hissed to her dad as she locked the cottage door behind them. 'The doctor told him – not until he's got the all-clear from his tests next month.'

Kip draped his arm round her shoulder as they walked down the back path to the rough hardstanding where Grandad kept his van, parked alongside piles of old bricks and sandbags that 'might come in handy one day'. The old man lunged at a ginger tom sitting on his bonnet, seeing it off with claw hands and a low snarl.

'I'm not going to argue with the old bugger,' Kip whispered back, and they clambered in the passenger side of the van, Nell sweeping dried earth and till receipts from her seat before giving her seat belt a tug to check it actually worked.

Pulling away, they passed along the rear gates of the small gardens belonging to their row of terraces, old 1930s council dwellings that backed onto the community allotments, where the morning sun now shone low over the distant hills and valleys of Highcap.

'So, how are you now, John?' Kip asked Grandad, inclining his head to see past Nell. 'It's been, what, three months since I last saw you. I hear you've been in the wars.'

Grandad threw a casual glance Kip's way. 'You know, me, son: it'll take more than a little bit of a heart attack to see me off.'

'Bloody hell, Grandad, you shouldn't joke about it,' Nell tutted, scowling at Kip. 'It's your third one in as many years.'

'Exactly! I'm unkillable!'

John Gale and Kip both laughed hard at this, and Nell couldn't help but join in, glad to be there in that moment, in a crappy old van, sandwiched between the two men she loved most in the world.

'Like the Terminator,' Kip said, and Grandad shrugged good-humouredly, clearly not having a clue what his would-be son-in-law meant.

Kip slotted his fingers through Nell's. 'It's nice to be back,' he said, casting his gaze across the open countryside they were now passing through en route to Dorchester. 'But I'd rather it was under better circumstances.' Again, he tilted his head to look past Nell. 'Nell's filled me in on the air crash at the campsite – but Cathy's message didn't tell me much more, John. What do you know? About Albie's condition?'

Grandad pursed his lips. 'No more than you, Kip lad. Doctors weren't saying much last night, were they, Nellie? Tight-lipped. But this one here,' he said, jerking his chin in Nell's direction, 'she was the one who told me about it – hours it was, after it happened.' He shook his head as though only now comprehending the seriousness of the situation. 'A plane crash, of all things. A plane coming down on *our* campsite. On our *boy*.'

'God, John, it's all so awful,' Dad said, with a catch in his voice. 'I just want to see Albie, see if he's all right. The thought of what might—'

But Grandad was on one of his rants and didn't acknowledge Kip's words, if he even took them in. 'If Nell hadn't come round and told me, I'd probably be none the wiser now,' he added gruffly. 'They treat me like a bloody invalid at times.'

'Mum wouldn't *let* any of us tell you, Grandad,' Nell replied, defensively. 'She was worried about your heart.'

'She wasn't worried about my heart.' He coughed. 'She didn't want the bother of me down at the hospital, getting under her feet. Didn't want to deal with anyone else's upset but her own. She's a hard one, our Cathy, at times.' He threw Kip a sideways nod. 'You'll know all about that, Kip lad.'

Nell felt Kip's fingers twitch slightly in her hand, and she gave them a little squeeze. He sighed, a sad sound. 'She wasn't always like that, though, was she, John?'

The truck turned into the hospital entrance, forcing Grandad to slow down as they approached a series of sharp road bumps. 'You're not wrong. She was a lovely wee girl,' he said. 'Had a smile for everyone, when she was a young 'un. Oh, and her laugh . . .!'

'Ha, that laugh!' Kip coughed. 'She'd howl, wouldn't she, if something struck her as funny? I used to call her the Howling Gale,' he said, shifting slightly to meet Nell's gaze, eyes alight. 'You know, as in her surname . . .'

Nell laughed now too. 'Yeah, I got that bit, Dad.'

Jerkily, Grandad pulled into a bay, stopping just short of mowing down a bollard.

Unbuckling his seat belt, Kip sighed again, his eyes drawn to the ominous spectacle of the Dorset County Hospital. 'I think it was her laugh that made me fall for her in the first place. Heard it across a crowded bar in Thailand. She was so . . . so . . .' He thought for a minute, before returning with words Nell would never use to describe her mother. 'She was free-spirited, Nell. A lot like you.'

For a moment, they sat quietly, all three seemingly contemplating the idea of a different Cathy, a free-spirited Cathy, a Cathy Nell had never had the advantage of knowing.

The morning sun was now hitting the upper windows of the hospital building, painting them a dazzling white. Somewhere inside, Nell thought, Albie was lying in a starched hospital bed, in God only knew what condition, what state of mind. She hoped he was still sleeping; she hoped he might sleep through it all, until everything was fine again, until the nightmare was over.

Now, beneath those windows, a slight figure emerged through the sliding doors of the main entrance. Pausing, the woman

34

turned to the wall to light up a cigarette out of the breeze, red coils spiralling from the top of her headscarf. As she turned back, Nell could see that her shoulders were up, tight with tension; she had the appearance of a small creature on high alert, ready to bolt.

'There she is,' Nell said, giving her dad a nudge, and the trio exited the truck and headed over, Nell flanked by her father and grandfather, feeling simultaneously invisible and spotlit beneath the bright blue Dorset sky.

When she recognised Kip approaching, a small lopsided smile touched the edges of Mum's mouth.

'*Ahh.*'

This was the sound that escaped Kip's lips as he locked eyes on Cathy. Nell felt her heart contract, at witnessing this proof of her parents' affection for each other. As Kip came to a halt on the pavement before Cathy, the pair seemed to study each other curiously before Kip took the cigarette from between Cathy's fingers and discarded it with a practised flick. A few steps back, Nell and Grandad watched on as Kip embraced her, and she gave in and allowed her face to pucker, and her tears to fall.

'Oh, darlin', come on, come on,' Kip murmured, rocking her gently, smoothing stray curls from her wet face.

'I wasn't expecting you yet,' she sniffled into his shirt before she pulled away, slapping his chest with the flat of her hand. 'You took me by surprise, that's all. I don't normally—' She gestured towards her tear-stained face.

'No, you don't,' he replied, and he planted a kiss in the centre of her forehead, and, ignoring her loud tut, took her hand and led them through the doors.

At the third floor, a hospital porter asked them to vacate the lift for a patient in a wheelchair, and he directed them to the stairs at the far end of a corridor busy with doctors and hospital staff darting about on morning rounds. Nell felt unnerved by the disinfectant smell of the place, and she wondered if the workers carried it home with them at the end of the day, seeped into their hair and clothes like a spectre of the ill and the dead.

In her pocket, her mobile phone vibrated, and she paused a second to check the alert on her home screen. The message was from an unknown number, and in her tired state, she clicked the attachment and an image filled the screen, accompanied by a jarring thrash metal audio. Her first reaction was regret at following the link – the zoomed section she could initially see looked like flesh, like porn spam. But as she adjusted the image to fit the screen, the assault on her senses was as visceral as a punch in the ribs.

Alley Dog, the anonymous message read. Nothing more. Just: *Alley Dog*.

Nell's receiving and viewing of this image had occurred in the space of just seconds, but already Mum and Dad and Grandad seemed very far away along the hospital corridor. With shaking hands and sickness swelling in her stomach, she fumbled with the phone, desperate to shut the image down, as feebly she called out to her family to wait.

Ahead, the corridor darkened as she leant into light-headedness. *Oh, God.* Was this really happening to her? She yearned to turn back time, to not have argued and stormed out on Mum that night, to not have let her brother down as she did. She was desperate for Albie to be fine – back home, winning his tennis match, like the little pro he was; she wanted Grandad to look after himself better and not die of a heart attack; and she wanted Mum to want Dad to stay put – to stay here, in Highcap, with Albie and Nell. Like a real family. She wanted not to have gone down that alleyway with God knew who the other night, not to have opened herself up to such shame and despair—

36

'Are you all right, love?' Dad asked, suddenly beside her, in a voice that sounded to Nell as though it came from inside a box.

Blindly, she reached out for the wall.

'Nell?'

'Uh-huh,' she replied with a small shake of her head, and she leant against the frame of a closed door, anchoring her focus on the small glass privacy panel as she fought the black mist dancing at the edges of her vision.

'Nelly?' Grandad said with more urgency, but she found she couldn't even turn to acknowledge him.

'We'll catch you up, Cath,' Nell heard Kip say, as he eased Nell into a chair beside the door, where they sat quietly for a few minutes, she bent over her knees, he with his hand on her back.

Behind the black of her eyelids, that image strobed like a spectre. Her fractured memories, the cold stone walls of the alleyway and that bright flashing light – it had all been real.

I wish I were dead, her mind whispered. Why hadn't she left Highcap when she'd had the chance? Instead of this – *all this* – she could be with Heidi on some sun-drenched island in Indonesia, whale-watching or snorkelling or working in a beach bar. Why had she let her mum guilt-trip her into staying?

By the time she'd caught her breath and was about to tell Dad she was ready to go on, an official-looking group rounded the corridor, striding towards them with purpose. Nell pulled her hoodie up and dropped her chin, not wanting anyone else to see her puffy eyes.

'Are you family?' a woman asked Dad, gesturing at the door to the room behind them, as the group came to a halt just feet away.

Nell recognised the voice and glanced up briefly to see the detective they'd spoken to last night in the canteen, now standing at the private door with three medical staff and a man in a corduroy suit. Nell lowered her face again.

'Er, no,' Kip replied, in his usual sunny manner, reaching his arm round Nell to give her a squeeze. 'We're just perched, catching our breath.'

There were a few moments of uncomfortable silence, which Nell took as their cue to leave. The group obviously wanted the seats they were occupying, or didn't want to talk in front of them, and Nell wondered who was in the room and whether they were one of the campsite casualties DS Samson had mentioned yesterday.

Dad leant in and whispered, 'Ready to go, love? The lift should be free now.'

They rose and set off back the way they'd come, and, sure enough, the group fell into discussion again.

'It's still touch-and-go,' Nell heard one of the doctors say. She slowed her pace a little, at once anxious to hear more. 'He's still very heavily medicated, so I don't think you can expect to get anything useful from him for at least a few days. The team say he hasn't spoken a word yet.'

A sudden recollection from the moments before the plane crash sprang into Nell's mind. She could see him clearly now, the bare-chested young man in the faded red cap, emerging sleepily from his tent, washbag in one hand, towel over his shoulder, ambling with no rush at all towards the shower blocks where Mum was cleaning. Nell had wondered about him in that moment, hadn't she? She'd wanted him to look up and see her; she'd wanted anyone to look up and prove to her that she was really there, and not a figment of her own imagination.

Moments later, that boy was simply gone – swallowed up by the building, by that great plume of black smoke—

'Mum said half the ceiling came down inside the shower block,' Nell said now, pulling her hood down as they entered the lift. She looked at her dad as the doors closed and the lift shunted upwards, and fleetingly, she saw real fear there in his eyes. 'She could so easily have died,' she said.

Kip gazed back at her for long moments before the lift halted with a sigh. 'But she didn't,' he said, softly, offering his daughter his hand. 'Did she?'

The doors opened onto another bleached corridor, and hand in hand the pair set off in search of Albie.

When the nurse showed them to the intensive care room where Albie had been moved to, he was not at first visible, his bed obscured by the hovering presence of Mum and Grandad at the foot of it, while another hospital worker bent over him, tending to his dressings.

Like Nell, Dad seemed at first unable to step over the threshold of the single room, the very fact of his being there telling them that Albie's condition was serious enough to keep him off the regular children's ward.

'Is he awake?' Kip asked, still holding on to Nell's hand.

As Mum and Grandad turned to answer, a gap opened up between them and Nell saw her little brother lying stretched out in the hospital bed, covers taut, eyes closed. From here, she couldn't tell the extent of his injuries, or what the nurse was doing exactly, but she could see that Albie's hair had been smoothed down horribly to one side, in the way that he hated. She wondered about all the dead people there must be who'd gone to their graves with their hair arranged wrong or dressed in their least favourite clothes or . . . or—

Rushing to her brother, Nell raked her fingers through his hair and pressed her lips to his brow. He smelled wrong. There was barely a mark on his face, and yet . . . and yet he looked so very close to death.

'Albie? Albie, mate?' she whispered, only then noticing the little heap of bloody swabs the nurse was collecting in her metal dish, and the breadth of the green sail-like sling elevating his right arm. 'Can he hear me?' she asked, breathlessly.

The nurse shook her head and indicated towards a drip connected to the back of his other hand. 'We're keeping him comfortable at the moment – lots of pain relief, so he can't feel a thing.'

Nell sank into the seat at Albie's side as a fresh wave of remorse rushed over her. At the foot of the bed, Kip had now joined Mum and Grandad, and to Nell, the three of them, standing there against the stark white walls with their drawn faces and silent dread, looked like some terrible vigil painting hung on a gallery wall.

She turned back to the nurse. 'Can you tell us anything? Is he going to be OK? How long will he have to be on the drip?'

The nurse glanced over at Cathy, as though deferring to her, but Mum seemed to have lost all the spark she possessed yesterday.

'When can he come home?' Nell demanded, her voice unintentionally rising. She stood to face the nurse, before realising with shame that she was doing exactly what Mum would do in a difficult situation: running in with her fists up.

Carefully folding a blue paper napkin over the blooded dish, the nurse returned a tight-lipped smile. 'The consultant will be doing his rounds shortly. You're near the top of the list, and he'll be able to fill you in on everything then.' She blinked at Nell across the bed. 'He's the one with all the answers, OK? Look, why don't you go and get your folks a hot drink or something? They look like they could do with one. While you do that, I'll go and fetch a couple more chairs and you can settle in to keep your brother company, yeah?'

The undeserved kindness of the nurse nearly broke her. With a taut nod, Nell accepted the twenty-pound note Grandad was already pulling from his wallet and set off in search of a drinks machine, thankful of the space to get her head straight.

Ever since the crash yesterday morning – no, ever since that black chasm of Friday night – it was as though the world had grown both more terrifyingly, teeteringly bigger and at the same time tighter-fitting and more claustrophobic. Was it really possible that it had all only happened yesterday?

Nell felt as though she'd tumbled into some terrible parallel universe, in which the rules of time had changed, where anything could happen. She thought about reaching for her phone again, to check if she'd imagined that horrible message, but deep down she knew it was real – and she knew she was powerless to do anything about it.

Who would want to do this to her?

At the end of yet another identical corridor, Nell reminded herself of the task at hand and realised she'd been walking for nearly ten minutes without spotting any kind of vending machine. Having no idea where she was, or even how to find her way back to Albie's room without help, she stopped a porter, who pointed her in the direction of the lift down to the third floor, where she could find a Costa machine.

Minutes later, she was stepping into the corridor she and Dad had stopped in earlier, recognising markers along the way, like the broken floor tile outside the gents' loos and the orange plastic seats they'd rested on earlier. Instinctively, she raised her hoodie again as she passed the private room, for fear of meeting those police officers who wanted her statement. It wasn't that she wasn't prepared to do it, just that right now she couldn't think of anything but fetching those drinks and getting back to Albie's room—

In her distracted haste, Nell ran headlong into someone coming out of the very same room, sending papers flying.

'Oops, steady on,' the woman said, smiling, as Nell raised a hand in apology and scrabbled to pick up the scattered documents.

Handing them back to the middle-aged woman, Nell glanced at the room she'd just come from and thought of that young man trapped beneath the ceiling of the shower block.

'Is he one of the ones from the plane crash?' she asked, indicating towards the closed door.

The woman gave a sorry nod.

Nell swallowed hard. 'Are you his mum?'

Now the woman's expression relaxed into one of kind amusement. 'No, I'm his doctor.'

'Oh!' Nell replied, embarrassed. The doctor was wearing regular clothes, with her hair rolled up in an old-fashioned pleat. She didn't *look* like a doctor. She looked like a mum.

'Ah, yes – no scrubs,' the doctor said, picking up on Nell's scrutiny. 'I'm just looking in on my way home. Do you know him?'

Nell was about to answer with a straightforward *no*, but she was at once gripped by an overwhelming need to find out more about this young man. 'I'm not sure,' she replied.

'That's a shame.' The doctor sighed, laying a hand on the door and pushing it open a crack. 'So far, we haven't been able to reach out to any family for him, as nobody seems to be able to tell us who he is.'

She stepped over the threshold, affording Nell a glimpse of the room beyond, similar in layout to Albie's, only this bed was inhabited by a full-size man, laid out beneath a different kind of canopy, obscuring him entirely. How bad was it? she wondered. How bad could it be?

Boldly, Nell stepped in behind the doctor. 'My family own the campsite where it happened. My aunt said a few people on the register were unaccounted for, so he should be one of those.'

42

The doctor's brow wrinkled. 'Your family own the site? So the young lad we took into surgery yesterday, he's—'

'Albie. My brother.'

For a moment, the doctor just stared back at her.

'Listen, I was there,' Nell persisted, indicating towards the bed, 'and I saw this guy right before the crash. So, if you let me see him, I might be able to help you work out who he is? I might recognise him?'

Picking up a clipboard from the end of the bed, the doctor appeared less forthcoming now. 'Look, I know you're trying to help, but you really shouldn't be in here. This patient is very poorly. I think you're unlikely to know who he is, and at any rate—'

'Tall, slim, in his twenties—' Nell blurted, frantic to gain access to the young man who suddenly meant so much to her.

'*No*,' the doctor was saying, gesturing for her to leave, but already Nell was rushing to the head of the bed to see, to see—

The patient was heavily bandaged, one side of his head bound heavily in gauze, the rest of the body in shadow beneath the strange canopy. It was a man all right, but immediately she could see that the visible side of his face was not the face of her young man; it was the face of a stranger, heavy-featured, dark-browed, and far from twenty-something. Nell took in the close-cropped hair on one side, silvery-dark, and the stitched-together gash over his temple – and all at once she knew exactly who he was.

'He's the pilot,' the doctor said gently, appearing at her side to escort her from the room. 'And you really shouldn't be in here.'

'*Alive*?' Nell gasped, taking a halting step backwards, as though terrified she might wake some sleeping monster.

'Yes,' the doctor replied, her face softening as she led her back to the corridor. 'He's alive.'

4. Cathy

Sunday

Nell came tearing through the door to Albie's room just seconds after the consultant had finally arrived, and she skidded to a halt at the sight of him, out of breath and with no drinks to show for her trip to the coffee machine.

'What—?' Nell looked from the doctor to her mum, her expression turning to panic as she took in the grave faces of the assembled adults in the room.

Cathy brought a finger to her lips and indicated towards Albie, asleep in the bed, his face a deathly beige against the starched pillowcase.

'Shall we take this into the family room?' the consultant asked, indicating towards the open door. 'Let the lad sleep?'

Already Cathy had forgotten the doctor's name. It didn't matter; she didn't need to know his name. Hell, she just needed to know how they were going to fix up Albie – she just needed to hear some good news. She followed the man across the hall to the vacant room, with Kip, her dad and Nell silently trailing behind.

Inside, the exterior grime of the large safety windows was depressingly illuminated. This side of the building seemed to have absorbed all the heat of the midday sun so that the space felt instantly oppressive, and, even though she'd been in the room several times before, there was now something about entering it that struck Cathy as doom-laden – something about the layout of the chairs, the carefully arranged out-of-date magazines, the—

The consultant shut the door and gestured for them all to take a seat, as he lifted a chair from the beneath the window and positioned it before them, as though he were an interviewee and they were a panel. Or he a head teacher, they kids on detention.

Shit, Cathy thought, already reading all sorts of meanings into this one small gesture, *what is it?*

'So,' he began.

Mr Freeman, that was it. Why Mr and not Dr? Cathy never really understood that—

'*So*,' he repeated, and she gave a brisk nod to indicate that she was listening. 'As you know,' he spoke slowly, carefully, 'we took Albie into surgery yesterday so that we could take a comprehensive look at the damage and see what could be done for him.'

Cathy swallowed hard, glancing sideways at her father and Kip. Both were leaning in, hands clasped over their knees, expressions earnest. To her other side, Cathy could almost feel Nell's held breath, and without turning to look at her, she opened up her hand and allowed her daughter's to slip into it.

No one spoke.

'Well, we have now carried out a thorough investigation.' Mr Freeman laid his notes at his feet and opened his hands like a politician. 'Albie's injuries *are* life-changing, I'm afraid.'

A small whine escaped Cathy's lips, and she found herself making moves to bolt from the room, as hands from either side held her steady.

'What the hell does that mean?' she uttered, incredulous, looking to the others for support. '*Life-changing*?'

Dad was on his feet in a hobbled instant, raising a placating palm, while Kip hung on to her arm and softly talked her down. Nell continued to weep silently.

'I'm sorry, doctor, my daughter's upset,' Dad said, sitting again. 'Just tell us, will you? We just want to hear it straight.'

But the reality was, Cathy *didn't* want to hear it straight. She didn't want to know what the man had to say, because, in truth, the word 'life-changing' already said it all, didn't it? He certainly didn't mean life-changing in the 'you've won the lottery sense'. Whatever it was this doctor had to say, it wasn't going to be good.

Still, he plunged on. 'OK. The damage to Albie's arm is irreparable. And, by that, I mean the humerus – that's to say the bone below the elbow – was so severely crushed by the impact of the . . . *the crash* – that the connecting tissue has, I'm afraid, no chance of repair.' He paused to allow the information to sink in. 'What that means, essentially, is that Albie's arm is unusable, and, if not dealt with, it poses a risk of infection and even possible—'

'We understand,' Kip said evenly, his eyes darting to Cathy, to Nell. 'So, what are our options?'

'There is only one option available to us,' the consultant replied, in a tone so funereal, Cathy wished she had the strength to choke it from him. 'It's Albie's best hope – and the good news is that there are all sorts of prosthetic options available now—'

'Oh, for Christ's sake, man!' Now it was Dad who reared, bringing a heavy hand down on his own thigh. 'Just spit it out!'

The doctor stalled for a beat, his eyes downcast. 'We're going to need to amputate,' he said. 'We'd like to do it this afternoon.'

Cathy slumped over her knees, wrapping her arms around her head, blocking out all the light of this new reality. This couldn't be real; it just wasn't possible. Beyond her huddle, the room expanded with unasked questions, and Nell wept, and Cathy wished it had been her hit by that plane, instead of her boy.

Forty-eight hours later, and on virtually no sleep since receiving the news of Albie's condition, Cathy rose before dawn, adrenaline pumping and determined to set off on foot for the holiday camp. What her purpose was, she wasn't yet sure; all she knew was that she couldn't stand another morning at her son's hospital bedside, desperately averting her gaze from the space where his arm used to be.

She dressed in the clothes she'd stepped out of the night before and crept down the stairs, her mind already racing with all the terrible new information that existed in her small world. Soon after the blow about Albie, further news had come, informing them that the pilot, the as-yet-unnamed man responsible for all this, had in fact survived and was now being treated in the very same hospital, just a couple of floors down – and that the two other fatalities the detective had mentioned were Howard and Elizabeth Warner, local visitors to the Golden Rabbit holiday camp for the past thirty years or more, but, oddly, not accounted for on Suzie's registration records.

Cathy thought her head, or her heart, might explode with the pressure of it all, and being near Nell and her grief only doubled that feeling. She wondered how they might have coped if in fact Albie had died, and that hateful unspoken voice at the back of her mind even dared to wonder if that might have been better. What was wrong with her? Surely a good mother would never have such a thought, such a cold, hard thought. She didn't mean it. The truth was, Cathy didn't know what she felt any more. All she felt for certain was that she'd do anything to make this all go away, to make Albie whole again.

Quietly easing open the back door, she grabbed her car keys as an afterthought. Now that the police had handed the crash site over to the air investigators, maybe she'd be able to drive her car back home, since it was parked outside their yellow tape.

As she headed on foot through the dark allotments, Cathy paused to glance back at the row of terraces from where she'd just come, and fired off a text message to Kip, asleep in Dad's spare room next door: *You can sit with Albie today*, she typed, feeling the need to punish her fair-weather partner for some undetermined failing. *I need a break. I don't think it's quite sunk in for him what's happened – he's not saying much. Talk to him, will you? The doctor said it's important to talk to him. Dad will let you use the truck if you ask.*

While her own home was still in darkness, next door at Dad's a light came on, glowing dimly through the upper curtains of the spare room. Cathy felt a jolt of guilt that she couldn't do more to unburden Kip of his pain – that, in fact, all she seemed able to do was jab at it. Albie was his son too; but in her usual hateful way, she couldn't seem to find it in herself to allow anyone else in – to share the weight of this monstrous grief.

Surely they'd be better off leaning on each other, to lessen the pain? Wasn't that something Kip had once said to her, many moons ago, before she'd finally driven him away with her lack of give, of warmth? Would he still be travelling the world, hawking his dreamcatchers and tie-dye sarongs like the oldest hippy in town, if Cathy had ever surrendered a little more of herself? Of course not; family was all Kip ever wanted.

She turned away and focused on the dawn trek ahead, out in the direction of Highcap Hill and the meandering coastal path towards the Golden Rabbit holiday camp.

As she crested the highest point, daylight was just breaking over the sea's horizon, and the true devastation of the plane crash came into soft focus in the valley dip below. So, this was what Nell would have seen, she realised: the small aircraft soaring in from over the ocean, and the appalling spectacle of it landing on the playground just minutes after she, Cathy, had driven in with Albie.

A sob filled Cathy's throat, and she leant against the hilltop marker and allowed her tears to fall, unchecked. It had been the same when she was younger, she recalled: only here – alone, close to the shore – could she truly let it all out, render herself vulnerable beneath the swooping of seagulls and the endless Dorset sky.

'Oh, Nell,' she murmured, continuing down the stony path, vowing to be kinder to her girl.

The night before last, just hours after they'd received the news that Albie's arm could not be saved, Cathy had stood in the darkness of their landing and listened to the muffled breath of her daughter's weeping beyond the bathroom door, and the snipping sound of scissors. Later, she had found the small bin stuffed to overflowing with Nell's beautiful hair – ten inches of luscious auburn waves, a sacrifice, Cathy knew, in the face of her brother's catastrophic loss. She should have gone straight to her, there and then, to comfort her, but she hadn't been able to. She'd known it was only her cowardice preventing her, that to go to her daughter was the right thing; but still, she just couldn't.

It wasn't lost on Cathy that she treated her daughter in much the same way as she treated herself: with impatience and disappointment and unrealistic expectation. Dad and Kip, and even Elliot, had pointed it out to her often enough – and she'd spent many a night awake in her lonely bed, staring at the crack of light through the curtains, wishing she could do something about it, wishing she could change. Because things had to change, didn't they?

But it was hard, because she recognised so much in Nell of herself: the enquiring mind, the fight, the fire, the fuck-it-all attitude. There were times when Cathy felt as though she were looking at her gentle younger self, reanimated from the past, teetering on the precipice, unaware of life's true threat, and foolishly leaping at every shiny new experience, as though danger wasn't even a thing. But danger *was* a thing, Cathy knew, and it was everywhere. How could a girl go out into the world with that brazen attitude and not get burnt?

Gazing at the campsite below, Cathy wiped her face dry on a balled-up tissue and started her descent to the grassy plain of the campground.

As she neared the crash site, the morning sun was now just high enough over the water to cast long shadows of the remaining debris, painting the devastation in muted tones and softening the harsh reality of it. While the first wing had been crane-lifted out to allow a thorough check for survivors, the body of the plane remained where it had landed, wedged onto the edge of the skate ramp, a large shard of its second wing still rammed through the window of the Warners' static caravan.

Yellow tape marked the investigators' 'no entry' zones, encircling the playground, the caravan and the shower block where Cathy had been cleaning at the moment of impact. The memory came back to her in a technicolour flash: the unreal spectacle of the ceiling slumping in, as a wall of debris and dust separated her from that young man who had entered the showers just seconds earlier. The young man the police couldn't seem to tell her anything about at all. He was only, what, twenty? Twenty-one at a push. And his little blue single-man tent was still there, lingering unclaimed in the middle of the now deserted hitch-'n'-pitch field, flapping loosely like some grotesque floral tribute laid at a roadside. Was it possible he was still buried beneath the wreckage, unclaimed?

Jangling the car keys in her fleece jacket, Cathy started towards the small parking bay on the coast side of the playground, where her Citroën Dyane sat cheerily in the morning light, a faded 1980s orange that once made a brighter splash wherever she went. *Ha, join the club*, Cathy often joked, and she wondered if this was what kept her so wedded to the old wreck: some weird solidarity of shared history and decline.

With purpose, she strode the perimeter of the vehicle, inspecting it for damage, and was surprised to find that, besides the gritty layer of displaced dust, it seemed intact. It was only when she got behind the wheel that she noticed the shard of light piercing through a six-inch gash in the soft roof, and a jagged metal object sitting on the passenger seat where Albie had last been.

For long moments, Cathy stared at the object, which in some ways resembled the distorted face of a clock, and she was again struck by the sense that this had to be some kind of cruel, surreal dream. Ever since this terrible thing had happened to them, she saw signs in everything, from the single winter glove snared by the hoover from beneath Albie's empty bed, to the flurry of fresh-kill bird feathers swirling around their back yard the morning after the crash, with no sign of a victim.

Just last night in the hospital, she'd passed a boy about Albie's age in the corridor, wearing the exact limited-edition white trainers he'd badgered her for last birthday, the very trainers he'd been wearing on the day of the crash. And now, here was her beloved car – the car Kip had bought her over twenty years earlier, an old banger even way back then – slashed by a piece of that fallen plane, much as Albie had been.

She turned her keys in the ignition.

'What the hell?' she snarled when nothing happened, furiously trying again, before realising the problem. '*Bloody lights.*

Bloody *bloody* lights! Why can't I ever remember to turn off the *bloody* lights?'

With a slam of the door, she exited the car, her feverish mind set on the long return walk home, but was halted by the sight of her sister-in-law's white Land Rover approaching on the main path. Instinctively, Cathy took a step backwards, so that she was obscured behind the plane's severed cockpit but could still see the vehicle as it neared. Suzie was driving, with a bandaged Elliot in the passenger seat, and it was obvious from their body language that they were arguing.

Conflicted by her need of a jump-start and the desire to bolt – to not get caught up with her older brother and his know-it-all wife – Cathy stayed put and waited for them to park. For two or three minutes, she watched as they apparently continued their argument, Elliot slump-shouldered, Suzie with hands gesticulating madly. Finally, they tumbled out, their words at once audible.

'I should've listened to my mum all those years ago.' Suzie snapped off her baseball cap and regathered her hair into its ponytail. 'God rest her soul.'

'Oh, not this again.' Elliot raised his eyes skyward.

'Yes, *this* again. I've made a lot of mistakes in my life, Elliot, and God knows you were the biggest. Or one of them, at least.'

Elliot stared at his wife across the bonnet. 'Why would you say a thing like that, Suzie? We're all suffering, you know? How do you think Cathy's feeling right now? Look at Albie—'

Suzie threw her arms in the air. 'Now who's bringing stuff up? *Cathy* is not my responsibility – and I suppose Albie's amputation is my fault, is it?'

From her hiding place, Cathy felt the sucker punch of those words. *Albie's amputation.* Suzie spoke them as though they were nothing, as though it were a case of the flu her boy had, not a devastating injury he'd never recover from.

'Of course not,' Elliot replied, with resignation. 'Anyway, I'm not saying I *didn't* renew the insurance; just that I can't remember. We've barely made a claim in all these years, have we? What I mean is, what are the odds, Suzie?' Elliot watched, deflated, as his wife retreated towards the office. 'I said,' he yelled, raising his voice, 'what are the bloody odds?'

Without turning back, Suzie raised a dismissive hand and disappeared inside the building.

'What are the bloody odds of what, Ells?' Cathy stepped out of the shadows, startling her brother, who jumped and grasped at his shirt front.

'God, Cathy! Don't do that, love.' He shuffled over and gave her a sheepish hug. 'Sorry about that. Didn't realise we had an audience. Oh, nothing. Just insurance stuff.'

Cathy blinked back at him. 'The Landie? Don't they believe it was *Suzie* driving when you crunched it?' she asked sarcastically. 'Because everyone else has sussed it was you behind the wheel, Ells.'

'All right, no need to be a smart-arse, sis,' he said with a grimace. 'No, not that. No problems there, thankfully. They've accepted the claim.' His eyes were puffy, his skin florid, and it was clear that he was drinking heavily again. 'So how are you bearing up?' he asked.

Cathy shook her head. After all, what could she say to him that really captured how she was feeling, what she was going through? 'So, what *were* you arguing about?' she asked instead, happier to talk about her brother's problems than her own. 'Just now – what's not your fault?'

That sheepish expression returned, as her brother glanced towards the office building and back to her again. He looked so ravaged, she thought. He might be fifteen years her senior, but right now he looked decades older. He didn't look well at all.

'It's the insurance on this place,' he said, simply. 'On the holiday camp.'

'Oh?'

'Well, obviously we're not liable – so we'll be putting in a claim against the pilot's insurance company. But no one's got the foggiest who the pilot even is, let alone the name of his insurers!'

'So, you must've phoned your insurance bods to get their advice – what do they say?'

'Not their problem.'

'What?' Cathy's mouth dropped, her brain leaping ahead to tot up the damage they'd need to put the Golden Rabbit straight if the campsite was to get up and running again. 'What d'you mean, not their problem? You've paid your premiums—'

Elliot groaned. 'That's the problem, sis. I can't find the paper-work, and the insurance company claim they don't have a record of our renewal. But I'm certain I paid it – I'm sure I wouldn't have messed up a thing like that.' He rubbed his nose with the heel of his hand, the crease between his eyebrows deepening.

'Does Dad know?'

'No, he bloody well does not – and that's the way it's going to stay for now. Until we work it all out. I mean, it might be fine. I think it's probably just an admin error . . .' he said, trailing off as he lost confidence in his own spin.

'Horrible news about the Warners, huh?' Cathy said, knowing she'd have to bring up the death of the old couple first.

'They hadn't signed in,' Elliot said with a shake of his head. 'They weren't even meant to be there. We had an air investigator here yesterday – you know, they reckon a large shard of the plane's other wing tore right through the window of their static. Killed them, just like that.' He snapped his fingers and grimaced guiltily.

'God, that's so awful,' Cathy said, recalling the quietly awkward pair who spent at least half their year caravanning here, not three miles down the road from their own family home.

Elliot nodded. 'Funny couple,' he said, and he turned in the direction of the Warners' static caravan with a distracted nod. 'It's all very sad.'

For a moment, the siblings looked on in silent respect.

'Guess you'll be needing a jump-start, then?' Elliot said, breaking the lull and dropping a heavy hand on his sister's shoulder. He nodded towards the keys in her hand.

'How—?' she started, but Elliot just gave a little laugh, and set about fetching the leads from the back of his Landie, the golden light of the morning setting him in silhouette as he went.

'It's not the first time,' he said with a smile in his voice, popping the rear bonnet of her Citroën, 'and I doubt it'll be the last.'

Once they had the engine idling over, the pair stopped off at the office to wash their hands. It seemed the welcome office was the only building that hadn't sustained any damage from the crash, being far away enough from the playground to have escaped flying debris. Suzie was sitting behind the large reception desk as they entered, scowling at papers and files spread out before her.

Cathy headed straight for the adjacent kitchen sink and called out over the sound of the running tap, 'What's all this rubbish about the insurance claim, Suze? You gonna give 'em hell?'

There was a long pause, before Cathy heard the explosion of Suzie hissing at her husband, furious at him all over again. 'Jesus, Elliot! What did I say to you? Not a word!'

Cathy turned on her heel, instantly ready to defend him – and herself – shaking the excess water from her hands, and intentionally spraying little droplets across Suzie's desk. 'I *am* his sister, you know?'

Suzie pursed her lips.

'I'm a real Gale, Suzie, unlike you! I've got more right to know about what's going on here than anyone – more right than you, for sure! How dare you try to keep it from me? Jeez, what is it with this family and its bloody secrets?'

'Hah!' Suzie coughed. 'If you only knew the half of it.'

Cathy witnessed the briefest glance pass between her brother and his wife, and she stood rooted before them, a new, unfamiliar panic rising in her chest. 'This is *my* dad's business you're talking about. If there's stuff going on here, I should know about it too.'

Suzie closed her binder with an aggressive snap. '*I* was working on this campsite before you were even born, Cathy – I earnt *my* right through sheer damned hard work. You've never done much more than your weekly cleaning shifts – and that's only when it suits you!'

'This? Again? *You* never gave me the chance to do more!' Cathy stepped forward, but Elliot was quick to catch her wrist. 'What the hell makes you think you're so much better than everyone else, Suzie? I've heard the way you talk to Elliot – it's *disgusting*. The only reason you stayed with him all these years is for this—' She swept her arms wide. 'You don't love him – he's your meal ticket!'

'God, you really are the bane of my life, Cathy. I swear, if you weren't family, I'd—'

'Ha! Family!'

'Whoa! That's enough, you two, please,' Elliot begged, tugging on Cathy's hand, cautioning her with a small shake of his head.

She slipped from his grip with a warning glare. 'No, Elliot, it's not. I bite my lip most of the time, but she . . . Jeez, she takes the piss, mate!'

Suzie gave a bored little scoff. 'You had your chance to be a part of this business, Cathy, just like me and Elliot – and you threw it away.'

'Oh, you *really* want to go over this again, Suzie? You were well into your thirties when Mum and Dad offered us the business; I was twenty-one, for Christ's sake! I wanted to travel, see the world outside of Highcap! What young person doesn't?'

Suzie shrugged, and Cathy saw red.

'Are you for real? It was *one summer*! I'd never been to university, or worked away, or travelled anywhere outside of Dorset. You don't give someone an ultimatum like that – *it's now or never* – and then wash your hands of them when they don't do what they're told. Even if you couldn't understand it back then, surely you can now? I mean, your Dylan – would you do that to him? Would you cut him out of the family business if he announced he wanted to go travelling for *one* summer?'

Not that Dylan would ever do anything so bold, Cathy thought spitefully. He was a computer nerdy shut-in, from everything she'd heard about him in recent years. Her own nephew and she barely knew the boy.

'That was Mum's call, not ours,' Elliot said softly. 'You know she made all the decisions when it came to the business. She was the one who said you couldn't expect equal treatment if you went off travelling.'

'You think I don't know that? She was a bitter, controlling old cow, right till the end – but you two didn't have to back her decision so bloody wholeheartedly, did you? Nor did Dad, for that matter, but that's another story.'

'We were only trying to protect you, Cathy. If you hadn't been so bloody-minded . . .' Suzie said. 'But, of course, you couldn't see that.'

'Protect me? From what? What business was it of yours? And you could have fought my corner, Ells, but instead the pair of you leapt on your *big opportunity* the minute I'd left the country – and when I got back, when I needed work the most, you just squeezed me out!'

57

'Yup, it's all our fault,' Suzie said glibly. 'And I suppose it was down to us that you came back from your travels pregnant, was it? To a man you'd only just met.'

Was there no end to this woman's venom? No one had ever loved Cathy the way Kip had back then – nor before or since – and here was Suzie, doing her best to belittle it as a childish whim.

'That's love for you,' Cathy replied, evenly. 'Not that you two would know anything about it. Anyway, it all worked out for you in the end, Suze: you're in your big cardboard cut-out on the hill, and me, I'm stuck in my crappy little terrace in Allotment Row, holding down three jobs just to pay the bills. Not to mention a fourth as unpaid carer for Dad next door, who insists on having a bloody heart attack every six months.'

Suzie gazed back at her impassively; at least Elliot had the decency to drop his head in shame.

'And the point of this rant is what, exactly, Cathy?' Suzie asked.

Exhausted, Cathy dropped her shoulders. 'I don't know. Honestly I don't. What I do know is, I'm going to drive home now, to feed Dad like I always do, so you two don't have to. And then, God help me, I'm going to try to talk to my daughter, who's in bits by the way, since her little brother nearly died, so—' She waited for some response, but none came, neither from Suzie, nor her own brother. 'Oh, fuck you, Suzie,' Cathy said, as disappointment washed over her. 'I actually hope the business really does go down the tubes, if only to see you get what you deserve.'

'Nobody wins if that happens,' Elliot said gently.

Cathy crossed the room towards the open door and the bright light of a summer morning in Highcap. 'Do you know what, Ells?' she replied, pausing in the door frame, and addressing only him. 'In my world, no one ever wins anyway.'

5. Nell

Friday

The morning's picking shift had been back-breaking under the ever-intensifying heat of mid-July, but Nell was grateful for the work over the past few days, if only to take her mind off Albie.

Albie, and the other thing, the shameful thing, she'd tried and failed to erase from her mind ever since evidence of it had landed on her phone, uninvited. She couldn't shake it from her thoughts, and, as the days had passed, it felt almost as though the horrifying events of Saturday's air crash and the alleyway incident of the night before had somehow merged into a single shapeless trauma that stayed close to her, like a haunting, at all hours.

Earlier today, as she'd set off for her summer job at Parsons' Nurseries, Mum had appeared at the top of the stairs, grey-faced, wanting to know where she was off to.

'You know, Mum? I'm due at work at seven,' she'd replied. 'I'm on earlies this week.'

Cathy had waved a dismissive hand at her, an *it's-all-right-for-some* gesture, and Nell's guilt had deepened. She'd heard her

59

arriving home late last night from her cleaning shift at the local carpet factory, and she knew she had two of her private clients to get to this afternoon over at the Starlings. The pressure of work and time spent looking after Grandad and fitting in visits to Albie in hospital seemed to have aged her in the past week.

Nell had raked fingers through her now cropped hair and wondered when, or if, Mum was ever going to acknowledge the dramatic change in her daughter's appearance.

'Listen, if Grandad doesn't mind me borrowing the truck, I'll drive over to see Albie when I get home, give you a break? Do you think they'll let me take him some stuff to eat? He's probably had enough of hospital food.' Nell had waited for a response, but her mum had already turned away, clicking the bedroom door shut behind her.

Now it was three in the afternoon, Nell's shift had ended and, still sweat-soaked and stinking of onions, she pulled up in the car park of the main hospital, snatched up the bag of treats and magazines she'd bought for Albie on the way home and headed into the cool reception.

She made a beeline for the lifts to the fifth floor, and it was only when the doors opened to let someone else on at level three that Nell found herself exiting early and wandering in the direction of the pilot's private room. The afternoon light cut dusty streaks through the high windows of the corridor, and it struck Nell how quiet this level seemed in comparison to the area Albie had been moved to since he'd come out of surgery and started to show signs of improvement.

Nell slowed her pace as she neared the pilot's room, cautious not to attract attention in case that same doctor happened to show up again. But the corridor was empty, and without thinking Nell reached for the door and eased it open, ready to claim she'd taken a wrong turn should she be met with nurses or auxiliaries on the other side.

Inside, still shrouded behind his blue canopy, the pilot lay, in much the same position as he had been when she'd first discovered him here five days earlier. Nell tiptoed to the foot of his bed, and was relieved to find he was sleeping and that the previously obscured corners of the room were indeed empty. She exhaled a slow breath, transfixed by the sight of the long, dark lashes that lay shut against his olive skin, the cropped head of silver and ebony hair; a stark contrast to the now unbandaged and gravely damaged left side.

Did he know about his boy yet? she wondered. About his disfigurement? Or did he have those fresh horrors still to suffer? Nell felt a sudden and overwhelming sadness, and, moving around to the side of the bed, she laid the tip of a finger on his unmoving hand and allowed it to rest there.

'Who are you?' she whispered softly.

What good could come of creeping about like this? she asked herself, as she gazed at the man's sleeping face, confused about her own motives. One thing was certain: her mum would go ballistic if she found out.

Nell retracted her hand as though burnt, and the pilot's eyes snapped open.

As the dark pools of his eyes locked on hers, a solemn crease formed between his brows.

'Do I know you?' An Irish lilt.

Nell gasped and shook her head. 'No,' she replied in a whisper. 'I just – just . . .' But the words wouldn't come.

'Oh,' he said simply, his eyes dropping away, and fleetingly he seemed to disappear inside himself. Now his gaze returned, with more fire, as his hand shot out and grasped her by the wrist, the touch of it fierce. 'Then, do you know *me*?' he asked.

'What?' Nell responded, still shaking her head, the intensity in this man's expression making her suddenly afraid. She pulled her hand free.

Unblinking, the pilot spoke again. 'Do *you* know who I am?'
Nell fled.

Up on the fifth floor, still coming down from the shock of her encounter, Nell was directed to the new ward Albie had been moved to that morning, where she was told his pain management was going well and that he was 'mending nicely'. Nell didn't think anyone should be described as 'mending nicely' when they'd just had their arm removed, but she resisted the temptation to point this out to the nurse, who had been otherwise nothing but lovely to her.

'Nelly-belly!' Kip called over when he spotted her making her way across the busy children's ward, and he leapt to his feet to sweep her up in a fulsome hug.

She missed him so much when he wasn't here; Albie did too. Why couldn't he just stay? Why couldn't Mum just let him stay?

'How's my little pixie?' He released her, ruffling her newly shorn hair and studying her expression briefly before fetching her a chair. He placed it on the opposite side of the bed, so that they faced each other across Albie, and, as she sat, Kip blinked at her, his chin pulling in in the tiniest of motions, silently signalling that things with her little brother hadn't been great that morning. Albie looked washed out and, quite unlike him, unsmiling.

'I've bought you some snacks, bro,' she said, cheerily, and for the craziest split second she went to pat his forearm and touched the empty space of his bedside instead. A groan caught in her chest, and she started talking to cover her alarm, the words tumbling out at speed. 'There are Doritos and a jar of sauce – super-spicy, your favourite, a pack of sweet and salty popcorn, some chocolate raisins and a bag of those disgusting Psycho Rats you can only get from the old-fashioned sweet shop.' She held the carrier aloft to show him, and Albie's mouth twitched at one corner, a concession of sorts. She took out the paper sweet bag and placed it on the bed on Kip's side, within reach of Albie.

'You'll be farting like a whoopee cushion with all that sugar inside you,' Kip laughed, nudging Albie's good arm. 'They'll think you're a methane hazard, pal – kick you out of the ward!'

This burst of normality prompted a bigger response in Albie. 'Good,' he said, in a raspy voice Nell barely recognised. 'I fuckin' hate it in here.'

'Albie!' Nell gasped, while at the same time laughing. 'I don't think I've ever heard you swear before! They'll be washing your mouth out with soap if you keep on like that.' She looked at Kip, whose expression had shifted into one of relief. 'But then—'

'If you can't swear when you've just had your arm cut off, when can you?' Albie asked, his eyes darting between his sister and their dad, waiting for their response. When none came, he laughed, his old, innocent laugh, and reached for the sweet bag, giving it a rough shake with his one hand, until the top crinkled wide. Placing a brightly coloured rat between his teeth, he twisted its head off. 'You look like a boy with your hair like that, Nell,' he said.

And that was all it took, that small shift in humour: Nell clamped her hands over her eyes and sobbed, all the while berating Albie for embarrassing her. 'I'm not crying, you little dickhead,' she laughed through snot and tears, 'I'm not!'

'Looks to me like you are,' he replied, awkwardly twisting his upper body to push a sweet into her wet hand. 'Looks to me like you've turned into a great big fat crybaby sissy since I've been away, and to be honest, it *is* a bit embarrassing, Nellie.'

'Ha!' Kip laughed.

'Oh, my God, you're *such* an idiot.' Nell gaped at her brother. 'I'd forgotten how annoying you can be—'

She glanced at her dad across the bed and was shocked to see tears now streaking down his face too. He waved her away, wiping his cheeks distractedly. 'Stop it,' he said, when Albie turned to him, wide-eyed. 'It's nothing.'

'*Oh, my God*,' Albie mumbled, reddening. 'Why are you lot always crying? Mum was the same yesterday. She said it was hay fever, but I could tell she'd been crying when she came back from talking to the doctors.'

'We're just . . . we're sad for you, that's all,' Nell replied, helping herself to another sweet. 'And relieved that you're still here. We don't know what to say.'

Albie pressed his lips together and he made a little goldfish noise, a nervous tic. 'Me neither. It still doesn't seem real. You know, I can't feel a thing, where they, you know—' He made a slicing motion through the air with his hand. 'So I'm not in pain, but, well, every now and then my stomach sort of flips when I think about it, when I go to do something normal like pick up my drink, or when I look down' —he lowered his gaze to where his arm should be— 'and I think maybe I'll wake up soon. Like it's a dream.'

Kip covered his mouth with a hand, inhaling a shaky breath.

'Oh, Albie,' Nell sighed. 'I can't even imagine how that feels. Have you talked to Mum about it? Told her how you feel? You can't keep these things to yourself.'

Albie shook his head. 'I don't want to upset her any more. She's really worried about work at the moment – she's worried she'll lose her cleaning jobs if she takes much more time off, and apparently the Golden Rabbit won't be back up and running until next season at the earliest, that's if it doesn't go bust altogether, she says, and then there's Grandad . . .'

Nell shook her head. 'That doesn't mean she doesn't want to talk to you about your stuff, Albie. She's just, I don't know, nervous about saying the wrong thing, I guess.'

Kip nodded. 'It's true, pal. Your mum's never been all that good talking about feelings, but it doesn't mean she hasn't got any.'

'Listen, Albs, Mum will probably keep trying to avoid talking about your arm, 'cause it makes her uncomfortable – but you're going to have to make her. Not for her, but for you.'

'Why do we have to talk about it at all?' he asked. 'It's a horrible thing to talk about.'

'Because, if you don't, it'll keep feeling like a bad dream,' Nell said, unsure where this piece of wisdom was coming from. 'I don't know, Albs. All I know is, if you let these things fester, they get the better of you.'

Albie nodded his head, looking like an earnest little owl in his hospital bed.

'You listen to this one.' Kip jerked his chin in Nell's direction. 'She's got a good head on those shoulders.'

Nell thought of that video and felt her stomach lurch sickeningly. All she wanted to do was run away, get away from this place, but how could she even think of leaving Albie now? Her old dreams of travel and adventure were gone, permanently now.

'No, I haven't,' she replied. 'I don't know anything. But I do know I love my little brother, and . . . well, I'm sorry I wasn't there for you that morning, Albs. If I'd been there for you, to take you to tennis practice like I was meant to, this would never have happened.'

Albie shrugged, as if it was nothing, as if she'd made some little mistake that had resulted in a minor inconvenience to him. But it wasn't little, was it? This was, in the words of that doctor, *life-changing*, and right now Nell couldn't think of anyone better to blame than herself. She was a total fucking car crash, in every possible way. She was too bloody lazy or scared to go to university; she'd let her mum talk her out of her travel plans; she'd slept with half of the under-twenty male population of Highcap; and now she had caused this – the loss of her own brother's arm. Of his future as a tennis pro or sports coach.

'The thing is, Nell,' Albie said, breaking her out of her self-absorbed train of thought, 'you don't *really* know that, do you? Nobody knows for sure. I mean, maybe you can't outrun the things that are meant to happen to you.'

'All right, Dalai Lama.' Nell scowled at him, wondering if her twelve-year-old brother had experienced some kind of spiritual awakening along with the bump to his head.

Albie scowled back. 'No, it's a thing! Like, what if you had got me to tennis in time, but that plane had taken a different turn, like just half a mile away, and landed on the tennis courts instead? I'd still be here, without my arm, wouldn't I? Or, if I'd gone inside the shower block with Mum, instead of onto the ramp, maybe the roof would've got me instead, *just so I could lose my arm.*' He stared at his sister, who was struggling to comprehend his easy acceptance of this dreadful new reality. 'Oh, you know what I mean. You're just being like Mum – trying to make this more horrible than it already is.'

'No, I'm not!' Nell protested, aghast at the comparison.

Albie huffed. 'I'm just saying, it's not your fault, all right?'

'You really can't argue with that, love,' Dad said with a proud smile. He picked up his empty coffee cup with a waggle and set off for the drinks machine. 'I'll leave you two to it.'

Nell stared back at her brother in awe. 'God, I love you, you little dipstick,' she said once Kip was out of earshot. 'I've been thinking, when you get out of here, I want to do something for you – something just for you.'

Albie frowned. 'Like what?'

'Like, anything you like. I dunno – a trip to London to Madame Tussaud's or the London Eye? Erm, a weekend on a canal boat – oh, tickets to Wimbledon! That kind of thing. Don't ask me to take you to New York, I haven't got that kind of cash, but you get what I'm saying. Whatever you like, within reason. On a budget.' She grimaced at the last bit, wishing she didn't have to say it. One day, maybe she would get to take him to New York or other places; one day, maybe they'd both escape this town and discover something new together.

Albie gazed off into the distance, with a tiny smile on his face, and it seemed to Nell he was perhaps imagining all the things they might do together too.

'What's the one thing you want more than anything else in the world right now, Albie?' she asked. 'Apart from the obvious.'

With a little frown, Albie tapped the home key on his iPad, to bring up his screensaver, which displayed a windswept Mum and Kip, smiling, arm in arm, the blue Dorset sea spreading out behind them. 'That,' Albie said.

Nell thought her heart might actually fall in, because 'that' – the one thing her little brother really yearned for – was completely beyond her power to grant.

'I said "within reason".' She smiled back at him, kindly.

Albie shrugged and offered her another Psycho Rat.

The Five Bells was starting to fill up by the time Nell got there at eight, and she scanned the front bar for anyone she might be able to sit with.

It was the first time she'd been back since the night before the crash – the night of the video – and, while her pulse hammered madly at the thought of who here might have seen it, there was a masochistic part of her that knew she had to front it out or risk vanishing altogether. Her talk with Albie earlier had echoed in her mind on the drive back home, shaming her into action. Man, if he could face up to the stark reality of his trauma, in which he'd lost a limb, she should be able to face up to hers, in which all she'd lost was some of her dignity.

But it wasn't that simple, was it? It wasn't just her dignity at stake here; it was so much more. In Nell's lone moments, snatches of that dreadful evening had started to come back to her in violent monochrome flashes, gathering momentum with each passing day, shattering her small sense of self-worth more with each recollection. These flashes were sensations more than images: the heat of hot breath on cold skin; the scent of piss and bins and hate and sweat; and the strobing threat of car headlights pulsing beyond the mouth of the alleyway.

There was something else, too, a feeling that just wouldn't leave her in her bleakest waking moments: the dark sense that she'd *known* they were being watched. It wasn't as though Nell had never done anything risky before, on an alcohol-fuelled whim with some strange boy, but this was different. This time, *someone* had filmed it – and now it was out there for anyone to see—

'Hello, love!' Uncle Elliot pulled out the bar stool where Nell stood waiting to get served. 'Didn't expect to see you in here. You with your mates?' His face was shiny and smiling, and the drink that landlord Ted was pouring in response to his merest nod would clearly not be his first of the day.

Nell looked about the dark-panelled bar but saw no one she knew, and she hadn't spotted any of her friends smoking out front as she'd come in. Were they really her friends? she wondered, not for the first time. They weren't close to her like Heidi or Holly – who might as well be on a different planet now they were off travelling – but they were a good laugh, an easy crowd who didn't ask too much of her on their pub nights out, drinking the dull hours away.

But not one of them had been in touch with her since that night when she'd gone off, wasted, with some strange lad she'd only just met, had they? In fact, none of them had tried to talk her out of it; quite the opposite, actually. They'd applauded as she'd left, she now recalled, as though she were just one of the lads who'd got lucky.

'Yeah. It doesn't look like anyone's here yet,' she replied, and she slid onto the bar stool her uncle had dragged over, wondering if she should just go home.

'I'll keep you company, love,' he said, slurring a little and patting her knee proudly. 'Ted, get one for my lovely niece here, will you? Nell's our Cathy's girl, remember? She's the spit, eh? Gale through 'n' through!'

Landlord Ted returned an unreadable smile, cautiously straight-mouthed, and not for the first time, Nell wondered if his expression was disapproval.

'Oh, do you need my ID?' she asked, reaching inside her thin parka. She'd never been asked for it here before, but she'd heard that some places in Highcap had started to clamp down lately, since a couple of fifteen-year-olds had got tanked up in the Anchor over Christmas and had to be rescued by the lifeboats offshore at Seatown.

Ted shook his head, but that look of caution still lingered. 'What can I get you?'

As he turned away to fix her a rum and Coke, Uncle Elliot drew down the corners of his mouth. 'Don't know what's got into him tonight,' he whispered conspiratorially, before raising his glass to Nell and taking a long draw. 'So, what about that pilot, eh?' he said, wiping beer from his sandy moustache. 'I can't believe he made it out in one piece. Well, not one piece, exactly. But alive.'

'I can't believe it either,' Nell murmured, thanking the landlord as he discreetly placed her drink on the counter. 'I had to physically stop Mum marching straight down to his hospital bed when she heard about it. He's been in a coma most of this time, so it's not like she could have it out with him.'

'What, d'you think your mum'd pull the plug on him or something?' Elliot chortled at his own joke, cutting it short when he realised the poor taste of it. 'No, she's hard, your mum, but she's not that hard. Anyway, she'd have to beat Suzie to it, the way she's on the warpath right now. I think they're both looking for someone to blame in all this. Best we lie low, eh, love?'

Nell smiled weakly and clinked her glass against her uncle's before taking a drink. 'So, how's Dylan doing these days?' she asked, for want of conversation. Her cousin was something of an enigma within the family – geeky, shy and rarely seen in recent years. They'd been in the same form at secondary school, but somehow their paths seldom crossed, and because of the tensions between Mum and Auntie Suzie, the cousins had never got to know each other beyond awkward small talk at Grandad's annual family barbecues.

'Oh, you know Dylan, love. He's a funny one. Barely leaves his room these days.'

'Did he finish his college course? What was it – media?'

Uncle Elliot rubbed his chin. 'Ha, well, he dropped that after the first term. Didn't like the tutor, or the other way round – I'm not sure. Anyway, he switched to computer programming instead, and now he's doing some distance learning. Reckons it'll get him into the games industry or something. Personally, I don't care what he does – I just wish he'd get out more, mix with people his own age. Real people, I mean, not people on the other side of a computer screen. Drives Suzie mad.'

'Has he got a girlfriend or anything?' Nell asked, nodding when Elliot indicated to Ted for two refills. 'I mean, he's a nice-looking lad, isn't he?'

Elliot laughed. 'Well, you know he doesn't get that from me – or your aunt, at that!'

'No, I suppose not!' She smiled, wishing she were the one who'd been adopted. At least that might excuse her mum for being so bloody cold towards her. She wondered whether Dylan was happy with his lot, or whether he, too, suffered strained relations with his mum and dad. 'Has he ever wanted to know about his birth parents?' she asked, hoping her uncle wouldn't be offended by the question. 'I mean, you can start finding out stuff once you're eighteen, can't you?'

Uncle Elliot's expression suggested he'd never even considered the possibility. 'Not as far as I know. I mean, I wouldn't encourage it. From what I recall, there were drugs involved. That's why he was taken into care in the first place – he was only a few months old when we got him, and already pretty neglected. Weedy little thing, he was. No, I wouldn't encourage him to look for that lot. That way heartache lies.'

Nell scanned the busy bar again and caught the eye of a middle-aged man in the far corner, who seemed to be pointing her out to his mates. Quickly they all looked away, before descending into laughter. She was being paranoid, she told herself, but still, the memory of that film clip reared up, forcing a rush of cold adrenaline through her body. Who else had seen it? Had it been sent only to her, simply to mess with her head in some sick way? Or was she the butt of some horrible viral prank, a video that everyone had already seen?

Of course, no one would be judging the lad, whoever he might have been. No, he'd be slapped on the back in congratulation, if anyone even worked out who he was. But Nell – well, *she* would be judged, wouldn't she? The *girl*, the *slapper*, the *dog*. That much she was sure of.

'Will you look after my coat?' she asked Uncle Elliot, forcing a smile as she dropped down from her stool and pointed at the toilet sign.

Elliot tipped her a salute and proceeded to order them a third round.

The toilets were situated out through the bar and up a creaky set of ancient, carpeted stairs that would have led to coaching inn rooms in days gone by. As she passed through the dim hallway alongside the men's loo, a couple of young lads bundled out laughing, startling her and carrying with them the scent of aftershave and testosterone. *Twats.*

'Don't mind me,' she muttered to herself, pushing open the door to the ladies' and coming face to face with the reflection of two girls she recognised from the year below her at school. They were both hard at work fixing their darkly drawn eyebrows, synchronised mouths formed into little 'o's of concentration. The short one was called Kasey, Nell seemed to think, and the other—

'All right?' the one called Kasey smirked into the mirror, holding her pencil aloft with her stubby little finger cocked.

Nell gave a brief jerk of her chin, already half inside the empty toilet cubicle. 'You?'

The girls sniggered. 'Yeah, *we're* all right,' Kasey replied.

Nell rolled her eyes and pushed the door shut on them. Bloody kids. This was why she had to get out of Highcap. Small town, small people. '*Good*,' she said from behind her door, hoping they'd hurry up with their stupid eyebrows and sod off.

Nell listened for the sounds of them packing up their make-up before her bladder finally relaxed enough to empty. It was only when she reached for the toilet paper that she realised they were still out there, laughing into their hands.

'All right, what is it?' she demanded, yanking up her underwear and cursing at the fiddly fly buttons on her jeans. Who the hell did they think they were? Throwing back the door lock, she lunged out at them, only to be met with a flurry of camera flashes from their twin mobile phones. 'Hey!' she shouted, but already the pair were out through the door and hurtling along the corridor towards the stairs. On the landing, several others halted their conversations to turn and stare in her direction, while another woman eased past her with a tut, trying to access the loos.

'*Nice* hair!' Kasey's friend yelled as she paused on the top step, emboldened by the distance.

'Dog!' Kasey shouted with a shrill laugh. 'Alley dog!'

And then, with a whip of their matching balayages, they were gone.

For a moment, Nell stood rooted, staring at the silenced landing, wondering if she was about to be sick. At least now she knew, she thought grimly. The film was out there, circulating in her home town, and she had nowhere to hide.

She thought about Mum, and what she would say. And Grandad. And *Albie*, for God's sake. What would Albie think? Because it was bound to get back to him too, some day, wasn't it? People just loved sharing this stuff. The evil fuckers couldn't get enough of it: other people's humiliation.

Pushing through the busy pub, Nell reached the place at the bar where her uncle had been, but found his seat now empty, his pint glass still half-full on the counter. She turned to the landlord behind the bar with a frown, and he slid her fresh drink across the countertop and leant in, not unkindly, and whispered, 'Someone just showed him the video, love.'

In what felt like slow motion, Nell glanced back towards the busy throng of drinkers, scanning their faces for signs of an enemy. She turned back to Ted. 'Has everyone seen it?' she asked in a quiet voice.

Ted grimaced and shook his head. 'I don't know, love. All I know is, one of the girls just stuck it under Elliot's nose, and he took off. I think it gave him a bit of a shock, is all.'

'It's been edited,' she hissed, leaning in to be heard, her anger rising. 'You know that? The boy's face – they've blurred him out, haven't they? But not me – not the girl – fair game!'

'But it is you, though?' came that voice again, this time right beside her. 'I mean, it's definitely *you*, isn't it? I guess, if you don't want people calling you a dog, you probably shouldn't act like one.'

'Who *are* you again?' Nell asked the girl called Kasey, feigning boredom as courage took the place of fear. Picking up her glass, she imagined smashing it into the little shit's smug face, but instead downed its contents in one. Easing on her jacket, jaw locked and determined not to rush, she ran her hands over her close-cropped hair, strangely emboldened by the lack of curls there. '*Fucking no one*,' she said with soft menace, 'that's who.'

Kasey and her friend sniggered, fuelled by alcohol and small-town self-righteousness.

Nell looked them up and down, before returning her attention to the landlord. 'By the way, Ted,' she said, jerking a casual thumb in the girls' direction. 'These two? *Underage.* You wouldn't want to lose your licence over a couple of silly little kids, now, would you?' Sedately, she pushed her empty glass over the counter into his waiting hand.

Ted nodded, and Nell left the Five Bells, eyes ahead.

It wasn't until she reached the far-off summit of Highcap Hill that she finally released her screams into the howling night sky. The tide was swelling high over the shore below, slapping against the craggy outcrops formed by decades of landslide and erosion. Nell edged closer than she knew was safe to do and peered over the edge, into the darkness. If it weren't for Albie, and the thought of leaving him all alone, with just Mum for company, the temptation to jump, to dash herself against those rocks, might have been just too great to resist.

6. Cathy

Friday

'I don't know where the bloody hell she is,' Cathy complained as she laid out Dad's cutlery and removed the foil from his steak and kidney pudding. 'She said she'd back in time to do your tea, but, as per usual, Nell is running to her own rhythms.'

'Go easy on her, love. She's more like you than you know,' John Gale wheezed, getting up from his easy chair to cross the room. 'You both think you're unbreakable, but you're not.' He eased himself onto the upright chair at the small dining table, exhaling through pursed lips as he caught his breath.

Cathy laid a hand on his shoulder. 'Are you all right, Dad? You don't look all that good. Want me to get Dr Rand to stop by and have a look at you?'

Dad waved a hand, shrugging her concern away as he picked up his knife and fork. 'This smells good, love.'

He was a right beggar when it came to admitting to physical weakness of any kind. It was a miracle he'd made it through the last couple of stays on the cardiac ward, considering how late he had left it before telling anyone how bad he'd been feeling. He of all people should know not to leave these things to chance; he was the one always telling them that if Mum had gone to the doctor's sooner, she might not have died so young.

'Elliot tells me they've taken the aeroplane away,' Dad said between mouthfuls. 'The investigators. Loaded the pieces up on a couple of trailers and drove it away. Farnborough. That's where they do the tests. So Elliot says.'

The clock over the mantelpiece read 7.30 p.m. Cathy pulled out the chair opposite and sat quietly for a few minutes while he ate. 'Uh-huh,' she murmured, not really listening. She'd spent enough time thinking about that plane, and the destruction it had brought down on them all.

After a while, Dad laid down his knife, and then his fork, and fixed her across the table. 'What is it?' he asked sternly. 'What's up?'

Cathy pulled her chin in. 'Does there have to be something "up"?' she replied.

'You don't usually have time to sit across the table and stare at me while I eat, Cath, so yes, I'm thinkin' that something's up.' He picked up his cutlery again and resumed eating. 'Is it Nell?'

'Well, yes. Among other things,' she replied. Nell had been under a black cloud since all this had happened, and Cathy knew it was wrapped up in her feelings of guilt about not getting back in time for Albie that morning. And then there was that self-destructive act of cutting off all her hair, something Cathy still hadn't even acknowledged, and which struck at her heart to even think about. But, frankly, Cathy didn't have time to deal with her adult daughter's self-pity when her twelve-year-old son had just lost his arm. 'She's wallowing,' she said.

Dad shook his head, and in that small movement Cathy knew his meaning, because she'd heard it a hundred times before: *You're being too hard on her, Cath; give the girl a break; she's a good kid; get off her back, will you?* But if Cathy wasn't going to keep her daughter on the straight and narrow, who would? You couldn't let them just run around doing whatever the hell they wanted *and* protect them. You either parented properly, or you didn't bother at all.

And from what Cathy could see, even across the emotional gulf that lay between them, Nell was as potentially self-harming as she herself had been at that age, and she still needed parenting, eighteen or not.

'Maybe it's more than just this thing with Albie,' Dad suggested. 'She's been losing her way for a while now, you said it yourself. Last thing I knew, she was going off travelling with that pal of hers, Heidi – what happened to that plan? I thought that's what she was going to spend her birthday money on.'

Cathy picked up the salt cellar, poured a small mound into the centre of her palm and proceeded to push it around with her index finger. 'Oh, that. It was all something and nothing. Heidi still went, but Nell changed her mind at the last minute.'

This wasn't exactly true, but it was the version Cathy was most comfortable telling.

The truth of it was, when Dad had offered to pay for Nell's long-planned gap year travel as an eighteenth birthday gift, Cathy had watched helplessly as the two girls spent hours huddled over Heidi's laptop, naïvely plotting their route through Indonesia and Australasia. The depth of Cathy's fear for them was limitless; anything could happen to them out there, alone. She knew this. *Anything.* She should have said something sooner, but, powerless in the face of their excitement, she had let Nell get right up to the eleventh hour, thinking she was about to book flights, before she'd finally put a stop to it.

There was no way she was about to let her daughter fly halfway across the world, with no one to look out for her but Heidi Reid, who was so tiny she'd blow away in a light breeze. Cathy knew what these places were like; she'd been there, seen it, done it, and she wasn't prepared to put her daughter at risk in that way.

At first, she'd tried to simply dissuade Nell, encouraging her to use the money to buy herself a nice little car instead and a weekend pass to Glastonbury. It was forecast to be a heatwave summer, and wasn't that every young person's dream? A set of wheels and a festival summer? Grandad's gift was a generous one, so there'd be money left over for some new clothes too . . .

But Nell hadn't been interested; she just wanted to travel, as her mum had – as both her parents had. 'You would never have met Dad if you hadn't gone to Thailand like you did!' she'd retorted. 'You'd never have experienced all those amazing things, and you'd never have had me! Dad says they were some of the best days of his life. Dad says—'

In the end, Cathy had drawn her last desperate card: they were broke, she'd told her daughter, penniless. She could barely afford the bills, let alone Albie's private tennis lessons, and she needed Nell's housekeeping contribution just to put food on the table.

'Why don't you ask Grandad for some help?' Nell had beseeched in a final, last-ditch hope. 'He can afford it.' But Cathy had just laughed, bitterly, and reminded Nell of her grandfather's life motto – the one, in fact, that had made him all that money he never spent: *neither a borrower nor a lender be*. The tight git even had it on a plaque that hung above the toaster in the kitchen, a silly seaside gift-shop trinket, picked up by Cathy's mother on a family day trip to Weymouth decades earlier.

Eventually, reluctantly, Nell had cancelled her grand trip, for the sake of her little brother, and Heidi had gone with Holly instead. That last conversation had been back in May, over two months ago, and since then, things between mother and daughter had never been worse, while Cathy's guilt swelled along with Nell's resentment.

'I don't understand the young,' Dad said now, looking irritable. 'Bloody hell, if someone had given me the money to go travelling when I was her age, I'd have leapt at it—' He stopped in his tracks and gazed distractedly across the table at Cathy, and, momentarily, she wondered how much he really knew about her own trip to Thailand all those years ago, about what had really happened out there. 'Did she say why she changed her mind?'

'Just cold feet, I think,' Cathy replied.

Out in the kitchen, the clatter of the back door signalled Kip's return from the hospital.

'How-do, Kip lad?' Dad called out over his shoulder, smiling to himself gently as they tuned into the sounds of Kip kicking off his shoes and hanging up the keys to Dad's truck.

It struck Cathy how easy her dad had always been with Kip, the hippy boy so unlike the rest of her family that she'd been nervous about bringing him home, let alone breaking the news to them that she was pregnant with his child just two months after meeting him abroad.

'How-do, John,' Kip replied. He looked exhausted.

'How was our Albie?' Dad asked, eager for news. John Gale was a man of few words, but he cared deeply about family. Cathy wished her love for her kids were as visible on the surface as Dad's was, but she feared she was more like her mother than she'd ever care to admit. There'd been no doubt old Irene had loved them all, but, God, she could be tough.

Kip dropped his rucksack on the sofa and pulled up a chair. 'He wasn't so good when I got there at lunchtime.'

'Penny's dropping?' Dad asked, tapping his own forearm.

'Was he upset?' Cathy asked. She could bear for him to be angry, but upset was another thing, because how were you meant to measure it? To deal with it?

'It's so difficult to tell with Albie, 'cause he's usually such a positive lad,' Kip replied. 'But for a few hours I hardly got a word out of him, and believe me, I tried. I asked him what he fancied doing when he got out of there – told him you'd promised us a little holiday away, John, when he was up to it, but he just wasn't interested. He's got his Switch game, and he's not playing it, he's got books, magazines – TV and films on that iPad you got him – but he doesn't seem to have the energy, or the interest, in any of it. Honestly, it's heartbreaking to see him sitting there like that, without his—' Kip dropped his gaze. 'Well, you know. Since the op.'

Cathy felt sick. She wondered if she should get in the car and drive back over, even though Albie had insisted she didn't need to stay every single night now he was off the quiet ward. 'Did he ask about the tennis tournament?' It had been the first thing he'd wanted to know about when he'd come round from the second operation, still groggy from the anaesthetic. *Can I still play in the match? Will I be out by then?* Nell had had to leave the room.

'No, he didn't,' Kip replied. 'Like you say, John, I think reality has started to kick in. Maybe that's why he was so quiet – it's a lot to process. Anyway, Nell turned up mid-afternoon, and you've never seen such a turnaround. That boy worships his sister, you know? It was like suddenly Albie was back in the room, more concerned that she shouldn't blame herself than he was about his own injuries. Honestly, Cathy, whatever it is you've done with those kids, you should be proud. They adore each other, and, God, they're such bloody lovely human beings.'

Cathy saw the moisture in his eyes and looked away. Any goodness in those kids had come from his influence, she was certain, not hers. 'You were around for a lot of it too, remember?' she said. 'Their childhood, I mean. I didn't exactly do it alone.'

'I know, I know,' he said, swiping at his eyes and making a show of eyeing up the remaining morsel of pie on Dad's plate. 'Cor, that looks good, Cath. I'm bloody starving. I haven't eaten since breakfast, give or take a gummy rat and handful of popcorn – and that hospital serves nothing but processed crap. I don't suppose . . .?'

Without a word, Cathy rose and fetched a second plate from the little kitchen, laying it down in front of Kip with an unceremonious clatter. 'Don't ask me to heat it up,' she said, in an attempt to defuse the grateful smile now radiating up at her, and she lingered just long enough to feel the warmth of Kip's hand as he reached up to brush her waist.

'You are a bloody marvel, Cathy Louise Gale,' he said, tucking straight in and hamming up his phoney Dorset accent through a mouthful of food. 'It's still warm – and, moy Gawwwd, it's delicious, moy lit'l darlin'!'

Unable to help herself, Cathy gave a small laugh, looking away, bashful in his presence, even after all these years.

'She's a marvel, all right,' Dad agreed, casting his gaze between the pair with what seemed to Cathy a meddling glint in his eye. 'You know, she'd make a lovely wife, Kip lad,' he said.

Kip looked up from his plate, fixing Cathy with a mischievous waggle of his eyebrows. 'That she would, Mr Gale,' he said. 'That she would.'

'Oh, sod off, you two,' Cathy muttered with a scowl, but that good feeling she'd been fighting made it through, and before she knew it, she was laughing, they were all laughing, and, for just a few short moments, her heartache over Albie receded.

As Kip cleared away the plates and headed into the kitchen, Dad leant in and lowered his voice. 'Cath? Why don't you two have a quiet night next door? Watch a film or something? If Nell's about, send her over to me for a game of backgammon. Tell her her old grandad wants some company.' He paused, waiting for her response, before punctuating his words with a sly wink.

'Dad!' Cathy laughed, feeling the flush reach her neck. 'Anyone would think you were trying to set us up.'

'Set you up!' he barked. 'You've been together nearly twenty years, you daft mare! Bloody Nora. If you want my opinion—'

Cathy raised her eyebrows.

'—which I know you don't – I think you two are wasting a whole lot of time apart, when you could be together. Life's short. Don't we know it? It honestly baffles me why you are the way you are with him. It's clear that your Kip's still as mad about you today as he was the day you met. He's smitten.'

Cathy fought the tiny smile she felt creeping onto her face, and Dad, immediately spotting the chink in his daughter's armour, called out to the kitchen, 'Here, Kip – our Cathy fancies a night in in front of the telly.'

'You haven't got a telly, John!' came the reply over the running water.

Dad shook his head in despair, raising his voice again. 'I don't mean with me, you pillock!'

Kip stuck his head round. 'Ohhhh,' he replied, his confused expression morphing into pleasure as he grasped Dad's meaning.

'Leave the poor man alone,' Cathy scolded, guilt flooding her as she realised just how much she'd like to flop down in front of a soppy film with her old Kip, to forget about this messed-up world around her. 'He's got bigger things to think about than watching a film with me.'

But before Kip could open his mouth to reply, Cathy's phone rang, the sound of it flooding her with the mixed emotions of dread and saved-by-the-bell relief. With a sharp intake of breath, she held up her handset to show Dad the caller ID and took the call.

'Suzie,' she replied, coolly. They hadn't spoken since that last confrontation at the Golden Rabbit a few days back, and, frankly, Cathy didn't care if she never spoke to her sister-in-law again. 'What is it?'

'Where are you?' Suzie asked. No small talk, then.

'With Dad. What's going on?' Cathy's mind raced ahead, imagining her brother dead from an undiagnosed brain bleed. He'd been so pale last time she saw him, and typically she'd just put it down to the drink. 'Suzie? Is Elliot OK? Is it his head?'

'He's fine. His head's fine. Listen, a friend at the hospital just messaged me to say they've been surrounded by news crews for the past hour. Loads of them – local *and* national, apparently.'

'What, because of *Albie*?' Already Cathy was up on her feet, scanning the room to locate her car keys.

'No. You know the pilot woke up a few days ago? He's well enough to talk now, apparently.'

'So?'

'So, I've been trying to get the police to release his name to me ever since – to submit to the insurers. We can't make a claim without it, and the bastards are trying their best to wriggle out of it as it is, saying we never filed our renewal last year. I keep asking the police for his name, and they keep saying they can't give it to me.'

'Suzie, I don't understand what this has to do—'

'You'd think the big story is the one where a reckless pilot ploughs into a campsite,' Suzie continued, ignoring Cathy's interruption, 'killing three people and maiming another—'

Cathy paced the living room in frustration, rolling her eyes at Kip and Dad.

'But *no*. Turns out he's *claiming* to have lost his memory – complete amnesia – to the extent that he doesn't know who he is, where he was coming from, or even that he had a kid in the plane with him. The sick part is, now the press have got wind of the fact that his own child was one of the ones who died, they're all over it – can't wait to get an interview with him.'

'Is he talking to them?' Cathy asked, aghast.

'No. I spoke to that DS Samson earlier and she told me if he's suspected of crash-landing intentionally he'll likely be charged with manslaughter, so he's been given a duty solicitor, who'll no doubt tell him to lie low. But the point is, if they can't get to him, those sharks'll be after anyone else connected for a statement, I'm sure – so we all need to agree: *no comment*. OK? Tell the others, yes? Dad – Nell – Kip. Anyone they're likely to contact.'

Cathy didn't know how to feel. There was her boy, lying in the very same hospital, his life shattered immeasurably, and another three dead, and all the press were interested in was the man who'd caused it all. The man who less than a week ago had smashed into their lives and left them devastated. 'Got it,' she murmured.

'Right.' Suzie exhaled a long breath. 'Good.' When Cathy didn't respond further, she added, 'You know, they're calling him the Unknown Pilot, Cathy, like he's some kind of modern-day hero. Anyway, I expect it'll all be on the local news at half-nine—' she added, and Cathy hung up.

No sooner had they all decamped to Cathy's next door than Nell arrived home through the back, appearing startled at the unusual spectacle of the three of them lined up on the sofa in front of the TV.

Remote control in hand, Cathy glared at her daughter in the doorway, the release of her anger following Suzie's call at once redirected. 'Well?'

'Ohh,' Nell replied after a beat, grimacing as realisation dawned. '*Shit*. Grandad, your tea. Shit. Sorry. Oh, God – I went to see Albie and then . . . I just, well, it went out of my mind.'

84

Grandad waved her apology away and patted his belly. 'It's all fine, Nellie, love.'

Cathy took in the dark rings under her girl's eyes, the dishevelled appearance. 'Have you been drinking?'

'Why?' Nell asked in response. Not exactly defensive, more guarded. 'Have you spoken to Elliot?'

Cathy glanced at her dad, who shook his head and gestured towards the TV, as Kip jumped up to offer Nell his seat.

'What's Elliot got to do with anything?' Cathy shunted along.

Nell's shoulders dropped, and she kicked off her dusty boots. 'Nothing. I'm going straight up,' she said, and Cathy wondered what secrets her daughter harboured. She knew that blank expression of suppressed horror; she'd seen it in her own reflection all too often over the years. There was no doubt to her that Nell was hiding something; she also had no doubt that she, Cathy, was the last person Nell would confide in. She wondered how far apart was too far, before it was too late to come back together at all.

'You might want to stay for this, Nellie,' Kip said, taking the remote from Cathy's hand. 'Suzie says the press are down at the hospital.'

Wearily, Nell accepted her dad's place beside Cathy, keeping a fist-sized space between them, and Kip perched on the armrest and switched the TV to the closing credits of the national weather. Seconds later, the news headlines were read over the opening bars of the regional programme.

One plane down, three dead and several injured – a week since the tragic Highcap air crash, police release a statement regarding the Unknown Pilot.

'*The Unknown Pilot*,' Cathy murmured above her father's cursing. 'That really is what they're calling him?'

As Kip shushed them both, the newsreader introduced the piece, and the screen moved to a live broadcast from outside the county hospital, where the light was now dimming.

'Jenny, I'm standing here outside Dorset County Hospital, where the man they are dubbing "The Unknown Pilot" has been treated since that fatal air crash we reported on last weekend at the Golden Rabbit holiday park on the coastal outskirts of Highcap. In the days following the air disaster, we were able to confirm that two elderly inhabitants of a static caravan were killed on impact, while another unconfirmed male is as yet unaccounted for. Perhaps most tragic of all, a child, believed to be the son of the pilot, was also pronounced dead soon after emergency crews arrived on the scene.'

The TV screen switched back to the newsreader.

'Nick, you say the man operating the aircraft has been dubbed "The Unknown Pilot", and I believe he is suffering from some kind of amnesia. Is that right? Tell me, what exactly do we know about him?'

Aerial footage filled the screen, showing a bird's-eye view of the smoking crash site and the full extent of the damage not long after the event. Cathy felt her stomach contract as she thought of Albie crushed beneath that skate park, and of the young man beneath the fallen roof of the shower block where she'd been cleaning. They still hadn't found him, had they? Only now did it dawn on her just how close to death she herself had come.

'Well, Jenny, this really is a mystery. So far, the police tell us they have nothing to go on, because, indeed, while the pilot

86

is now awake, he is currently suffering from an acute form of amnesia. As the cockpit of the plane was at the centre of the explosion, unfortunately any personal items which might have shed light on his identity have been destroyed.'

'And, Nick, what about flight records – many of our viewers will be wondering how it's possible for a plane to come down and no one notice it missing. Don't all flights have to be logged before take-off?'

'You'd think so, wouldn't you, Jenny? But, in fact, within the UK, if a light aircraft is flying from a small private strip with no air tower, it is actually possible to take off without speaking to any human form of air traffic control at all. Of course, as well as carrying out thorough tests on the recovered aircraft itself, the AAIB – that's the Air Accidents Investigation Branch – will be looking for any other clues that might come from transponder records, radar sightings or communications with a destination airfield.'

'And any news on the casualty – the pilot?'

'Yes, hospital staff have confirmed that the patient suffered third-degree burns, as well as fractures to his collarbone and leg. And let's not forget that up until forty-eight hours ago he had been held in a medically induced coma while they fought to save his life – so there is hope that his memories will return in time. But, Jenny, most mysterious of all is that, so far, no one has come forward to report a father and son missing – and it is this detail that police believe will be key to unlocking his identity. Someone, somewhere, must be missing them.'

'Now, Nick, what do investigators think happened to cause the crash in the first place?'

'Well, this really is an unusual story all round, Jenny. While the investigators are yet to publish their findings,

we've learnt that CCTV cameras set up to capture rare bird footage further up the coastal path at Kite Hill managed to film the plane coming in on that fateful day.'

The television screen filled with the grainy CCTV footage from the viewing post up at Kite Hill.

'I was there,' Nell murmured. She sounded numb, like a person in shock. 'Right below that camera, as the plane came over. When you phoned me, Mum – I was right there.'

The journalist narrated over the film.

'As you can see, in this footage it appears that initially the pilot circles once over the campsite – here – as though assessing the location.'

For a few moments, the reporter was silent, letting the film speak for itself.

'And then, as we see here, he heads back out over the water as though retreating, only to swoop back and strike, nose-first, into the children's playpark.'

In the silent film, so grainy that no sign of Albie, or indeed anyone else, was possible, the plane went down, and a cloud of grey smoke puffed up, like a small match strike.

The screen returned to the newsman outside the hospital.

'This footage has led to the theory that the aircraft, or indeed the pilot himself, had encountered some sort of difficulty while in the air, and that his intended emergency landing spot had in fact been the large open field just beyond the holiday camp.'

'And so far, no suggestion from investigators as to what kind of difficulty that might have been?'

'There's been plenty of speculation, Jenny – everything from engine failure to fuel loss, to some kind of medical emergency such as a stroke or heart failure. It was a bright morning, and it's been suggested that the pilot may have been dazzled by the reflection of the sea, or even, one local resident speculated, by the glare of the large golden rabbit figure recently erected on the entrance path to the holiday camp.'

The screen flashed up an image of the toppled statue, with the 'Welcome to the Golden Rabbit Holiday Park' billboard cheerily displayed against the backdrop of rubble and destruction.

'What the—' Cathy shunted forward in her seat. 'They're blaming us?'

'Steady.' Dad brought a hand down on her knee, squeezing it firmly, silencing her.

'The one thing we can be sure of, Jenny, is that the police and air investigators are working round the clock to get to the bottom of this tragic accident, and to identify the Unknown Pilot and child. More on this story as we get it.'

As the news anchor moved on to the next local update, Cathy sprang from her seat, her heart racing with rage and confusion.

'Calm down, Mum,' Nell pleaded, reaching out for her. 'It's the press – they always get it wrong.'

'What about Albie?' Cathy yelled, snatching her hand away. 'Did any of you hear them mention Albie? His loss? Our grief? How dare they – how—?'

In a rush, she strode through the living room and into the kitchen at the back, snatching up her keys and pulling on her trainers.

'Where are you going, Cath?' Kip asked, pursuing her to the back door. 'It's nearly ten o'clock!'

'I'm going to the hospital,' she barked over her shoulder. 'And I'm going to find out from that fucker – that "Unknown Pilot" – what really happened when he crashed his plane.'

Cathy slammed the back gate and headed off into the night.

7. Nell

Why did her mum always have to have someone to blame? Wearily, Nell said goodnight to Grandad and Kip at the back gate and returned to the house alone, fearful of the havoc Mum was almost certainly leaving in her wake.

Of course the hospital staff weren't going to let her anywhere near a patient – a complete stranger – at this time of night, or in that kind of state. It was just another of Mum's useless point-making exercises, and the only thing she would end up with, as always, would be a deeper sense of injustice and upset. It never seemed enough for her that bad stuff happened in the first place; she always had to go off in search of an aggressor – real or imagined – to what, eclipse her own pain? Nell wasn't sure, but in this, at least, she knew she and her mum differed.

Conversely, Nell had always been one for an easy life. A conflict-avoider, according to Mum. A peacemaker, according to Kip. A pushover, if you were to listen to her best mate Heidi. They were all right, she knew, in one way or other. Because if

91

trouble came looking for Nell, why, the best response was surely to stick her head in the sand, wasn't it? Hope that if she averted her gaze from whatever it was for long enough, the trouble would go away.

Had that served her well, she asked herself as she locked the back door behind her and switched off the kitchen lights, this conflict-dodging? Probably not. It was almost certainly the reason she'd always been the kid who ended up with the bashed-up leftovers at the school cake sale, too polite to push to the front. It was why she hadn't attended her school prom at the end of Year Eleven, having been too reluctant to ask out the boy she really liked, in case he said no. In case she embarrassed *him*.

Self-destructive, was what one school counsellor had suggested, when Nell had passed out in the toilets after taking a pill some boy had given her on the playing field at lunchtime. Apparently he'd already tried it out on several other girls that term, and some of them hadn't been lucky enough to make it back to the school before he did God knew what to them at the back of the pavilion.

'Why would you take a pill without knowing what it was?' the counsellor had asked.

'I didn't want to offend him by saying no,' had been Nell's pathetic reply.

What the hell was that all about? Her own mother had gone through her entire life seemingly not giving two tosses about offending others, and yet to Nell it was unthinkable. It was perhaps why she – and she knew this to be true because she'd heard the catcalls with her own ears on more than one occasion – had already got herself a reputation among the boys in town, since she'd never been able to work out how to say no, even when *no* was exactly what she wanted to say.

Nell tasted blood, and realised she'd bitten down on her lower lip as thoughts of that video leaked to the front of her mind. She would cry, if she had tears to spare, but she'd shed them all on the dark coastal path over Highcap Hill, and now all she felt was numb.

As she ran the tip of her tongue over her sore lip, she thought how strange it was, the way everyone in the family banged on about how she possessed her mother's fire, yet the two women really were so different in so many ways. Unlike Nell, her mother certainly knew how to say no; she said it all the time.

Up in her bedroom, the smell of old-fashioned roses drifted in through her open window, and she stood for a while gazing down at the patch of light thrown across Grandad's cluttered patio. She imagined him and Kip together inside his kitchen now, pouring tea from the pot and dissecting the events of the day. The day as they knew it. Because Nell's day had taken on a different shape altogether since that hour spent in the Five Bells this evening.

Despite her uncle having seen the video first-hand, poor sod, news of it hadn't yet reached the rest of the family, and Nell prayed that Elliot had just moved on to the next pub up the street and carried on drinking until he'd forgotten about it entirely. Her heart juddered icily every time she thought of him seeing her in that video – his niece, for God's sake.

Still feeling nauseous, she dropped onto her bed and opened her tatty laptop, instinctively navigating to Facebook – an app she had barely glanced at in the past few years. For what felt like an age, she stared at the log-in box, trying to recall her password, when suddenly it came to her: *Arsebook1:)* She and Heidi had set their accounts up together years ago, for some social media project their year group were working on in secondary school, and they'd quickly embarked on a shared mission of competitive 'friend'-collecting. Heidi's password, from memory, had been *Cockbook2;)* which had, naturally, been the source of much hilarity between them.

Typing in her own password now, Nell was surprised to discover it worked, and within moments she found herself staring at the timeline of the old Nell, a timeline full of childish chat, Pokémon pics and schoolgirl silliness. It felt like a window into simpler times, and it made her profoundly sad to think of all that had happened in the years since, and all that she had become, and hadn't become. She missed Heidi, and wondered if she missed her back, or whether she even thought of her at all, a thousand miles away on her adventures.

With a cautious touch, Nell typed in the name of the girl who had cornered her earlier that evening in the Five Bells, trying to imagine how on earth she thought she was going to track her down without a surname. *Kasey.* With a 'y' or an 'ie'? A never-ending list of worldwide Kaseys, Kacies and Kaceys populated her screen. Of course, Kasey no doubt favoured other platforms, like Instagram or TikTok, rather than the housewife's choice everyone thought Facebook had become, but so far Nell had failed to find her on either. Still, Nell reasoned, Facebook was worth a try – it was a superior stalking platform, and it was possible this Kasey or her mate had had an account in the past, even if they didn't use it now. If Nell could find her on here, she could at least work out her full name and reach out to her, to ask exactly where that video had come from. Judging by Kasey's animosity towards her earlier tonight, Nell wasn't sure she'd co-operate, but it was worth a shot. Anything was worth a shot if it meant Nell could get to the source of that video and get it taken down.

She searched for Kasey using Highcap as a location, without success. She searched for Kaseys in Dorset, at the high school, in Dorchester, but still, nothing. She looked up the Five Bells, and found they had an active page, with over two thousand followers, and in desperation she typed the name into the search bar there, to see if she was a contributor.

But before the results had even scrolled, Nell was startled by the long-forgotten 'bing-bong' sound that signified a new live message arriving in her Messenger inbox. Her cursor hovered over the red bubble, as she deliberated over whether to click it or shut the app down once and for all, never to know. Her pulse raced. What if it was from someone else who'd seen that video? What if it was from the person who'd filmed it – or the boy she'd been with? What if she was just about to open a fresh world of hell for herself—?

Nell clicked on the inbox and the sender's name appeared: Dylan Cat.

Dylan? She stared at the unread message for a while, squinting at the profile picture of a cat wearing sunglasses, which gave away nothing. There was only one Dylan that Nell knew, but it couldn't be him, could it? Dylan *Gale – cousin* Dylan? Sure, it was a long time since she'd used this account, but Nell had absolutely no memory of being 'friends' with her cousin back then – any more than she'd been friends with him in real life.

Reluctant but now unable to look away, she opened the message and began to read.

Hi Nell, hope you don't mind me messaging you but I saw your status was active so I thought id try. I heard about Albie and the plane and wanted to say hi it must be really horrible for you all right now and I just wanted to say hope you are ok. I know we dont really know each other v well but anyway if you ever need anyone to talk to you can talk to me. Only if you want to, thats what I wanted to say. Dylan (cousin)

Nell stared at that last word, in brackets, and it seemed to her to be profoundly tragic that Dylan had needed to type that.

How was it possible that their families lived so close by, that all these years they'd gone to the same schools and supermarkets and doctors and dentists and village fêtes, and yet they'd grown up virtual strangers, because of the frostiness between their mums? Nell had always yearned for a closer family; maybe Dylan had too?

Hi, Dylan, thanks for your message. It's weird seeing you on here – I haven't used Facebook for years. How are you? I can't remember the last time we saw you – maybe Grandad's birthday bbq at Golden Rabbit year before last? My mum and yours aren't that good at keeping in touch, are they, haha. Albie is still in hospital, and he's putting on a brave face, but, I don't know – how do you get over something like that?

She pressed send.

Immediately, Nell could see the dots signifying that Dylan's reply was being written, and a minute later it arrived.

Yeh they dont get on all that well do they. Doesnt mean we shouldnt be friends though does it, thats what I think. Dad said you saw the whole thing the crash I mean. What was that like. They said three people died maybe four and the pilot is burnt but alive. Did you see the news tonight. They reckon he cant remember a thing. Not even his own name. The pilot i mean. Thats insane.

Nell wondered about Auntie Suzie's theory that Dylan didn't do so well at school because he was gifted. By gifted she meant super-intelligent, but his tone was childlike, stilted, and he certainly wasn't gifted in the punctuation department. Maybe he was dyslexic? Maybe this wasn't even him.

How do I know this is really you? she typed.

For a few seconds, nothing happened, and then a fresh message popped up in the form of a passport photo. It was Dylan all right, showing a photograph that must have been taken a couple of years back, around the time she would last have seen him.

OK, she replied. *You're right. It IS insane. I'm OK, but my mum's been off her trolley with worry ever since, and you know Kip – my dad – came home from his travels to be near. And Grandad is being his usual self, but I can tell he's worried about Albie too. It feels like a bad dream, tbh.*

When Dylan's reply didn't immediately arrive, Nell typed, *I was thinking about your mum and dad. Uncle Elliot must be really stressed out, with all that mess to sort out at the holiday camp.* She stared at her own words and added, *Have you seen him today?*

The typing dots returned, and Dylan's message winged in. *I dont really speak to my mum and dad all that much. I havent seen him today so I expect hes down the pub or the pool club. You know my mum reckons hes an alcoholic that's what she says anyway and I think shes probably right. I just stay out of there way really. All they do is argue and I cant be arsed to get in the middle of it. Makes me want to go find out about my real mum and dad lol. I mean my birth parents. Cos they cant be any worse can they lol.*

Nell stared at the words a while, trying to work out how you were meant to reply to a statement as big as that. *Do you know anything about them at all?* she asked.

Nope but I might soon. I did ask once and mum said they were addicts so they might even be dead. I dunno. How is your mum btw? Sounds like they all had an argument down at the site earlier in the week. My mum says auntie Cathy told her she hopes the business goes down the pan. Mum was spitting feathers! Lol

Nell sighed heavily; it certainly sounded like the kind of thing her mum would say. *God, I don't know why they can't all just get along. I don't really understand why Grandad didn't give Mum more to do in the business – I think that's what causes all this bad blood. There's definitely some jealousy thing.*

Its cos shes not a real Gale isnt it? Dylan replied. *Which really sucks cos it makes me wonder if everyone thinks that about me too.*

Confused, Nell read and re-read the message over, trying to decode Dylan's words. *What do you mean?* she typed.

Well like cos Im adopted too.

Nell stared at the last word *too*, trying to formulate a response. *My mum's not adopted*, she finally replied.

She watched as the typing dots rippled on the screen, then off, then on again, until at last Dylan's response came. *Sorry my mistake. It was just something I heard mum say thats all I musta got it wrong.*

What did she say? Nell typed, now with growing urgency. *What did you hear?*

Long seconds drew out, before Dylan at last replied. *It was a while back now and im sure I got it wrong. I think my dad lent your mum some money for Albies tennis lessons and my mum found out about it and gave him an earful. She said she was fed up with bailing Cathy out and she didnt know why he was such a soft touch cos Cathy wasn't his problem. She said – actually I dont think I should say anything else Nell. You should ask my dad maybe.*

Nell screamed in frustration before typing, *You have to tell me now, Dylan, or I'll just go and ask my mum myself! What did Suzie say?*

Ok ok. She said and this is word for word – Elliot shes not your problem. Your dad's the one with all the money – let him bail her out. Hes the one who bloody adopted her. It's not for you to interfere.

Adopted? Nell stared at the word, trying to find any other possible meaning but coming up with none.

That's what she said Nell. I'm not making it up.

Carefully, she composed her reply, desperately casual, to conceal her horror. *That's weird, isn't it? I'll have to do some subtle digging my end* ☺

Whats your mobile number? Dylan asked. *Maybe we can text – meet up even?*

Sure, Nell replied, adding her number and a wave emoji. *See you soon.*

She navigated away from the inbox, her stomach churning with hunger and nerves, and was startled when her phone immediately chimed, as a message from Dylan landed. *Heres my number cuz. Lets meet up soon.* Barely had she had the chance to add him to her Contacts when a second message pinged through: *How about tomorrow?*

She sighed heavily, already regretting sharing her number with her weird boy cousin. *I'm working,* she typed without enthusiasm. *Tuesday's my next day off. I can take you to visit Albie if you want?*

With a sinking feeling, she switched off her phone, shut her laptop and flopped back against the pillows. Kasey and the video would have to wait. For now, Nell had a new problem to unsettle her mind: who was her mum, really, if she wasn't a Gale? And if any of what Dylan had said about Cathy being adopted was true, did her mum know? Did she even have the slightest clue?

8. Cathy

Saturday

Cathy had been sitting at the bedside of the Unknown Pilot for most of the night.

She felt curiously serene, sitting in the quiet of dawn, as fingers of sunlight began to filter through the hospital blinds of his room, bathing his white bedsheets in soft stripes of buttery gold.

The night before, she had set off from home in so violent a fit of rage it was a wonder she managed to find her way to his hospital room without being ejected by security staff alerted by the pounding of her furious heart. What was she going to do when she found him? She hadn't a clue. But one thing Cathy was clear on: she needed to look into the face of the man who had done this terrible thing to her boy.

When she'd arrived, Cathy had been surprised to find the hospital short-staffed, and, concluding the man must be somewhere on the Acute Care floor, she was soon hurrying along the corridors unchecked, locating his private room with ease, marked as it was with the giveaway moniker: *John Doe*.

All night long, the lights in the corridor were kept burning on low, and all night Cathy had watched closely as the pilot slept, one side of his face a livid charred red, the other a chiselled work of art, deeply tanned and just old enough to be scored with the evidence of a life lived.

When a clocking-on night nurse had found her at his bedside on her midnight rounds, Cathy had whispered that she was his sister, just flown in from overseas, and she was, miraculously, left alone; the nurse must have been an agency cover, somehow oblivious to the nationwide interest in the man at the centre of the Highcap air crash.

There was a madness to it, but Cathy had felt compelled to stay and watch him through the night, her chair pulled up close to his side, so close that she could hear his breath as it escaped his dry lips.

As minutes had turned to hours, and the darkness outside gave way to daybreak, she had found herself almost imagining she knew him from another life. All night long, she'd sat like this, gazing at the Unknown Pilot, and what had started within her as raw hatred had somehow morphed into something else altogether.

In the surreal hours of early morning, her memories had, without permission, travelled back to those early days in Thailand, where she had first met Kip, a barefoot youth juggling empty beer bottles in the light of a fire at a New Year full moon party on Ao Nang Beach.

She'd been alone, having only just arrived the night before and checked into a cramped apartment over the Satay Tiger bar, and tonight, this laughing, dreadlocked man called Kip had been the first to smile at her, the first to invite her into the circle. Until the early hours, they'd sat together, each edging closer by small, cautious increments, talking, talking, talking, never running out of things to say, and Cathy had felt the strongest sense that this was her man, her love, her forever.

Was he? she pondered now, in the quiet dawn light. Had Kip turned out to be her 'forever'? The atmosphere that night was surely hypnotic, spreading its light over the tranquil Andaman Sea. Had that been to blame for the way they had fallen into each other's lives, so immediately, so trustingly, without life-back-home hesitation?

Kip wouldn't say so. Kip would say they were made for each other, that they were twin stars, meant to find each other there on that beach, under that full moon sky. There was an album that belonged to that season of love on Ao Nang Beach, 'their album', and Cathy recalled it now as the morning light shifted to throw highlights across the pilot's olive complexion. *Pink Horses* was the title, a strangely out-of-step album of folksy songs that sounded as though they hailed from another time, long before them, a gentler time. The haunting melodies had become the soundtrack to those sun-soaked weeks, of snorkelling and swimming, of lazing in hammocks, drinking beer from the bottle and falling deeper into each other under leaf-woven canopies by night.

Somehow, this stranger's face wove with her memories of that album cover, on which a lean and long-haired man-boy stood on a dusty road, open-shirted in a pool of sunlight, one hand around the neck of his guitar, the other held cocked in hope of a hitch. Just the memory of that album cover had the power to reignite those feelings of falling in love for Cathy, and that made her feel both nostalgic and powerless – two emotions she worked hard to avoid these days, at any cost.

From along the corridor, the sounds of hospital staff drifted in, moving about for their morning rounds, and Cathy wondered how much longer she had before she was ejected once and for all.

Later, she would wonder what had possessed her, but there, in that moment of madness, she leant over the pilot's bed, so that her face was as near to his as to a lover's, and she laid a kiss on his lips, closing her eyes and holding the moment, one, two, three long seconds, before realising the insanity of her actions and withdrawing.

The pilot's eyes were open.

With a gasp, Cathy brought her hand to her mouth, ashamed. But the pilot's eyes were soft on hers, and to her astonishment he reached out, touching her hand with the tips of his fingers, drawing it into his.

'I dreamt of you,' he said sleepily, in a voice raspy with lack of use, but undeniably Irish. 'I dreamt you came before, and you were but a slip, an elfin. And you touched my hand, and you asked me who I was.' His words had the sound of poetry.

'What did you answer?' Cathy whispered, swept, unaccountably, into the pilot's dream. 'When I came before?'

Gently, rhythmically, the pilot's thumb massaged the lines of her palm, a quiet rotating pressure that felt like a song. 'I—' he started, but then he withdrew his hand, and raised his other, which was bound and blackened at the tips, and the serenity of his expression fell. 'I don't know,' he murmured, his eyes slowly misting over, and all at once Cathy knew this was no ruse. This man could no sooner tell her his name than she could reverse her son's dreadful injuries.

She stood, suddenly sickened at herself as she recalled the rage that had brought her here last night. This man had lost everything. On one side, his face was burnt beyond recognition. His memory wiped. But worst of all, Cathy reminded herself by way of penance, he had *lost his son* in this terrible disaster. Not a 'life-changing injury' like the one Albie had to face; but death. This man's son was gone forever. If he was ever to regain his full self, how could he hope to survive a loss of that magnitude?

'I'm sorry,' Cathy whispered, as she picked up her sweater and started to leave.

The door to his room opened and a new nurse appeared, a frown travelling across her face as she checked her watch.

'Will you return?' the pilot asked Cathy, following her with his eyes, forcing her to look back. 'Will you come again?'

'Visiting hours are two till four and six till eight,' the nurse said with unconcealed disapproval.

Without acknowledging her, Cathy gazed back into the sorrowful eyes of the Unknown Pilot and nodded. 'I'll come again,' she said, and she set off towards the fifth floor, where her sleeping son lay, battered and bandaged, with one arm less than he was born with, but alive, thank God, alive.

9. Nell

Tuesday

Nell hadn't really thought it through when she'd offered to pick up Dylan, and her heart sank when she spotted Uncle Elliot's truck parked on the sweeping gravel driveway outside their house. Her mind had been replaying Friday night in the Five Bells, over and over, and by this point her fear of bumping into her uncle was so intense as to be paralysing. She'd expected him to be at work today as usual, but, of course, right now there was no holiday business to speak of, not until the builders were allowed in.

She messaged her cousin. *I'm outside. Ready?*

When his thumbs-up emoji bounced back in return, Nell released a sigh of relief, and for the next couple of minutes she sat quietly behind the wheel of Grandad's truck, watching the house and praying her uncle or aunt wouldn't come out to say hello. Their home was – certainly compared to their own run-down little terrace – imposing: a new-build, commissioned by Suzie, according to Mum, after a bonanza year at the Golden Rabbit, right before Covid had socked it to them.

It had been built on a four-bedroom Georgian model, apparently, in red brick, with wide sash windows and painted bargeboards; built to last. But the way it was positioned in its big walled plot, back towards the coastline, in a great expanse of shingle driveway, with not a sprig of greenery to be seen – well, Nell had to agree with her mum: it was all a bit depressing. Rumour had it, they'd taken out a massive bloody mortgage to fund it, this 'smoke and mirrors' project of theirs – Mum's words – and Cathy missed no opportunity to bring up the fact that they'd been struggling to make payments since lockdown had cut off their income at the knees.

Grandad said his son was a fool. Elliot had been given the same as Cathy after Grandma had died: a small three-up, two-down on Allotment Row, near the rest of the family, mortgage-free – but it wasn't enough for him. Or, rather, it wasn't enough for Suzie, in Mum's opinion; nothing was ever enough, *She always wants more than she needs.* But Nell wasn't so sure they could lay all of Elliot's problems at his wife's door. Suzie always appeared to have life under control; Elliot, on the other hand, seemed perfectly capable of messing things up without anyone else's assistance.

Now, Nell gazed up at those freshly painted windows and wondered, like her mum, why a family needed four bedrooms when only two of them ever got used.

'Nellie!'

Nell shrieked, and turned to see her Uncle Elliot knocking on her window, smiling widely.

He reached for the handle and yanked open the door. 'What're you doing out here on your own? Come in!'

Her mind raced as she tumbled out of the truck, swept along by her uncle's enthusiasm. *He doesn't remember*, she thought, hopefully. There was no indication whatsoever that he remembered a thing.

'I was really made up when our Dylan said you were going to take him to see little Albie,' he said, draping an arm over her shoulder as they walked across the gravel towards the front door. He smelt stale, she thought, like a damp beermat, and she wondered if he'd already had a drink today or whether it was just the fumes of the night before.

He stopped a little way from the house and laid a gentle hand on her elbow.

'I'm sorry you two haven't seen so much of each other over the years – it was never meant to be like this. You were lovely little playmates for a while. When you were tots.'

'We were?'

Uncle Elliot nodded sadly. 'We tried for a while, but your mum – well, you know. Still, it's not too late. You and Dylan could be good mates, I think. Family should stick together.'

Nell was quite taken aback by the sudden outpouring of feeling, unused to it in a family who barely knew how to say *I love you* to one another. 'I mean, we don't really know each other all that well—' she started to say, just as Dylan appeared through the front door a few feet away, wearing a backpack as though he were just setting off to primary school.

'Well, now's as good a time as any to fix that,' Uncle Elliot replied with a decisive nod. 'I'd hate to think of you not having anyone to confide in, Nell,' he added, and he held her gaze in such a way as to tell her that he recalled exactly what he'd been shown in the Five Bells last week. He just didn't know how to talk about it.

Nell's stomach turned over. 'Does Mum know?' she whispered. The words were out before she could stop them. 'About the video?'

Uncle Elliot gave a grave shake of his head. 'Not from me, love. She'll never hear it from me.' And then he headed off towards the house in short, lumbering strides, slapping his son on the back as he passed.

Nell stared after her uncle and watched him disappear behind his grand front door. What now? Ignoring her cousin's perplexed expression, she jerked her chin towards Grandad's truck. 'You need to give the handle a thump,' she yelled over, as she slid behind the wheel and started the engine.

Dylan climbed in on the passenger side and proceeded to clear the seat of receipts and soil pots. 'What was that about, back there, with my dad?'

'Just catching up,' she replied, avoiding eye contact as she reversed the vehicle in a neat arc, spitting up white gravel in her wake. 'You know, after the air crash. Lots to sort out, I'd imagine. I was just asking him how he's doing.'

'Huh,' Dylan grunted as he clunked his seat belt in place. 'I coulda told you. Same as ever. Brain-dead.'

Pulling out onto the main road, Nell glanced at her cousin with fresh eyes. He'd grown about four inches since she'd last seen him, but he still had that same 'surly nerd' look about him, and it was hard to think of him as eighteen, as a fully grown young man, even with the wispy goatee.

'Got any music?' he asked after a few moments' silence, pointing at the dashboard.

Nell smiled to herself. 'You do know this is Grandad's truck, right? The only thing you'll find in his glovebox is a bunch of unfiled paperwork and a few packets of seeds. I once found some mushrooms growing in the footwell.'

Dylan rolled his eyes. 'Yeah, right.'

'Honestly!' She laughed, pointing to the space beneath her cousin's feet. 'Right there! It was disgusting – God knows how they got there, but he hadn't even noticed!'

Dylan's face broke into a smile. 'Yeah, it does sound possible, now you say it. He's funny, isn't he, Grandad? Not like the rest of them.'

'What do you mean?'

'Like, I think he'd be happy if you just left him to it – you know: his little house, his allotment, his veggies and bird feeders. I don't think he cares about the money at all.' There was a pause, while they both thought about this, the rarely-mentioned-and-never-seen Gale family fortune. 'That's what I like about him most.'

Nell nodded her agreement, momentarily stumped for words. It had never occurred to her that anyone else could know Grandad in the way she did, or, bizarrely, that anyone else really occupied the role of *grandchild*, other than her and Albie. Because Dylan was so absent in her life, it seemed extraordinary to think that he should play a role in her grandfather's.

'Do you see a lot of him?' she asked. 'Grandad?'

Dylan shrugged. 'They used to sometimes drop me off with him at the allotment, when I was at primary school. To, you know, get me outside more. They're always so obsessed with *getting me outside.*'

A hazy memory came to Nell then, of a small school-uniformed Dylan sitting at Grandad's kitchen table, shucking beans, and she wondered what else she'd forgotten over the years. Memories were like that, she decided. The mind had a way of clearing out plenty of perfectly decent ones, while cruelly hanging on to more than a few you'd rather be shot of. It wasn't fair.

The truck idled as they waited for the Poundbury roundabout to clear. 'Don't you like being outside, then?' she asked. Outside was where Nell felt most free, up on the hills, with the coastal breeze blowing clarity through her hectic mind.

Dylan wound down the window and hooked his elbow over the door frame. Nell could tell he was looking at himself in the side mirror, trying to formulate an answer. 'I don't mind the outside *per se* – I guess it's the people I don't really like.' When

Nell laughed at this, Dylan's head snapped round, his expression wounded. 'You wouldn't understand. You're probably one of the popular ones.'

'I'm not laughing at you, you idiot,' she quickly countered, worried about offending him so soon into their reunion. 'I'm agreeing with you. *I'm agreeing.* People are, on the whole, knobheads. So, I get it.' She flipped her indicators for the hospital turn-off. 'And, for the record, Dylan, I am *not* one of the popular ones. Far from it.'

As they pulled into the car park and located a space, Dylan started fiddling with his phone. 'You look pretty popular here,' he muttered.

Nell engaged the handbrake and turned her frown on him, but before she had a chance to ask him what he meant, he held up his phone, displaying the dark alleyway that now haunted her waking hours.

Momentarily paralysed, Nell watched the girl with the long red curls, the girl she used to be, gazing blankly over the shoulder of the man pinning her to the shadowy walls. If it weren't for the almost imperceptible rhythm of his movements, you could be forgiven for thinking it was a still photograph, until, with a clownish movement, he turned to look towards the camera to reveal, not a face, but a smiling emoji.

With a strangled cry, Nell snatched the phone from Dylan's hand, cursing as she fumbled to stop it, instead knocking the pause button and rendering herself a gape-mouthed monster on the screen. *Oh-God-oh-God-oh-God.* Had everyone in Highcap seen this?

'What the *fuck*, Dylan?' she screamed. She twisted to challenge him square-on, oblivious to the tears already springing to her eyes. 'Is this why you wanted to meet up? To show me this? To humiliate me? For fuck's sake, you little perv!'

Blankly, he stared back at her and reached to retrieve his phone, but Nell lashed out, as if keeping it from him might somehow contain this shitstorm. As her knuckles glanced the side of his head, Dylan's hurt expression shocked her into releasing the phone.

She dropped her face into her hands. '*What the fuck?*' she murmured into the dark space. '*What the—*'

Beside her, Dylan didn't say a word, but instead put out a hand to shake her shoulder gently, persistently, until she lowered her guard and looked up.

'I'm not a perv,' he said, quite simply. 'And I didn't meet you to humiliate you. I want to help. That's all. I'm sorry I did it like that – I don't really know how to, you know, handle stuff very well. That's what my mum says. She says I don't always read the signs. She says sometimes I come across as cruel. Unintentionally, like.'

Nell blinked back at him. Was he being truthful? Or was this just a trick – a chance to have fun at her expense?

'What do you mean, you want to help? How can you help me? If even *you've* seen the video, Dylan, the whole of bloody Dorset's probably seen it by now. Everyone knows what a dirty slut I am.'

Dylan's brow creased. 'Why would they think you're a dirty slut?'

'For that!' she replied, raising her voice again, gesturing towards the phone. 'What else would they think?'

'They might feel sorry for you. They might think you didn't deserve it.'

'Huh? I was happy enough to go down that alleyway of my own accord, wasn't I? Who *wouldn't* think I deserved it?'

'But you didn't ask to be filmed. And you don't *look* very happy in the film.'

'Seriously?' She stared at her cousin, aghast. 'You've watched it that closely?'

111

'You don't *look* like you want to be there.' Now, he returned to the screen, scrolling the time bar back to the start. Nell tried to look away, but Dylan was insistent. 'Just look, Nell. Just ignore what's going on in the film and look at your face.'

He zoomed in closer, so that only Nell's ghostly features filled the screen.

Under duress, she watched as, like a scene from some terrible silent movie, her downturned mouth moved wordlessly, beneath eyes that remained closed throughout. She felt nauseous; she wanted Dylan to stop talking about it and just get out of the fucking truck.

'I don't know what you're trying to show me, Dylan! I was off my face, and I look like a sad druggie slut whore – so what?' she demanded, pushing the screen away again, and snatching the keys from the ignition.

'So,' Dylan replied, more cautious now. 'So, you say you went down that alleyway willingly, but do you really remember? Like, *actually* remember? 'Cause – well, you saw it, didn't you? You look completely out of it.'

'It doesn't matter what I remember,' Nell said flatly. 'I chose to meet the bloke. I chose to spend the evening getting smashed on vodka-cranberries. And I chose to go down that alleyway of my own free will. I've only got myself to blame.' She stared across the car park, towards the looming hospital building beyond. 'Now can we just drop it, and go and see Albie?'

10. Cathy

Tuesday

Albie was sitting up in his hospital bed, with his dad and grandad one side, Cathy to the other, a game of Monopoly balanced on the bed tray between them.

All around, the noise and bustle of the hospital ward carried on, as the family did their best to create an atmosphere of togetherness, politely picking out their Monopoly pieces and placing them on the board. Dad had the boot, Cathy the car, Albie the dog, and Kip had the iron, the least popular of all the playing pieces. Nobody had chosen the hat, Cathy realised, perhaps because they all knew that one was always Nell's.

Always. *Ha!* They probably only ever played the game once a year, at Christmas, and never outside of the holidays. Cathy didn't feel good about the fact that this was certainly down to her, and her inability to sit still for five minutes when there were always more pressing things to do.

'You always choose that one, Dad,' Albie said, shifting position awkwardly, his bandaged upper arm still elevated in a hoist contraption beside his head.

'I feel sorry for it,' Kip smiled back at their son, throwing the dice. 'I always used to get picked last in games at school, so I can relate.'

Despite the grey hair now streaking through the dirty blond of his grown-out short back and sides, he still looked so young, Cathy thought, following his movements as he skipped his piece around the board. There were crow's feet at the edges of his eyes, and his skin had taken on the texture of a man who'd spent many years in the sun, but still the boyish Kip shone through when he smiled. She didn't think he'd gained or lost a pound in weight in all the years they'd known each other, and as a result of his daily yoga habit, his posture and gait appeared unchanged. Sometimes it felt to Cathy as though she'd been hauled across the coals of life several times over, while Kip simply leapt over them, ever bright-eyed and optimistic. It wasn't fair.

'I don't know why I got the sports car,' she said with a scowl, moving her own piece along the board. 'It's not exactly "me", is it?'

Albie laughed. 'Maybe when we win the lottery, Mum,' he said, echoing the words she routinely threw back at the kids when they asked for something unattainable.

'We don't even do the lottery,' she replied, echoing back his, and he gave a little chortle that took her back to easier times. She picked up his hand and kissed it; it was warm and smooth.

'A sports car and a dog and a holiday to the Galapagos Islands to see the giant tortoises . . .' he said, continuing the fantasy.

'A yoga retreat by the sea for your old dad,' Kip added.

Grandad patted his chest. 'And a new ticker for me.'

'"If I only had a heart",' Cathy sang, laughing as Dad joined in.

Albie's face lit up. 'And a bionic arm for me!'

Like a punch to the guts, Cathy's smile slid from her face.

'What?' Albie laughed again. 'Dad's been telling me about the Six Million Dollar Man.'

'You think this is funny?' she asked, glaring at Kip, whose light expression instantly dropped.

'No, we—'

'Bloody hell, Cathy, love,' Dad cut in. 'Lighten up, will you? Stop jumping down everyone's throat any time they say anything about Albie's arm. We can't pretend this hasn't happened. Albie, son, do you want us all to pretend this hasn't happened?'

Albie shook his head. 'I mean, it's a bit hard to miss, isn't it?' He jerked his head towards his shoulder and widened his eyes at his mum. Cathy was caught off guard.

'Yeah, Mum, you really should lighten up a bit.' It was Nell, suddenly at her mother's side, and with her cousin Dylan in tow. 'I mean, if Albie's all right talking about it, we should be too.'

Gulping back her instinctive reaction, Cathy gave her daughter a tight smile and conceded defeat. 'Hi, Dylan,' she said, grateful for the opportunity to change the subject. 'How are your mum and dad? I don't think they've been in to visit Albie yet, have they?'

Her nephew gave a bemused shrug. 'I dunno. Probably not. I don't really see that much of them . . .'

'They'll come when they're ready, Cath,' Dad said with a careful tone. 'There's a lot to sort out at the holiday camp.'

'Lovely of you to come, Dylan,' Kip piped up, ever the peace-maker. Jeez, Cathy recalled, wasn't that the source of many of their past arguments? *Why do you always have to seek out conflict?* he'd ask her. *Why do you always have to be such a bloody hippy?* she'd throw back.

'*An-y-way,*' Nell interjected, 'I said I'd bring Dylan down here to see Albie, but the nurses said we can't have more than three at the bedside at once, and there's only an hour left of visiting time, so . . .?' She eyed the group, giving her dad a *go-on-hop-it* signal.

'No problem!' Kip was already getting out of his seat, offering a handshake to the nephew he barely knew.

Cathy stayed seated. 'We're in the middle of a game,' she said, avoiding her dad's stern gaze.

With a wheeze, Dad pushed himself up against the bedframe, steadying his balance. Still Cathy remained in her chair. God, she hated herself sometimes.

Nell cocked her head to one side. '*Really*, Mum? Albie, are *you* going to be upset to put your game of Monopoly on hold for half an hour?' She held up a carrier bag and gave it a little rustle, exaggeratedly mouthing the word *popcorn*.

'Oh, for heaven's sake,' Cathy tutted, getting to her feet as an uninvited rush of love for her children threatened to show her up. She grabbed Nell into a stiff embrace, kissed Dylan drily on his already embarrassed cheek and indicated for the others to leave them to it.

'Must be time for a bite to eat, Kip lad,' Dad said, checking his watch, as he leant in to squeeze his grandson's toes. 'We'll be back tomorrow, Albie, mate. See if we can't break you out of this horrible place sometime soon, eh?'

Albie gave them a thumbs-up and Cathy, Kip and her dad headed for the ward exit, leaving Nell to catch up with her brother. As she turned the corner, Cathy glanced back. Already, Nell was up on the bed beside her brother, pinching his pillows and nudging him to scooch up, while he laughed and winced at the discomfort of his arm hoist and an awkward Dylan handed out popcorn and bottles of pop.

A warm hand slipped around her waist, and Cathy knew without looking that it belonged to Kip.

'Gorgeous, aren't they?'

She nodded, afraid to answer for the sob that was caught in her mouth.

'We did that,' he murmured, his face so close to hers she could feel his breath on her skin. 'We made those two amazing human beings, my love. And whatever happens next doesn't matter, because we did that, and it is a miraculous, beautiful thing, and we should take pride in it. Yes?'

Kip was right; Kip was always right. He was telling her to count her blessings – something she generally failed at – and he was right. With a sigh, she left her children to look after each other and trailed alongside her limping old dad, Kip's arm still safely wrapped about her waist, like an anchor.

As the lift descended to the ground floor, Cathy told Kip she'd rather hang about at the hospital, to make sure Albie had everything he needed before she left.

'There's some quiche and cold potatoes in the fridge,' she said, walking them out to the front exit and handing Kip her car keys. 'I'll just get a ride home with Nell in an hour. OK?'

Dad raised a hand and shuffled ahead, looking somehow older this week; slower, she thought.

The moment they disappeared beneath the covered walkway, Cathy, too impatient to wait for the lift, jogged up the stairs to the third floor and out onto the corridor that had become so familiar to her over the past few days.

She eased her head around the pilot's private door to see him sitting in a more upright position than he had been yesterday, his attention firmly held on the open pages of the dog-eared paperback she'd brought for him on Sunday.

'Hi,' she said, softly, careful not to startle him. 'Hi, it's me again.'

The pilot turned to look in her direction, a small wincing movement which drew attention to the tight restriction in the skin of his neck, caused by those terrible burns. 'It's you again,'

117

he murmured in the soft Irish gravel of his voice. 'Three days on the trot.'

'Four,' she corrected him.

'I'm honoured.' He held her gaze, today more lucid than yesterday. It was a gaze of longing, yet not one of desire. What was it, that look? *Yearning*, Cathy thought. Or perhaps hope. The intimate connection between them when he regarded her in this way felt strangely akin to nostalgia, and, as with all things nostalgic, once you turned a page to peer in, you were lost to it.

'You know, one of the nurses spotted you leaving yesterday. She wanted to know who you were,' he said.

'Oh, really?' Cathy replied, sitting at his bedside.

'I told her I didn't know your name. Which is true. I told her you were investigating my accident,' he smiled. 'She seemed happy enough with that. I think the police have them keeping a close eye on me.'

Cathy reached into her pocket and pulled out a small KitKat she'd brought in for Albie but forgotten to give him when Nell arrived. 'I brought you some chocolate.'

The pilot's mouth turned up in a small lopsided smile. '*Have a break*,' he said, recalling the words of a long-ago advertisement. For long moments, he stared past Cathy, out through the windows to the cloudy sky beyond, as though trying to conjure up more of where that memory came from. 'Will you share it with me?' he eventually said, his focus returning to her face.

She peeled back the red paper and ran her thumbnail down the centre, scoring open the tin foil. The pilot nodded approvingly, and she snapped the bar in two, and passed him a stick.

For a while, they sat and ate, slowly, as the hospital beyond his door buzzed on regardless; he quietly savouring the long-forgotten delights of a childhood chocolate bar, Cathy simply happy to just be. When had she last felt this way? This sense of unhurried contentment? Of calm?

Into the silence, he finally spoke. 'Why do you come? Have I asked you that already? You must have someone here? A loved one in the hospital?'

Cathy dropped her eyes to her lap, uncertain how to respond.

'Ah. A lover, perhaps?' She looked up again, and his eyes were twinkling with mischief. 'A *secret* lover?'

When she blushed and denied it, he closed his eyelids with a sigh and dropped his head against his pillow, that playful smile still lingering on his lips.

'Ah, I'm pulling your leg,' he said, inclining his head to look at her side-on. 'It gets a little dull around here, if you hadn't noticed. I'll take whatever entertainment I can get.'

Cathy felt cut to the quick, and it must have registered in her expression, because the pilot's face fell too.

'Ah, man, I don't mean *you're* the entertainment, you ninny! I meant, me larking about like that.' He shook his head in mock regret. 'I mean, look at me. I should be grateful to have so beautiful a maiden as you gracing my bedside. And I've no manners, have I? I haven't even asked you your name – or maybe I have. Have I?'

'I'm Cathy,' she replied, although she'd already told him several times before.

'Of course,' the pilot said, raising the book between them, her old A-level copy of *Wuthering Heights*.

Cathy shrugged bashfully, and offered her hand to seal the acquaintance, not predicting the strangely intimate finger tangle that would result from him only having the near hand to offer back. 'And you?' she asked, hopefully.

'Me?'

'Your name?'

'Oh, my name. Wouldn't that be a grand thing to offer you?' There was a slight shift in his tone now, as though he were mocking himself. 'Heathcliff?' he laughed, setting him into a hoarse coughing fit.

She gave him her best withering look.

'Haven't you heard?' he asked, once he'd caught his breath. 'Who I really am?'

Cathy's heart beat faster as they edged closer to the great monstrous event that had really brought them together.

'I'm nobody,' he replied. 'So they say. And missed by no one, to boot. Isn't that the most depressing thing you've ever heard? Isn't that the most tragic thing?'

'No,' Cathy murmured, her eyes locking on his. 'I think the most tragic thing is to have lost a child.'

In the long silence that followed, it was the pilot's turn to drop his gaze.

'Oh, Cathy, my maiden. It truly is. It is the saddest thing in the world, to have lost a child and yet to have no sense of them at all. Nothing at all, except for the sure knowledge that I have loved.' Tenderly, he reached for her hand again, and she took it. 'Cherish your loved ones. Promise me? Never let them go.'

11. Nell

Sunday

Mum was being weird.

For some inexplicable reason, her mood had lifted over the past week, casting an oddly cheery aura over the Gale family cottages in Allotment Row. She seemed to have stopped worrying about all the lost work her visits to the hospital were causing; she'd even stopped talking about money – or the lack of it – which, for as long as Nell could remember, had been her most pressing source of stress.

In Nell's waking hours – and there were many – she even wondered if perhaps Mum had dropped her pride and asked Grandad for a bit of help, just to get them through this rough period. But in the clear light of day, she doubted the idea; such weakness would surely make her mum more stressy to be around, not less.

Only this morning, Nell had woken early to the sound of music drifting up the stairs, and she'd headed down in her bare feet to find Kip sitting at the tiny kitchen table in his pyjamas, muss-headed, drinking iced coffee as Mum removed a tray of fairy cakes from the oven.

'You know it's the weekend? Mum's never out of bed before nine on a Sunday,' Nell said, more bemused than annoyed at being woken so early. She stared at her dad. 'Did you stay over last night?'

Kip laughed and shook his head, and Cathy ignored the question.

Instantly hungry at the rare smell of fresh baking, Nell reached in for a cake, only for her mum to push away her hand with a good-humoured slap. 'Wait for the icing,' she scolded, transferring the cakes to the cooling rack before messily dusting them in icing sugar.

The music she'd heard was playing through Mum's phone, and Nell picked it up to see what it was. '*Pink Horses* by Jago,' she said aloud. It was an artist she had never heard of, with a folksy cover that suggested the album was decades old. Nell liked it; it felt like the soothing sounds of an altogether different era – an era she suspected she might have been better suited to.

'They don't make 'em like this any more,' Kip sighed. 'Died young, didn't he, love? Drowned. Tragic.'

Mum gave a sad little nod. 'Another member of the 27 Club.'

'So, if you didn't stay over last night,' Nell asked, ignoring the music trivia, which they were clearly using to divert the conversation, 'what are you doing here in your pyjamas at seven in the morning?'

'We,' he said, casting Mum a playful smile, 'are taking a trip down Memory Lane.'

'Huh?'

'Your mum sent me a text message last night, reminding me of this album – we played it that whole summer we spent on Ao Nang Beach, when me and your mum first met. It was the music we fell in love to.'

Mum was now firmly busying herself at the kitchen counter, trying to conceal a smile.

'Every morning, we'd have breakfast at DanDan's, wouldn't we?' he said, forcing her to turn back with a tug of her sleeve cuff. She returned a warm expression, and leant back against the counter, her arms folded lightly across her slight frame, her eyes distant. 'And we'd have iced coffee and warm madeleine cakes, and talk about marriage and babies and a smallholding on the coast . . .'

Now Cathy met his gaze, and they locked, just briefly, momentarily lost in the memory.

Nell stood in the doorway, witnessing the love circulating in the space between her parents, and she took a breath. 'You know what Albie said, when I asked him a few days ago what he wished for most in the world?'

They both turned their eyes on her, their expressions at once pinched.

'He didn't say, "I want my arm back",' she said.

Kip tilted his head in question.

'He said he wished you could be together.'

Dad turned to look at Mum; Mum looked at her feet. And Nell left them alone with the thought.

For the rest of the morning, Nell lay motionless on her bed, listening to the sounds of her parents moving around in the kitchen downstairs.

These days, her every waking moment – whether she was working, eating, showering, driving, sitting at Albie's bedside – was occupied with obsessing about that video clip circulating the phones and laptops of Highcap. How long would it be before it, or, at the very least, news of it, reached her mum, her dad and, God forbid, her grandad?

She couldn't bring herself to rewatch the video alone, but as she lay there in her small box room, staring at the damp patch on the ceiling above, it occurred to her that, while the shame of the situation was as overwhelming as ever, sharing it with another person – Dylan – had brought her a little comfort. He was strange, her cousin, and yet there was something so humourless and solid about his pared-back view of life that she knew she could trust him. When *he* looked at that disgusting clip, he wasn't shaming her or ogling the action – he was analysing it, trying to decode it, looking for answers.

Sitting up, she picked up her phone and messaged him.

What are you up to? I'm not working today. I was thinking – maybe you're right. Maybe we should hunt down those tossers behind the film.

Nell knew she wouldn't have to wait long for a reply; it seemed Dylan lived every waking hour through his tech. A message pinged straight back.

Mum and Dad are out. Come here if you like and we can trawl the net. Bring chips.

Nell laughed at his sign-off and returned a French fries emoji before swinging her legs from the bed and getting herself dressed.

At Gale House, Dylan answered the front door in his customary gamer's uniform: black joggers, Nintendo hoodie and socked feet. Nell handed him the still-warm wrap of chips.

'I hope you like salt and vinegar?' she said, following him to the kitchen, where he dumped the contents into a big sharing dish.

'Of course,' he replied, and she watched as he squirted portions of ketchup into two ramekins, handing one to Nell. 'I won't tolerate double-dipping,' he said, and Nell gave a nod, reining in her natural urge to take the piss.

Up in Dylan's bedroom, the curtains were still drawn, but his bed was made to military standards, and the room, while decidedly muggy-smelling, was spotless.

'Sorry, mate,' she said, drawing back the curtains and pushing open a window. 'I can't eat in the dark. Do you mind?'

Dylan cleared a space on his desk and pulled up a second chair, and together they sat in front of his blank computer screen, eating chips, and not double-dipping.

'Where are your folks today?' she asked, noticing that both their vehicles were missing from the driveway below the window.

'Down at the holiday park. They've got the insurance people and the air crash inspectors coming again tomorrow, so they need to sort out some paperwork.'

'My mum said the insurers might not pay out,' Nell said. 'That can't be right, can it? I mean, what do you pay your insurance for, if it doesn't cover a thing like this? It's not as if they could've done anything to prevent an aeroplane crash-landing on their business.'

Dylan shook his head. 'Dad forgot to pay the premium this year,' he said, simply.

'*Really*?'

'That's what Mum says. Not to me, to him – they're always arguing, and you might think you could do it privately in a house this big, but not them. Dad says he's sure he must've paid it – he says he's sure he had it on auto-renew. Mum says clearly he didn't, because the insurers never received the payment. Dad says he wouldn't screw up something that important. Mum says he's so pissed half the time it's surprising he hasn't screwed up something this big before now. I swear they hate each other. God knows why they even live together.'

Nell thought about her own parents, who clearly loved each other after all these years but still couldn't seem to live in step together. Why was the world so bloody complicated?

'Dylan,' she ventured. 'Has your dad said anything about the video?'

Dylan frowned. 'I haven't shown him, if that's what you mean.'

'No, no. It's just, last week, when I was down the Five Bells, your dad was there—'

'Naturally.'

'And this girl – this Kasey something – she had the video on her phone. And the stupid little twat went right up and played it to him.' She waited for Dylan's reaction, but he only looked thoughtful. 'I came back from the loos and he'd already gone – didn't even finish his pint. God only knows what he thinks of me now. He must think I'm disgusting.'

Nell's blood pressure surged as she relived the moment. She loved her Uncle Elliot; despite the distance between Mum and Suzie, Elliot had always stayed close, regularly dropping in to check on his sister and slipping the kids the occasional tenner when he could see that Mum wasn't flush. The thought of him seeing her like that – it was almost too much to bear.

'Kasey Clapton,' Dylan said robotically.

'You know her? I couldn't find her on Facebook, but then I didn't know her surname.'

'The year below us at school. Yelled "freak" every time her lot passed me in the corridor. One of the popular girls. Makes sense she'd do that. She's not nice.'

'Where do you think she got the video from? I mean, you can't share this sort of thing through social media, can you? It'd get reported – taken down.'

'You'd be surprised,' Dylan replied, picking up the empty bowl and depositing it outside his bedroom door. 'I think there are all sorts of private groups on Facebook where you can share pretty much anything, so long as all the members aren't the kind who'll report.'

'It's risky, though, isn't it?'

'Not really, not if you get a group run by pervs and populated by pervs. All they want is perv content – none of them will report it, 'cause that's what they're there for. And, of course, no one uses their real names if they're into dodgy stuff.'

Nell thought of Dylan's moniker, 'Dylan Cat', but thought better of questioning him on it. 'Well, wherever it started, someone downloaded it from somewhere and sent it to Kasey.'

Dylan switched on his PC monitor. 'Yup, I think first we find out what Kasey Clapton knows, and from there we work backwards. Until we reach the original source. And we get it removed.'

In a rush of gratitude, Nell reached out and touched Dylan's wrist. He flinched. 'It's really good to have someone I can trust,' she said, unperturbed, gently withdrawing her hand. 'Thank you. Oh, and by the way, you're not a freak.'

With a flat smile, Dylan nodded. 'Any time. And . . . you know, thank *you*,' he said, at once looking away, and Nell knew that he meant it.

12. Cathy

Monday

The consultant had asked Cathy to attend the hospital for an update Monday lunchtime, and so, with several anxious hours to spare, she popped into Dad's to sort out his lunch and told him she was off for a work shift before visiting Albie that afternoon.

She hated lying to him, but, honestly, how on earth could she even start to explain that she'd been visiting the Unknown Pilot, the man who had single-handedly caused all this heartache? How could she explain that in his company she felt more alive than she had in years, or that they talked and talked, about anything and everything, without judgement or history or fear.

Cathy knew she should be concerned about the hole in her income, since she'd had to drop most of her cleaning shifts these past two and a half weeks, but somehow she couldn't care less. Whether it was the enormity of Albie's accident or the light that this stranger had brought into those short hours they spent together each day, something had shifted in her since meeting him, and it felt good.

'Has your sister-in-law been to visit our lad yet?' Dad asked as she placed a foil-wrapped meal in the oven and set a reminder alarm for him to switch it on at 11.45 a.m.

Cathy shook her head. Even her rage towards Suzie, if not entirely vanished, had ebbed. 'She's got more important things on her mind, Dad,' she replied, stopping short when she remembered they were meant to be keeping the insurance problem from him.

'More important than family?' He coughed.

Cathy sighed. 'Come on, Dad. Suzie's never really seen us – me and mine, anyway – as family, has she? Ever since I was a little kid, she's done nothing but criticise me. Put me in my place. You've seen that, surely?'

'She only wants what's best for you,' Dad replied, sitting heavily in his recliner. 'She just doesn't know how to show it.'

Cathy made a little scoffing sound. 'We both know that isn't true. She's always been jealous of me and Elliot. Don't you remember, when I was only just in Infants and he first started working full-time down at the campsite, he was always buying me little treats on payday – and she was always telling him not to. Telling him they were meant to be saving – for the wedding, for the house, for the holiday. Not to waste his money on me. Tight cow.'

Dad shook his head, though his face said he recalled it well enough.

'Anyway, that's the past,' Cathy said firmly, plumping up a cushion and indicating for him to lean forward so she could position it behind his back. 'We should be more concerned with the here and now. Shouldn't we? With getting Albie back home.'

She picked up her bag and headed for the back door, feeling the beam of her father's scrutiny as she turned to say goodbye.

'You've got a secret,' he said. 'Damned if I know what it is. But you've got a secret all right.'

129

'Ha!' Cathy barked, turning quickly to hide her blushes. 'I'll see you later, Mystic Meg.'

Out on the back path, she checked her watch and hurried to make more time with the pilot before her meeting that afternoon. Today she would tell him exactly who she was; no more secrets. Not between them, at least.

On Falcon Ward, Cathy lingered in the corridor for fifteen minutes or more, concealing her face behind a battered old copy of *Hello!* magazine while she waited for the pilot's visitors to leave, anxiously wondering who they could be. Burns specialists? Well-wishers? Relatives who'd finally noticed he was missing, ready to swoop him away?

When they did eventually vacate his room, Cathy recognised the female detective she had talked to on the day of the crash, along with another woman in doctor's scrubs and a suit-clad man with a serious expression. While the doctor disappeared along the far corridor, the other two walked slowly together in Cathy's direction, deep in conversation as they headed towards the lifts. Quickly, she brought her hand to her chin, striking the pose of a woman deep in concentrated reading.

'Thank you, DS Samson,' the man said, as they passed, pausing long enough to shake the detective's hand. 'I'll send you a copy of my report as soon as all the test results come in. It could take a few weeks – but I'll let you know if we have any significant breakthroughs.'

DS Samson thanked him and strode ahead to take the stairs.

The moment they were gone, Cathy rushed, without knocking, into the pilot's room, and found him sitting upright in his bed.

'What did they want?' she asked, pulling up her chair. His expression was bleak. 'Are you all right?'

For a long while, he didn't reply, and Cathy studied him, breath held, waiting to hear the news that had affected him so. And then, just like that, his focus returned, and he broke into a smile. 'Cathy,' he said in his melodious voice. 'Wonderful, wonderful Cathy.'

'Your visitors?' she asked, with obvious impatience. 'That looked official. What did they want?'

'Oh. That was nothing. Nothing I want to tell you right now, at any rate.' He smiled again, more sadly this time. 'Now, you, on the other hand, look as if you have something to tell me.'

Outside, the sun was breaking through the grey morning, the midsummer breeze blowing the clouds along at a pace. Cathy could feel the warmth of its rays pressing in against her back.

'We're friends now, aren't we?' she asked him, her voice low.

'Like the oldest of friends,' he replied with a slow blink. 'Don't you think?'

Cathy nodded, swallowed her anxiety. 'It's about my son,' she said. 'That's who I visit here. His name is Albie, and he's twelve, and he's the most amazing lad you'll ever meet. But the reason he's here – well, he was in the wrong place at the wrong time, and now, well . . .' She watched as comprehension slowly filled the pilot's eyes. 'Two weeks ago, he was standing on the skate ramp at the Golden Rabbit holiday park, and . . . and, he lost an arm. He was lucky to survive.'

The Unknown Pilot gazed back at Cathy, his jaw slack, his eyes moist with tears. 'I—' he began, but Cathy interrupted.

'At first, I wanted to kill the man who was flying the plane. But then, I realised he had lost as much as – no, more than – we had, and gradually I think I'm making peace with it.' She covered his hand with hers and spoke softly. 'Now you tell me something.'

Slowly, brows knotted in anguish, he gathered his words. 'That's fair, Cathy. A fair trade for your truth.' He hesitated, studying her closely, putting the hazy pieces together, perhaps. 'I have three things to share with you today. That man you saw leaving just now? He's one of the air accident investigators – he's been working on the case these past couple of weeks, trying to get us all some answers.'

'And?'

'Well, the plane is apparently a pretty old model, so there's no transponder – that's the thing that sends out a signal for air traffic control. It explains why we weren't picked up in the air. He says they're struggling to find a legitimate cause for the crash . . .' He paused, as though thinking this over.

'They think you did it intentionally?'

The pilot lowered his gaze, and Cathy nudged his hand, urging him to continue.

'I think maybe they do. And the detective – she came to ask me more about the little boy, to see if she couldn't jog my memory. She couldn't.' The pilot paused at this, his eyes on the joined hands between them. 'But I *know* he's mine – with every fibre of me. When I close my eyes, I can recall the weight of him in my arms; the scent of his hair as he sleeps against my chest. But how is it possible that I don't know his *name*? That I can't even conjure up his face?'

'You will,' Cathy told him. 'In time, you will, I know it.' Finally, after long moments had passed in silence, she asked him, 'And the third thing?'

'Oh, yes, the third thing,' he responded, regaining his focus. 'They want the bed back.' He gave a small sorry laugh. '*The good news is, Mr John Doe, you're well enough to go home.*'

'*Home*?' Cathy murmured.

'Home,' the pilot echoed.

Cathy shook her head, anger suddenly rising. 'No! They can't just kick you out – look at you! Do they know your situation

– that you don't even know your own name, let alone your address?'

'Of course. But that doesn't change the fact that they need this bed back – for someone who needs it more than me.'

'*You* need it!'

With some degree of effort, he lifted his injured arm and flexed his charred fingers. 'Look. They X-rayed my collarbone this morning – it's mending really well, they say. And the burns – I know they look monstrous, but the docs are right, Cathy. They can be looked after at home. And the leg is only a hairline fracture. It's weak, but it'll mend.'

'But you don't *have* a home!' she cried out, slamming her palms together. 'It's ridiculous! Who's your doctor?' she demanded. 'I'll go and have a word. The very least they can do is get you moved onto a main ward, until you've worked things out. I mean, how are you going to dress your wounds if you're on the street, for God's sake? Before you know it, you'll be back here with an infection – or worse. This country is a bloody mess—'

'They won't put me out on the street,' the pilot said, with an infuriating smile. 'My – what do you call it? Case worker? My case worker says there's a halfway house just outside of Dorchester. The police want to know where I am after I check out of here, and, you know, it's a roof over my head.'

'A halfway house? Where they send the homeless? Ex-cons? Drug addicts! They think that's a suitable place for a man who's been through what you have? I can't believe what I'm hearing—' Cathy was heading for the door.

'Cathy – I can't expect you to fight my battles, not after everything I've already put you through—' the pilot tried to protest, but Cathy's fire was up and she wasn't in the mood to be dissuaded.

'I'll come back later,' she said, drawing a calming breath and holding up a hand in apology. 'I'm just a bit stressed out, that's all. I've got an appointment with Albie's consultant in fifteen minutes, to talk us through his options. But I'll chase down your doctor straight afterwards, make sure you're looked after here. I promise. OK?'

The pilot sank back against his pillows, and Cathy left him, bathed in leaf-dappled light, the bright white of his bedsheets painting him like some broken angel. Whatever happened, she promised herself, she wouldn't allow them to kick him out onto the street. Not after everything he'd been through. Nobody deserved that. She'd threaten them with going to the press if she had to, if it meant securing his bed until he was fit to leave. She could see the headlines now: *Grieving Amnesiac Pilot Failed by County Hospital*. Yes, that should do it.

Resolved, Cathy set off, the melody to 'Pink Horses' meandering through her mind. Something was shifting in her, she knew, something she could neither see nor understand, and it was opening up so many doors to her past, both good and bad. It was as though, in the presence of this stranger, all the threads of her history were converging, weaving together in this one moment in time. Kip's return and talk of their long-ago romance on Ao Nang Beach, a reminiscence Cathy had denied herself for too many years. Nell's secret pain and the mirror she held up to her mother – and her own inability to reach into it. Dad and Elliot and Suzie and the bitterness surrounding the business, and the harm her mum was still doing, even beyond the grave – all these things felt connected and not connected, and important and fleeting, and all at once hard to look at.

Cathy didn't understand what any of this meant, this torrent of memories and feelings, but one thing she felt sure about was that, this time, she couldn't look away. It was the stranger; *he* wouldn't let her look away.

By the time she reached Albie's ward, her pace accelerating with every step closer, a light film of sweat had covered Cathy's face as she anticipated the update she was about to receive on the state of her son's recovery. Turning the corner, she cursed at the sight of the consultant already there, standing at the foot of Albie's bed, a wad of notes in his hand.

'Ah, Mrs Gale!' the doctor smiled broadly as Cathy took her seat beside Albie in the noisy ward. 'I hope you're ready for some good news?'

13. Nell

Monday

When Mum phoned from the hospital, Nell was next door with Grandad and Kip, making a pot of tea and helping them polish off the breakfast cakes.

'You're all there?' Mum asked, uncommon excitement in her voice. 'Will you put me on speakerphone – make sure Grandad's close enough to hear!'

Nell beckoned the others to gather around the phone on the countertop and turned up the volume for Grandad's benefit. 'OK, we're all here,' she said, making wide eyes at her dad, who already looked as though he might cry – whether it be good news or bad.

'I've just this minute seen the doctor,' Mum announced, 'and they're really pleased with Albie's progress – with the way he's healing.'

'That's great news, love!' Grandad shouted, still not fully *au fait* with the workings of a mobile phone.

'How is he, in himself?' Kip asked, wiping his eye.

'He's fine – *really* fine now, actually, because we've just had some good news.'

'You have? What's that, love?'

'Well, they've just told us, so long as one of us is there throughout the day to look after him – which, between us, I said is completely manageable – he's ready to come home! Albie's coming home!'

Nell jumped on the spot, grabbing on to Dad and Grandad in a joyful clench. 'When?! How soon?'

'Today!' Mum's relief poured down the line, and Grandad's tiny kitchen felt to Nell, in that moment, as though it were bursting with happiness. 'They've got some final checks and medication to prescribe – and I promised to run an errand for someone here at the hospital, which might take another hour or so. But we should be with you by five or six.'

'We'll get his room ready!' Nell said. 'Grandad, we should get some party food in for him – and some balloons, or something?'

Already, Grandad was dipping into his breast pocket for his wallet, as Mum said her goodbyes. 'Don't go too mad,' she replied, with a huge smile in her voice. 'He'll be tired. But, Nell, he wanted me to say – he can't wait to see you back home.'

Nell reached out and touched her dad again, who was smiling and sniffing and wiping his eyes. 'Tell him from me, Dad's blubbing like a baby, and we can't wait to have him back home where he belongs.'

The brief pause was filled with a whisper of inhalation Nell knew only too well as the sound of her mum taking a drag from a cigarette, before she replied with a catch in her voice, 'He's going to be all right, you know? Albie. He's going to be just fine.'

It hadn't taken much to persuade Grandad that they should mark Albie's arrival home with a proper family gathering – including

Elliot, Suzie and Dylan – since, for once, they had something really good to celebrate. No sooner had they hung up the call from Mum than Nell started putting together a shopping list of things to pick up at the supermarket on the edge of town.

'Right, food,' she said, leaning on the kitchen worktop to scribble her notes. 'Pizza slices are good. Everyone likes pizza, don't they?' She wrote it down and looked at the twenty-pound note in her hand. 'We're gonna need a bit more than this if the others are coming too.'

Sheepishly, Kip handed her the last ten-pound note from his wallet, and without ceremony Grandad pulled out another forty. 'You'd better get some fizz in, I suppose,' he smiled. 'Get that stuff your mum and Suzie like.'

'Prosecco? What about you and Dad? Bitter for Grandad – craft beer for Dad. Sausage rolls, crisps, nuts. Should I get a cake?'

'Definitely,' Grandad replied, patting his stomach. 'I'll give Elliot a ring now, let him know he's expected.'

Nell didn't bother to ask what her uncle would like to drink, as she already knew the answer. Anything – and everything – given half a chance. 'Make sure Suzie comes too?' she said, tearing her shopping list from the pad and indicating to her dad that she was ready to leave. 'I know Mum won't be keen, but it's not about her, is it?'

'Course,' Grandad replied, already dialling out on his landline.

'Tell them six o'clock,' Nell said, as she and Kip stepped out through the back door with the keys to Grandad's truck. 'And tell Elliot that Nell says Dylan has to come too. No excuses!'

She started up the engine and turned to smile at her dad on the truck bench beside her. Right now, she couldn't care less about that stupid video, or what Uncle Elliot saw or didn't see, about the fact Heidi was travelling in Indonesia without her or that her life felt as though it had ground to a dull, thumping halt. Right now, all she cared about was the joyous news that her little brother was to be released from hospital; Albie, coming home at last.

By six, everyone was there, including old Mrs Jenkins from next door but one, who'd asked after Albie every single day since the accident, Albie's best friends Asha and Hannah, and Mr Moore, Albie's devoted tennis coach from the age of six.

Nell hadn't been aware of it as she'd made the phone calls, but, seeing them all assembled in the now balloon-festooned living room of her home, talking and laughing and buzzing with anticipation, she thought perhaps she'd unconsciously invited them to create a safe wall between her mum and Auntie Suzie and whatever it was that drove them to fall out time and again. At least, with all these guests in the room on Albie's special day, they were more likely to keep their dignity intact.

On his arrival, Nell had set Dylan in charge of handing out drinks, and he'd taken to it with uncommon enthusiasm, politely asking those he wasn't acquainted with what they'd like to drink and how they knew Albie. Suzie, ill at ease in her sister-in-law's home, hovered at Uncle Elliot's elbow as though at a wake, and it struck Nell how tired she looked.

'Are you all right, Auntie Suzie?' she asked, offering her a top-up as Elliot went off in search of a fresh bottle of beer. 'I heard there were problems with the insurance – down at the campsite?'

Auntie Suzie rolled her eyes. 'You heard right, Nell. It's been a complete nightmare – but at least we've sorted our side of it now. Your uncle switched companies at our last renewal, but – can you believe this – he completely forgot! So all this time we've been trying to argue the toss with the wrong insurance firm. Honestly, I was all set to throw in the towel this time last

139

week.' She glanced about the room distractedly. 'Do you think they'll be much longer?'

'Albie and Mum? No, she messaged me half an hour ago, saying they were just setting off. I think there's lots of paperwork when they sign you out – you know, with prescriptions and all that.'

Suzie gave a humourless nod. 'I can imagine.'

'Anyway,' Nell said, glancing about in search of Kip, 'they'll both be really stoked you all came – they're only expecting me and Kip and Grandad to be here, so it'll be a big surprise. Don't forget to cheer when they arrive!'

Nell left her aunt with a full glass, and worked her way around the room, handing out party poppers and instructing everyone to arrange themselves in the direction of the galley kitchen, ready to shout 'Surprise!' the moment Albie and Mum walked in through the back door.

'All set?' she asked her dad, who was loitering near the stairs checking his phone. He looked as nervous as she felt and, glancing at the time on her own phone for the hundredth time, Nell slid it into her back pocket and gave his arm a tug. 'Come on, we'd better get to the front with Grandad, so we're the first they see when they get in. You got your party poppers? They'll be here any minute.'

Kip put down his bottle and wrapped his arms around her, nestling his chin into her shoulder. 'You're the best daughter a man could hope for,' he said, and Nell could tell from the tremor in his voice that he was getting emotional again. 'And you're the best big sister a boy could hope for, too. Albie's very lucky. You know that, right?'

He pulled back to look her in the eye, something he always did when he wanted a point to land firmly with her or Albie.

Nell blinked back her own tears. She couldn't tell her dad that the reality was, she felt like the worst sister in the world, after

140

what she'd done to Albie, causing him to be there at the time of the crash, when he shouldn't have been. And she couldn't tell him that he might not think so much of her as a daughter if he knew what shameful deeds she'd been caught up in lately, or if he'd seen even a glimpse of that grotesque film circulating on the internet as they stood there.

She couldn't say any of those things, and so instead she simply nodded, grateful for the buzz of chatter in the room, drowning out her thoughts.

She pulled back, anxious that they should hurry to position themselves near the back door for Mum and Albie, but Dad held on to her a moment longer.

'Nell, what Albie told you, about wishing me and your mum could get back together?' he said, with new exhilaration in his expression. 'Well, I really think—'

Behind them, the rarely used front door swung open with a clatter, and everyone in the room spun round to see Mum and Albie in the doorway, unaware of their audience as she helped him over the front step, his shortened arm glaringly signposted in its fresh white sling.

'*Surprise!*' Grandad bellowed, firing off the first popper as a volley of voices followed.

'Surprise!'

'Surprise!'

'Surprise!'

Albie's smile almost broke his face in two, as his best friends rushed forward to greet him, to draw him in, like two little ducks bobbing in the water around him. Mum simply gaped.

'You never use the front door!' Nell laughed, approaching, arms outstretched.

But no sooner had she reached her than another figure stepped over the threshold, to inhabit the space at her mother's side. As

141

tails of brightly coloured streamers drifted in slow motion to the rug, Nell felt the party atmosphere be sucked into a void as every last person in the room fell silent.

It was the pilot. Hobbling on crutches, with livid burns streaking wildly up one side of his face, he entered Nell's home.

Her mother had brought the pilot home.

'The hospital needed the bed back, and he's got nowhere else to go,' Mum announced to the room, her chin jutted defiantly. '*So.*'

Beside Nell, Kip's hand slipped into hers, and she felt the silent weight of their assembled family and friends pressing in behind her, witnessing her mother's affront to decency. '*What*?' she mouthed at Cathy, her head shaking slowly back and forth as though the motion might make this all go away. 'Mum? So *what*?'

'So,' Cathy replied archly, reaching out to rest a hand on the pilot's shoulder, 'so, he'll be staying here with us for a while.'

Behind them, Nell heard the sound of the back door slamming, of Auntie Suzie leaving the party in disgust.

PART TWO

PART TWO

14. DS Ali Samson

Tuesday

The 1950s bungalow on Joy Lane was a conventional box, in an avenue of identical homes each set back from the road on neat patches of identical low-walled lawn.

DS Ali Samson parked a little further along the kerb and switched off the engine, scrolling through Benny's digital briefing as she waited for him to join her from the station two miles away. Another girl attacked; another video circulated. What the hell was wrong with the world?

When her phone rang, she expected it to be Benny telling her he was on his way, but instead the name 'Suzie Gale' came up – one of the managers of the Golden Rabbit holiday camp where that plane had come down two weeks ago.

'DS Samson speaking.'

The woman on the end of the phone sounded breathless. 'Hello, it's Suzie Gale here.'

'Hello, Mrs Gale.' It was rare that Ali took against people so quickly, but there was something about this woman that put her hackles up. She had a self-serving quality to her, and it hadn't escaped Ali's notice that in the days after the crash she'd not once asked after the families of those who'd died in the disaster. 'What can I do for you?'

'I thought you ought to know that *that man* – the pilot who crashed into my holiday business – has just moved in with my sister-in-law.'

Ali was momentarily caught off guard, as her mind lined up the various players to work out how this could be. 'Your sister-in-law – Cathy Gale?'

'Yup.'

'Whose son lost his arm in the crash?' Ali moderated her tone to mask her own astonishment at the revelation.

'The very same one. We got together for a welcome-home party yesterday afternoon – for Albie – and Cathy just turns up, bold as brass, with the pilot in tow. "He's staying for a while," she said! Detective—'

'Call me Ali.'

'If you're sure.' Suzie Gale cleared her throat, wrong-footed by the informality, as was Ali's intention. 'Isn't there something we can do about it? I mean, you're investigating him and the crash, aren't you? Surely it's a . . . I don't know, a *conflict of interest* to have him move in with one of the wronged parties?'

'Mrs Gale, no one's been charged with anything in relation to the air crash. The AAIB investigators are still looking into it, and most likely they're going to find it to be a tragic accident. You might not like it, but your sister-in-law is allowed to invite anyone she likes into her own home. It's a free country, as they say.'

'But people *died*! What about the Warners? Howard and Elizabeth. Don't you think their family are going to demand answers? And that little boy? Someone must be to blame!'

'Not necessarily,' Ali replied, with studied patience.

'You know he's faking it, right? The pilot. Amnesia – ha, that's a joke!'

Ali spotted Benny parking his squad car a few hundred yards up the street. 'And you have what proof of that?'

'Proof? I don't need proof – it's obvious! He tried to kill himself and his son, and when it all went wrong for him, he thought it was better to pretend not to remember anything! That's a criminal offence, isn't it? To kill your own son? Can't you arrest him for that? You have no idea what grief he's caused this family. What we've lost! We're missing out on yet another peak season's trading – how do you think that feels, when we're only just getting back on our feet after lockdown?'

Ali chose not to answer, letting the silence do its thing.

Eventually, a huff made its way down the line. 'How long will this investigation of yours take?' Suzie Gale asked. 'It's not right that we should be made to suffer because of one man's suicidal crusade!'

Ali took a long breath and held up her hand to halt Benny from opening the passenger door. 'Mrs Gale, it's not the police investigation we're waiting for. It's the Air Accidents Investigation Branch. They're working on the aircraft as we speak, and, once their report is in, we'll have more information. But, you know, these air investigations can drag on a bit.'

She was about to bring the call to a close when Suzie released an audible scoff on the other end of the line, causing Ali to see red and divulge a detail she'd planned to save until after the investigator's report was in. 'But there is something we'd like to ask you and your husband, about the conditions you maintain at the park.'

A pause. '*Conditions*?'

'It's just that one of my first officers on the scene made note of the presence of gas canisters very close to the crash site. As you know, the plane exploded and burnt out very quickly, which is unusual for a craft of its size. The AAIB are looking into the possibility of accelerants being the cause of the explosion, so these canisters are of interest to us.'

'I . . . This isn't our fault, you know—'

'Of course it's not your fault that a plane landed on your camp-site. But the insurers *will* want to check that the way in which you store your flammables didn't contribute to the damage.'

Ali gave Benny the nod and he bundled into the seat beside her, still eating a slice of cold toast.

'As I say, Mrs Gale, we're still awaiting the results of the full investigation, but it might be worth checking the conditions of your business insurance, to make sure any negligence on your part doesn't render your policy void.' When Suzie didn't reply, Ali signed off. 'Anyway, all the best – I'll be in touch.'

She slid her mobile phone back inside her jacket and turned to Benny with a weary smile, running a palm over her eyes and mentally separating her last conversation from the next. Her day hadn't got off to the best start as it was, after a disagreement with Margo over their anniversary plans a fortnight away.

'It's a popular restaurant, Al!' Margo had pressed as Ali had raced to get out of the door. 'We need to book or we'll never get a table. We've been wanting to go there for months!' She still found it hard to accept that Ali's working hours meant forward planning was always going to be a struggle.

'Can we talk about this later?' Ali had stalled as she'd snatched up her keys to go, and Margo had returned a look that told her she was hurt and disappointed and doubtful of a happy result, ever.

'Sorry about that, sarge,' Benny said by way of greeting, distractedly searching through his document case and pulling out a clutch of paperwork. 'Kid's got a stomach bug. I would've come straight from home, but I wanted to pick up another file.'

He handed it to her, a manilla folder, a different case, several months ago. 'This is the one I was talking about. You'll remember it, back at the start of April – Easter weekend. Poor kid came in as a date-rape case, in which the assault was recorded, circulated online *and* sent to the victim's mobile phone.'

'How could I forget?' Ali lifted a photograph from the file, in which a seventeen-year-old girl displayed a puffy eye and a split lip, inflicted by her attacker when she fought back. This case had affected all those who had been on duty the evening the teenager came into the station, persuaded into making a statement by her ballsy best friend – exactly the kind of friend a girl needed in a situation like that.

'Dahlia Alberts,' Ali said. 'Met her attacker via a dating app. *Matt*, he called himself, from my recollection. Up until their first meeting, she'd done everything right – got to know him for a while online, arranged their first face-to-face in a public place, kept her eye on her drink, and told her parents what time to expect her home. But after a few hours with him she let her guard down – just enough to accept his offer to walk her from the pub to the bus stop, when instead he dragged her down an alleyway and raped her.'

'Makes your blood run cold, doesn't it?' Benny retrieved the photograph and slid it back into its folder.

'Especially when you factor in the presence of a second man hiding in the shadows filming the attack. Unbelievable.' Ali sighed heavily, remembering the girl's defeated assertion that they'd never catch the man who'd raped her: nobody knew who he was, he'd been careful not to leave any DNA, and his profile had vanished from the dating website overnight. 'Have the tech guys had any luck following the trail of the video?'

Benny shook his head. 'Nah. It's encrypted, so no way of getting to the source info, and we're not even sure where the media was first loaded for circulation. As you know, Dahlia's rape kit failed to bring up anything useful, apart from a few clothing fibres that could've come from anywhere – the perpetrator took precautions – so the case hasn't progressed at all in the four months since the crime. And you'll remember the pub, the Bassett, had no CCTV coverage.'

'So, you think there might be a connection with this one?' Ali said, nodding towards the bungalow. 'Why?'

Benny closed the file. 'It was the brother who called it in, early this morning. It wasn't his sister who told him about the attack – he learnt about it after being shown a video of the assault last night down the pub. We haven't seen the tape yet, sarge, but from his description, it sounds a lot like the same crime.'

Ali glanced back at the ordinary-looking home, centring herself for the interview ahead. 'Come on, then, Benny. Let's do this.'

It was the brother, Adam, who answered the door, ushering Ali and Benny through the gloomy hall with funereal grace. As her eyes adjusted from the bright light outside, Ali saw that he was in his early twenties at most, clean-shaven in a crumpled shirt and chino shorts, with the creased expression of someone who'd spent several hours crying the night before.

At the back, the kitchen opened up into a sunnier extended space, largely decorated in whites and neutrals – white units, white furniture and white walls, decorated extensively with studio photos of the family, dating from baby days to more recent ones in which the two children were almost young adults. A mother, a father, a girl and a boy, with a world of prospects and happiness ahead of them. And now this.

Adam gestured to the seats at the kitchen table and offered the officers a hot drink.

'Thanks,' Ali replied. 'I'll have regular tea, if you've got it? Milk, no sugar.'

Benny raised a hand and cast his eyes around the spacious room.

'Where are your parents?' Ali asked.

Adam moved about the kitchen with a slowness you'd more likely see in an elderly man. 'Sardinia,' he replied, pouring milk into Ali's cup with studied concentration. 'It's the first time they've been away without us.' He placed the cup on the table in front of her, pulling out his own seat and finally raising his gaze to meet hers. 'You know, since before having kids.'

Ali gave him a small smile, reassuring him, she hoped, that they were there to help. 'So, it's just the two of you here?'

'CeeCee's in her room. I'll go and get her in a minute. She's . . . well, she's not OK, to be honest. And she won't talk to me. Normally, well, she can be a bit, you know, annoying. Obnoxious even.' He gave a small, embarrassed laugh. 'I've never seen her like this.'

'She's had a traumatic experience,' Ali replied. 'It's not unusual to shut your loved ones out, at first.'

'The officer you spoke to said you're home from uni at the minute?' Benny said. 'What're you studying?'

'Um, media, second year. At Falmouth. I only got back a couple of days ago – my tenancy's up for the summer. Mum and Dad flew out the day before, knowing I'd be back to keep an eye on my sister.' At this, he lowered his gaze, his thumb worrying away at the edge of the table. 'She's only just turned seventeen.'

These animals; they had no idea of the ripples they sent out, the harm they inflicted on so many more than just their victims.

'You know there's nothing you could have done to prevent this, don't you?' said Ali.

'Isn't there?' he replied, looking up now with hurt in his eyes. 'They asked me if I could come back a few days earlier, to

151

be here before they left – but I said no. There were end-of-year parties I'd said I'd go to, and a girl I liked and – and . . .' He shook his head, muttering angrily. '*Such an idiot . . .*'

Benny pulled a packet of tissues from the inside pocket of his jacket and pressed one into the boy's hand. 'It's all right, lad. This isn't your fault. Even if you'd been here, you'd never have known what was going on, OK? Now, why don't you show us that video clip, and then we'll get your sister in, yeah? Get this over with as quickly as we can, so you can get on with looking after each other?' He nodded encouragingly at the boy, and Ali was grateful to have an officer as compassionate as Benny on her team.

Opening his phone, Adam lined up the media player and put it down on the table, not quite ready to launch it.

'And you say some friends showed the clip to you in the pub last night?' Ali asked, sensing this lad needed careful handling. She really didn't want to view the contents of the video; she'd seen enough bad stuff in her years on the force to last a lifetime.

'Well, kind of. I mean, it's not like they'd been sitting around watching this stuff or anything. They're not like that – I've known most of them for years, since primary school. But last night, we were just sitting there, down the Five Bells, a few pints in, when one of them had a message ping up on WhatsApp from a hidden number. The video link was in it.'

'And did the message say anything?'

'It said, *Alley Dog! Pass it on.* That was it.'

'Why send it to your mate and not you?'

'Probably didn't have my number. I'm not a big fan of social media, so I don't put my details out there much. Or maybe it was just a coincidence that it came through when I was sitting there with Dan – maybe that video's doing the rounds everywhere, and he was just one of the, you know, recipients.'

'Do you think it could be personal, Adam? Someone you know?'

The lad shrugged, exhausted. 'I don't know. I doubt it. I mean, I really don't have any enemies. And it's got nothing to do with Dan or any of my other mates, if that's what you mean. They're good guys, honestly. I mean, I figure if someone *was* trying to get it to me, they were probably more concerned with making sure CeeCee got to know about it. Maybe it was sent to shame her?'

'Shame her?' Benny asked.

Adam released air through pursed lips. 'It's a thing, isn't it, these days? Revenge porn – humiliation porn . . .' His words trailed off.

Ali glanced at the phone on the table, her mind trying to put together the two attacks they knew about. He was right: humiliating the victim seemed key to this crime. It wasn't enough to simply attack the girls. The rapist wanted to make sure his victims knew their humiliation was out there for anyone to see.

'And your sister hadn't said anything to you about the attack before this – before you saw the footage?'

Adam shook his head ruefully. 'To be honest, I barely saw her in the twenty-four hours after I got home. She was in her room when I got back from the train station – I shouted hello to her, but she never came out, just shouted "hi" back – and after I'd made a sandwich, I went straight out to meet an old mate at Burton Bradstock. The surf was good that day, so . . .' He looked completely wretched. 'I should've checked in on her. She was in there, hiding in her room all that time, on her own, not knowing what to do. You should've seen her face when I asked her about the video. She thought everyone would think she'd asked for it somehow, because she'd signed up to meet him on a dating app. She thought everyone would just think she's a slag, or a dog, like it said in the video.' He blinked at Ali, uncomprehending. 'She's had a few boyfriends before, but this was the first time she'd ever gone on a blind date like that.'

He trailed off, and silently pushed the phone across the table. Ali exchanged a glance with Benny and pressed play.

The scene played out, very much like the scene from the Dahlia Alberts video, in which the girl was held against the shadowy walls of a building, in this case unresisting, while the attack took place. While her expressionless face could be made out, his was digitally obscured from view by an animated emoji, as a manic thrash metal soundtrack blared over the top of the disturbing scene, all viewed and filmed by another unseen perpetrator.

The video ended and Ali returned the phone to Adam.

'What height is your sister, Adam?' Benny asked. 'It'll help us to establish the height of the perpetrator, in contrast.'

'Oh, yes. Um, five foot two or three, maybe?' he said, scratching his head distractedly. 'You should ask her; I'm not exactly sure.'

'We will, no problem, Adam. Benny will get a download of the video from you before we leave. Let's talk with your sister now, shall we?'

The young man swallowed hard, retrieving his phone and polishing its screen against the cotton of his shirt, as though stalling.

'Adam, I promise we'll be gentle with her,' Ali said. 'We've done this before, and we know how hard it can be – not only on the victim, but on those who love them. Go on and get her. Yes?'

The lad nodded and disappeared along the hall to his sister's room.

'Sarge, I think we could have a serial rapist on our hands,' Benny murmured to Ali as soon as Adam was out of earshot.

Ali cast her gaze over the happy family photographs adorning the walls and exhaled a resigned sigh. 'I think you could be right, Benny. God only knows how many more of these poor girls are out there, too ashamed to come forward.'

15. Cathy

Saturday

The homecoming party, interrupted as it had been by Cathy's shock announcement, had lasted all of twenty minutes before the last of the embarrassed guests had made their excuses and scurried away home.

What the hell was Nell thinking, organising something like that without checking with her first? In her arch defiance, it was somehow lost on Cathy that *her* crime, that of bringing a strange man into the family home – and not just *any* man – was of far greater severity than that of a loving sister throwing a surprise party for her recuperating kid brother.

Cathy had been left reeling, confronted by so many faces, collectively expressing their disapproval, and in no time at all her shame had turned to anger. *How dare they judge me?* her inner voice had screamed, suppressed only for the sake of Albie, and for fear of scaring her pilot away. *How dare they condemn my actions before they've walked in my shoes?*

Suzie and Elliot, the cowards, had been the first to leave,

with Dylan following behind, signalling their departure with a slam of the back door before Cathy had even put her bag down. And while Nell, ever her father's daughter, had done her best to smooth things over, everyone from Mrs Jenkins next door to Albie's pals Asha and Hannah had felt just too uncomfortable to remain any longer than they had to.

As soon as it was just the immediate family present, Cathy had asked the pilot if he'd mind sitting outside a minute, rightly assuming that all hell was about to break loose at No. 33.

'*Mum*?' Nell had lost it the moment the back door was closed, casting her outraged gaze this way and that, as though inviting the rest of the family to pile in. Kip had stood at his daughter's side, leaden-armed, the deep crease between his eyebrows the only sign of his confusion. When no one else had spoken up, Nell had thrown her hands in the air. 'Mum? What the actual fuck is going on?'

At this, Albie had gasped, then covered his mouth, and his older sister had eyeballed him to warn him this was no laughing matter.

It was this outburst from Nell that had finally provoked a response in her grandfather, who heaved to his feet and slammed a meaty palm down on the dining table before Cathy had a chance to retort. 'Nell Gale!' he'd bellowed. 'You're not too old for a soapy mouthwash, my gal! I'll have none of that talk under my roof.'

Cathy had considered correcting him – he might have paid for it, but this was *her* roof they were under – but thought better of it. Her dad's vehement abhorrence of swearing from anyone of the female sex was legendary, and quite unconsciously Cathy's mouth had turned up at the corners in an inappropriate display of pride for her girl. Caught mid-smirk, she had met her dad's gaze and was at once chastened to see the raw dismay in his eyes. Helplessly, he'd cast about between her and the rest of

156

the family, finally lingering on his grandson, who was perched quietly on the edge of the sofa now, staring at the carpet, a loose hand gently cradling the bandaged stump of his right arm.

'You'll not stay here alone with that man,' Dad had told Cathy; a statement, not a request. 'And I'll not allow Nell to sleep under the same roof as him, either. He's done enough damage to this family already, without – without . . .' His words had trailed off.

Cathy had shaken her head.

'Grandad's right,' Nell had weighed in then, hands on hips. 'I'm not staying. It's me or him!'

Wanting to put her daughter in her place and hating herself as she did it, Cathy had merely shrugged at her dad. *Whatever*.

'We don't know him from Adam, Catherine.'

Cathy had stiffened; he hadn't called her Catherine since she was a child. Lowering her voice then, she'd eyed each one of them, lest they misunderstand her resolve, and spoken low and slow. 'He's staying, and that's that. I've already explained this to Albie. It's just for a few days, until they find him a bed somewhere. It's a kindness, that's all. His child is dead, Dad,' she'd said, and John Gale had dropped his gaze.

It was Kip who had stepped forward then, finding his space in the conflict. 'I'll swap with Nell, John. Nell, you take my bed at Grandad's, and I'll stay here. You'd like that, wouldn't you, Albie, mate? I can help you with that school project you're behind on.'

Albie had nodded quietly, his delight close to the surface. And it was settled. Without further discussion, Nell had headed up to pack a bag, while the rest of the family had stood rooted in discomfort. As Nell had bashed about in her bedroom, Cathy had waited at the foot of the stairs, feeling more than ever like an outsider in her own home. How had it come to this?

'He's *not* sleeping in my bed.' Nell had hissed the words as she brushed pass, and Cathy could do no more than watch as her daughter kissed Albie on the top of his head, hooked her arm through her grandad's and marched the old man across the room before pausing in the galley kitchen to address them all. 'Why is nobody stopping this?' she'd demanded, tears glistening in her eyes. No one replied. 'Why does nobody in this family ever talk about the important stuff? What in God's name is *wrong* with us?'

With a final shake of her head, Nell had led her grandad out past the broken pilot on the mildewed bench, and away through the back gate.

Those words pricked Cathy more than any other Nell had spoken that day. Five days had passed since, and with Nell and Grandad keeping to themselves next door, and Suzie and Elliot behaving as though Cathy were dead to them, life at No. 33 had begun to find its own new rhythm. Kip had taken Nell's bed – the only concession Cathy had made to her daughter's protest – and the pilot, grateful to sleep anywhere other than 'that damnable hospital bed', had taken the sofa. Like a trained soldier, he rose each morning at dawn, to roll up his sleeping bag and stack his bedding in the cupboard beneath the stairs, before putting on the espresso pot and setting out the breakfast dishes.

In his calming presence, the uncommon shyness that had been developing between Kip and Cathy since his return only intensified, and, while they still slept in separate beds, some inarticulable thing between them was rekindled, in part by their shared devotion to Albie's recovery, and in part under the tranquil gaze of their Unknown Pilot.

When they came down for breakfast on Saturday morning, he was already up and sitting at the small dining table, plates and cups laid, his brows heavy in solemn concentration.

'Do you think I have more family out there?' he asked Kip, who took the seat opposite. 'Do you think I'm missed?'

Kip glanced at Cathy, now standing at the entrance to the kitchen.

'Everyone's got someone,' she said, turning to fetch the milk from the fridge.

'Perhaps I don't,' he mused. 'Perhaps that little lad of mine – perhaps he was all I had? Nobody seems to have missed us. No one has reported our absence to the police, have they? Maybe I really am alone.' And the pilot dropped his face into his hands and wept, in his first open display of grief since arriving at Cathy's home five days earlier.

Cathy and Kip moved to comfort him, hunkering down either side, their hands on him.

'Don't cry.' The three adults looked up, to see Albie standing in the entrance to the living room, having navigated the stairs himself for the first time since losing his arm. His eyes were darkly hooded, from sleep interrupted by the night terrors he claimed to have no memory of by morning, despite the all-consuming horror that seemed to grip him as they played out in the midnight hours. 'Things seem bad now, but you survived, didn't you?'

The pilot ran a hand across his eyes. 'Sorry, lad,' he said softly, a small laugh in his Irish accent. 'Take no notice. I'm just feeling a little sorry for myself.'

Cathy reached behind the pilot for Kip's hand, squeezing his fingers and taking strength from his touch. How had Albie grown up so much without her noticing? How could he be so young and yet so wise?

'You said you were all alone,' Albie said with a shake of his head. 'But you're not. Not really. You've got us.' He looked from his mum to his dad. 'He's got us, hasn't he?'

'That's right,' Kip said, his voice thick, and he beckoned for his son to join the huddle, and for several long, peaceful moments, they held on to each other, each taking comfort from the contact, with no need for words.

The following morning, a day without work, Cathy and Kip were drawn out from their separate rooms by the sound of guitar music, drifting up from the living room below. In the preceding moments, Cathy had been lying in bed, staring at the chink of morning light breaking through the curtains, and reluctantly giving in to feelings of guilt over Nell's displacement, but, also, selfish regret. Without Nell here, Cathy was quickly realising just how much parenting her daughter took care of for Albie, in terms of homework and stability and, really, just being there. Albie's boring family tree project was still sitting on the table downstairs, unlooked at, even though he'd begged Cathy to sit down with him to talk through it. 'If you want to know about your family history, Grandad's the one to ask,' she'd told him, when his school friend Asha had delivered the project to his hospital bed a few days back. 'You should get him to come over.' But, of course, Grandad wasn't exactly keen on spending time in Cathy's company right now, was he?

As Cathy gradually realised that the music was live, not recorded, she rose and met Kip on the landing, both in pyjamas and simultaneously noticing the open door to Albie's empty bedroom.

'Is that *The Dark Side of the Moon*?' Kip asked.

Cathy frowned, following the tune. 'Yeah. It's "Breathe".'

In wonder, the pair descended the stairs on bare feet, to quietly stand in the doorway to the lounge, where the pilot sat cross-legged on a pile of cushions, playing Kip's acoustic guitar, beautifully, to Albie, his audience of one. The morning light from the kitchen fell on the unblemished half of the pilot's face, casting the livid scars of his damaged side in dark relief, allowing Cathy to see the whole of him: the serious cheekbones, the pensive brow, the lips that knew sorrow. There was something so familiar in that face, and yet so *unfamiliar*. Was she falling in love with him? Cathy didn't think so. So, what was this, then?

When the song ended, Albie spun to face his parents, an expression of unfettered delight on his tired face.

'Did you hear it?' he asked, excitedly, hugging his knees up beneath his chin. Just as he used to do when he was little, watching a favourite TV show, or playing audience to one of Nell's funny dance routines. This was the first genuine display of happiness Cathy had seen in her son since the accident, and it took all her power of control to not crumple at the sight of it. 'He plays just like the guy on the album, Dad!' Albie went on, not seeming to notice his mother's lack of response as he turned back to address the pilot. 'It's one of my dad's favourite albums, so I've heard it, like, a million times. More, probably!'

'It's true,' Kip said with a conceding nod. 'I mean, it's a classic, isn't it?'

'Dad said he was gonna teach me to play the guitar, but I never got round to it, 'cause of tennis and everything, but, but – I wish I'd done it now.'

The room fell silent. Cathy wanted to say something to comfort her son, but what could she say?

Breaking the sombre atmosphere, the pilot stood and held the guitar towards Kip, laid across his palms like a Japanese sword: an apology. 'I should have asked,' he said. 'That was rude of me. A man's guitar is a sacred thing.'

Kip laughed at that and waved his apology away. 'Man, I never played it like that. That was out of this world. Did you tune it up or something?'

The pilot gave a little nod and lowered the guitar, cradling it against his body as though to play again.

'How did you know you could play?' Albie asked the question on Cathy's mind. Did this mean his memories were starting to return?

The pilot gazed along the arm of the instrument, and silently moved his fingers over the strings, as though trying to work out a puzzle. 'I don't know. When I woke this morning, the guitar was the first thing I saw, propped up in the corner of the room over there, and maybe I was still half-sleeping – but I knew I knew. What was that song I was playing?'

'Pink Floyd,' Albie replied, with proud authority. 'Man,' he said, aping his dad's turn of phrase, 'that was just so awesome.' Gingerly, he rested his upper arm on the edge of the sofa and stared at it awhile.

'You know there was a famous drummer who only had one arm,' the pilot said, his brow crinkling as he spoke.

'Rick Allen,' Cathy said.

'AC/DC,' Kip said.

The pilot nodded thoughtfully. As though synchronised, the three adults turned to look at Albie.

'Nah,' Albie replied, roundly waving the idea away. 'You'd lose your mind, Mum. Can you imagine? You say you want to chuck my PlayStation out the window when I've got it too loud.'

'I know, but . . .' She started to protest, but then stopped, knowing her son was right. A drum kit would send her batty, once and for all. She glanced towards the back door, craving a cigarette. Her kids had been begging her to give them up for years, and she'd always argued that she only smoked four or five a day, but for the first time in her life, she was really thinking about giving them up for good. Life was too short, after what had happened to Albie. Not to mention that the pilot had smelled it on her breath in the hospital once or twice and he'd gazed at her, confused, and asked, 'What's a smart soul like you doing that for?'

'He's right,' Kip said, rubbing Cathy's shoulder affectionately and bringing her back from the thought. 'You'd hate it, love. But how about a piano? He could play that with one hand, couldn't he?'

Cathy scoffed. 'And where exactly will we keep this piano, hm?'

'Or a keyboard, then,' Kip quickly replied, noticing Albie's expression of interest.

Cathy pursed her lips. 'And who'll pay for this keyboard – let alone the lessons, Kip? Neither of us are exactly flush right now, are we?' These days, Cathy's own bank account was rarely in the black for longer than a week at a time, and the casual nature of Kip's working year meant that his own existence was little more reliable than hand-to-mouth.

Kip scratched at his stubble with a grimace. 'We could always ask your dad? It's not as if you ever ask him for help, Cath – and he'd do anything for Albie right now.'

'Ha!' she barked, drawing her chin in. 'I'm not asking that old fucker for anything!'

'Mum! Don't call Grandad an old fucker!' Albie gaped from the sofa, shaking his head as though scolding a small child. 'He's not an old fucker.'

She crossed her arms defensively. 'Well, he kinda is, the way he's treated . . .' And she gestured towards the pilot, who looked up from the guitar as though waking from a dream.

'Maybe I could teach him?'

For a moment, all eyes were on him, and no one spoke.

'Do you know how?' Albie asked, breaking the lull as he shifted to the edge of his seat.

At this, the pilot threw back his head and laughed. 'I don't see why not,' he said. 'I mean, I just taught myself how to play the guitar in a morning!'

Albie jumped up from the sofa and grabbed the pilot's shirt sleeve. 'I bet you know.'

'I bet he does,' Kip agreed with a wide-open smile that immediately put Cathy in mind of the young man she'd first met on Ao Nang Beach. 'Let's do it!'

'Do it! Do it! Do it! Do it!' Albie chanted, tugging on the pilot's sleeve with each beat.

Clapping their hands to Albie's rhythm, Cathy and Kip joined in the chant, and when the pilot threw his hands up in mock defeat, they all fell about laughing, loudly, raucously.

At that moment, the back door swung open, and Nell appeared, with Grandad close behind, her neutral expression shifting darkly on finding the pilot still in her family home, at the heart of such mirth.

The mood plummeted in an instant.

'He's still here, then?' she muttered, before making quote marks in the air. 'The "Unknown Pilot".'

'Actually,' Albie offered up, clearly desperate to break the atmosphere, 'we've decided on a name, haven't we?' he said, gesturing towards the pilot, who returned a grave nod. 'It's Griffin – like in that book, *The Invisible Man*, 'cause of all the bandages he had on his head . . .' When no one replied, Albie's shoulders dropped. 'Well, we can't keep on calling him the pilot. It's just weird. So from now on it's Griffin, OK?'

Kip patted Albie on the shoulder. 'Griffin it is,' he murmured.

Nell glowered on. 'Bit more than a few days, eh, Mum?' she snarled, pushing through the group and towards the stairs. 'I thought after nearly a week I'd be safe to come back home. But clearly not.'

'Nell! Do you realise how rude you're being? I brought you up better than this, young lady!' Even as she said the words, Cathy knew they were for his benefit. For the pilot. But still, she *had* brought Nell up better than this.

'Oh, rude, is it?' Nell spun in the doorway, her short red hair sticking up at angles, making her look like some small, angry wood fairy. 'I think it's rude to kick your daughter out in favour of the man who maimed your son!'

'Jeez,' Kip breathed out with a shudder. 'Come on, Nellie—'

'I did NOT kick you out!' Cathy yelled, her fury breaking loose. 'It was your choice, Nell!'

Infuriatingly, Nell gave a casual little shrug. 'Yeah. If that's what you want to tell yourself, Mum, that's fine by me.' She turned and disappeared up the stairs, to bash about and gather a new set of clothes for the week ahead.

Showing little sign of discomfort, the pilot – *Griffin* – turned to Cathy's dad and offered his hand. Wrong-footed, John Gale took it and shook it.

'I'm sorry about this, sir,' the pilot said. 'I really am.'

Dad gave a solemn nod.

'Your daughter Cathy here,' the pilot continued, gesturing to her with the arm of the guitar, 'she wants to ask for your help. Your grandson needs a piano keyboard. He wants to learn music. They think it'll be good for him.'

Cathy took a step back, raising her hands. 'No, Dad, I didn't—'

But, without hesitation, John Gale reached into his shirt pocket and took out his wallet, thumbing note after note, pausing to look up only to say, 'Two hundred do ya?' before counting on and handing Cathy a small wad. 'Make it three, and you can get him one of those stands, can't you?'

In stunned silence, Cathy accepted the money and Albie threw himself at his grandad, who dropped a kiss on the top of the boy's head before turning away and leaving through the back door. 'Enjoy it, lad,' he said, in a choked voice.

Moments later, overstuffed bin bags swinging, Nell pushed back through the room and out through the kitchen door with a slam.

Cathy reached for Kip's hand, and then for Albie's. 'Thank you,' she told the pilot.

'Thank you, *Griffin*,' Albie corrected her.

But the pilot wasn't really listening, as his gaze lingered on the back door. 'I shouldn't be here,' he said. 'Your daughter – it's not right.'

'She'll come round,' Kip murmured softly. 'You're a good man, and she'll come round.'

The pilot handed him his guitar. 'I'll put the coffee on, shall I?'

16. Nell

Tuesday

Since Albie had returned from the hospital and she'd been forced to move in with Grandad, Nell had taken every available shift going at work, just to get away from them all.

With Mum now officially at war with Auntie Suzie and Uncle Elliot, she was almost glad to have been kicked out of her own home, and she could only imagine the vitriol spilling from her mother as she defended her corner and the ropey choices she made. That said, Grandad seemed to be getting it from both sides.

Only a couple of nights ago, when Nell had served up their microwaved fish pie and peas, she'd caught the tail end of a phone conversation with Suzie, who'd been speaking so loudly on the other end, it was a wonder Mum didn't hear her through the neighbouring wall. 'I'll not set foot in that street until your Cathy chucks that murdering bastard out, John!' was the general gist of it. 'Fair dos,' was Grandad's reply, and he'd hung up without another word on the matter, and picked up his fork.

'She's got a point,' Nell had said, sitting down across the table to eat her own dinner.

'Your mother will work it out, girl,' was all he had replied, and they'd eaten their meal in silence, the spectre of the Unknown Pilot hanging between them where conversation should have been.

In the end, Nell had reached for the backgammon set, and despite their earlier something-and-nothing, they'd spent the rest of the evening harmoniously enough, silently pushing black and red pieces about the board.

According to Albie, who Nell messaged several times a day, the pilot – or Griffin, as her brother was now calling him – was 'a cool cat' (clearly Kip's words), who was now making them breakfast every morning and teaching Albie to play the keyboard 'for free'. If she'd only give him a chance, she'd see, Albie insisted. Ha! 'Griffin' was not doing anything 'for free', Nell was quick to point out, not when the lagger was sleeping on their sofa every night, eating their food, showering in their bathroom, breathing in their sodding air . . .

Now, it was 2 p.m. on Tuesday, over a week since that cuckoo had pushed her out, and Nell was cycling back on the coastal low road after another early shift, glad of the ocean view and the traffic-free path ahead. The shift itself, back-breaking as ever, had been uneventful, right up until she'd looked up from her solitary tuna salad in the works canteen, her attention caught by an animated group of casual workers on the far table. One of them was looking pointedly in her direction, a boyish smile of interest coming right at her.

He was good-looking, in a scruffy veg-picking kind of way, and, caught unawares, Nell had returned a smile, warmth flooding her as she'd wondered how she'd pass by his table without blushing. But, moments later, as she'd slid her tray onto the empties trolley near the exit, he and another one – an oily-faced teenager in a lumbering great body – had leapt up, blocking her path, and she'd flinched as the good-looking lad's smile had morphed into a sneer. "Scuse me, can you tell me the way to Cock Alley?' he'd said, ramming his tongue into his cheek at the exact moment the second lad reached out, quick as a snake, and patted her crotch through her shorts.

Just as her mum had taught her, she'd struck out, landing a sharp kick on his bare shin, all the while wishing she were wearing something more punishing on her feet than rubber-soled Converse trainers, which chose that moment to flap apart at the sole.

'I'll report you for that,' the dickhead had hissed, rubbing at the reddening dust mark on his pasty leg as his friend had rocked back on his heels, laughing.

Nell had leant in close and hissed back, flashing her eyes at the pair of them, 'I'll report you more, you dirty little perverts,' and then she was out of there, back on the onion patch, her silent fury raging as she'd picked away, onion after onion after onion under the blistering sun.

The more she thought about the injustice and shame of that video, the more it somehow merged with the arrival of that plane on Highcap Hill, and with the disgrace her mother had brought upon them all, inviting the pilot – the very architect of Albie's trauma – back home from the hospital.

And then there was her dad! *Jeez*! What the hell was Kip doing – or, more to the point, not doing – by supporting Cathy in all this madness? Yes, Auntie Suzie could be a selfish cow, and yes, Uncle Elliot was a useless soak most of the time, but, really, they had a point, didn't they? That man should not be allowed anywhere near their family!

But the really sad thing was, her uncle and aunt's anger wasn't in defence of Albie, as Nell's was. Theirs was wrapped up in the damage to their business, and in the fact that the accident had highlighted grave shortcomings at the Golden Rabbit holiday camp. Shortcomings that were, according to Dylan, being investigated right now.

As Nell switched up her bike gears and steeled herself for the distant uphill stretch home, these feelings of anger blossomed behind her ribs, turning over like bile as she pedalled. Overhead, the sun was relentless, on one of the hottest days of the year so far, and despite the sunblock she had applied at six this morning, the scorch of it was singeing her bare shoulders as she pressed on towards the crest of the hill, her only incentive the promise of the downward stretch home that would follow. *Home*, whatever that was.

She pedalled harder and harder and thought of her family – her mum and dad, her little brother – on the other side of the wall from her bleak little room at Grandad's, laughing and joking and making music with that man, while she and Grandad spent evening after evening eating at six, with nothing to entertain them other than the radio or a few tall tales of Grandad's life in the Navy over fifty years earlier.

She imagined Heidi, travelling around Bali under a golden sky, lounging in a hammock under a straw hat and sarong, making new friends-for-life from faraway places, maybe even falling in love. And then she thought of herself, grubby-faced and sweaty, on her knees gathering onions under the same old Dorset sky, lodging with an octogenarian in a house where the carpets dated back to 1965. Shagging randoms in alleyways and getting posted online, like a dirty bloody tramp.

What was wrong with her, that she'd give herself away so easily? She wasn't even nineteen and already her life was an almighty screw-up. Maybe this was all there was for her? Maybe the world with all its treasures was not for the likes of Nell Gale.

If it were, wouldn't it feel easier to access? Wouldn't it be hers for the taking? Perhaps this, and only this, was her destiny. *Look at my mother*, she thought. *She never escaped, did she? Not really.*

At last, she crested the hill, and in an upward spray of gritty dust, Nell's front wheel buckled in a pothole and she hit the tarmac, bare shoulder scraping heavily along the rough surface as the bike skidded to the other side of the road. 'Faaaaaaaaaaaaaaak!' she screamed, furiously kicking off the knackered Converse trainer that now hung from one foot, its sole finally detaching from its upper. 'Fuck-fuck-fuck-fuck-fuckedy-fuck!'

Glancing about the coastal road, she quickly gathered up her backpack and dragged the bike onto the verge, only then spotting her mobile phone lying face down on the other side of the road.

Ignoring the searing pain in her bloodied shoulder, she started to limp out to fetch it, at the exact moment that a roaring refuse truck thundered past, whipping dust into her face, its enormous tyre flipping her phone through the air to smash against the tarmac for a second time. It landed near her shoeless foot, and gingerly she bent to turn it over, her mind only just kicking in with the fact that she might have been killed by that truck if she'd stepped out a second later. To Nell's dismay, she found the screen not just cracked but smashed – and completely blank.

For several long moments, she sat on the verge beside her crumple-wheeled bike, holding down the power button to no avail. Home was another three or four miles away, her shoulder was bleeding more than she'd first realised, her shoe was busted and her bike was totalled. Pushing herself to standing, she brushed off her cargo shorts, straightened her top, snatched up her useless shoe and began the half-hour walk, cross-country, towards Dylan's house. Family feud or no, they'd give her a lift home, wouldn't they?

*

When she arrived at Uncle Elliot's front drive, Nell wondered where everyone had disappeared to. Both vehicles were gone, and the front door stood wide open, with a pile of clothes dumped on the top step, as though burglars had rushed through on a smash-and-grab, dropping some of their loot on the way out.

'Hello?' she called into the unlit hallway, wondering if it was safe to go inside. 'Anyone home? It's me – Nell!'

From overhead, she heard the sound of a door opening, and Dylan appeared at the top of the marble *Hello!* magazine (according to Mum) staircase.

'You all right?' she asked, gesturing towards the open door as her voice bounced around the large hall.

'Yeah,' Dylan replied, not moving to come down, a headphone set dangling from one hand. He looked pale, as if he hadn't left his room in days, which, Nell thought, might actually be the case. 'You?'

As she started up the stairs, Dylan let out a low whistle. 'What happened to your shoulder?' he asked, grimacing at the wound as she passed him on the top step. 'That looks bad.'

'Bastard bike. Or bastard pothole, I should say. I've left it on the roadside up there. The wheel's fucked. My shoe's fucked. In fact, everything's fucked.'

'All right, Sweary Mary,' Dylan said, and, uncharacteristically, he laughed.

It was true: Nell always got more foul-mouthed under pressure. It was one of those things she knew she definitely *did* get from her mum.

He glanced at her shoeless foot.

'Let's just say it's been one of those days,' she said, heading for the main bathroom and unhooking the shower head to rinse off her shoulder. She winced at the stinging cold of the water.

Seeing her struggle, Dylan bent in and took over, instructing her to lean in so she wouldn't get her clothes soaked. It was a strangely tender moment, Nell felt, from a boy who until very recently she'd thought posed a high risk of becoming a future serial killer. He fetched her a clean towel, and together they headed downstairs to apply Savlon and make pizza in the enormous *Country Living* (Mum again) kitchen at the back of the house.

'So, what's new?' Dylan asked as they hopped up on shiny chrome stools to sit at the breakfast bar and drink Coke from ice-cold cans.

'Oh, you know,' Nell replied, easing back the ring pull. 'Since Mum brought the Murdering Pilot home, I've moved in with Grandad – at Grandad's insistence, actually, not that I needed any persuading. He seemed to think the bloke might ravish the womenfolk if we stayed under the same roof with him alone – which is also why Kip has swapped with me: to protect Mum from the ravishing, obvs.'

'Sounds like quite the ladykiller,' Dylan said drily, sounding so much like an old-timer that Nell almost spat her mouthful of Coke across the polished countertop.

'Meanwhile, over a week has passed since she brought him home – God, that was embarrassing, wasn't it? – and now Albie, Mum and Kip seem to have all fallen completely under his spell and are busy bending over backwards making sure he's comfortable enough to stay on forever. Oh, and Albie's given him a pet name – *Griffin* – so everything is, apparently, hunky-dory. Even Grandad is starting to fall for it!'

'Really?'

'*Yup.* I went to get him his dinner last night, and he was nowhere to be seen – not in the house, not in the garden or over the allotment. It was only after I'd been out back to check if his truck was still there that I heard his voice coming from next door. So I stood on a chair and stuck my head over the fence, and there he was sitting at the outside table with a glass of stout, chatting away and playing backgammon – with the effing pilot!'

Dylan shook his head in wonder. 'My mum is gonna lose her shit over this.' He stared at his can for long seconds, before looking up. 'I thought Grandad had more sense.'

In a rush of anger, Nell slammed down her can, causing liquid to spout out over the top. 'You know what I think? I think he – the pilot – I think he's one of those . . . what do you call them? Like at Waco – a cult leader! He's got these eyes – and, I mean, he dropped out of the sky in a bloody aeroplane, didn't he? You don't get much more cult leader than that.' Glancing down at her stinging shoulder, she released an exhausted breath. 'Anyway, that's my news. Same old, same old. So, what about you?'

Dylan shrugged. 'Dad's been on a week-long bender – since that detective woman told them they might get investigated for the gas canisters found near the explosion, you know?'

Nell nodded.

'Mum's been down the park all morning, replacing the carbon monoxide detector batteries in all the statics. Apparently Dad was meant to do it six months ago, but he forgot. Course, I'm not meant to tell anyone that.'

'Huh,' Nell sighed, rolling her eyes in sympathy. Uncle Elliot really was a bit of a liability.

Dylan took a long drink. 'Anyway, upshot is: Mum's kicked him out. Hence the mountain of clothes on the doorstep out there. I think he's gonna be sleeping on Grandad's sofa for a while.'

Nell ran a hand across her forehead, as she imagined the living space at Grandad's closing in with the addition of Elliot's beer-smelling clothes mountain. 'Great,' she said. 'That's just the cherry on the top, cuz.'

For a little while, they sat together, drinking Coke in amiable silence, until Dylan took out his phone and placed it on the counter between them, and pressed play on the alleyway video again.

After the day she had just had, this casual action felt like an open-handed slap. Nell glanced at her cousin, at the benign expression he displayed as he watched, and she picked up his phone and threw it across the kitchen in a powerful overarm lob, where it landed on the York stone tiles with a terminal crack. 'What exactly are you trying to do to me?' she demanded, dropping from her seat, gesturing wildly at her head in an exploding motion.

'I just—' he tried to reply.

'You just *what*? You just like watching your cousin getting screwed in an alleyway? Is that it? Some messed-up incest shit?'

'No!'

'What, then? You like seeing me squirm, watching it again and again? Are you some kind of shame-junkie?'

'No! You shouldn't feel ashamed—'

'What?! Of course I'm ashamed, Dylan! I'm ashamed of *everything*!' Nell was at full out-of-control volume now. 'I'm ashamed of myself! I'm ashamed of my mother and that pilot! I'm ashamed that the Gale family will now forever be associated with killing three people! Aren't you?'

She didn't wait for an answer, just continued to pace around the kitchen, gesticulating madly and raising her voice higher and higher, while her dumbstruck cousin watched on. 'I'm ashamed of Uncle Elliot falling down drunk in the street! I'm ashamed that my grandad is apparently a millionaire who drives around in a truck and belts up his trousers with a baler twine! What else? Oh, yeah, I'm ashamed of letting my mum talk me

175

out of going travelling – and more than that – get this – I'm ashamed of my own fear of actually going. And, you know what, Dylan? I'm ashamed of you, and how fucking award-winningly weird you are! And *yes*, I'm ashamed that I'm a dirty little slag who'd let someone screw me in an alleyway *and* film it!'

'But *did* you let them?'

'Well, I didn't fight back, did I?' she spat, hating herself more at the acknowledgement of those words. If her mum had taught her one thing, it was this: *always fight back*.

At that, Dylan leapt from his own seat and grabbed Nell's wrists in his hands, fixing her with a firm stare. 'But that's exactly my point, Nell! I don't think you *could* fight back – and I don't think you *did* let someone do that to you. Don't you see? I've watched that video over and over again, and I don't think you were there of your own free will.'

Without warning, all Nell's strength and rage seemed to leave her body, and she slumped against her cousin's shoulder, where she sobbed uncontrollably.

'I don't think I was either, Dylan,' she whispered into the damp fabric of his hoodie. '*That's what I'm most scared of.*'

17. DS Ali Samson

Wednesday

Ali arrived at the station early on Wednesday morning, to go over the reports that had just come in for the crashed aeroplane and prepare an update for DI Trelawney in relation to these recent sexual assaults. Annoyingly, he was already in his office and, despite her attempt to slip behind her desk without being seen, he was out in an instant, striding across the office with the clear intention of perching his brown slacks on the corner of her desk.

'Morning, Samson!' he called in an unusually jocular tone as he approached. 'You've been a busy girl lately, I hear!'

'Er, sexist!' she replied, not looking up as she typed the password into her PC and navigated to her emails. She and Trelawney had grown more comfortable around each other over the past year, ever since he'd helped her get through the difficult period of her assailant's trial, and she had gradually come to terms with the fact that her boss was, despite his obvious flaws, a fairly decent man.

He scoffed. 'Suppose I'm meant to say "person" these days?'

'Or "officer", maybe?'

He pursed his lips and frowned, before deciding on an approving nod. 'You'll make a new man of me yet, *officer*.' And, sure enough, he plonked his arse on the corner of her desk and drank from his coffee mug with a loud slurp. 'So, what've you got for me?'

Ali clicked on a new email received from the Air Accidents Investigation Branch and opened the attachment. 'Right,' she said, scanning the document as he watched. 'I was hoping for a bit of time to get things together before I saw you this morning, boss, but as you're here—'

'Give me what you've got.'

Ali unlocked her drawer to remove the Golden Rabbit air crash file and opened it up on the desk between them.

'OK. So, you know the basics: almost four weeks ago, a light aircraft crashed at the Golden Rabbit holiday park and subsequently burnt out. The site is owned by the Gale family, whose premises took a heavy hit – the accident pretty much wiped out the playground and some of the main buildings, so it was a miracle that no more than three people died in the crash.'

'I know John Gale from way back,' Trelawney said, gravely. 'I was at school with his son, Elliot. Decent family. I heard John's grandson was hurt – lost an arm?'

'That's right, sir. The cruel part is, he shouldn't even have been there – he was meant to be at tennis practice that morning, training for the regional championships or something. He had quite a talent, I understand.'

Ruefully, Trelawney shook his head.

'So, the three casualties: the first two were an elderly local couple, Howard and Elizabeth Warner, long-time users of the holiday camp, who had a rolling lease on a static caravan there.

Oddly, they were not expected that week, and they hadn't signed in, which was, apparently, unusual. The campsite manager, Suzie Gale – married to Elliot – thinks perhaps they arrived late the night before, with the intention of signing in in the morning. But, of course, morning didn't come for them – a few hours after the disaster, the pair were found dead inside their caravan, both still in bed and crushed by the wing of the aircraft.'

Trelawney released a whistle of air. 'What a way to go.'

'We've had a bit of trouble with the couple's family, in relation to the funeral. They've been keen to just get on with it, but the coroner wanted to see post-mortems after the responding paramedics apparently reported very little blood loss at the scene. Which raised questions . . .' She trailed off as she checked her inbox again, spotting an email from the right department. 'Ah! This could be it – I'll take a look in a mo. Anyway, the third casualty was a young boy, approximately five years old and, so far, identity unknown. One of the witnesses, another Gale, says she saw the pilot lifting the child from the cockpit of the aircraft just seconds before it exploded, and so, with the pilot still unable to remember anything, and no one coming forward to report a missing son, we're working on the assumption that the child is his.'

'Ah, yes,' Trelawney nodded. 'The Unknown Pilot. Still no information on him, then?'

'Nope. He suffered bad burns down one side of his face and arm, and, while we've requested permission to release his image to news agencies in the hope that someone will come forward and identify him, so far he's refused. We can force the issue, if need be, but we've been proceeding with caution in the hope that he'll tell us himself. Did you know he's moved in with Cathy Gale? It was her son who lost his arm.'

'Moved in?'

'Well, he's staying there, at least. Pretty weird, huh? Can't imagine that's gone down well with the rest of the family.'

Trelawney scratched his stubble, bemused, and nodded at Ali's screen. 'So, what does the air crash report say?'

Ali scrolled back to the start of the report. 'So, this says that because it's an older aircraft, there was no transponder – the thing that allows air traffic control to spot it in flight – and, due to the extensive fire damage, there's very little else to identify it. However, a serial number was eventually retrieved, which appears to have led to the name of the plane's owner – a man with a residential address on the Isle of Wight.'

'So, you can narrow your search for the child's ID to the Isle of Wight, for starters.'

'Yep, that's if the island is his place of residence. Which it might not be – it is the summer holidays, after all. Of course, we've already registered his description with national and international missing children databases, so I'm hoping that, even if a family member doesn't come forward, we'll get a hit from one of them before long.'

'Hmm. And the registered owner of the plane?'

Ali located the details. 'Andrew Belgo. Date of birth March 1945.'

'So, we have our man?' Trelawney slapped his thigh: job done.

Scowling at the screen, Ali made a counting motion on her fingers. 'No. No, I don't think we do. If this owner's date of birth is correct, that makes him seventy-nine years old. Our guy is fifty at most.' She slumped against her chair back and crossed her arms. 'Who the hell is he?'

'Well, you just need to locate the owner, don't you?' Trelawney said, stating the obvious. 'Find Andrew Belgo and hopefully you'll find your answers.'

He stood and started back to his office, nodding to other officers who were now making their way in.

Ali turned back to her inbox, feeling frustrated at the complexity of what should really have been a straightforward light air crash, and she opened the forensic attachments her colleague had sent over late last night. The young child, thank God, had died on impact and would therefore not have suffered in the blaze. Whereas the couple in the caravan . . .

'Hey, sir!' Ali called over, drawing Trelawney back before he turned into his office. 'Take a look at this. It's the report on the elderly couple.'

Trelawney reversed back and leant in to study her screen. According to the covering email, the family had now been informed of these details.

'So – what? Is that right? They were already dead?' Trelawney murmured.

'Very much so,' Ali replied, suddenly impatient for answers. She grabbed the file and stuffed it inside her messenger bag. 'I'm going to head down to the Gales', sir – I promised them an update, and it'll be a good excuse to see if that pilot has remembered anything new. I think it's time to put the squeeze on him a bit.'

'Oh, and what about these video assaults you've been investigating?' Trelawney asked, hoiking up his trousers as he stood, and giving off a waft of fresh cologne. 'Are you still convinced it's the work of a serial rapist?'

'I'm certain of it. The tech guys are still working on the videos – early suggestions are that these could be made-for-profit attacks, originally uploaded to pay-per-view sites hosted on the Dark Web and later leaked. Apparently, "Dog Tag" is the name of one of these sites, so we're zoning in on that, as both videos labelled the victims "Alley Dog" – but you know the Dark Web: it takes time.'

Trelawney nodded thoughtfully. 'Sexual predators tend to work up to this kind of risky activity – he, or they, certainly won't be a first-time offender. He's bound to have a police record – got anyone in your sights?'

Ali sighed heavily. 'No one, yet. And we shouldn't rule out that this is someone with a clean record, guv. You're right that this'll be someone with an offending background – but it doesn't necessarily mean he's ever been caught. I'm worried we've got a smart one here.'

'You can buy me a drink if I'm wrong, Samson. But no one's that smart. A pint says he'll have a rap sheet as long as your arm.'

Ali shrugged. 'Anyway, I've got one of the team cross-checking nationwide, to see if there are similar attacks across the country, on the basis that this might be some kind of network or ring. And now we've got a real victim to compare to the perpetrator in the film, we've established we're looking for someone close to five foot nine, which narrows things down a bit. Listen, I need to get off to see the Gale family now, so I'll give you a fuller update later.'

She stood, giving her boss the side-eye as she switched off her PC.

'What?' he said, pulling in his chin.

'Have you got a date later or something, boss?'

'Well, I—' he said, growing instantly flustered.

Ali gestured towards his neck. 'It's the aftershave that's the giveaway.'

'Sod off, Samson, and don't be so bloody impertinent.' DI Trelawney scowled and waved her away. 'Oh, and, sergeant, I want this doing by the book – no cutting corners or putting yourself in harm's way again, OK? I know what you're like when you get the bit between your teeth, and I'm starting to think this sexual assault case might be one of those occasions.'

Ali signalled a mock salute and set off for Allotment Row.

*

At No. 33 Allotment Row, DS Samson got no answer, so she tried next door at No. 31 where she knew John Gale lived. It was his grandson Albie who answered the door, to the backdrop of a small dog yapping.

'Oh,' the lad said with a little gasp. 'I thought you were Amazon—'

Ali held out her left hand. 'Were you expecting something good?'

Albie shook her hand lightly and nodded, and stood back to let the detective in. 'I've been learning the keyboard – Dad ordered me some new headphones, so I don't drive my mum barmy.' A puppy, something between a sausage dog and a scruffy terrier, nosed between Albie's ankles. 'Oh, and we ordered some toys for my new puppy.' He grinned widely.

'Name?' Ali smiled, hunkering down to pet the dog.

'Lump,' Albie replied, hooking the pup beneath the collar to make room for the detective to enter. 'Grandad got him from one of his mates down the Legion.'

'Lump. I like it,' Ali laughed, and she followed Albie through to the little living area at the back of the house, gloomy in the mid-morning light, where John Gale sat at a small Formica table, across from the Unknown Pilot, a backgammon board between them. On the sofa, Elliot Gale was lying with a blanket over him, apparently fast asleep, while in the small kitchen, a fair-haired man was fetching out a tray of warm pasties from the oven.

To Ali, it had the feel of an all-male barracks dorm, with the scent of mothballs and dust and coffee in the air, and a distinct lack of frills or decoration. The puppy ran through to the kitchen and promptly peed copiously on the lino floor.

'Albie, mate! They're ready!' the fair-haired man called out, clearly oblivious to Ali's presence until she alerted him with a loud hello, and then, already smiling, he looked round.

'Mr Gale,' she said, addressing John Gale with a friendly don't-get-up wave of the hand, 'we met before, at the hospital. I'm DS Ali Samson. I just tried next door, but there was no answer. I wanted to give you all a quick update, and perhaps have a few minutes with our pilot here?'

'How-do,' said John Gale, genial enough, and the pilot nodded, inclining his head to one side. Elliot Gale, roused either by the sound of their voices or the promising smell of the pasties, stiffly lowered his legs off the sofa and rubbed his crumpled face.

'I'm Kip – Albie's dad,' the pasty-maker said, setting the tray down on the hob and gesturing towards the space on the sofa next to Elliot, as casually as though having a visiting police officer was an everyday occurrence. 'Everyone for a cuppa?'

For several kettle-boiling minutes, Ali made small talk with Albie, about music and the summer holidays and his family tree project, while the rest of the family quietly rearranged themselves to give her their full attention.

'Right,' she started once they were all gathered, with mugs in hands. 'I promised to keep you in the picture, as and when I had information. Where's your wife, by the way?' she asked Kip.

'Cathy? We're not actually married,' he said, looking almost surprised at the news himself. 'She's at work – she'll be back at four.'

Albie, perched now on his dad's knee, gave him a playful nudge, and she suspected Kip's calm demeanour was all for his son's benefit. The lad was too big, really, to be sitting on his dad's lap, but she knew from years in the job just how regressing trauma could be. Luckily for this kid, he had family who loved him.

'Are you sure Albie shouldn't . . .?' she said, with a gesturing hand. 'I'm going to be talking about the air crash.'

'I'm fine,' Albie replied before his father had a chance, and he slipped off his dad's lap to sit cross-legged on the rug between them.

Ali glanced at the pilot now, who gave a small but distinct nod for her to continue, and she returned an understanding smile and tried to work out exactly what the situation between Cathy Gale and her pilot visitor really was. He hadn't spoken a word since she'd arrived, and his brooding silence, together with his dark and damaged good looks, lent him the air of some mysterious character from an old-time movie.

'Right,' she began again. 'So, I've only really got one thing to update you on – and I'm sorry if this is upsetting for any of you: we've had the coroner's report back for the couple in the caravan.'

'Mr and Mrs Warner,' Elliot said in a gravelly voice. He had the expression of a man on his way to the gallows. 'Their poor family,' he added, and he rubbed his face again with both hands.

'Well, it would appear that the couple were already deceased when the plane came down.'

All eyes were on her. 'You mean I didn't—' the pilot spoke now, his Irish accent foreign in the room. 'It wasn't the crash that killed them?'

'It wasn't,' Ali replied.

'So . . . so, what was it then?' Albie's father asked. 'How did they die?'

'We believe they'd been . . . that they'd passed away at least forty-eight hours before the plane crash. The coroner has ruled it as asphyxiation.'

'*Asphyxiation*?' John Gale murmured. 'But, how . . .?'

Elliot Gale seemed to fold, doubling over his knees, and Albie jumped into the space between them and took his uncle's hand. 'It's OK,' the boy murmured quietly.

Conscious of the need for discretion, but realising the family needed reassurance, Ali added, 'Don't worry, we're not looking for any external party. Once the full findings are ready for release, we'll let you know. Oh, and by the way . . .' She turned to Elliot beside her. 'They're now sure that the explosion was caused by the fuel in the aircraft itself. The gas canisters weren't involved.'

In a silent burst of dust motes, John Gale stood, leaning heavily on the edge of the table, saying nothing, but radiating a kind of alpha support into the room. The relief was palpable, and Ali regretted that call with Suzie Gale a few days back, when she'd egged up the presence of the canisters just to shut the woman up. It wasn't *not* true, but neither was it a serious consideration; yet, clearly, Elliot Gale had thought about nothing else since. Despite Ali's update, the man still looked haunted, as though it hadn't quite sunk in that he was not to blame.

'And the missing fella?' John Gale asked now. 'Our Cathy's been fretting about him – the young man who went into the showers before the crash. She's been having nightmares about him still being trapped under there.'

'Well, it's been almost four weeks, and no one has been reported missing. Suzie said you do get a lot of one-night campers, hill walkers and so on, so we think he probably just moved on. Tell Cathy not to worry – we checked the site thoroughly and he's definitely not in the wreckage.'

Ali stood, still cradling her half-finished tea in her hands, and locked eyes with the pilot, who seemed to be anticipating her words.

'Shall we have a private chat?' she said, crossing the small room and lowering her voice. 'About your son?'

The pilot gestured towards the back door and, moving with a steady grace, he followed her out to the picnic bench on the unkempt patio, where they sat on opposite sides, the sun-bleached wooden surface between them.

'Do you *know* that he's my son?' he asked, fixing her with his good eye. The other was still concealed beneath a patch of sorts, while the livid skin of his burns was now out in the open, to heal, and shock.

'We're working on that assumption, for now, Mr – I'm sorry, I don't know what to call you.'

'Neither do I,' he murmured apologetically. 'But the lad, Albie, he calls me Griffin, so that'll do.'

'OK. *Griffin*. If you're happy to give us a saliva sample,' she said, taking a kit from her bag, 'we'll be able to tell you for certain. We'll be able to compare and match your DNA with the boy's. Are you happy to do that?'

'Can I refuse?'

The man's mistrust of authority was perplexing. If he really had no memory of his own identity, why would he be so keen to protect it?

Ali gave a curt nod. 'You're not under arrest, so your co-operation would be entirely voluntary.'

The pilot held her gaze a moment, and then turned away to fill the vial. Ali took out a ballpoint pen and completed the sample envelope, with the name 'John Highcap Doe', the working name they had given him from the moment he was taken into hospital, identity unknown. She added the name 'Griffin' in brackets at the bottom.

'The coroner's report,' he said cautiously, as he turned back and handed her the vial. He seemed to stall for a moment, as he searched for the words. 'I assume there was one for the boy too?'

'There was.' Ali dropped her gaze, a kindness. 'The pathologist said it was instant. He didn't suffer, after the crash.'

When she looked up, the pilot's expression had shifted again, and she knew that if it weren't for her position here she would want to embrace him, to comfort him, to offer soothing words.

'Sir, do you know a man called Andrew Belgo?' she asked instead.

The pilot blinked at her, uncomprehending. 'No,' he replied.

Was his amnesia real or was this man just buying time? she wondered. Was he hiding something, as Suzie Gale suggested, faking it, just to dodge justice?

Ali took a breath.

'Look, we really need to find out who you are. Whether that boy is yours or not, someone's going to miss him eventually – his mother, grandparents, family friends. It's the summer holidays now, and it's conceivable he might be considered as simply away on holiday with his dad. But, come September, someone is going to notice him missing, aren't they? Don't you want to spare them the pain of finding out about his death through the national news?'

The pilot dropped his head. 'Will there be a funeral?'

Ali was shocked by the question, as she acknowledged for the first time that the boy could not be given even a memorial service until he was identified. 'Not until we find out who he is.' She waited for a response. 'Listen, I want your permission to release a photograph – of you – to see if we can locate anyone who knows you.'

In a beat, the pilot looked up, shaking his head. 'I can't do that.'

'Why not?'

'I don't know. I don't know,' he repeated, his calm exterior at once fractured, panic streaking his expression. 'I just know I can't do that.'

Turning out of the front gate, Ali glanced along the quiet path and spotted the Gale daughter, Nell, who had witnessed the air crash from the top of Highcap Hill. Dressed in khaki shorts and a grubby black vest top and boots, the girl looked as though she'd come off a construction site, her hair a scruffy cropped auburn that drew attention to her big green eyes.

Recognising that it was the detective at her front step, the girl slowed, cautiously sliding her thumb under the strap of her army surplus rucksack to readjust it on her shoulder.

'Hi,' Ali said, holding open the little gate for her.

'Hi,' Nell replied, appearing simultaneously scared or guilty, or both, as she waited for Ali to move out of her way. 'What . . .?'

Ali gestured back at the house. 'Oh, I was just giving your family an update. On the crash.'

The girl's shoulders seemed to relax a little, and awkwardly she manoeuvred around Ali and in through the gate.

'I like your new puppy,' Ali said. 'Lump!'

Nell gave a little smile. 'Yeah, he's cute. Apart from all the peeing and pooing.'

'They do that,' Ali replied, and she paused a moment, taking in Nell's appearance, an unformed question floating just outside of her reach. 'Have you changed your hair or something?' she asked. The girl had worn her hoodie up the previous time they'd met, but, for some reason, Ali had imagined her with a longer style.

Nell bobbed her head, already walking on. 'Oh. Yeah. Summer job – all that hair was a bit, you know, sweaty.'

Ali laughed. 'Yeah. Would be.' She started to walk away, and then that floating thought drifted a little closer. Nell was about the same age as the girls in those videos. Maybe she'd heard something?

Glancing back, she watched as Nell turned her key in the lock and pushed her grandfather's door open, her weariness almost visible in the slump of her shoulders, the incline of her head. 'Hey, Nell?'

Nell Gale looked up, her eyelids scrunched against the early-afternoon sun. 'Yeah?'

'Do you know the Five Bells?' For a moment, Ali thought she hadn't heard her. 'Nell?'

'Why?' the girl asked, defensive.

With that one word, Ali's suspicion was piqued enough to push further. 'Because I'm investigating some attacks, the most recent of which took place near there.'

'Attacks?' Nell repeated.

Ali nodded and waited, one beat, two. 'Well, do you ever get down there?'

Nell pushed open the door. 'No,' she finally replied, confidently returning the detective's gaze. 'No. It's a dive.'

And she stepped out of the sunlight and shut the front door.

18. Cathy

Wednesday

After Wednesday's double cleaning shift out at the Starlings, Cathy, hoping to simply collapse for a few hours, stepped in through her kitchen door and managed just thirty seconds alone.

Because flying in through the back gate behind her came Nell, who had clearly been watching out for her from Dad's first-floor window next door.

'You're back, then?' she yelled, standing on path, hands on hips, expecting Cathy to know by some kind of telepathy what the problem was.

Cathy glanced about the living room, surprised to sense the house otherwise empty, which was strange, considering the time, just after eight o'clock. She reached into the back of the kitchen drawer and foraged for a half-pack of cigarettes she'd stashed there soon after she'd announced she was giving up once and for all. She never could abide waste. Lighting up at the gas stove, she dropped to sit on the back step to the small garden space and faced her ferocious daughter.

'Right. What is it?' she asked before taking a long, bored drag on the cigarette. Her daughter's expression remained fixed and furious. 'What could I possibly have done to offend you, Nell,' she asked, in the jaded tone she knew drove her daughter insane, 'while away working my six-hour cleaning shift this afternoon? Hmm?'

Nell dropped her hands to her sides and released a sarcastic cough. 'You're priceless,' she said. She gestured over the fence to her grandad's house. 'It's not enough that you kick me out of my own home so you can move your fancy man in—'

Cathy raised her fag hand, like a defendant swearing on the oath. 'Er, *not* my fancy man.'

'But then you swan off to work and let everyone just get on with it, with no – no—'

'No what, Nell? Spit it out, for God's sake!'

'No bloody rules! I got home from work today – you're not the only one, you know – and guess who was round at Grandad's? Every bloody one! Your pilot playing backgammon with Grandad like they're old mates, while Dad cooks them all dinner. Albie taking over my room with his keyboard. And Elliot – when he's not going on about having killed the Warners – snoring off his hangover on the sofa and stinking the house out.'

'Elliot didn't kill the Warners, the bloody idiot.'

'Try telling him that. According to him, it was carbon monoxide poisoning. Asphyxiation.'

'What? No – I mean, *yes*, it was asphyxiation – but caused by a suspected overdose. They're all talking about it over at the Starlings.' One of the neighbours there was an admin at the police station, and a loose-lipped one at that.

'Well, maybe someone could tell Uncle Elliot that? He's losing his mind over it.'

Cathy made a move towards the back door.

'Not now – he's gone out. And anyway, that's not what we're talking about! I want my room back. How long's that fucker gonna be staying? I've got no space. Oh, and did I mention that that stupid dog Grandad bought Albie is pissing everywhere?'

Cathy let out a groan. 'Sounds perfectly harmonious to me, Nell.'

Nell threw up her arms. 'I don't know where I'm supposed to go! Where do I belong? Huh?'

Cathy stared back at her.

'You should've let me go travelling, Mum. I don't know why you made me stay, 'cause you don't need me like you said you did. You've done nothing but make me feel unwanted since all this happened, and now that pilot has moved in, it's like I'm invisible to you. What is it about him that makes you hate me so much?'

'It's not Griffin,' Cathy said, standing to grind her cigarette butt underfoot. She met her daughter's gaze.

'*Griffin.*' Nell shook her head, and took a little step backwards, her bare arms appearing to Cathy to be suddenly so thin and vulnerable that she wondered how she had it in her to treat her own daughter so cruelly. 'I get it.' Nell backed off towards the gate with a small dismissive wave of her hand. 'I'm sorry, Mum. I wish I could undo it all – Albie, everything.'

There was no antagonism in her tone now, just regret, and Cathy wished she could turn back the clock, back to a time when she and her daughter had had nothing but love and admiration for each other. What changed it all? Was it as simple as Nell just growing up, not being a child any more? Or was it more likely that the rot had set in once Nell had started to see Cathy for who she really was: a flawed woman, just making her life up as she went along.

'They don't give you a manual, you know?' Cathy said, trying to find a way in. 'Parenting, Nell. No one tells you how to do it, and it's not always easy—'

Nell blew air between pursed lips. *Stop talking,* her look said, *just stop.* 'Look, you blame me for not taking Albie to tennis that day,' she said. 'I get that – because you're right. But you know what? *I* blame me too – for letting you talk me into staying in Highcap. Because if I'd just gone, like I wanted to, none of this would've happened. To Albie, to you, to me—'

'To you?' Cathy scowled, her defence autopilot already rearing up. How could Nell compare *her* guilt to the loss that Albie had suffered?

Nell looked defeated. 'I just wish we could talk more, Mum, like we used to. I just wish we—'

In Cathy's back pocket, her mobile phone rang, and she reached for it, to see a number she didn't recognise. 'Hello?' she answered, turning her back on Nell.

'Auntie Cathy?'

Cathy spun round, gesturing to Nell and putting the call on speakerphone. 'Dylan? Nell's here with me. What is it?'

'It's Dad,' he replied breathlessly, before launching in without pause. 'I just got a call from the Five Bells – Ted, the landlord – says Dad's in a right state and there might be a fight and you know I can't drive yet, but Mum refused to go and get him because she's already had two gin and tonics, and anyway she's kicked him out so—'

'So, what are you saying, Dylan?' Cathy demanded, feeling fresh rage at her soak of a brother and his selfish wife.

Nell reached out and snatched the mobile from her hand. 'Dylan, it's me. Sorry, I haven't sorted a new phone yet. What can we do, mate?'

'We need to go and get him,' he replied, seemingly soothed by the sound of his cousin's voice. 'The landlord said he was completely out of it, shouting the odds at some idiot who was getting up in his face. I'm scared he's gonna get himself killed.'

Nell looked at her mum. 'We're on our way,' she said.

The volume of the public bar reached them even before they pushed open the door of the Five Bells. It wasn't yet nine, and already the place had the bawdy atmosphere of last orders on a full moon in midsummer.

At the bar, Elliot was slumped over the counter, his ruddy forehead resting on his hands, apparently passed out.

'Ted.' Cathy nodded curtly. He had been a few years older than her at school, another who'd never left his home town and had spent the rest of his life looking cheated by it. Cathy remembered him as a player back in the day, and now he was one of those men who'd once been good-looking but whose looks had faded too fast for their conceited brains to catch up with. 'Problems with Elliot?'

He gave a roll of his eyes and indicated to his barman – a lad so obviously his son that Cathy had to give him a second look – to take over serving. 'Come on, Elliot,' Ted said, raising his voice in an attempt to rouse him from his drunken slumber.

At the mention of Elliot's name, another, younger man's interest was piqued and he slid along the bar, draping louche eyes over Nell, who stood at her mother's elbow, looking uncomfortable.

'You his sister?' the man slurred, addressing Cathy.

''S'right,' she replied, avoiding eye contact. 'Come on, Ells,' she said, giving her brother's shoulder a little shake.

'Come to take the old cunt home?' the younger man snorted.

Cathy felt Nell stiffen at her side.

'Don't start with me, mate,' Cathy replied icily. 'I might be half your size, but I'm twice as sober.'

She looked at Ted with a sharp jerk of her chin, but he did little more than shrug. 'Get him out of here,' he said, nodding towards

Elliot. 'These two have been pushing each other's buttons all night. The place is packed, and I haven't got time to break up some stupid playground argument.'

'You the one whose kid lost his arm?' the sleazy bloke asked with a smirk, wriggling his butt onto the bar stool beside them.

'He didn't "lose" it, you dickhead,' Nell spat.

The man lunged at her with an open hand. Instinctively, Cathy pulled her fist back, but her punch hit only empty space, because Nell got there first, darting between them to jerk the stool leg from under the man, spilling him across the sticky carpet with a heavy, '*Oof.*'

After a couple of stunned seconds, the drunkard pulled himself to standing, just as Elliot also managed to stagger to his feet on the other side of the two women. Swaying, the man jabbed his finger in the air, first at Cathy, then at Nell, and then at Elliot. 'You're a fucking Gale, you're a fucking Gale, and you're a fucking Gale, so you can all fucking—'

'Dean!' Ted bellowed now, midway through pulling a pint for another nervous-looking customer who was trying hard to stay away from the action. 'Either pack it in or get out!'

Dean gave an unsteady salute and turned his gappy smile on Cathy and Nell. 'Yous twos don't know who I am, do you? It was my mum and dad in that caravan, y'know?'

Oh. This was Dean Warner, Cathy at once realised, and all her combative energy slipped away. *Elliot*, she thought with an inner sigh, *you idiot*. He just had to go and get pissed up and bump into Dean bloody Warner of all people, just days before his parents' funeral.

'Take him out to the car,' she whispered to Nell, indicating to Elliot.

Nell hooked her arm through her uncle's and attempted to get him moving. He wasn't having any of it.

'I'm really sorry about your mum and dad, Dean,' Cathy said, tempering her tone now. 'But – well, you do know it was nothing to do with us?'

Dean laughed manically and threw back his drink, thrusting the glass high in a wordless request for a top-up. Astonishingly, Ted's son took down a fresh glass, which he began to fill at the bar tap.

'We've always been really fond of them,' Cathy continued. 'They've been coming to us for years. But we couldn't have done anything to stop them, could we—'

Without warning, Dean raised his empty glass and smashed it on the bar top, provoking Ted to at last sprint out and ready himself to restrain the man.

'No!' Dean yelped, batting the landlord away, never tearing his eyes from Cathy. 'You're just like my sister, saying shit that isn't true! She says there was a letter – bullshit! Why would they? Why would they? They were happy! They wouldn't do that!'

Nell laid a hand on her mother's shoulder. The touch was tender, and so familiar and longed-for that, quite without warning, Cathy's eyes filled with tears.

Misreading her emotion, Dean Warner folded against the bar in a fit of uncontrolled sobs. Ted escorted him outside to sit on the bench and cool off, as the Gale family waited in silence for the landlord to return.

'What did it say?' Cathy asked Ted when he returned, glancing at Nell and Elliot, who were now finally exiting the pub in a zigzag fashion. 'Do you know – the Warners' note?'

Ted glanced towards the door. 'Didn't tell anyone they were going away, apparently, and when the sister couldn't get an answer on the phone after a day or so, she called round the family home and found a suicide note on the fridge. She – the mum – had terminal cancer, and they decided to check out early, together.'

'Jeez,' Cathy murmured. 'Everyone's been saying it was an overdose.'

Ted gestured towards the open door. 'It was. They'd collected up Elizabeth Warner's pain meds, apparently. But old Dean there is having trouble accepting it. When your Elliot came in, already half-cut, he just started spouting rubbish to rile him up.'

'Bloody hell. What is wrong with these men? God, Dean can hardly blame Elliot for his parents' death. Elliot just runs the place.'

Ted poured himself a shot and knocked it back in one. 'Oh, Dean wasn't saying stuff about his parents. It was about your Nell, and that alleyway business. He asked Elliot . . .' He hesitated, glancing beyond Cathy, alerting her to the presence of Nell in the far doorway, anxiously waving to hurry her mum along. Ted leant in to lower his voice. 'Dean asked if he could have a go on her next time she was in.'

After a silent drive home, they let themselves into No. 31 and Nell headed directly upstairs to bed, while Cathy poured Elliot a pint of water and covered him with a blanket on the sofa. She thought about going up to Nell's room, knocking on her door, sitting on the edge of her bed and asking her, 'What's going on, my darling girl?' but she didn't act on it. She couldn't; she was terrified of the answers her questions might unleash.

Locking the back door behind her, she returned to her own home, softly creeping in her own identical back door, through the kitchen to the little living room, where moonlight sliced soft shadows across the sleeping form of the pilot on the sofa. She'd almost forgotten about him in all this drama, and now she found herself standing in the darkness, watching the rise and fall of his breath, her gaze wandering over the perfect and imperfect contours of his broken face.

'He's beautiful, isn't he?'

Cathy didn't start at the voice beside her. She'd been aware of Kip appearing silently at the foot of the stairs, and now, in the darkness, she felt for his hand, and for long moments, they stood, watching the pilot, together.

'Stay in my room tonight?' she whispered, and she felt his fingers tighten gently around hers.

As he led her through the small house, to her bedroom upstairs, Kip could never have imagined the turmoil raging inside Cathy's head. Nell needed saving; how could Cathy ever save Nell? In the darkness, she slipped out of her clothes and into the arms of the only man she'd ever felt safe with; the only man she'd ever willingly given herself to, without a fight.

19. Nell

Thursday

The day after Uncle Elliot's punch-up, Grandad called a family meeting at Tino's Italian in town, where everyone was expected for lunch at 1 p.m. sharp. It was unusual; while he was always generous with the odd ten- or twenty-pound note here and there, Grandad was famously tight with his money when it came to 'lording it up'. He'd cough up for barbecue food, for birthdays and emergency motor costs whenever Mum's old Citroën broke down, but as far as luxuries were concerned, his wallet full of cash stayed firmly in his breast pocket. He was set to be the richest man in the graveyard, if Auntie Suzie was to be believed.

The owner, Tino, knew Grandad – everyone knew John Gale – and he arranged a private dining area upstairs, where they could all fit comfortably around the large rectangular table, without the distraction of other diners. Grandad took the central seat, with Mum and Kip to one side, Elliot and Suzie to the other, and Dylan, Albie and Nell filling the space between.

'Do you think he's dying?' Dylan asked Nell, as he distractedly rearranged his cutlery on the tablecloth.

'Jeez, Dylan!' She gaped at him sideways. 'This is a good example of one of those "keep your thoughts to yourself" things I've told you about. Course he's not bloody dying.'

Albie, who was listening in, made wide eyes at Nell across Dylan, and she scowled back at him to stop herself from smirking.

'Grandad will outlive the rest of us,' Albie whispered discreetly. 'That's what everyone says, isn't it?'

'Yup, that's what they say,' Nell replied, and Dylan just blinked, non-committal.

She watched as a waiter placed a bottle of red wine on the table, alongside two jugs of water and a pint of ale for Grandad. Without missing a beat, Suzie leant in for the water, filling Elliot's glass to the top, before reaching for the wine to pour herself a glass. Unceremoniously, she passed the bottle across Grandad to Kip, who poured for himself and Mum before returning the bottle to the centre. With a rush of nervous adrenaline, Nell swooped it up to fill her own glass, and offered to pour for a startled Dylan, who she knew didn't drink.

'Not for Dylan, please!' Suzie announced, louder than necessary.

'All right, Mum,' he responded through gritted teeth, reddening as he poured himself and Albie a glass of water, ignoring his cousin's smirk to the side of him.

'Do you think Lump'll be all right?' Albie asked Nell.

'Huh?'

'The *puppy*, Nell. Lump. D'you reckon he'll be OK without me?'

'Lump?' Suzie echoed. She was the only one not to have met the new addition to the Gale family. 'What a strange name for a dog.'

'It was good enough for Picasso,' Mum retorted archly.

'He'll be fine, Albie lad,' Kip called across, placing an affectionate arm around Cathy's shoulders. 'Griffin's there, isn't he? He'll be just fine. He's got a warm lap to sit on.'

Nell felt her irritation rising at the mention of that name. *Griffin*; he was even muscling in on the dog now. What was wrong with this lot, that they couldn't see how messed up the whole situation was?

As she glanced about the assembled family, two more waiters passed through, laying out bread and plates of salami and cheese and dips, and momentarily the room went quiet. Elliot nudged Suzie to pass him the wine, and she hissed at him to drop it. The moment the waiters had cleared off again, Suzie spoke up. 'I said we shouldn't order wine,' she said, addressing her complaint to Cathy. Elliot sat silently staring at the tablecloth before him, compliant as a child and looking every bit as hungover as he probably was.

'Well, you don't seem to be steering clear,' Cathy replied, with a nod towards her sister-in-law's full glass.

'Come on, Cath,' Kip said. He took her hand in a bid to avert a confrontation, and she threw a small smile his way.

Albie's face lit up, and he leant back to reach behind his cousin and tug at his sister's sleeve. 'Oo-ooh, look at Mum and Dad,' he said with a waggle of his eyebrows.

Nell took a slug of her wine and followed his gaze. Their parents were sitting very close, and it was true: you'd almost be forgiven for thinking they were together. 'You're such a little dickhead,' she laughed at her brother, and she slapped his hand away and took another drink.

'*You're* a dickhead!' he laughed back.

Grandad banged a palm on the table, and the clamour died down. 'So, you'll be wondering what this is in aid of,' he said. All eyes were on him. 'Well, there are two things. First, it's the

Warrens' funeral tomorrow. I hear we had some bad blood with their youngest last night, is that right, Elliot?'

Elliot nodded gravely.

'As you'll all know, Howard and Liz have been customers – and friends – of this family for longer than some of you have been around. Thirty-odd years they've leased a caravan at our place. Now, you've all heard about the sad circumstances of their . . . their – passing . . .' Grandad stuttered briefly. 'But you'll be comforted to know I spoke to DS Samson this morning, and she confirmed that there is no suspicion levelled at anyone – at all – in connection with the way things ended for them. I don't need to go into detail, but needless to say, the last thing we want is bad feeling connected to the campsite, or the Gale family. So, I paid the family a visit this morning and sat down with their eldest three, the girls, and passed on our sincere condolences.'

Cathy blinked at Grandad, and Nell wondered what her look meant.

'You gave them money, didn't you?' Cathy said.

Grandad gave no response.

'After what that little tosser Dean said last night—' Cathy began, but Elliot shook his head and threw an anxious glance towards Nell.

'What?' Nell asked, immediately paranoid.

'That's enough,' Grandad continued. 'I just gave them a little help towards the funeral costs. It's the least I could do, as a friend. Now, hear this: I expect to see every one of you at the church tomorrow, to show our respect, as a family. As the Gale family. The Warner girls said we'd be welcome – that they'd see to it that Dean behaves. It's the right thing to do. Understood?'

With some eye-rolling and murmurs of dissent, the family begrudgingly agreed, and the matter was settled as the plates of nibbles circulated around the table. Not for the first time,

Nell felt herself quite apart from them all, as though she were a distant relative, just passing through.

'What was the other thing, Grandad?' she asked.

'Oh, yes, the other thing,' he replied, loading up a hunk of bread with salami and cheese and all the things he was meant to avoid. 'The docs reckon I've got three months to live,' he said, taking a large bite and chewing thoughtfully, as though considering something as inconsequential as the weather. 'Six, if I'm lucky.'

'I don't . . .?' Mum murmured, her hands instinctively balling into little fists. 'Dad?'

'Pancreas,' Grandad replied, simply. 'And before you ask, no, I'll not be having any of that bloody chemo rubbish, not at my age. I've had a good innings.'

Around the table, everyone stopped eating and laid down their forks, and Elliot burst into tears.

The Warren funeral was an old-fashioned affair, a burial at the local church, where their family had been laid to rest for generations, shoulder to shoulder with the Gales and a handful of other local families who'd stuck around long enough to continue the tradition and fill up the plots.

Sitting in the church, a few rows back from the grieving daughters, Nell held her brother's hand as the service came to an end and whispered to him that she would never be buried here. That she'd never be buried, full stop.

'Me neither,' Albie whispered back, giving her fingers a squeeze. 'I was just thinking, I wouldn't want to be buried without my other arm, so I reckon cremation would be better. It would be sort of like it never happened, if there was just ash at the end of it.'

Nell felt her chest heave as tears sprang with ease, under the comforting guise of neighbourly empathy. She wondered how much more she could take, without collapsing under the strain of it all: Albie, Grandad . . . the other thing.

As they waited for the front rows of the congregation to file out, Nell closed her eyes and imagined her own death. She'd be cremated and scattered from the top of Highcap Hill, so that the wind might take her, across the water, far, far away, to all those places she'd ever dreamt of visiting; far, far away from here. She took a breath, mopped her face dry and followed the crowd to the graveyard outside.

As the congregation had relocated to the graveside, the Gale family had spread out, so that the united front Grandad had insisted on became more of a scattering. Mum and Kip stuck close to Grandad, who since his announcement yesterday appeared suddenly years older, while Suzie and Dylan on the opposite side kept an eye on Elliot, who had arrived already smelling of alcohol and slurring his words. Still hanging on to her little brother's hand, Nell lurked at the back, feeling sick with nerves as she noticed that detective woman in the crowd, the one who'd stopped her to ask about the Five Bells.

'Let's go,' she whispered to Albie.

'What?' He scowled, but he followed her anyway, and the pair of them broke away to wander quietly among the overgrown gravestones at the back of the churchyard.

'I couldn't take any more of that,' she said, perching on a fallen headstone and drinking deeply from her water bottle. 'Want some?' she asked.

Albie took the bottle, and in turn reached into his trouser pocket and handed her a Chupa Chups lolly. 'From Mrs Jenkins next door,' he said. 'She keeps bringing me sweets since the accident. She shouts for Grandad over the fence, then drops them over.' He did that funny fish mouth thing and shrugged. 'Silver linings and all that.'

Nell smiled, despite her horror. 'You've got a sick sense of humour, Albie Gale.'

Albie sat down beside her. 'I know. But, like Grandad always says, if you can't laugh, what can you do?' Without warning, he began to cry, and he allowed his sister to pull him close. 'I'm gonna miss him so much, Nell. He can't die,' he sobbed. 'It's not fair.'

When a shadow fell over them, for one horrible moment, Nell thought it would be that detective again, somehow on to her. But when they looked up, it was another, older woman, one Nell didn't know but had noticed around town these past couple of years. Thrusting a tissue into Albie's hand, Nell stood.

'Oh, darlings, I'm so sorry to intrude on your grief!' the woman gasped, as she realised the pair were both crying. Her eyes fell on the space where Albie's arm used to be, and her hand fluttered to her neck. 'Goodness. You're John Gale's grandchild?'

'We both are,' Nell said, and all at once the woman's arms were about them, drawing them in as she cooed her sympathy.

Across the graveyard, the coffin was lowered, and the vicar's solemn words drifted inaudibly across the leafy plot as the woman released them.

'I'm Ginny LeFevre,' she said, perching her expensive bottom on the slab between them. 'Your mum cleans for me – over at the Starlings.'

Ah, so *this* was Ms LeFevre. Cathy had often mentioned her, bringing home the occasional bottle of perfume or silk scarf that the woman had tired of, and passing on little snippets of information that she had gleaned in her two hours there a week. Nell seemed to recall she'd had a glamorous life in London, once upon a time, before returning here to her childhood town.

'She does a few places there, doesn't she?' Nell replied, out of politeness.

'She likes you,' Albie said. 'She doesn't always like the posh ones.'

Ms LeFevre laughed, a full and authentic sound, before putting her hand over her mouth with a little 'Oops! Well, I like your mother very much too. And your grandfather – I knew him a little when I was younger.' She gazed across the churchyard, where the mourners were now starting to break away from the graveside, to move about in small clusters of polite chatter. 'You know we're sitting right beside your family plot?' she said, and she pointed to a large, ancient headstone to Nell's right.

Albie got up to investigate. 'It says William George Gale, I think. Died 1856! And his wife, Mary – 1877.'

Nell joined him, and, lost in the moment, the trio wandered through the Gales, trying to work out the connections to their Grandad and themselves.

'I'm doing my family tree at school,' Albie said. 'It's our summer project and I've hardly done anything on it. Hey, Nell! I could come down here and take photos and dates, couldn't I?'

'That's a lovely idea,' Ginny LeFevre said. 'I'm very interested in this kind of history too – I've been tracing my own family tree, of sorts. Would you believe, I found a long-lost sister, just two or three years ago, through research and DNA. It's extraordinary what's possible these days!'

'DNA,' Nell repeated, recalling the weird thing Dylan had said about Mum being adopted. Of course, the idea was ridiculous – Cathy *looked* like a Gale; they all did – and she certainly had Grandad's impatience and lack of sentimentality. If anything, Uncle Elliot was the odd one out. 'Was your sister adopted?' Nell asked. 'Or were you?'

'She was,' Ms LeFevre said. 'She'd been one of the children born at the mother and baby home – many years before it was renovated into what we now know as the Starlings. Back then, unwed young women went there to have their babies in secret

– to avoid the scandal – and then they'd leave, empty-handed, while the baby got moved on to a new family.'

'Wow,' Albie gasped. 'That's so sad. Nell, if Mum had been alive then, she would've had to give us away, 'cause her and Dad weren't married, were they? We would've ended up somewhere else. We might never've known each other.'

They came to a stop at a tiny gravestone, laid flat against the grass.

'Who's this, then?' the woman asked, stooping to read the inscription. 'Lisa Anne Gale, 3 May 1976 to 15 June 1981.'

'Beloved daughter of John and Irene, taken too soon.' Nell stared at the words. 'She was five,' she murmured.

'Huh?' Albie glanced across the graveyard, where the Gale family were now clustered around Grandad in the shade of the great oak tree, as he leant heavily against the trunk. Mum appeared to be scouring the crowd, perhaps looking for her absent children. 'That would make her Mum's sister. Do you think she knows?'

'She would've said something, wouldn't she?' Nell replied. 'Although these dates – it was three years before she was even born. Let's go and ask her.'

Ginny LeFevre laid a gentle hand on Nell's wrist. 'Now's probably not the time, darling. Save it for another day?' She gave them a friendly little wave and continued on her solitary walk around the gravestones, heading away from the crowd.

Nell and Albie rejoined the fold.

'Nell,' Mum said quietly, dropping Kip's hand and breaking aside as her daughter caught up with the family group. 'Ted at the Five Bells said something the other night. Something I've been worrying about.' She hesitated. 'He said there were rumours – about you.'

'*Mum*,' Nell gasped through gritted teeth. What was wrong with her? She chose *now* to confront her? At a funeral? 'Whatever he said, it's bullshit. You know what this place is like. He's never liked me. He's just stirring the pot!'

At the sound of their whispered exchange, Kip snapped his head in their direction, and Nell shook her head at him – *don't get involved* – and turned back to her mother. The path was getting crowded as people prepared to move on to the wake – at the Five Bells, of all places – and Nell felt hemmed in, panicked by her mother's confrontation.

She lowered her voice further still. 'What did Ted say?'

Cathy regarded her carefully. 'He said there's a rumour about you getting caught up to no good in the alleyway there at the Five Bells. With *two* men.'

'Ha!' Nell coughed and crossed her arms. 'Go on, then. What else?'

'Nothing else. He said I should ask you if I wanted to know more.'

Did this mean Mum hadn't actually seen the video? Or just that Ted didn't mention it? A monochrome image of the man with the phone camera – the other man – suddenly flashed from the back of her mind; his face was in darkness.

'Well, as I already told you, it's bullshit,' she said, feigning indifference, while her blood pounded in her ears. Was she about to faint? 'So now you know.'

Turning from her mother, she scanned the busy path and spotted Dylan near the gate, as ever wearing his backpack over both shoulders, like an overgrown schoolboy. She pushed through the crowd to reach him.

'Fancy dodging the bloody wake?' she asked.

'Yes, I do. My dad's already very drunk, and I don't fancy watching the disaster unfold.'

'OK. Let's go back to mine,' Nell said, leaning in to speak low. 'I've got to get out of here. Mum just asked me about the alleyway. *Oh, my God.*'

'How much does she know?'

'I don't know – but I do know that tosspot Ted down the Five Bells said something to her.'

'Does she know about the video?' Dylan asked, in too loud a voice, but before Nell could tell him to shut up, she felt a hand on her shoulder and she spun around, coming face-to-face with the very detective who'd asked her about the Five Bells.

'Hello, Nell,' she said, her face impassive.

Had she overheard their conversation? *Had she?* There were so many people jostling about, it was possible she hadn't heard a thing.

DS Ali Samson turned her attention to Dylan. 'And who's this?'

'My cousin, Dylan.'

Dylan hooked his thumbs into the straps of his rucksack, forming an unconvincing smile for the officer.

'Dylan. OK. Dylan Gale?' She narrowed her eyes, as though unpicking some problem, then threw a friendly smile at them both before striding through the church gate and into the car park beyond.

Nell stared after her. 'I don't think she—'

'She heard,' Dylan said, his voice flat. 'She definitely heard.'

Back at Allotment Row, Nell, without thinking, went to the rear gate of her own home, but was halted by the sound of the pilot in the back yard, calling to the new puppy, his stranger's voice now so familiar to Nell's ears.

'Lump!' He was calling the dog's name, in between little starts of laughter and praise, the name coming out as '*Lomp!*' in his soft Irish accent.

Cursing under her breath and signalling to Dylan that they should go to Grandad's house instead, she found herself almost hating the little puppy by association, and her rage at her mother and the rest of her hopeless family swelled again, intensified by the visceral fear that that woman from the police was closing in on her dirty secret.

On soft feet, Nell and Dylan retraced their steps, and let themselves in through Grandad's front door. Without a word, Nell raced up the stairs, with Dylan close at heel, and the pair of them stood back from the bedroom window, furtively watching the pilot play with the puppy in the back yard of her house. Leaning up against the bench was the expensive wooden walking stick they'd bought at Christmas last year; Grandad had refused to use it, complaining he wouldn't be made an old man of yet, and they hadn't seen it since. But here it was now, gifted to this interloper.

'That *fucker*,' she growled. 'Fucker' – the name Nell had given him from the moment he'd turned up in her living room had stuck, after she'd figured that if the lying bastard wasn't going to tell them his name she might as well choose one for him. And she was damned if she was going to use Albie's new name for him, *Griffin*. So 'Fucker' it was. After a couple of weeks of this, even Mum had stopped correcting her, and Nell wondered how easy it would be to stop calling him it once his real name was revealed.

But the more time she had spent around him, the harder Nell was finding it to keep hating him. There was something about him that seemed to unite her mum and dad – she hadn't seen them so close in years – and even Albie lit up in his presence, as his new love of music filled some of the gap once filled by his passion for tennis.

But still, it wasn't right, was it? To invite the man behind all their recent woes into their lives like that. If Nell wasn't going to hate him, then who was?

'You know,' she said, 'the police offered to put his picture out on the news and stuff, to try to help him find out who he is. But he said no. Why would he say no, Dylan? Why would anyone say no, if they had nothing to hide?' She turned to look at her cousin, who was scrutinising the man carefully.

'Well, the only reason I can think of is if you *do* have something to hide. Right?' He scratched his wispy chin. 'How good's the camera on that new phone of yours?' he asked. 'Could it get a close enough picture of his face from here?'

Nell shook her head. 'I could only afford a cheap one. But I've got a pretty decent digital camera I got for my art A-level. It's here – Grandad was mending the strap on it last week.'

'Go and get it, then,' Dylan said, with a pleased nod. 'We'll see if social media can tell us who Mr Fucker really is. Right?'

Out in her tiny family garden next door, the pilot stood in a pool of light, cradling the little puppy against his neck, face turned to the sun, as though posed, ready for his picture to be taken. With creeping doubt, Nell set off downstairs to fetch her camera.

20. DS Ali Samson

Ali hadn't even arrived back at the station when Benny's call came in.

She'd been thinking about the snatch of conversation she'd just overheard between Nell Gale and her cousin, in which they had distinctly mentioned a video and the Five Bells pub. Could they be involved, somehow?

The only thing their team knew with certainty was that the man carrying out the assaults was in both videos obscured by a smiley emoji Photoshopped over his face, and that there had to have been at least one other person involved, filming the attack.

To date, they'd assumed, perhaps incorrectly, that that other person must be male. But what if their assumption was wrong? What if Nell Gale and her cousin – who certainly fitted the attacker's height profile – not only knew something about the assaults, but were behind them?

'Sarge?' Benny sounded as if he was chewing. She'd noticed he was never without something in his mouth these days, and his waistline was suffering for it. 'We've got another video – looks like the same alleyway, but this time the tech team have been able to zoom in on an address attached to a delivery carton in the foreground—'

'Don't tell me, Benny? It's the Five Bells again?'

'How'd you know?'

Ali pulled out onto the main road back towards Highcap, putting her foot down in her impatience to find out more about that new video. 'Just something I picked up at the Warner funeral this morning. Listen, Benny, can you run a check on Nell Gale and her cousin Dylan, same surname? I also want anything we've got on the Five Bells. Any altercations, drug offences, sexual assaults, licence warnings – anything at all in the past year or so. And check out the landlord. I don't know his name, but you'll find it easy enough. Get the team onto it straight away, will you? I want as much info as you can gather – then come and join me at the Five Bells in, let's say, an hour. The Warren family are holding the wake there. It won't be a surprise when I turn up – one of the daughters just invited me along – and it'll give us a chance to grill the Gales and anyone working in the pub. Anyone who might have heard about these videos. Someone connected to that pub has to know something.'

When Ali arrived at the Five Bells, she discreetly moved from group to group, making herself known and repeating her condolences to the family. Clusters of mourners were arranged around the bar, and Ali noticed that the Gale family group was somewhat reduced now, with Nell and Dylan nowhere to be seen.

Behind the bar, the landlord and two assistants were busy serving up drinks, while a couple of kitchen staff ferried finger food back and forth to the buffet table laid out beneath the window. There were plenty of locals here, to mark the Warners' passing, and Ali was glad to go unnoticed among their number.

Sitting on a corner bar stool and waving an empty glass was the Warner son, Dean, who had not made it to the funeral itself, an absence Ali noted did not go unremarked among the congregation. From what she could gather from snippets overheard while the mourners lingered outside the church, the sisters had prevented him from attending, for fear that he'd make a scene. And judging by the slump of his shoulders and the two empty glasses in front of him right now, they probably weren't too far off the mark.

Dean Warner was, Ali estimated, around forty years old, skinny as a teenager, with a pale complexion and thinning, mousy hair. She offered him her hand. 'Hi – Dean, isn't it? I'm Ali Samson – I'm one of the team who investigated your parents' deaths.'

Unconsciously, Dean Warner wiped his hand on his trouser leg. 'Huh,' he said. 'Your lot said it was an overdose, right?'

'That's right,' she replied, keeping her voice kind.

'Huh.'

'It's a lot to take in. I understand you weren't convinced by the verdict?'

'Yeah, well, that was before I knew that Mum was ill. *Terminal.*' He gave a harsh little laugh. 'Didn't have a clue, did I? Everyone knew 'cept me. But, then again, that lot never told me anything, so no news there. I'm the black sheep.'

Ali smiled sympathetically. 'Every family has to have one.'

Dean laughed openly at that, and Ali took her advantage to pull up a stool, feeling an uneasy stomach flip as the edges of his mouth turned up in an unreadable smirk.

'Dean, are you a regular here, at the pub?' she asked.

'As clockwork,' he replied, catching the landlord's attention and jabbing his finger in the direction of his empty glass.

'So, you must notice things. They always say, if you want to know what's going on in a town, just go to your local pub and chat awhile, right? Expect nothing passes you by.'

Dean's smirk grew. 'Could say that.'

'So have you heard about these videos that are doing the rounds?'

'Videos?' Dean dropped his gaze.

'We think they're local – people having sex in an alleyway – the man's face always obscured. I say "sex" – but we think it may in fact be non-consensual.'

'Yeah, I've seen 'em,' he replied, unruffled. 'What d'you mean, non-conshenshial?' He slurred the last word, barely getting it right.

'The girl in one of the videos has come forward to make a statement, so for now we're treating them all as possible assaults.'

Ali watched his reaction closely, but he showed no emotion. 'Wouldn't know about that,' he replied, taking a noisy sup of his fresh pint.

'And how did you come to see the videos?'

Now he pulled his chin in, defensively. 'Jesus, I don't know! That kind of shit does the rounds, doesn't it? People see funny stuff and pass it on – WhatsApp and all that.'

Funny stuff. Ali set her jaw and did her best not to let her contempt show. 'So, do you have anything like that on your phone?'

'No! I didn't say *I'd* been sent them. I don't know – maybe someone showed me on their phone or something. There were two of them – two videos. No, three. *Alley Dogs.* That's what the captions said. I just thought they were, you know, couples who'd got caught shagging or something.'

Ali decided it was time to change direction, if she was to keep Dean Warner on side. 'What do you know about the landlord here?'

'Ted? He's all right. Bit of a moody bugger when he wants to be. He's always banning me, just for being a bit pissed. But he always lets me back in. Well, he would – I pay his wages, don't I?' Dean smiled broadly, revealing several dark gaps where his back teeth should be.

'And the Gale family?'

He glanced across the bar at the family group, where Elliot now appeared to be dozing on the sofa as the rest of them talked discreetly. Old John was standing with the Warner group, chatting with the daughters, a small buffet plate in one hand, a pint of bitter in the other. 'Think they're something special,' Dean sneered. 'They say the old man, John, is a secret millionaire. Owns all this land and property, but lives in a shitty old ex-council house and drives a twenty-year-old rust bucket. My mum used to think he was some kind of bloody hero, just 'cause he chucked a load of money at the village hall and stopped it from getting demolished.'

'Sounds like a decent bloke to me,' Ali replied.

Dean shrugged. 'Anyway, they've been around here since the dinosaurs, so they think they own the place. Whatever. Elliot's an arsehole, and his wife's a stuck-up cow. Cathy – she's probably the only OK one among 'em.'

Ali hadn't been expecting such an unfiltered outpouring of information, but she wasn't going to let the moment pass. 'And what about the grandkids? Dylan? Nell Gale?'

Dean's mouth puckered nastily. '*Nell Gale*. She's a little slapper, from what I've heard. Puts it about, you know?'

'Could she have anything to do with those videos, do you think?'

With a snort, Dean took another draw on his drink. 'You'd have to ask her yourself,' he replied, glancing in the direction of the landlord before dropping down from his stool and staggering away to sit alone at the edge of the room.

The landlord wiped down the bar top, erasing the lager slops Dean had left behind, and addressed Ali with a sullen nod. 'What can I get you?'

'A Diet Coke,' she replied, glancing casually about the bar as he poured it. Beyond the window, Benny's car pulled up in the parking bay. 'Actually, make that two.'

She scrolled through her text messages, sent through from Benny moments earlier, in which she learnt the landlord's name was Ted Flowers, a forty-four-year-old ex-serviceman who had done time in prison for domestic violence in the past ten years, as well as a short stretch for handling stolen goods, some two decades earlier.

'You're Ted, aren't you?' Ali asked, as Benny joined her at the bar.

'That's right,' he replied, narrowing his eyes.

Ali showed him her badge. 'We're looking into some assaults we think may have taken place in your alleyway outside,' she said, keeping her voice low, and getting straight to the point. 'Some *serious* assaults.'

The landlord scowled, and he too lowered his voice. 'It's not exactly *my* alleyway. People get up to all sorts in alleyways, as you probably know. Use it as a cut-through – as a public toilet – a knocking shop, for all I know. I wouldn't wonder if a few drug deals took place while I'm busy in here running my pub.'

He paused, clearly hoping his nonchalance would do the trick and get rid of the pair. When neither responded, he sighed heavily.

'Look, I've got enough to keep my eye on in this place. I'm not exactly in the business of policing stuff that happens *outside* of my premises.'

Ali exchanged a surprised glance with Benny. 'OK. Um, you don't sound all that alarmed about the fact that I just said there may have been assaults carried out. One of the victims says she met her attacker here first, *inside* your pub. Are you concerned to hear that?'

Ted straightened up and crossed his arms. 'Of course,' he said, but his face didn't match the statement.

'Right. So, anyway, we're looking into it – and yes, I understand that you don't *own* the alleyway, so we're just here asking if you've heard anything or seen anything or know about any rumours, et cetera.'

The man nodded, to indicate he'd heard her and understood.

'Well, have you?' Benny asked, his impatience unchecked. 'Heard anything? Or seen anything on your CCTV?'

The landlord snatched up a couple of empty glasses from the counter and loaded them into the dishwasher below. 'Nope,' he replied, shoving the glass drawer back in with a loud clatter. 'Not a thing. And the CCTV camera is out of action. We've got one out back, but it's been vandalised four times in the past six months.' He blinked dispassionately. 'Sorry I can't help.'

'In that case,' Ali replied, draining her drink, 'all we need from you, Mr Flowers, is a list of your employees over the past year.'

The landlord released a harsh laugh. 'Do you know how fast staff turns over in the hospitality industry?'

'That's what you keep records for,' Benny replied. 'You must keep staffing records, for your accounts?'

The landlord wiped down the bar top again, unnecessarily. 'Give me an email address and I'll get them over to you.'

Ali and Benny exchanged another of their glances. 'We don't mind waiting. We really do want that list today.'

With no further acknowledgement, Ted Flowers pushed the cloth into his barman's hand and swaggered out back to gather up the information the detectives had requested.

'I don't like him,' Benny said, grabbing a packet of cheese and onion crisps from the basket on the counter and indicating to one of the staff that he wanted to pay.

'Me neither,' agreed Ali. Ted Flowers was shifty and unhelpful, and in her book that was always cause for suspicion.

About ten minutes later, the landlord reappeared with a handwritten list of a dozen or so names, which he pushed across the counter before turning to serve a waiting customer.

'Recognise any of the names?' Ali asked Benny, running her pen down the list.

'Nope. Oh, except for Nell Gale.'

'Mr Flowers!' Ali called over, and he returned with a glower. 'Can't you see how busy we are?' he huffed.

Ali gave him one of her flat-line smiles. 'Yup, we won't keep you.' She tapped the list. 'Nell Gale – does she still work here?'

He rolled his eyes. 'Only lasted a fortnight.'

'Oh?'

'Bad attitude. Thought washing up was beneath her.'

Benny gave a warm laugh. 'I know the type.' This was where Benny would always score points over his superior officer. Men *liked* talking to men like Benny.

At once, Ted Flowers relaxed, and he addressed his answer to Benny. 'Yeah. Thought she was something special.'

Ali tapped the list again. 'OK. I just need you to circle the names of all the staff who are currently employed here, sir. We may need to talk to them at some point.'

Without a word, the landlord leant over the bar and circled six names, his own included, before turning back to the queue. 'Who's next?'

Outside the pub, the street was quiet, just another day in Highcap for anyone not attending the funeral. Benny looked up and down the quiet side street, tucked back adjacent to the main high street, with the pub positioned halfway up between a residential townhouse and a second-hand shop selling designer womenswear. The pub had once been a coach house, but all that remained of its legacy was the arched rear entrance to a small car park hosting a handful of bays marked 'Paying patrons only'.

As they walked around the premises, Ali and Benny quickly located a side passageway leading to the back entrance of the flats above this section of high street shops. But their hopes quickly evaporated when they realised this could not be the location in question; it was too narrow, there were no bins or markings on the wall, and the aspect was all wrong.

As they doubled back through the small car park, Benny indicated towards a second alleyway running the far length of the Five Bells, a high-walled passageway, cluttered with bins and packing boxes, and leading, they assumed, to the back entrance of the pub kitchens. Benny powered up his iPad and located the latest video, which showed a new girl, face half hidden by long curls, held up against the same brick wall by a man whose face was obscured with a smiling emoji. They had no idea who this new victim was, or where she could be found. How long before this awful video reached her, and further tore her life from beneath her feet? This man – these people – had to be caught.

Benny pointed out the matching arrangement of kegs and bins on the screen, and, just visible on the wall behind the couple, the faded ghost mark of some decades-old graffiti, the swirling tail of its tag a perfect match to the one on the wall in front of them now.

'This is not a cut-through by any stretch,' Ali said. 'It's tucked away back here – no one's going to be stumbling past it, as our landlord here reckoned – and I'd argue that Ted Flowers *does* own it. Anyway, it's more or less a dead end. Anyone leaving the pub is heading away from this passageway, not towards it.'

'And it's not exactly a perfect dealing spot, either. There's too much risk of getting spotted by one of the staff coming out to the bins.'

'So, how do they manage to film these attacks, unseen? Do they wait till after closing time? Till after all the staff have gone home?'

Squeezing through the space beyond the kegs and wheelie bins, Benny headed off to investigate the far end, just as the door to the kitchen swung open and a man in chef's whites stepped out to drop a trash bag in the wheelie bin. He started at their unexpected presence and Ali raised a hand, apologising for making him jump.

'Sorry! We're with the police. Just checking something out.'

The man seemed to relax, and on a whim Ali pulled out the handwritten list of names Ted Flowers had provided her with minutes earlier.

'Are you on this list?' she asked, holding out the sheet. 'Nothing to worry about. We're investigating some recent assaults in the area, and we're trying to get the lie of the land.'

The cook pointed to his own name – Joe Boyle – and shrugged.

'Did you work with Nell Gale?' she asked, pointing out her name on the paper.

The lad shrugged again. 'I've only been here for three weeks. She might've been before me.'

'OK. Anyone on the list you think we should take a look at? Anyone, you know, a bit odd?'

The lad took the sheet and scrutinised it carefully. 'Nope,' he said, finally, handing it back. 'Oh, but if that's a current list, you've missed off Andy.'

'Andy?' Ali repeated.

'Yeah. Andy Flowers,' the lad replied, hand on the door as he readied to return to work. 'Ted's son. He works behind the bar. You've missed him off the list.'

As the door closed behind the chef, Ali locked eyes on Benny at the far end of the passageway. 'What d'you think of that?' she asked.

In turn, Benny held his pen aloft, to display a used condom dangling from the end of it. 'What d'you think of *that*?'

Nothing surprised her these days. 'Bag it up, Benny.'

21. Cathy

Saturday

Cathy woke in the dark pit of early morning, dry-mouthed, blood pressure surging as her hangover took a grip.

She had the strongest sense that all was not right with Dad next door, and, try as she might to return to the comfort of sleep, she couldn't shake the unsettling image of him at his front step last night, as they said goodnight after the wake. It was late, the afternoon having drifted, for some, into evening, and by the time they'd all poured out of the pub and into taxis home, Dad had grown grey-faced in the full moonlight outside Allotment Row.

His cancer diagnosis had, of course, come as a blow to Cathy, but it was only now, in the lonely space of insomnia, that she really took on the gravity – the finality – of his sentence.

Leaving the warmth of Kip's bed, she crept downstairs to fetch her mobile from its charger, careful not to wake the sleeping Griffin as she padded past the sofa on bare feet. In the darkness of the kitchen, she checked her phone: no new messages – no missed calls.

She gazed from the back door, across the moonlit patch of garden she'd been meaning to transform for years, and she wondered what life was. It was a huge question, she knew, but the events of the past few weeks had seen her scrabbling for patterns in everything, and searching for meaning and connections in the most banal of moments.

She'd realised, stupid as it might sound, that she loved her family deeply, that they really were everything. And, strangely, it was not Albie she feared for the most, Albie with his crushed dreams of becoming a tennis pro, with this life-altering physical loss and trauma. No, Albie was going to be fine, she was sure. It was Nell.

Every time Cathy looked at her daughter, she saw danger, and she met it with ferocity, lashing out as though she were the predator, not the prey. Cathy knew Nell was not to blame for what had happened to Albie, but still she would hint and prod at that idea in Nell's presence, either overtly or inside her own head – and to what end? Did she believe that Nell would stick around for a mother she could no longer love, let alone tolerate? Kip said she was too hard on her; Cathy agreed. And Cathy disagreed.

Nell wanted the world – she wanted to see it, taste it, smell it, *absorb* it. But she had no idea of the danger she faced, no idea how the world saw her. And now there was this thing Ted had said to Cathy, about Nell and some men in an alleyway, and Cathy wondered whether the danger had found her daughter anyway, despite her attempts to keep her from it, to keep her safely home.

'What are you worrying over, lovely girl?'

In the dim light, Cathy could see the faint outline of the pilot, now sitting up on the sofa, the flints of his eyes watching her from across the room.

'It's Dad,' she replied. 'I'm worried about Dad.'

Crossing the room, she sat beside him, the seat still warm from his sleeping body.

'What would Dad do, if he woke and needed help?' she asked, keeping her voice low so as not to wake Kip and Albie upstairs.

'He'd call out for Nell,' he replied.

'But what if she didn't hear? Elliot's there, but he'd be no use in a crisis, would he?' Cathy conjured up a vision of her brother asleep, slack-jawed, on the sofa next door. Suzie had left hours before the rest of them last night, and, subsequently, Elliot, finding himself off the leash, had got so drunk he'd thrown up in the street outside the taxi rank, nearly costing them their ride home. 'Should I phone Nell?' she asked. 'Dad looked so tired last night – I'm worried.'

'Want me to go check on him?' Griffin asked without hesitation, and Cathy nodded. She wanted to say, *And while you're at it, check in on my baby, will you? Check Nell's room to make sure she's home, that she's safe from harm. Check in on her and tell her that her mother loves her very much, no matter what she says or does or doesn't do.*

Cathy realised she must look desperate, because Griffin was already up and pulling trousers over his boxer shorts in the half-light, gingerly easing his arm through his charity-shop shirtsleeve and stepping into Crocs donated by the hospital friends.

He held out his hand. 'Keys?'

At the front entrance, Cathy lifted Dad's keys from the rack. 'I'm coming too,' she whispered, and she stepped into her own welly boots, shrugging on Nell's fake fur jacket as she eased the door open.

Minutes later, they would be standing on the neighbouring doorstep, watching paramedics loading her father into the back of an ambulance. *I knew it,* she would berate herself later, over and over again. *Why do I never go with my first instinct?*

By daybreak, every one of the Gales was once again congregated in the family room at Dorset County Hospital, muted by the unknowable. When the pilot had knocked gently on Dad's bedroom door just hours earlier, something in Cathy had caved, and she'd pushed past him, knowing already that her father was dead.

Except he wasn't. He had been pale and unresponsive, but Griffin, sensing life in John Gale, had set about reviving him immediately, administering CPR and mouth-to-mouth, while at the same time delivering instructions for Cathy to call the emergency services and rouse the family. Of course, everyone, including Nell, who had been drinking with her cousin all afternoon the previous day, was still over the limit, and so, after depositing the pup with a startled Mrs Jenkins next door, Kip had gone in the ambulance with Dad, while Cathy and the kids had squeezed into the old truck, with Griffin behind the wheel, wincing at every bump in the road.

Now it was a quarter to seven, and Cathy found herself in that same depressing family room, staring at that same clock, memories of Albie's surgery suddenly at the front of her mind. She couldn't believe that only a month had passed and here they were again.

Only this time there was an addition to the family group, sitting just feet away: the very man who'd crashed his aircraft into her son. She watched him, sitting across the room beside Albie, nodding along as he showed him some geeky website or other, chatting quietly, like an unobtrusive fairy godfather, a member of the family.

In the furthest corner, Elliot and Suzie sat in their own little huddle, with poor Dylan between them like a punctuation mark,

227

none of them speaking. It occurred to Cathy, not for the first time, that they were the strangest little family, and she wondered how different things might have been if they'd adopted a second child, or had managed to have one of their own all those years earlier, when they'd first started trying. But Suzie was too selfish for the one she had, Cathy thought. Too selfish for the husband she had, at that, although God knew Elliot couldn't be easy to live with, could he? The clock ticked on: 7.55 a.m.

To Cathy's one side, Kip was dozing, upright, with his hand upturned on Cathy's lap, a cradle for her own. And on her other was Nell, her arm slotted through her mother's, her fear and love for her grandad silencing her.

'He'll be fine,' Cathy said, softly, kissing her daughter on the top of her head. 'He'll outlive the rest of us.'

Nell nodded gently, not looking up. And then, quite out of the blue, she asked, 'Why have you never told me about your dead sister?'

For a moment, Cathy struggled to work out what she was talking about.

'Is that why Granny and Grandad had such a big gap between Uncle Elliot and you?' She sat back and looked at Cathy. 'I saw the gravestone,' she said.

The gravestone. The truth of the matter was that Cathy had barely thought of the fact of her dead sister for decades or more, so unimportant – so unaffecting – had it been in her life. She'd been gone three years, apparently, before Cathy came along, and, as with so much of that generation, the gaping loss of her parents' first daughter was rarely ever spoken of again.

'They gave me Lisa as a middle name,' Cathy said. 'I didn't know until I was much older – in my twenties, I think.'

Nell straightened up now, interested. 'How did she die? Lisa Anne?'

228

This was something Cathy had never really had to put into words – avoided doing so, for the pain it would cause others. But years ago – many, many years ago – Elliot, then in his thirties, had called on Cathy in a terrible state, having come across historical news records from the time of Lisa's death. To her shame, the teenage Cathy, not knowing how to handle her much older brother's guilt and pain, had told him to forget it, to put it back in the past and leave it there.

'She was taken,' Cathy said now. 'Someone took her, and the next day a dog walker found her on the rocks at Highcap.' Discarded, for some poor soul to find at dawn, she recalled now. The news reports said she'd been strangled, but the detail had stopped just short enough to allow the nation's imagination to do the rest.

'Where was she taken from?' Nell asked, her grip on her mother's arm tightening.

Cathy glanced across at her brother and dropped her voice further still. 'From our back yard.'

'In Allotment Row? Grandad's house?'

Cathy nodded. 'Your Uncle Elliot was babysitting while Mum and Dad were down at the campsite, and . . . well, someone just walked straight in through the back gate and snatched her away.'

'Is that why Elliot's . . . you know,' Nell whispered. 'A bit messed up?'

Cathy gave a little nod and squeezed her daughter's arm beneath her own. She suspected it was also the reason her own mother had always been so hard on her, so controlling – desperate, perhaps, to guarantee that her replacement daughter wouldn't go the same way. Because that was how Cathy had always felt: like a poor replacement. Better than nothing, but a disappointment all the same.

'So, you've never thought you were adopted, or anything – because of the big age gap?' Nell asked, polishing her new phone on the sleeve of her top.

Cathy smiled. 'No – no more than any other kid, fantasising they'd been put with the wrong rubbish family!'

Nell gave a little murmur.

'And anyway,' Cathy said, pointing to her own face, 'have you seen my nose? Gale through and through.' She gently thumbed her daughter's nose, just as she used to when Nell was little, and bit down on her cheek to rein in her emotions. 'Love you, Nellie.'

'Love you too, Mum,' Nell replied, and she dropped her head against her mother's shoulder and rested her eyes.

For a while, Cathy dozed too, but when the doctor arrived with an update, she stood up with a start, nudging her daughter awake beside her.

'Are you all here for John Gale?' the doctor asked, glancing about. 'Quite the fan club!'

'How is he?' Elliot asked, standing to join Cathy, unconsciously draping an arm about her shoulder, the way he used to when she was a kid.

'He's awake,' the doctor replied. 'We're going to have to keep him in for a few days – but the good news is, he's eating breakfast, and he seems to have his sense of humour intact. He told me to tell you all to halt the funeral plans, he's not going anywhere just yet!'

Cathy and Elliot clung to each other, sobbing openly, and one by one the rest of the family joined them, quietly urged on by Griffin, who Cathy could see working his magic in the background, gesturing for them all to approach. Cautious as foals they went, a huddle of Gales, hugging and crying and giving quiet thanks that their beloved John Gale had been, at least for now, spared.

'I'm so relieved,' Suzie breathed into Cathy's hair, the first gentle words she'd spoken to her in many years.

'Me too,' she replied, and she hugged her back, and it felt right.

As they broke apart, Cathy glanced at her pilot, discreetly watching from the sidelines, a soft expression on his face. *He fell from the skies*, Cathy thought, *and we believed he was our destroyer.*

But, in fact, he's an angel.

22. Nell

Friday

The day after he arrived home from the hospital, Grandad insisted on throwing one of his famous family barbecues, something they hadn't done for at least a year or two, what with lockdown and the various family quarrels, not least this latest one surrounding what Auntie Suzie politely dubbed 'Cathy's life choices'.

Now here they all were – Mum's family and Elliot's family, easy together, breaking bread in Grandad's back yard to the soundtrack of his favourite Beach Boys album.

Even Nell, though determined to maintain a healthy hatred of the man who had maimed her brother, was finding herself inexplicably drawn to Griffin, easy as he was to be around, with his gentle lilting accent and his calm response to what must have felt like a world of strangeness. Hard to believe he had lost a child in all this; even harder to believe that he had no memory of the child, or of having a child at all. What would that do to a person, the not knowing? As she watched him now, tending to the barbecue coals with Kip and Grandad, laughing lightly, Nell had the strangest sense that he'd been here among them all along, almost as though the air crash had merely brought him into focus.

Beside the back door, Elliot was filling a large tin bath with bags of ice and bottles of beer, while Albie stood at the picnic bench, deftly spearing chunks of cheese and pineapple onto cocktail sticks with his one hand, and arranging them around a foil-covered half-grapefruit. The smell of charred sausages drifted on the warm breeze, under a clear blue sky, empty but for the occasional crying gull soaring high overhead.

In the next-door garden, Mum was just visible passing chairs over the fence to Suzie and Nell, and Dylan, oddbod that he was, was busy sweeping the cracked old patio to within an inch of its life.

'That'll do, lad,' Grandad called over to him. 'Get yourself a drink and relax!'

But Dylan swept on, and Grandad gave a good-humoured shake of his head and accepted a beer from Kip before returning to his grill. No one said he should be watching his cholesterol; no one said he shouldn't have a drink.

Heading inside to fetch tablecloths and cutlery, Nell paused for a moment, taking in the scene, and was at once pierced with guilt about that photograph of the pilot she and Dylan had posted up on Facebook last week – sneakily captured without his consent. She'd barely given it another thought, since the rush to the hospital had occurred only hours later, and she'd long ago deleted the app from her phone, so there'd been no alerts to tell her if anyone had responded at all.

But what they'd done wasn't right – Nell knew that now, as she watched the pilot with her parents, smiling between them, the happy matchmaker – because that was what he was, wasn't he?

He'd come into their lives, and, robbed of the capacity to grieve for all that he himself had lost, he'd channelled in on the lives of these strangers around him. There was no doubt he'd ignited a new love of music in Albie, something that steered him from self-pity and challenged him anew. And in Cathy and Kip he'd spotted the residual spark between them, discreetly nurturing it over these past few weeks, nudging them closer, quietly singing the praises of one to the other, showing them how to be kind again, how to love.

Mum had even announced last week that she was ditching the cigarettes, once and for all, and for the first time Nell actually believed her. That was his doing too, galling as it was to admit. Through the filter of her anger, Nell had watched Griffin quietly bringing them together, healing them, and, just like her mother at her very worst, she had chosen not to acknowledge it.

She cursed beneath her breath, wondering if she had time to sprint upstairs and log in to her PC, delete the post from Facebook before anyone else got wind of it.

'Nell!' Albie called over. 'Grandad wants to know where you've got to with laying the table!'

'Tell him to ask me himself!' she yelled back, poking out her tongue at the old man when he blew a raspberry in her direction. Facebook would have to wait.

She fetched the faded gingham tablecloths and a bunch of knives, forks and serving spoons, which she and her mum arranged over the picnic bench, extended with an old wallpapering trestle they'd set up to accommodate their number. Kip set out two vases of peonies from Grandad's allotment over the back, while the rest of the family carried bowls of bread rolls and potato salad and coleslaw in through the gate and out from the kitchen. The pilot transferred the cooked sausages and chicken pieces to large dishes and placed them on the table, before standing back to let everyone else sit down, lest he should take the wrong seat.

'I hope it's all right if I say a couple of words?' he said, taking a step back, one hand resting on his walking stick, the livid red of his facial burns shaded by the old straw trilby Grandad had gifted him just this morning. He wasn't overly tall, but his straight posture and elegant stance rendered him imposing, and the weirdness of his appearance – a full head of silvery-black hair to one side, hairless scalp to the other – was an arresting sight in anyone's book.

Grandad gestured for him to continue.

'I want to thank you all for your kindness, and your hospitality, and your heart. I know it can't have been easy for you all – to let me into your lives, after everything. After everything I've put you through.'

He halted momentarily, scanning the table, as though desperate to communicate this message to each and every one present.

'I'll have to move on soon, I know, but I just want to say that I'll never forget you—' He laughed at that, a small warm chuckle, tinged with irony. 'This, from the man who remembers *nothing*.'

They all laughed now, and for a moment Nell thought he might sit down. But instead he held out a theatrical hand and Albie moved to his side.

'We've been practising a song,' Albie said proudly. 'For Grandad. I'm on keyboard, he's on guitar – we borrowed yours, Dad. You don't mind, do you?'

Kip gave a little smile. 'He's far better on it than I am, son.'

Albie beamed proudly. 'It's "Danny Boy" – one of your favourites, Grandad.'

He and the pilot fetched the keyboard and guitar and set themselves up in the shady light of the garden gate. As the pilot's voice lifted, in haunting harmony with Albie's, Nell had the strongest sense of recognition, as across the table she watched the expression on her parents' faces shift from wonder, to joy, to confusion.

The sound that came from the pilot was almost celestial, and Nell wondered how it was possible a man with a voice like that could forget who he was, or where he came from. The tenor of it, the depth, the tone; Nell had never heard anything like it before, and yet, the sense of having been here before was intense.

When the last bars were played and the final words sung, the garden fell to awed silence, before Grandad stood to incite uproarious applause and whoops of congratulation.

'Oh, man,' Kip exclaimed, rushing over to hug his son and pump the pilot's hand, quite overwhelmed. 'Do you remember Jago – the singer?' he asked the blank-faced pilot. 'From the early 2000s?'

'It's uncanny,' Mum said, turning to address Nell and the rest of the family. 'Honestly. It's *uncanny.*'

That was when the sound of hammering at the front door sounded out, a noise so loud as to suggest an emergency in progress. From the living room, Dylan called, 'Grandad! It's the police!'

It seemed to Nell that every member of the family stood frozen in that moment, shocked into inaction, uncertain what this meant. But that inertia was short-lived.

'Mr Neill?' a voice shouted over the back entrance to the garden, a voice among many. The rear gate swung open, and a mob – a real mob – of journalists and photographers appeared on the other side, like a scene from a film. 'Mr Neill? This is Jay Tooley from *ITV News.* We wondered if we could have a statement from you?'

All eyes were on the Unknown Pilot, who could do nothing more than gaze back in confusion, guitar rested loosely across his body.

'Jago?' another journalist called out, pushing forward with a microphone in hand. 'Jago Neill? Our viewers want to know: did you fake your own death back in 2006?'

PART THREE

PART THREE

23. DS Ali Samson

Friday

Folk Legend Jago Back from the Dead

The 'Unknown Pilot' at the centre of Dorset's recent Highcap air disaster has been named by police officials as missing folk star Jago Neill.

Neill, who rose to fame as 'Jago' in the early 2000s with his chart-topping album Pink Horses, *was declared dead in 2009, after going missing at sea three years earlier. His haunting combination of folk nostalgia and contemporary lyrics hit a chord with the listening public at the turn of the century, an antidote, many a music critic suggested, to the feverish dance and trance trends of the decade before. But fame came to Jago at a cost, and his battles with mental health and addiction are well documented.*

In November 2006, exhausted at the end of a sell-out tour of Europe, Jago is said to have taken his small yacht, the Julianne, *out alone from Falmouth harbour in Cornwall. The following day, the yacht was found floating in the English*

Channel, two miles off the mainland, an apparent suicide note pinned to the wheel, and Jago was never seen again. Jago Neill became, it seemed at the time, yet another member of the infamous '27 Club', a group of celebrities, such as the likes of Jim Morrison, Amy Winehouse and Kurt Cobain, who all died tragically at the age of 27.

Neill's wife, Julianne, a talented ceramicist, inherited his considerable fortune, and has in the years since remained out of the limelight. Little is known about Julianne these days, except that it is believed she entered into a new relationship and became a mother.

The breaking news that the 'Unknown Pilot' is in fact Jago Neill has rocked the nation, presenting more questions than answers. Where has he been all these years? And why has no one come forward to report as missing the child who died in the tragedy? With his continued claim of amnesia, Jago Neill is not yet in a position to answer these questions himself.

The police are now appealing for anyone with information about Jago in recent years, or who witnessed the plane crash at Highcap, to come forward and help them with their enquiries . . .

In the stifling early-evening heat of the interview room at Highcap police station, DS Ali Samson and DC Benny Garner wait silently across the table from Jago Neill as he finishes reading the article.

Neill's solicitor reads his own copy once and leans in to whisper into his client's ear. Jago makes no response, but continues to read the piece two, three times, finally pausing to rest his fingertips on the main photograph, before looking up. The image on the desk is a press photograph of a leaner, longer-haired Jago Neill, eighteen years earlier, eighteen years younger. Is that recognition in his expression, or confusion?

'Does this mean anything to you, Mr Neill?' Ali asks.

'This is me,' he replies. Absently, he runs the back of his wrist across his brow. It's impossible to know if the beads of sweat are the result of stress or the oppressive August heat of the room.

'Is that a question?' Benny cuts in.

Jago Neill's eyes return to the image. 'I can see that it's me. But, still—' Now he looks up and meets Ali's gaze directly. 'But no, not really. It doesn't mean anything to me.'

His expression is hooded, his burnt side a permanent mask of sorrow, his good side a chiselled image of something like loss or regret. Does she believe him?

Ali stares across the table at the man for a long time, long enough to make Benny uncomfortable beside her. Unlike many of her colleagues, Ali was not previously aware of Jago, either as a musician or as a cult icon. She would have been around fifteen years old when Jago was at his height of fame, and certainly more interested in pop music than folk. And because of Ali's ignorance, he holds no mystery, so, to her, Jago Neill is just an ordinary man – a man who, quite possibly, intentionally took the life of a child and caused the destruction of others.

'Now, Mr Neill, we've had the DNA results back from the lab, and I can confirm that the child who died in the crash was indeed your son.'

Jago Neill swallows hard, and, while his expression registers something like pain, he says nothing.

'Jago, when you took that plane out from the Isle of Wight, did you intend to kill yourself? Did you intend to kill your son?'

'I don't know,' he murmurs, shaking his head. 'I don't even . . . I can't even conjure up the smallest memory of having a child. I don't think I could do that to another human being, even at my lowest – I don't . . .'

Benny shifts in his chair, and Ali puts down her pen, their unspoken signal for the other to step in.

'Soon after you came round in hospital, after the crash,' Benny says, 'we offered to put your image out to the news agencies, to see if we could identify you that way. Do you recall?'

Jago nods.

'We made that request to you, what, two, three times? And every time, you flatly refused to let us use your image. Why?'

'I don't know. I was scared. I just knew it would be unwise—'

'"Unwise"?' Benny echoes. 'Can I suggest that you refused because you hadn't, in fact, lost your memory, and you knew, full well, that the moment your image was out there, someone would recognise you as Jago Neill, the musician. You've been missing for eighteen years, declared dead for over a decade – and I think you are completely aware of it. Why else would you have fought to protect your anonymity so fiercely?'

Jago shakes his head sadly. 'I can't explain it. I can't remember details, but I have senses, you know? A sense that I mustn't be seen. A sense that I've lost everything. A sense that I'd never willingly hurt a child. That I'm not a bad man.' He hesitates. 'That I'm not a good man, either. That I'm nothing. And no one.'

Ali is somewhat disarmed by the man's words. There is so much grief in him, it's hard not to believe his assertion that he doesn't remember a thing. But she's been fooled before, and she won't risk it again.

'May I ask how Mr Neill *was* identified?' the solicitor asks.

'Social media,' Ali replies. 'Someone took it into their own hands to post a photo, it was widely shared – and a member of the public – a fan of his music, in fact – recognised him. We could've saved a lot of time if Mr Neill had allowed us to make an appeal in the first place.'

The solicitor merely blinks. 'So, what now?'

'Well, I can tell you that the Air Accidents Investigation Branch have not found any definitive fault in what remains of the aircraft Mr Neill was piloting, but nor have they found compelling evidence to suggest he is culpable.'

Ali turns her attention on Jago. 'What this means is, while there are strong suspicions that you may have crashed that plane intentionally, we have more work to do, now that we actually know who you are. Mr Neill – Jago – is there anything you can tell us at this stage that might help us to work out where you've been living all these years, and who else needs to know about your son? Did you live on the Isle of Wight, or were you just visiting?'

The pilot drags a heavy hand across his brow. 'There's nothing. There's nothing I can tell you.'

Ali and Benny both lay down their pens. 'OK. Well, as you might have gathered when we picked you up, there's fairly heavy media interest in your story. It's quite possible we'll get all the answers we need about you once it's public knowledge tomorrow morning. Needless to say, we don't want you leaving Highcap until we have more information and you have a confirmed address to go to. Will you be remaining at the Gale family residence for the time being?'

Jago nods.

'Good. DC Garner here will take you to the duty officer out front. And then we'll want you to report in to the station twice weekly – and contact me the minute you remember anything, yes?'

Jago Neill stands and steadies himself. 'You have my word,' he says, and, with his solicitor on one side and Benny on the other, he leaves the room.

Ali remains a moment longer in the uncomfortable heat of that small space, tuned in to the distant voices from the corridor beyond. Does she believe him? Right now she couldn't put money on it either way, and if it weren't for the dead child at the heart of this tragedy she might happily close down the case without another thought.

Her mind flips seamlessly onto the other case she's working, this god-awful sexual assault spate she and Benny have been following over the past month. They're still understaffed, with this latest Covid wave creating a bigger gap in the workforce than ever before, which means Ali's having to do a lot of the slow work herself.

They need to chase down the results of that discarded condom Benny had bagged in the alleyway outside the Five Bells, and then there's the follow-up with the tech guys to see if they've had any luck in locating the original source of those videos. They haven't even had background checks back on Ted Flowers' employees at the Five Bells, to know if any raise concerns, including Nell Gale, who's clearly hiding something or other, and Ted's son Andy, who was notably omitted from the staff list.

Ali checks her watch, and realises it's too late to chase anything today. Those guys will all have gone home long ago, like the sensible family folk they are, she thinks, and she sets off towards the car park, resolved to be more like them. In her car, she taps out a message to Margo.

Hey, doll. Sorry, I'm on my way home. Shall I pick up a bottle of anniversary fizz?

A celebration is the last thing on Ali's mind right now, but she can't let Margo down again. If she doesn't have Margo, what's it all about?

And chocolate, comes the quick reply.

Ali smiles, softens, turns the key in the ignition. As she drives round to the front of the station, she spots a group congregating around an old flatbed truck parked in one of the visitor bays. It's a surprise to see such a gathering at this time in the early evening, and as she draws parallel, she recognises them as the Gale family, en masse, clearly here in support of Jago Neill and waiting to take him home.

Ali pulls on her handbrake and waves over. 'Hi!' she calls, but none of them approaches.

Cathy Gale is there, untypically wearing her long, curly red hair down, standing to the side of the truck with Kip. They both raise a hand, polite but not exactly welcoming. Just beyond them, Ali can make out the legs of old John Gale, resting side-on in the passenger seat, while Albie sits cross-legged on the flatbed, and the daughter, Nell, perches beside him, cradling the pup, legs dangling, her face, framed beneath that pixie haircut, impassive.

Realising none of them is coming over, Ali gives a nod and is just releasing her handbrake when, from nowhere, a stark image from Benny's latest video pushes to the front of her mind – an image of the victim, the girl with the long, curling hair.

She slams her foot on the brake pedal, and lingers a moment longer, staring out across the forecourt at Nell – the girl who she had suspected might be involved in the offences – and she knows, without a doubt, that Nell is the girl in the video.

'Cathy!' she shouts over, with a beckoning gesture.

Cathy shoots her partner a brief glance before jogging over. As she comes, Ali keeps her eyes on Nell, who drops down from her seated position and now stands in a cross-armed pose, her Doc Marten-clad feet planted wide, her young face unreadable.

Cathy comes to stop a foot from Ali's open window. 'Yup?'

'Your Nell,' Ali says. 'When did she cut her hair short?'

Cathy purses her lips. 'Why?'

Ali raises an eyebrow, a so-you're-questioning-a-police-officer kind of eyebrow, and lets the question hang.

'I dunno, a few days after the air crash.'

The low sun casts a golden hue across the car park, illuminating the likeness of the mother's hair to that of the girl in the alleyway.

'I think she, you know, did it to punish herself,' Cathy says, stepping a little closer, her tone milder now.

'To *punish* herself?'

'Because of her brother.'

Ali looks again over at Nell, who is now pacing restlessly, snatching furtive glances in their direction. 'Poor kid. How's she been lately?'

'Not great.' Cathy drops her gaze. 'Not great at all.'

Ali's every instinct is to march over and question the girl, but her rational head tells her she needs to bide her time, to go away and look at that video again, and carefully calculate her next steps. If Nell Gale is indeed a victim of these vile creatures, it is clear she's told no one in her immediate family, and Ali senses she'll not admit to anything without a fight.

'Well, look after her, eh?' She gives the mother a warm smile.

Cathy Gale nods, and steps back from the vehicle with a small wave.

Mind racing, Ali drives out through the entrance gates and releases the clip from her neat bun in a practised motion, setting off along the coastal road home, hair billowing, grateful for the wide-open skies and the boundless sea air.

'Nell Gale,' she says aloud. Nell Gale is the key to cracking this case.

24. Cathy

Friday

Back at home, Cathy and Kip quietly fuss around Jago, this fresh revelation of his true identity casting a strange new deference over the most mundane of actions. The press intruders have mostly gone for now, eager as they were to tail the arresting officers who'd escorted Jago to the station, only to be seen off by a canny duty officer, who'd apparently spun them a line about interviewing Jago overnight.

Jago. It's still impossible to take in. All this time, with him under her roof, and Cathy and Kip never knew. Well, she says she never knew, but there was *something*, wasn't there? Enough to spur her to invite a complete stranger into her home, despite all the harm he had caused. Enough to make her send that text to Kip, asking him if he recalled the name of the album they'd played all season long on Ao Nang Beach, the season they met and fell in love.

What Kip doesn't realise is how she's avoided listening to that album these past two decades, given how that trip had ended for her. But, hearing it again, in that present-day moment in her kitchen with Kip – well, it had felt right, untainted by the bad thing she's kept to herself all these years.

But *Jago*, there in the house with them – the pilot. Even as they'd sat and relived those good memories, listening to that music while the pilot slept on their sofa or boiled coffee on their stove, neither one of them had made the full connection.

'I can't believe it's you,' Kip says now, placing a mug of tea in front of Jago Neill. He gazes at the man across the table, wide-eyed. 'I mean, right up until you sang that song – "Danny Boy" – with our Albie, I could never have imagined it. I mean, now, it's obvious, isn't it, Cath?' He turns to smile at her, his boyish expression an echo of the young man she'd first met. 'And the guitar – man, no ordinary fella plays the guitar like that.'

Around the room, the rest of the family sit on sofas or lean in doorways, all of them together now, even Elliot and Suzie, who are apparently trying to reconcile their differences, though you wouldn't know it from the physical space between them. They all watch Jago, like some awful interactive theatre audience, and it strikes Cathy that it must feel horrible, to one minute be just a man in a room full of people who offer you kindness, and the next a celebrity, an icon, a *resurrection*.

Jago brings the cup to his lips. 'How could you imagine it?' he asks, now meeting Kip's gaze across the table. 'I was dead. Wasn't I? That's what they tell me. How could you imagine, in a million years, that I was this famous man they tell me I am? I was *dead*; lost at sea; a ghost on the outside, looking in.'

On the sofa beside Cathy, Nell draws her woolly cardigan close, and gives a little shudder. She's pale, tormented-looking, and it strikes Cathy that as time goes by, while the rest of the family have slowly begun to come to terms with Albie's injuries, Nell is growing more withdrawn. Her lustrous hair is gone, the golden glow of her summer skin appearing sallow, and her eyes – what is it about them that bothers Cathy so? They seem empty.

'Have you lost weight?' Cathy whispers, easily encircling her daughter's wrist with her thumb and middle finger.

Nell shakes her off and rubs her wrist, as though stung. 'No. I'm fine.'

'That officer today – Detective Samson—'

'*What*?' Nell stiffens and pulls back further. 'What about her?'

'She wanted to know when you cut your hair.' Cathy keeps her voice low. 'Why would she ask me that, Nell?'

'I dunno. Because she's a nosy cow, maybe? Because she doesn't like me. Because she's got nothing better to do . . .'

Cathy knows when she's beaten. 'Probably,' she agrees.

Dylan steps in through the kitchen, having been out at the garden bench with Albie, helping with his family tree project, and he stops to run himself a glass of water from the tap. Albie plops himself on the sofa arm and drapes his hand on Cathy's shoulder, so affectionate still, so open and easy. She covers his hand with her own and swallows back the emotions that so frequently threaten to engulf her these days. Last night, in bed, she'd asked Kip if he thought she might be experiencing early menopause, wondering if it could explain her teetering anxiety and off-the-handle temper these days.

'What, a gorgeous young whippersnapper like you?' he'd joked, biting her neck in the way he knows sends her weak. 'I doubt it. You're only forty, darlin' – way too young.'

'God, I'd forgotten how clueless you were,' she'd rebuked, pushing him away. 'I'm serious, Kip. And forty isn't too young for some women.'

At that, he'd grown serious. 'No, love, I *don't* think you're menopausal. I think you're a gorgeous forty-year-old woman,

251

with a son who just lost his arm in a horrific accident, a daughter who's busy blaming herself, and a dad who's just announced he's dying of cancer. Who wouldn't be frantic with worry?'

Kip was always right. She'd folded back into his arms then.

'Marry me?' he'd asked, for the thousandth time.

'It's still a no,' she'd replied. Nearly twenty years later, it was still a no, and even to Cathy the reason was a mystery.

'Mum?' Nell brings her back to the room, nudging her elbow and pointing over to the corner. 'Grandad looks a bit, you know—'

Dad is sitting at the circular table with Kip and Jago, but he isn't joining in the conversation. Just a week after his announcement at Tino's restaurant, his cheeks appear more hollowed, his energy on the wane. Has he given up?

Cathy crosses the room and quietly tells him she's got a pie to put in for him next door, and does he want to head back now? Something like relief crosses his face, and with a slow, wincing motion, he rises to his feet and heads for the back door.

'Mum, we can do it,' Nell says, jumping up. 'Can't we, Dylan? Albie wants to look at Grandad's photo albums for his homework, so we could do that while dinner's cooking. You don't mind, do you, Grandad?'

John Gale leans a heavy hand on the kitchen worktop and gives the smile he reserves for his grandchildren alone. 'More the merrier,' he says, and he continues towards the open back door as Cathy gives her daughter hasty instructions for his meal.

As the last of the kids trails out behind him, Suzie, silent until this point, pipes up, directing her pent-up fury at Jago. 'So, how do we know you're not just feeding us a pack of lies? How do we know you didn't mean to kill yourself that day?'

Cathy is mortified. Elliot, who has now taken Dad's place in the corner seat, simply covers his eyes in a gesture of despair.

252

'For fuck's sake, Suzie,' Cathy growls, flopping back onto the sofa like a petulant teenager, while Kip busies himself filling the kettle again.

Jago raises his hand, sending dust motes dancing through the slice of early-evening sunlight that cuts through the room. 'No, no. It's a fair question, Cathy.'

Seconds pass as those dust molecules separate and collide, and for a moment, Cathy thinks he might actually say it's all true.

'Well?' Suzie presses. 'How can we know you're not just faking it?'

Jago returns a regretful shake of his head. 'I'm afraid you can't, Suzie,' he says, his tone imbued with more warmth than Cathy believes her sister-in-law deserves. He levels his good eye at her, and smiles softly, genuinely, even the crooked pull of his burnt side not detracting from the beauty of the man. 'For now, you're just going to have to take my word for it.'

'Well, you can't live here forever,' Suzie mutters without confidence, clearly disarmed by Jago's directness, by his intimate use of her name. 'With any luck, they'll work out where your home is soon. I hope so, for Cathy's sake.'

Cathy rolls her eyes at Suzie's mock concern. *I hope they don't work it out*, is the thought that pops into her head. She glances at Kip in the kitchen, filling the teapot with studied concentration, and she is almost overcome with her love for him, and a desire to make him happy.

Would she feel the same about Kip, she wonders, if Jago disappeared from their home, if life returned to the way it was before, albeit a more damaged version of the family they once were? Is Jago, as she fears, the only glue that is holding this whole fragile family unit together?

25. Nell

Friday

Before Grandad heads up to his bedroom for a lie-down, he directs Albie to the cupboard in the sideboard, to help himself to the box of old photos he needs for his school project.

'Take what you need, lad,' Grandad says, indicating to Dylan that he could do with a hand getting up the stairs. 'Just put 'em back when you're done.'

'Which box is it, Grandad?' Albie shouts after him, as Nell gets to work peeling spuds at the kitchen sink. 'The shoebox? Or the big brown one?'

'Yup,' comes the distant reply, and Albie looks to Nell for help.

'He can't hear you,' she says, dropping the last of the potatoes into the pan and switching on the hob. 'Just have a rummage around – he won't mind.' She sets her phone timer for the spuds, and, at the sound of Dylan's tread returning downstairs, opens her laptop at the little dining table.

Dylan slides into the seat beside her, and, careful not to alert Albie to their activity, they discreetly move around the internet in search of Kasey Clapton, one of the girls who'd foisted that foul video of Nell onto Uncle Elliot in the Five Bells.

'I've checked Instagram, and TikTok too,' Dylan murmurs, unzipping his backpack and taking out a small book of notes, 'but nothing there either. You never found anything on Facebook?'

'Nothing.' Nell glances over at Albie, who is thankfully too engrossed in Grandad's photo boxes to take any notice of them. Beside him, a little pile of pictures is forming, as one by one he finds images to attach to the poster-sized family tree chart Nell helped him to sketch out last week.

Dylan clicks back through to Facebook. 'What if we trawl through the profiles of some of Kasey's old school friends? I can definitely remember the names of a few of them. She might be in *their* photos. And if she's in their photos, then she might be tagged. And if she's tagged—'

'Then we've got her,' Nell agrees, feeling sick at the thought of actually confronting the girl. She checks the timer on her phone and leans in closer.

It was only this afternoon, after she had spotted that policewoman talking to her mum down the station car park, and under pressure from Dylan's insistent badgering, that Nell had finally agreed to start looking for Kasey again. He's talking sense, she knows; if they can just find out from Kasey where that video came from and who it was that was sharing it, maybe they can get it removed before anyone else gets to see it. Before the rest of her family sees it.

She flushes at the imagined shame, at the thought of that image seared into the memories of her loved ones forever. She thinks about DS Samson, and wonders about the way she looks at her, with questions in her eyes, and she tunes into that voice at the back of her mind, telling her this video has something to do with it. *Oh, God.* If they could just find Kasey—

'Wow, that's *weird* – Nell, look at this!' Albie holds a faded piece of paper aloft, but Nell can't make it out, and she's too busy to get involved right now.

'Save it, Albie,' she mutters.

Dylan clicks through to the profile of another girl Nell recognises from the year below at school. Star Bennett. And another, Jodie Downes. And another . . . The sucked-in cheeks and pouting poses and shiny prom dresses all begin to look the same.

Nell feels her short-lived resolve waning. 'We're never gonna—' she starts to say.

'Yeah, but this doesn't make any sense,' Albie interrupts, still scowling at that paper in his hands. 'It's about Mum, I think, and—'

'For God's sake, Albie, button it!' Nell throws her hands into the air. 'Can't you see we're in the middle of something?'

At that precise moment, the potatoes boil over, spewing starchy grey foam over the hob in the tiny adjacent kitchen. Albie leaps up, rushing to remove the pan from the ring, and threatening to slip on the tiles in his socked feet.

'Albie, leave it!' Nell yells, but this time it is concern in her voice, not irritation. She grabs him away from the heat and kisses him on the head. 'Sorry, bro, I've got a lot on at the moment. I'm, you know, a bit distracted.'

God, she sounds like her mother.

Lowering the temperature on the hob, she turns back to Albie. 'What was it you wanted to show me?'

'Well—' he starts, instantly forgiving his sister's impatience as he returns to his photos and lifts one off the top.

But before Albie even starts to explain, Dylan brings his hand down on the tabletop and yells, 'Bingo!' – loud enough to make Nell shriek.

Albie and Nell turn to study their cousin, probably the person in the world they'd both vote least likely ever to use the word 'bingo'.

'Jeez, mate—' Nell exhales.

'I've got her,' Dylan says, looking up, his expression displaying something close to excitement.

'You've got who?' Albie asks.

Dylan rotates the laptop and Nell leans in, purposely obscuring her brother's view. There, dominating the screen, is a large photograph of that little cow Kasey Clapton, standing by a low wall, in a fluffy lilac prom dress from the year before – and looking just as pleased with herself as she did when Nell last saw her, that night in the Five Bells. Dylan points to the profile name at the top of the screen: Sharon Clapton. *So proud of our baby girl*, the caption under the photo reads.

'Her mother, I presume,' Dylan nods. 'But the picture – Kasey Clapton, without a doubt.'

'God, I was starting to think we'd never find her,' Nell says.

'Find who?' Albie demands.

Nell flips the screen back towards Dylan, ignoring her little brother.

'And there's something else rather interesting about this picture,' Dylan says.

Ignoring Albie's tuts from the living-room floor, Nell slides back into the seat beside Dylan. She scrutinises the photo, taking in the girl, the dress, the proud parents waving in the background. Dylan zooms in on the picture, stopping at what appears to be the first two letters of a street name, the rest of it obscured by Kasey's meringue dress.

'I know where this is,' he says. 'I know where she lives.'

26. DS Ali Samson

Saturday

The morning after they release Jago Neill without charge, Ali drives to the station, having picked up a message that the owner of Neill's aircraft has finally made contact.

Over a fortnight since his name came up in connection to the disaster, Ali reflects as she turns into the station forecourt and parks her car in the shade, and the man has only just deigned to return their calls. Apart from showing a blatant disrespect for the officers who have been trying to track him down, Ali wonders just how rich a person has to be to not get straight on the case with an insurance claim for a burnt-out borrowed plane.

But it's not really the Jago Neill case that has compelled Ali to drive to work on her day off. She's been awake half the night, turning over the words from their consultant profiler's report on the serial assault cases.

If these cases are indeed related, I see no reason why the perpetrators will stop. In fact, past studies indicate that, if not arrested at an early stage, criminals of this nature tend to gain in confidence as each of their crimes goes unpunished, gradually escalating in severity. In answer to your specific question, yes, I think it's possible these offenders have the capacity to kill, given the sociopathic nature of their attacks. It is clear they do not see their victims as people.

The longer she'd struggled with sleep, the more anxious she'd grown about young Nell Gale, and, with no physical evidence to lead them to these men, Ali fears that this case is in danger of going unsolved.

But she can't let that happen. Not with so many girls already damaged by the sick pair behind those terrible videos; God only knows how many more there might be, not to mention the countless others at possible risk.

Finally, it had been Margo who'd given her gentle permission to give up on sleep, to get up. 'I know what you're like when you get one of these cases inside your head,' she'd said sleepily. 'Just go and do what you need to do.'

Inside the station building, Ali is relieved to see Trelawney's office empty, and she heads straight for her desk and opens up the 'Golden Rabbit Air Crash' file, to locate the original notes, giving the plane owner's name as Andrew Belgo, a resident of Fishbourne on the Isle of Wight – 'one of those swanky sea-facing villas', Trelawney had remarked when they'd first received the details. 'We used to holiday there a lot when the kids were little. They're the big houses you can see as you take the ferry into Fishbourne Harbour, hidden among the trees. Bloody gorgeous, some of them. Second homes of actors and rock stars, mostly.'

And 'long-dead' folk icons? Ali wonders. Seems perfectly likely to her that someone like Jago Neill could disappear from view in a place like that.

When Andrew Belgo fails to answer Ali's call on the fourth attempt, she turns her attention instead to the assault case, lining up the files she believes are connected on the desk in front of her: Dahlia, aged seventeen – April; met perpetrator calling himself Matt, via a dating app, in the bar of a respectable Highcap hotel; kept an eye on her soft drink all night; unsuccessfully fought back when she was attacked by 'Matt' on the walk home; video circulated widely.

CeeCee, aged seventeen – July; also met perpetrator, this time called Mac, via a dating app; believes her drink was spiked, and only understood the full extent of her assault when the film was circulated, too late to collect any meaningful DNA samples.

And now there is this latest video: Unknown Victim No. 3 – the girl Ali strongly believes to be eighteen-year-old Nell Gale – visibly intoxicated to the point of unconsciousness, her attack, like the others, captured on film by some unseen accomplice.

'Nell Gale,' Ali murmurs, as her eyes bounce between the case files. Did she meet her attacker via a dating app too? Benny's background checks on Ted Flowers' employees at the Five Bells – including the son he'd conveniently omitted from the staff list – have turned up precisely nothing of interest.

Ali flips back through the older notes. Dahlia's file clearly states that the dating site she used was a little-known app called Authentically Blind, whose unique selling point is the absence of photographs on their user profiles. *We believe true love IS blind*, the sales page tells would-be daters. *Here at Authentically Blind, we aim to match you with the person, not the face . . . for, we believe, that way, true love lies.*

Not only an idyllic set-up for true romantics to meet, Ali thinks, but also a perfect hunting ground for catfishers and con artists. She picks up the phone and dials.

'Hey, Benny?'

There's an audible throat-clearing at the other end of the line, before Benny speaks. 'Sarge?'

'Oh,' Ali says, checking the clock and realising it's only just gone seven. 'Sorry. Did I wake you up?'

Good-humoured as ever, Benny ignores the question, as Ali makes out the sounds of him throwing back the covers and leaving the bedroom. 'What can I do for you?'

'Benny, did we ask CeeCee – the victim on Joy Lane – did we get the name of the dating app she used?'

'Yeah, sarge, it should be in the notes.'

'Well, it's not. You wrote it down, I'm sure. Can you check your notebook, in case you just missed it off your typed report.'

Benny puts down the phone and returns moments later, riffling through pages in his notebook. 'It's here. Sorry, sarge, I can't believe I missed that—'

'Forget it. What's it called – the dating site?'

'Authentically Blind.'

'*Ha,*' Ali replies. 'And the notes here say her date called himself Jac. Is that right?'

Benny flips another page and hesitates, cursing under his breath. 'Sorry, sarge, I've got to work on my touch-typing. My notebook says Mac. You know, the J is just above the M on the keyboard—'

Matt. Mac. At last Ali sees a pattern forming. She hangs up, grabs her keys, and returns to her car before its engine has even cooled.

*

At Allotment Row, Ali sits in her car until the clock on her dashboard passes 8 a.m., conscious that even this hour is too early to be calling on unsuspecting members of the public on a Saturday morning. Really she should wait until Monday, or phone ahead at least, but impatience is getting the better of her. And, anyway, Jago's face is all over the papers this morning, so they're bound to have been roused early by calls on the subject.

It is the pilot who opens the front door to Nell Gale's home, surprising Ali into a display of false cheer. 'Hello, Mr Neill!'

'Oh, good morning,' he replies, his heavy brow knitting as he tries to work out what the police might want from him now. 'I thought you were another hack,' he says, bringing a hidden jug of water from behind the door. 'I was about to, you know . . .' He makes a throwing motion, and then stoops to pour the water into the geranium pot on the front step.

'I'm here for Nell Gale,' Ali says, trying to see past him into the dark little terrace.

Overhead, a sash window flies up and a crazy-haired Cathy Gale leans out, quickly joined by Kip. Are they together or not? Ali wonders. Is anything straightforward with this family?

'Hello? Sergeant, um, Samson?' Cathy says, clearly trying to sound less grumpy than she's managing.

'I'm after your Nell,' Ali repeats, concentrating on keeping her tone light.

'She's staying next door at the moment, at Dad's. What do you want with her?'

Ali steps back down into the road, casting her gaze over John Gale's adjoining terrace. 'Just a few words.'

'About the air crash?' Kip asks, draping an arm around Cathy's shoulder.

'No,' Ali replies, meeting their scowls with an impassive nod.

John Gale's door eases open to reveal a pyjama-clad Albie standing on the threshold, balancing a big poster-sized roll of paper over the crook of his bandaged arm.

'Are you after Nell?' he asks, with a helpful smile.

She nods. 'Can I come in?'

Albie looks over his shoulder and back at the detective again. 'No point.'

'She's not there?'

'She was. But then, when she saw you knocking, she told me to give it a couple of minutes before I opened the door. You know, to let her make her getaway out the back.'

Ali is momentarily struck dumb; Jago Neill's face creases into a broad, crooked smile, and across the threshold of their adjoining front steps, Albie leans in to knock knuckles with him, sending his poster tumbling onto the path.

'She took Grandad's truck,' Albie continues. 'Don't know where or why, but, well, she definitely didn't want to talk to you.' He shrugs, good-humouredly. 'Sorry 'bout that.'

In the window above, Cathy Gale gazes down, and it's clear she doesn't share in the amusement. 'Go back inside, Albie,' she calls down, curtly, and her son and Jago Neill close their respective doors.

'Cathy,' Ali says, lowering her voice now they are alone. 'I can't tell you what this is about – Nell's over eighteen, so I need to talk to her directly. But—'

'But what?' Cathy urges, her eyes filling with fear.

'Do you know if Nell has ever used any dating websites?'

Cathy blinks back at her. She shakes her head.

'No?' Ali confirms.

Cathy's hand hovers over her mouth, as though she's putting some terrible puzzle together.

'Is there anything I should know, Cathy?'

'I don't know,' she murmurs. 'I really don't know.'

Back home, over lunch, Margo helps Ali set up, Margo and Ali set up a fake dating profile on Authentically Blind, placing their fictional Polly's age in the broad 18–25 bracket, and listing her as a single student living in Highcap. Her interests are music, baking, the cinema and socialising – a combination of the interests Ali knows CeeCee and Dahlia included in their profiles. She adds 'walking' for good measure, as she pictures Nell, looking out across the hills of Highcap the day that plane came down.

'I'm not actually going along, if someone replies,' Ali says, pouring them both a glass of red. 'God, they'd suss me in a second. I mean, I'm clearly not under twenty-five, for starters.'

'You could definitely pass,' Margo says, reaching around to pull Ali's hair into a high ponytail. 'Definitely.'

'Anyway, even if I found the bastards, cornering them like that would be unlikely to stand up in court.'

'Why not?' Margo asks.

'Entrapment? Coercion? Trelawney would do his nut.'

'You don't know that—'

But Margo doesn't get to finish her sentence, because, with a resounding 'bing!' Ali receives her first Blind Alert. The username is 'Happy Chap'.

Hey Polly. You sound absolutely lovely. I've been on here for months and I swear I haven't found anyone I fancied meeting up with until now. It's amazing – you're into all the same things I'm into! Most girls I know don't even own a pair of walking boots!

His message is unnervingly courteous, and, for someone of his generation, notably absent of emojis and slang. Ali blinks wildly as Margo reads the message too. 'Just "like" his message!' she urges. 'Go on! Let him do the talking.'

So, what kind of music are you into?

'What shall I say?' Ali asks, at once aware of the likely age difference between her and this stranger.

Margo shrugs. 'I dunno. Um, soul? Reggae? Just say you're into all sorts.'

Ali types her reply.

Me too, Happy Chap replies. *You should see my Spotify account. #Eclectic*

Ali shakes her head, barely believing what she's getting herself into. *Same* ☺, she types.

'Flirt a bit!' Margo laughs. Ali can't believe she's taking this so lightly. 'Oh, I forgot; you don't know how to.' She grabs the phone from Ali's hands and takes over.

We'll have to compare notes, Margo types. *They should have a Spotify dating site, shouldn't they? Bet the matches would be more accurate if they were based on musical tastes.*

Haha, too right! I love that idea!

Margo holds back for a moment or two, before returning with a simple heart emoji.

Listen, Happy Chap replies, quickly snatching up the silent bait. *Your profile says you live in Highcap? Don't suppose you fancy meeting at the Five Bells tomorrow night? I know it's short notice and a Sunday and everything, but I'd really love to meet you! Before anyone else snaps you up. Joking! (Not joking!) My real name's Max, by the way.*

Max. Ali and Margo stare at the message, barely breathing. 'Matt. Mac. Max,' she murmurs. 'It's him.' Before she can change her mind, Ali types into the reply box and presses send.

OK. What time?

27. Cathy

Saturday

For twenty minutes or more after she steps back from the window, Cathy doesn't leave her room. The moment she saw DS Ali standing on the doorstep below, her chest started to tighten in ever-increasing increments, and now, as she tunes into the peaceful rhythms of Kip and Jago in the kitchen downstairs, she wonders if this is how a heart attack feels.

Should she text Nell? See how she is? *Where* she is? Or, better still, phone her? She thinks back to what Ted the landlord had told her that night at the Five Bells when she'd gone to fetch Elliot: about rumours of Nell messing around with some lads in the alleyway there. Cathy thinks about the reasons Nell might find herself in such a situation, and her guts run cold.

'Cathy, love?' Kip calls up the stairs, stirring her into action. 'Cath? Are you coming down for breakfast?'

As she enters the living room, still belting her robe, Albie returns through the back door with the pup at his heel, dragging his interminable homework with him, forcing a smile from her. For a child who knows every excuse going to avoid homework of any kind, he's grown uncharacteristically invested in this family tree project. Maybe it's the accident; or maybe it's the novelty of being able to ask questions in a family that rarely talks about the past.

'Hey, Super-Alb.' She beckons him to her, cupping his head against the crook of her shoulder, breathing in the bed-mussed baby scent of his hair. Has he grown again? Will he soon, like Nell, be too big and too embarrassed to give in to her fickle emotional demands? What will tomorrow look like; or the day after that? The sands just keep on shifting.

'You OK, Mum?' he asks, looking up. 'Your heart's pounding.'

She releases him and pours herself a coffee from the pot Jago has just brewed. 'Yup, all good. Apart from that bloody nosy copper waking up the whole sodding row.' She sends an exaggerated eye-roll his way. 'Anyway, what were you doing next door so early? Is Grandad up?'

'He's having his breakfast.' Albie drapes his poster over the back of the sofa. 'I wanted to ask Nell about my homework, but as soon as I got to her room, we heard the door. She legged it when she saw it was the police again. Like a fugitive,' he adds with a little chuckle.

Cathy pulls out a chair and sits opposite Kip, pushing away the toast Jago sets down before her. *Jago Neill*, in Cathy's little house, serving her toast; maybe this is all a dream? The events of the past month still feel so surreal, and things just keep getting stranger.

As though channelling her thoughts, Jago's eyes land on Cathy's, and he tilts his head, just slightly; a question.

'You think I should go after her?' she asks, her tone bordering on defensive.

Jago is unrattled. 'Do *you* think you should?' he returns, with kindness.

Cathy glances at Kip, who is quietly eating, his face unreadable, and she wonders how much he knows about his daughter, whether he too has heard the disturbing rumours about her and those men. Cathy turns her attention to her son, latching on to him like a lifebuoy. 'What did you want to ask Nell, Alb?'

Albie has claimed Cathy's unwanted toast and now stands messily peanut-buttering it at the edge of the table, while Jago takes over feeding the dog in the kitchen. 'Do you think I should add Lump to the family tree?'

'What? No, silly. He's a dog. Alb, you said you wanted Nell's help with your homework – is it something I can help you with?'

For a few seconds, Albie doesn't answer. He takes his plate and perches on the edge of the sofa next to his giant family chart, and studiously avoids her gaze altogether. 'Um, no, thanks. You're fine.'

'*You're fine*?' Cathy scoffs. 'Since when did you ever turn down help with your homework?'

Albie shrugs and takes another bite from his toast. 'I think Jago's right, Mum.'

Scowling, Cathy looks to Kip for support.

'We *should* at least phone her, love,' Kip agrees. 'Find out what she's running away from.'

Beyond the kitchen, Jago is now sitting out on the wooden bench with the guitar resting against his body, not playing it, but just sitting there, face turned towards the sun.

Cathy sends her daughter a text message.

Call us, Nellie. We're worried about you x

At midday, Kip heads off to fetch Grandad, to ferry him to the hospital for a follow-up appointment with his oncologist and the support nurses who'll be working with him over the coming weeks. Cathy had wanted to go, but Dad had refused, telling her she'd make any bad news all the worse, with her worrying and hand-wringing, and in the end she'd agreed Albie could go along for the ride, so long as he promised not to badger Grandad about that blessed family tree any more.

With Nell still AWOL, and Elliot and Suzie still keeping their distance, the house is quiet, and Cathy finds herself standing at the washing-up bowl as Jago Neill dries, wondering if this is perhaps the loneliest she has ever felt. Without warning, she breaks down, head bowed over the sink to create a shield of her hair.

'Oh, Cathy, darlin' – is it Nell?' Jago soothes, pushing back her curls to study her face. 'Is it your wee girl?'

She tries to brush it aside, to push him away, but Jago won't hear of it, won't let her go. He holds her, in a gentle restraint, until her tears subside and she has the strength to break free, to wipe dry her face and blow her snotty nose. At the front of the house, the door knocker goes again; another journalist. Another intrusion.

'Let's go out,' he says, throwing down the damp tea towel. 'I could do with a walk, my maiden. I'm feeling stronger; I could do with the exercise, before these poor weedy legs of mine waste away once and for all.'

Jago smiles at her with a sadness Cathy can't ignore, and within minutes they are driving out towards the Golden Rabbit holiday camp of all places. Nothing has changed since Cathy was last here, except for the new 'Danger Keep Out' signs, and several large floodlights erected around the site, in preparation for the start of the autumn rebuild, when the evening light will fade early.

As they drive along the welcome path, past the derelict shower blocks and demolished playground, neither speaks, two sets of eyes fixed on the shimmering horizon of the sea ahead. It is what Kip would call 'a day of days': a perfect day, neither too warm nor too cool, too breezy or too still. *Ah, it's a day of days*, he'd say, and Cathy would know what he meant, and that the day ahead would surely be a good one.

For a moment, the pair just sit behind the windscreen of Cathy's old Citroën, gazing out at the water, following the passage of a lone speedboat as it flies over the surface, leaving curving white arcs in the otherwise peaceful canvas of blue.

'Do you remember anything, Jago?' she asks, not looking at him, thinking of the way he pored over the headlines on Albie's iPad this morning. His younger face on the front page of every tabloid. 'Sometimes . . . sometimes I think perhaps you know exactly who you are. Sometimes I think you remember it all, but it hurts too much to admit it.'

For a long while, he doesn't answer. 'Is that the coastal path?' he asks in reply, and he looks past her, indicating across the campground towards the man-made steps leading up towards Highcap Hill.

Cathy nods, a sense of foreboding at once crushing in on her, as she thinks of her daughter, Nell, standing up there on that fateful morning, a lone witness to her brother's destruction and the new shape of their lives to come. What must she have felt in that moment? Has Cathy even asked her?

Leaving the car, they set off on foot, Cathy pointing out the various landmarks that can be seen at the crest of each new incline. Back over the town, inland, thin white cloud-cover stubbornly obscures the church spire, despite the brightness of the day here at the water's edge. To the west, the clocktower of the Starlings dominates the horizon, while to the east, the empty green pitches of the Golden Rabbit holiday camp roll beneath them, like a dream of the past.

'You're worried about your Nell,' Jago says, sitting on the stone bench at Kite View, where the sea spreads out, travelling from the fossil rocks of Lyme Bay all the way to the sun-dappled sands of Chesil Beach.

'The world isn't kind to girls. To women,' she replies.

'This is true,' Jago replies. 'It is cruel, in the extreme. And unfair.'

'When I met Kip,' Cathy says, all at once calm in the certainty that she is about to share something with Jago Neill that she has never told a living soul, 'I was in my early twenties – old enough, but still pretty green. My family tried to talk me out of travelling, but I just wanted to get out of this place, see the world. You know?'

'I do know. I did it too; I'd do it again.'

'I'd not really had many boyfriends, nothing serious at any rate. But when I met Kip, it was – well, it was something else. We talked endlessly, about everything and nothing, and laughed – oh, my God, did we laugh!'

'That's love. It doesn't come along all that often, my Cathy.' Jago sighs. For a while, he is silent, his fingers raking over his jawline as he disappears inside his own private thoughts. 'What was it, then? When was it you stopped laughing?'

Cathy studies her hands, resting in a neat stack on her lap. 'When I left Thailand, a few days ahead of Kip, I already suspected I was pregnant.'

'With Nell?'

Cathy nods. 'I hadn't told him yet. We'd only been together a couple of months, and we were young, and anyway, I wanted to wait till I got home, to be sure. I knew he'd want it, what-ever happened – I mean, we were young and stupid and . . .' Overhead, a kite soars, before dipping low in pursuit of some prey. 'But on the morning of my flight, I overslept. Stupid. We'd been out late the night before – the bar we worked in had thrown a farewell party for us on the beach – and I missed the taxi I'd pre-booked for the airport.'

'Ah. So, you took an unlicensed one?'

Cathy turns to look at him. 'The one thing they tell you not to do. Travellers' Guide Rule Number One: be on your guard.'

Jago turns to face her, his eyes darkly intense, and it seems to Cathy that he is looking right inside her, into the core of her truth. 'He raped you?'

She gives a little shrug, only realising now that she's never before named it, only ever allowing her mind to briefly linger on the word *attack*. The real word was too brutal, too debasing to attach to herself. Yet here is Jago Neill, a virtual stranger, naming the atrocity for what it really was.

'Yeah,' she replies, with a grim nod. 'But he was kind enough to drop me at my destination, as promised, after clearing the cash from my wallet and splitting my lip when I put up a fight.' She exhales through pursed lips. 'I'm not sure I've ever looked Kip square in the eye since, even when I told him we were expecting a baby; even when Nell was born. That man, that irrelevant little man – he took it all from me. My clean, clear view of the world, my silliness, my innocence. That's when I stopped laughing, Jago Neill. Because, the truth is, the world *isn't* fun; the world is shit.'

Jago stares back out at the wide blue horizon. Long, silent minutes pass and Cathy watches him, witnessing the shift in his expression, as his darkly lashed eyes dart across the bright horizon with something like urgency. 'It was a day like today,' he murmurs, but, when he turns to face her again, his expression is blanked off, unreadable again. 'You know, it can be both,' he says, his eyes glinting with unshed tears.

'Jago—?' she starts, but he shakes his head resolutely, forbidding her to step inside his pain.

'Life, Cathy,' he says. 'It *can* be shitty, just as you say. But it can still be good, and joyous, and loving. It can still be safe, and full of things to keep you going. Like your kids. Like Kip.

They're precious to you, aren't they?'

'Why do you think I'm so scared for them?'

'But you can't protect them from everything, Cathy, love. Your experience in Thailand was a terrible thing, and of course it still haunts you. But Nell's her own woman, and she needs to follow her own path. You won't protect her by clipping her wings. Just because something bad happened to you, that does not mean something bad will happen to Nell.' Again, Jago places his hand on top of hers, enclosing it in his warmth. 'Cathy, darlin', she's not you.'

'But that's the problem, don't you see?' Cathy cries out, finally voicing her darkest fears. 'She *is* me. She's so like I was at that age that it scares the hell out of me. And she's so like me, Jago, that I *know* something bad has already happened, that I'm already too late to save her. I just don't know what it is.'

28. Nell

Standing on the pavement outside Kasey's house, her cousin by her side, Nell swipes her damp brow and curses the heat of the midday sun. Dylan is wearing his stupid 'Be prepared' backpack over both shoulders, and it occurs to Nell that he might actually hamper their chances of talking to Kasey, odd as he is.

'This is a bad idea, Dylan,' she murmurs, distracted by yet another call from DS Samson, which she rejects before switching her phone to silent. 'I think we should just forget it. Forget the whole thing.'

Dylan stares at the house, as though it is a beast to be slayed. 'After all that work finding her? You want to get that video taken down, don't you? You want to give effing Kasey a piece of your mind?'

They'd talked about this over the past twenty-four hours, about nothing else, and yes, Nell wants all those things. But, at the same time, she wants none of it. She wants to ignore it, shrink it, bury it; pretend it never happened at all.

274

She looks at her cousin, and back at the bungalow. 'It did happen,' she says aloud, and Dylan leads them up the path, pressing the doorbell once, twice, ready to do battle.

A young man answers the door; Nell hadn't anticipated anyone other than Kasey on the other side. This guy, nineteen or twenty at a guess, looks pale, hungover even, and for a moment, Nell worries that they've got the wrong house altogether.

'Does Kasey Clapton live here?' Dylan demands robotically. 'We are looking for her.'

Inwardly, Nell cringes.

'Erm, yes,' the lad replies, suspiciously. 'She's my sister. Who shall I say—?'

'School friends,' Dylan states, adding an unconvincing smile as an afterthought. 'We were just passing.'

Still appearing uncertain, the young man steps back into the hallway, leaving the door slightly ajar, with Nell and Dylan waiting on the other side. 'CeeCee!' they hear him call. 'CeeCee?'

'Oh, I get it.' Dylan gives a self-satisfied nod. 'It's Casey with a C. Casey Clapton. *CeeCee*. I bet that's the name she goes under on Facebook.'

Beyond the obscured entrance, there are the sounds of doors opening and closing, of hushed voices and '*I-don't-know*'s and '*tell-them-to-go-away*'s – but then, to Nell's surprise, there is the echo of a different pair of footsteps passing along the hall, and the door is cautiously eased open.

Standing on the other side is not the brash Casey Clapton Nell last encountered, publicly shaming her in the Five Bells, but another, frailer shadow of the girl. When Casey sees it is Nell on her doorstep, she does not flinch or slam the door in her face, but instead her mouth works wordlessly to form the word: *sorry*.

And Nell recognises the look in her eyes, and she understands. 'Casey, do you think we can come in?'

Adam, Casey's older brother, brings Cokes and crisps to her room and leaves them alone, as though some unspoken agreement has passed between them in the few moments since Dylan and Nell entered the house.

All the things Nell had planned to lecture the girl on – about violence and rape culture, about the sisterhood and shame – all those rehearsed conversations, designed to reduce Casey to a position of humiliation herself – evaporate the moment Nell recognises that Casey is a victim too.

'Do you want to talk about it?' Nell asks, sitting on the edge of the bed beside her, ignoring Dylan's blank expression.

Casey drops her head. Nell notices her fingernails are a perfectly manicured silver, except for a single jagged one, which she worries away at with the thumb from her other hand.

'Your nail,' Nell asks. 'Did that happen when—?'

'When what?' Dylan demands, confused.

'Dylan, just let Casey talk, all right?'

Casey nods. 'I scratched him, I think.'

'Is there a video?' Nell presses, and, after the initial flinch of shock at Nell's direct line of questioning, Casey begins to talk; before long, Nell and Dylan know as much as the detectives who took Casey's statement just over a fortnight earlier.

As horrible as it is to admit, for Nell there is some small, strange comfort in knowing she's nothing special, that she was not alone in being targeted, because her assault meant almost nothing to the men who demeaned her.

For some inexplicable reason, the image of Jago Neill fills Nell's mind, a flashbulb snapshot of that desolate pilot reaching into the smoking cockpit of his fallen plane, reaching for his child as her own tears bled into the sun-baked earth way up overhead on Highcap Hill. So much loss; so much suffering.

And just like that, her fear turns to simmering rage.

'Casey, we can't let them keep doing this,' she says, in a voice so cool and calm, it sounds as though it comes from somewhere outside her own body. 'You didn't deserve this. *We* didn't deserve this. We didn't ask for this.'

Casey meets her gaze, her chin trembling. 'I don't understand. Why are you being so nice to me – after the way I treated you? Showing your uncle that video – calling you a slag – *blaming* you.' Shame pours from her, and all Nell knows to do is to wrap her arms around the girl and tell her that it'll be all right.

'They treated us like pieces of meat. They used us and threw us away, and we didn't ask for any of it,' Nell murmurs into the girl's hair, telling her all the things she herself had needed to hear in the days after her own attack. 'You're better than this. You're better than this, OK?'

'I told the police I wouldn't go to court,' Casey says, pulling back. 'That I just wanted to forget about it. But—'

'But you can't forget?' Nell says.

Casey brings her fingers to her temples, tap-tap. 'It's all I think about. Some days, I think I'm actually going mad with it.'

Nell nods slowly, even now blinking away the shadowy images that have haunted her days and nights. 'Me too.'

Awkwardly, Dylan sits down on the rug at their feet and clears his throat, as though asking for permission to speak. 'The brain doesn't work like that,' he says, as though reading from a textbook. 'Memories don't just go away because you don't talk about them. The worse they are, the bigger they get. In my experience.'

Nell looks at him, quite taken aback by his sudden show of empathy. 'You're right, Dylan,' she says. 'The thought of facing up to it – admitting it – is terrifying. But, Casey, now we know there's two of us, and the worst has already happened—'

On the bed beside her, Nell's phone vibrates, and, guiltily expecting it to be another anxious message from her mother, she flips it over. DS Samson's name flashes across her screen. She holds it up for Casey and Dylan to see.

'Should I take it?' she asks. 'Dylan? Casey? Should I take it?'

Dylan reaches out and presses the green button, and finally DS Ali Samson connects with Nell Gale.

'Hi,' Nell says, bringing the receiver to her ear. 'You've been trying to reach me?'

The tiniest intake of breath at the end of the line betrays the detective's surprise at actually getting through. 'I have,' she replies, after a pause. 'I want to talk to you about a recent date you went on,' she says, and now it is Nell who is caught off guard. 'Through the Authentically Blind website.' When Nell fails to answer, she adds, 'And a man whose name I'm guessing begins with an M.'

Mal. That was his name; or the name he gave, at least. The name Nell has been trying to erase these past five weeks.

'He called himself Mal,' she says, casting a glance at Casey.

'Mal?' DS Samson repeats, her tone gentle.

'Yes.'

'How about we meet up this afternoon and you tell me everything? Nell, whatever you've been through, I want you to know you're not alone. You're not the only girl this has happened to. There are others.'

'How many?'

'At least two that we know about. Possibly more. We have to stop this, and we can't do it without witnesses. Without victims coming forward. You want us to catch them, don't you?'

'Yes,' she replies shakily, as her eyes meet Casey's. 'I want to nail the fuckers for what they've done to us.'

278

'Me too,' DS Samson replies. 'And I've got a plan. Where shall I pick you up?'

'Joy Lane,' Nell replies.

'*Joy Lane*? But that's—'

'Joy Lane. No. 1. I'm with Casey Clapton.'

29. DS Ali Samson

Saturday

Within half an hour, Ali and Margo are pulling up outside No. 1 Joy Lane, having been out grocery shopping when Ali's call-back to Nell Gale finally got through.

Not only are CeeCee Clapton and Nell Gale together, but Nell's strange, quiet cousin is also in tow. Ali gets out of the passenger seat and greets them, explaining that her partner is going to drop them at the Breezy Café, where they can chat discreetly. She senses that a casual environment is a good starting place for Nell, who, so far, has dodged Ali's every attempt at a straight conversation.

'I can drop you off on the way,' she suggests to Dylan, before looking to Nell and CeeCee for their agreement.

Dylan gives a knowing bob of the head. 'I can walk.'

As the two girls take the back seats, Dylan pauses alongside Ali's open passenger window and raises a finger, like some teenage Columbo. 'Officer. Casey Clapton lost a fingernail in the struggle with her attacker at the Five Bells. She believes she may have scratched him, so the lost nail may provide a good source of DNA.'

Ali glances into the back seat, where CeeCee raises her hand to display her broken nail. Bloody hell, how had they missed that? She thanks Dylan, and Margo drives on.

Weekend or not, Ali types out a message to Benny: *URGENT – can you get down to the Five Bells alleyway in the next hour, to search for a broken fingernail, painted silver – possible DNA source for the CeeCee Clapton case. Reply pls!* She presses send and prays for a quick response.

At the Breezy Café, Ali orders a round of tea and cake and sits with the girls at the furthest corner table, overlooking the ocean. There is enough noise in the café to drown out their conversation, and she notices a shift in both the girls' demeanours, as though finding each other has brought them some peace.

'Did you know each other, before?' she asks.

'Not really,' Nell replies.

'We went to the same school. Different years,' CeeCee says.

'Yeah. And we weren't exactly fans. Of each other. But, you know – adversity, and all that.'

'*The enemy of my enemy is my friend*?' Ali asks.

She watches the two consider the phrase, and, while neither smiles, Ali detects something like warmth in the space between them.

The waitress places a tray on the table and Ali sets about pouring while the girls cut the cake selection into threes.

'Now, Nell, I'm not going to ask you about your experience here – I'd rather do that down at the station, where I can take a full and uninterrupted statement. OK? But I do want to ask you both about the dating app Authentically Blind, and about the usernames Mac and Mal.'

Both girls nod.

'So, to be clear – you both, independently, used the app, which led to a blind date for you, CeeCee, with a person calling himself Mac, and you, Nell, with a person calling himself Mal.'

Again, they both nod.

'He deleted his account straight after – you know,' Nell says, clearly not yet in possession of the words needed to describe her attack.

'Same,' says CeeCee.

'Which suggests that he's creating a fresh account for every new encounter,' Ali says. 'And can you remember how he first made contact? What were his words?'

Nell looks embarrassed. 'He said something like, "Wow, we're into so many of the same things. You're the first girl I've actually wanted to chat with on here."' Her tone grows sarcastic. '"You sound *really* special . . . When can we meet?"'

CeeCee has paled visibly.

'What is it?' Ali asks.

'What she just said – it's exactly the same. Almost word for word,' she murmurs. 'I can't believe I fell for it. *Oh, my God. I'm such an idiot, DS Samson.*'

'It's Ali. And, no, you're not.' Now, Ali shows them a screenshot of her own conversation as 'Polly', virtually a replica of the one Nell just described. 'You're not an idiot,' she says, levelling her eyes to meet CeeCee's, to meet Nell's. 'He's cold and he's calculating. And he's found a method that works.'

'Whose is that account?' CeeCee asks, gesturing towards Ali's phone. 'Another girl? Did you get to them in time?'

Ali puts her phone down on the table. 'Her name is Polly, and she hasn't had her date yet. But – and this is completely irregular, so my boss would go insane if he knew I was suggesting it – I think you can help.'

'Help?' says Nell. 'How?'

'How would you feel about coming along on the date – at a distance, of course – and seeing if you recognise Max? My colleague Benny will be there, keeping an eye out for the second offender, so you'd be completely safe.'

'But what about this girl, Polly?' There is panic in Nell's voice. 'You can't put her at risk like that!'

Ali reaches out for a slice of apple cake. 'Polly's going to be just fine, Nell.'

'Ohhh,' CeeCee says, and Ali sees her smile for the first time. '*You're* Polly.'

When they're done, the girls decline Ali's offer of a cab, and instead head off to Nell's together on foot, so she can drive CeeCee home from there. Ali watches them, setting out towards the soft horizon of the coastal path west, an unlikely pairing brought together by trauma.

She thinks about her own losses; about the baby, about her hopes of ever being a mother. And then she thinks about Margo, and the safety she represents.

In her pocket, the tinny ring of her phone brings her back to the moment, and she sees Benny's name pulsing on the screen.

'Sarge, I'm here at the Five Bells – in the alleyway,' he says, before she's even had a chance to say hello. 'And I've got it!'

'Slow down, Benny!'

'The silver fingernail. I've got it! It was between the cracks of the paving slabs, perfectly preserved!'

Ali stamps her foot on the pavement, restraining herself from screaming out in celebration. '*Yes!* Benny, you bloody star!' In a case completely absent of DNA evidence, this could be the piece they're looking for.

'I've bagged it, and I'm about to drop it into the station, so the guys can fast-track it.'

She thinks about the condom sample they found in the same alleyway, which came up with no known criminal match, and she thinks about Trelawney's assertion that it's unlikely this is a perpetrator with no previous convictions. But what if this pair are just so slick, they've never been caught before? The sad truth of it is, no conviction does *not* mean no crime. Many a sociopath has been uncovered with a previously spotless copybook. Sociopaths are invariably organised, and careful at covering their tracks, so it stands to reason they might have, instead of a criminal record, a long history of getting away with it.

'Benny?' she adds. 'Get them to check it against that condom sample, will you? It's a long shot that they'll match, but worth a look.'

'Right you are, sarge. I'll see you tomorrow – we're still on for Operation Polly?'

'We are. And remember, not a word to Trelawney, OK? If he gets wind of it, I'll take the fall. He doesn't need to know about it until we have something positive to tell him.'

Without questioning her judgement, Benny hangs up, and Ali feels grateful to have a friend like him on her team. Striding out, she heads for the pier, where the views of the ocean stretch wide, the shimmering sun lighting up the water like mercury. It is worth it, isn't it? All the heartache and worry that comes from doing a job like hers? If only for the hope of sweeping away just a few of the world's parasites?

Far out on the coastal path, two tiny figures crest the distant mound of Highcap Hill and disappear from view.

30. Cathy

Sunday

Elliot wakes Cathy early on Sunday morning, ringing her mobile in a nerve-shredding start to her day.

'Elliot?'

'Hi.'

'What is it? God, it's only just gone eight.'

'I know,' he replies, sounding more sober than Cathy's heard him in a long time. 'It's Dad.'

Cathy sits upright, shaking Kip by the shoulder as she throws back the covers. 'Where are you? Next door?' she rattles off, sliding her feet into flip-flops and already grabbing for a jumper in her haste to race to her father on the other side of the wall. 'Is he – has he . . . taken a turn?' she demands, already at the foot of the stairs.

'No – slow down, Cath,' Elliot says, tuning into her panic. 'I'm at my place. Dad's at his. Asleep probably. Everything's fine.'

She flops against the kitchen worktop, her eyes only now falling on Jago in the darkness of the adjoining living room, stretched out under his sleeping bag on the sofa. He raises a sleepy hand; she rolls her eyes in return, as though he's party to the whole conversation and might have an opinion of his own. Cathy snaps on the kettle and fetches down a mug. 'Then, why the dawn bloody wake-up call, Ells? Do you know how many lie-ins I get each week? *One*.'

'Sorry . . .' Elliot pauses, and Cathy wonders if Suzie is there in the background, listening in. 'It's just, Dad called me late last night. He's been talking to Albie about our family tree, and it got him thinking about, you know, the end . . .'

'The end?'

'Come on, Cath, don't make this harder. We all know he's only got a matter of weeks . . .'

She sighs, angry, sad, hating her brother for putting words to the facts. 'Go on.'

'And he wants a family meeting, at his, tonight. I don't know what the doctors told him yesterday, but this is only going in one direction, sis – so we're to get supper together for half-six, seven, and then he's going to go over his will. And talk about some important stuff.'

'Important stuff?'

'Family stuff. That's what he said.'

Cathy's mind is galloping ahead, a hundred thoughts and images pouring in at once. 'What do you want me to cook?'

'Suzie says if you do a big chicken casserole, she can do cheesecakes. Dad said there's lots of veg wants picking at the allotment, and can one of us go over and spend an hour there, picking and weeding a bit.'

'Kip'll go. Bloody hell, Dad's at death's door and he's worried about the allotment?'

'You know Dad. He asked me to get in some bottles of wine and some beer, which I'm going to have to ask Dylan to get, as

286

Suzie's put me on a ban from even buying the stuff. See you at six, to get the food on, yeah? Make sure Nell's there too.'

'I don't know what Nell's up to,' Cathy says, with a deep sigh, 'but I'll ask her when she gets up. She came home yesterday with some strange girl, and then went straight out again in the car, and didn't get back till late. She's been, I dunno . . .' Cathy can't begin to explain what she means; what she fears.

'Dad said everyone,' Elliot reiterates. 'Except the pilot, of course.'

Cathy gives a sorry shake of her head. 'His name's Jago,' she murmurs, turning to the back door and lowering her voice.

'Yeah. Jago,' Elliot replies. 'Family only. Six o'clock. See you later, Cath, OK?' He waits for her response, and when it doesn't come, says, 'Love you, sis,' and hangs up.

31. Nell

Sunday

Out on the main high street, Nell and Casey sit in the back of DC Benny's undercover car, all attention on DS Ali, who is earnestly instructing them through the gap in the headrests.

It was a miracle Nell had managed to get away from home at all, what with Mum fussing about some 'important' supper at Grandad's tonight, and Jago Neill doing his best to persuade her to join him and Kip picking veg over at the allotment. The strange thing was, she'd actually really wanted to; the idea of digging carrots in his gentle presence had seemed infinitely more attractive than what she'd committed to here.

But, in the end, in danger of being late to pick Casey up, she'd had no choice but to simply grab the keys to the Citroën and leg it, batting away Mum's questions as she made her escape.

'OK, you two?' DS Ali asks, checking they're focused on the task. Her hair is worn loose, and she's wearing trendy tortoiseshell specs and casual clothes; she looks completely different from her normal police self. 'Right, I'm going to go in through the front entrance, and Benny's going to park the car in the bay at the back, where you'll both have a good view of the bar through the window. I want you two in the front, Benny in the back – and I'll do my best to get a table as close as I can to your viewpoint. Of course, it's quite possible "Max" will come in through the rear entrance, next to where you'll be parked, but the windows of the car are tinted, so there's no chance of you being spotted, OK? You'll be able to see out, but he won't see in.'

'And what if we recognise him?' Casey asks.

'Then you let me know,' Benny replies. 'DS Samson will have her phone on her, so if we get a positive ID, I can message her straight away.'

'What if he spikes your drink?' This is Nell's greatest worry. 'Like he did us?'

'I've checked,' Ali replies confidently. 'They do table service here – you can order at your seat with an app, so there's no chance of him slipping something in at the bar. And, anyway, I'll be watching him like a hawk.'

'If it *is* him, will you arrest him, there and then?'

'Let's see who turns up first, shall we?' Ali replies with a smile. 'Where's your car, Nell?'

'Oh, it's up the next side street. It's my mum's – I thought people might recognise it, so I've parked it out of view.'

'Good thinking.' Ali checks her phone. 'It's five to seven, so I'll get off now. And remember, whatever happens, you're to stay in the car. I don't want one of you jumping in and wrecking our chances of a conviction, OK? You're just here to ID anyone you recognise. And if you don't recognise him, that's fine. But the main thing is, stay put. OK?'

'Got it,' the girls chime, and, after Benny has moved the vehicle into the little car park round the side of the pub, they switch places, wind the windows down just an inch so they don't overheat, and wait, with DC Benny in the back slurping on the giant Diet Coke he picked up on the way here.

Inside, DS Ali manages to get a seat at a table right beside the window they're facing, where she sits and waits, giving no indication that she's aware of them at all. It seems surreal to Nell, to be sitting here in a tinted police car, next to her fellow victim, part of the swat team out to catch a predator. *Their* predator. To their right is the alleyway that leads to the pub kitchens and bins; the alleyway where, she now allows herself to recall with more clarity than ever before, she was brutally assaulted and filmed.

A member of staff emerges, clocking off for the night. A lad around her age, in skater jeans and a hoodie.

'Guys?' Benny asks.

'No,' they both reply.

In Nell's hand, a text vibrates on her mobile. It's Albie. *Where are you? Grandad said we ALL have to be here tonight. We're about to eat. Mum's doing her nut.*

Won't be long x she replies quickly, not wanting to take her eyes off the scene for a moment.

Another message drops in: Dylan. *Everything OK? I can see you on Find my Phone – at the pub right? Keep me posted.*

She returns a thumbs-up and pushes the phone into her pocket, resolving to ignore it for the next hour, as another employee emerges from the alleyway, stopping to lean against the wall and take out a cigarette.

'That's Andy,' Nell says, eyeing him just a few feet away, as he gazes in their direction, unlit cigarette dangling from the corner of his mouth, and checking through his pockets as though his life depended on it. 'The landlord's son.'

'Looks a bit jumpy. What's he like?'

Nell shakes her head. 'Never had much to do with him. I only worked there a couple of weeks. Quiet. Chain-smoker. Think he usually lives with his mum somewhere round the New Forest.'

Inside, DS Ali is still sitting alone, waiting, and it seems impossible to imagine anyone's going to turn up at all. What if this is all a waste of time? Someone on the dating app just messing Ali about?

In the passenger seat beside her, Casey stiffens, and Nell is alerted to another male, leaning in to give Andy a light for his cigarette. She can't see his face from this angle; his physique is lean but broad-shouldered, and he's dressed in denim shorts and a plain blue T-shirt. The bright white trainers he wears remind Nell of Albie's tennis sneakers, and the baseball cap is a faded red, just like—

Nell gasps. *Surely not?* But it's true – it's the lad from the campsite; the one she'd seen from high above the holiday camp, just moments before the plane came down. The guy who'd disappeared beneath the fallen shower block and never turned up in the searches that followed. She recognises the shape of him, despite having only ever seen him from a distance, from behind. Having relived that scene a hundred times in the weeks that have passed since the crash, the picture of him crossing the grassy plain, she has no doubt at all. It's definitely—

'It's him.' Casey exhales. 'That's him.'

'I don't—' Nell starts to protest, but then the lad turns, laughing at something Andy has said, and she sees his face, the cruelty in it – hears the sound of it drifting in through the gap in the window – and she knows it's true. It's him. Her hand reaches for Casey's.

In silence, they watch, as the two men exchange a couple of words, before 'Max' leaves Andy smoking, to disappear through the rear entrance to the lounge bar, where he greets DS Ali with

291

a hug. In the back seat of the car, DC Benny taps out a message, and, seconds later, a ping returns.

'OK, she's in the picture,' he says simply. 'Now, let's just wait it out.'

The next hour seems to move at half-pace, as the trio watch Ali put on the show of her life, pretending to smile and laugh at the things her companion is saying, things only Nell and Casey can imagine, having been in that situation before her.

Nell tries to pull together the threads of her nightmare experience, struggling to comprehend how she failed to recognise the lad from the campsite as the same person who had attacked her the night before the crash. Her date had been dressed differently, smartly, she recalls, and, of course, there'd been no baseball cap to obscure his hair. And then there was the fact that for at least forty-eight hours after the attack she'd struggled to remember many of the details, with whatever drugs he'd put in her drink still muddying her grip on reality.

Inside the pub, one round of drinks follows another, Ali sticking to soft drinks, her 'date' on half-pints. Inside the car, no one speaks, and Nell has to remind herself to breathe every now and then. Even Benny in the back seat gives off a nervous energy, his knee bumping up and down to an anxious rhythm.

As the clock on the dashboard passes eight, he peers between the headrests with a sheepish expression. 'Sorry, girls, I'm gonna pee myself if I don't go. D'you know where the toilets are?'

Nell directs him, explaining how he'll need to cross all the way through the main bar and up the staircase to the first floor, and she tries not to think of the last time she was in those loos herself, being heckled by Casey and her friend.

'It's a bit of a hike,' she says, eyes still fixed on Ali and the rapist. 'Just follow the signs.'

'Bloody fizzy drinks. Sorry. I'll be quick.'

As Benny jogs in through the back entrance, Nell and Casey allow themselves a moment to meet eyes.

'It's really him, isn't it?' Casey asks, a whisper.

Nell nods, never more certain of anything. 'It's really him.'

Turning their attention back to the window, they see DS Ali rising from her seat, pointing to her phone, apologetically, as Max makes a no-worries signal, and the detective unexpectedly appears through the back exit of the pub.

'What's going on?' Nell asks.

'Is she phoning for back-up, or something?' Casey wonders. 'Are they about to arrest him?'

Please God, Nell thinks. *Please let this be it.*

32. Ali

Sunday

Of all the times for him to return her call, he chooses now.

The 'date' with Max is progressing well, and the swift update from Benny that the girls have both ID'd the man as their attacker has put vigour in her conversation, a thrill of a different kind of chase from the one this lowlife has in mind. Already, she has admitted to being a couple of years older than her profile claimed, and he's forgiven her, saying he's not so keen on the girls closer to his age anyway. *They're shallow*, he tells her. *Not like you.*

They've been chatting for an hour now, and when Andrew Belgo's name flashes up on her screen, Ali feels an uncommon rush of elation and makes her excuses to step away for a moment.

'God, Max, I'm *really* sorry – it's a work thing,' she says in a rush, and he smiles broadly, fine with it, as she dips out through the back entrance, where Benny and the girls are parked. Giving them a discreet *everything's OK* signal, she positions herself against the wall, where she's able to keep an eye on both the back door and the alleyway while she takes the call.

'Hello, Mr Belgo?' she asks, before he even has a chance to speak, fumbling as she activates the recording device on her phone. The car park is now in near darkness, the setting sun having disappeared behind the towering spire of St Jude's. Autumn is whispering, Ali thinks, her mind wandering.

'DS Samson? Yes, Andrew Belgo here. You've been trying to contact me, I believe?'

Ali gives a little laugh; she feels strangely giddy, and with effort she resets her formal tone. 'For some time, Mr Belgo. You know, it's usual to return police calls with a bit more urgency—'

'Ah, well, I've been a bit indisposed,' he replies, his voice frail. 'I've been on a ventilator since mid-July. Covid. Thought all that nonsense had ended, but no. Caught it in Cowes, and, well, let's just say I'm lucky to be here.'

'Since the start of August? So – and, oh, I'm really sorry to hear about that – that would coincide with the time Jago Neill flew your aircraft from the Isle of Wight and crashed it here in Highcap.'

'Well, it would appear so. Except, I don't know the man as Jago Neill. The man I know – have known for the best part of ten years, in fact – is Neil Jacobs. And the boy, God rest his soul, is Sonny. *Was.*' He exhales audibly. 'I was very fond of the lad.'

'I'm really sorry for your loss,' Ali replies, desperately trying to hide her impatience to speed things along. 'So, you'd describe yourself as . . . as, um, friends?' There is a resounding echo in Ali's ears that's messing with her focus.

'More than friends, I'd say. In fact, he was a witness at our wedding – not long after my wife and I moved to the island. We became quite close.' Andrew Belgo sighs sadly.

This is just the kind of breakthrough Ali has been waiting for. 'And where exactly does Neil Jacobs live?'

'He's my neighbour – next place along, here in Fishbourne. On the island. I knew he used to be something in the music industry, but I always thought he was a producer or something – not a rock star, or whatever people are saying.'

'And you let him borrow your plane?' It's not lost on Ali how bizarre it is to her, the idea that a person could be so well off, they borrow planes from friends, the way ordinary people borrow sugar.

'Yes, he has a licence, so it's not unusual, in fact I'm glad of it getting a good run. I keep it on a small farm strip I own over near Compton – he'll have flown it out from there.' Belgo falls silent for a moment. 'I live alone since my wife died, and I don't see many people. Neil and I spend a good deal of time together. Even more so recently, since the funeral.'

'Your wife's funeral?'

'Oh, no, my wife died a few years back. I'm talking about *his* wife, Julianne. Not even forty years old. The man was devastated.'

Ali glances back towards the pub, where she can just make out Max still sitting at their table, watching her.

'Devastated enough to take his own life?' Ali asks, her heart rate rising inexplicably. 'To kill his own son?'

'*No.*' Belgo's answer is firm. 'Absolutely not.'

'How can you be so sure?'

'One, because I know he'd never do a thing to harm his child. And two, I can prove it.' He pauses a moment, to catch his breath, the after-effects of his illness perhaps lingering still. 'A few days before my hospital dash, Neil had asked to use the plane, just to take Sonny out over the water for the afternoon, and that morning he'd dropped in beforehand to check if I needed anything for what I thought then was just a bad bout of the flu. Soon after he and Sonny had set off – actually, within the hour – my housekeeper had me in an ambulance. Within twenty-four hours, I was on a ventilator, and out of it for the next three or four weeks.'

'Mr Belgo, I don't understand how this proves the plane crash was an accident?'

'Well, when I eventually got home this week, my housekeeper helped me to access the voice messages on my mobile phone. There were a good few – and, horrific as it is to say, one of them was from Neil. Mid-flight – I don't think he realised he was talking to my voicemail, not me – sheer panic in his voice, asking what this warning light meant, saying they were starting to lose height, circling over the coastline, that he didn't think—' Belgo breaks off, the upset in his voice rising. 'And then, well, the message just cut out. Not like you'd imagine, not like a crash or explosion, more like a soft thud as the line went dead.'

Ali sways a little, her mind fogging as she imagines the scene. Her tongue feels dry, her head full of cotton, and for a moment she almost forgets who it is she has on the phone.

'Mr Belgo,' she says, reining in her concentration as she zooms in on the sight of Max getting up from the table and peering from the window in her direction, 'do you still have that recording?'

'I do.'

'Well, keep it safe, please.' It takes her full focus to finish the conversation. 'Someone will be in touch with you. Thank you.'

For a moment, Ali stands staring into her handset, a brief sensation of euphoria rising within her at the idea of this tragic case coming to a close, of Jago Neill being released from his torturous self-doubt in the aftermath of such loss. She must let him know immediately.

The man they're calling Max leans out of the doorway, hanging on the frame with a rakish smile. 'Everything all right?' he asks.

Ali returns an apologetic smile, a nod.

'Happy to stay for another one? Listen, don't run away – I'm just gonna head up to the gents' a sec.' And he returns inside, buying Ali a free moment in which to make her call.

Jago Neill answers on the first ring. 'DS Samson? I don't suppose you've seen Nell Gale, have you? Her mum's been looking—'

'She's fine,' she replies, cutting him off. 'She's with me. Are you free for a sec?' she asks, at the same time glancing along the alleyway to the open kitchen door, from where the landlord's son is approaching at pace, on his way out for another cigarette, no doubt. 'I've just had a call—' she starts, but confusion derails her, and she turns sharply as Andy Flowers' pale face looms in at her from the darkness.

In a flash of pain, his hand is on her wrist, vice-like, forcing her to drop her phone as she yelps in shock. It hits the gravel path with a crack.

'Hey! Get your hands off me!' Ali cries out, but her words sound muddled and weak. 'Hey! Whadoyou think you're—?'

And before she can even lash out at the boy, to caution him, to pin him against the wall in arrest position, as she's done with others a hundred times before, her knees buckle and her legs give way, and she's caught by another set of waiting arms, and Ali sinks, heavily, like a stone dropped in a pond.

33. Cathy

Sunday

By seven, there's still no sign of Nell, and Dad says they're going to have to eat without her.

Cathy is working hard to disguise the icy spear of anxiety that has crept in over the past hour, but it's there, lodged in her chest cavity, and she feels like a mother whose toddler has vanished on a busy beach. But how to explain this baseless sense of foreboding to anyone else, without sounding like a lunatic?

Just two hours ago, Nell was here, having stuck around for most of the day, helping set up the trestle tables and avoiding Albie's badgering requests for her to look at his family tree. Cathy had watched from the sidelines as Nell chatted comfortably with Jago, even laughing at some small joke he'd made, and for a brief moment she'd allowed herself to imagine they were coming out the other side at last, that harmony might finally be within their reach.

But then, at five, after some whispering in corners with Dylan, Nell had disappeared, announcing that she'd do her best to be back in time for Grandad's dinner but to go on without her if she was late. Cathy had chased down the garden path after her, demanding answers, but Nell had just hopped into the driver's seat of the old Citroën, shutting the door between them.

'Mum, I'll be back, I promise,' she'd said, turning over the engine with a twist of the choke. There was something changed about her; her eyes were still shadowed with something unspoken, but a new energy had broken through, a raw determination. 'I can't explain, but a friend needs me, OK? DS Ali will be there, so you don't need to worry. It's important.'

'Your *grandad* is important,' Cathy had called after her, but the car had already reached the end of the path and turned out onto Allotment Row and away. Jago, who had witnessed the entire exchange through the open back gate, had silently led her back inside and deposited her in the arms of Kip before disappearing himself to leave the family to their private dinner.

The meal itself, with the family gathered around the hotch-potch square of trestle tables and benches in Dad's little back yard, is as upbeat as could be expected considering the uncertainty felt by most about what is to come. Cathy and Kip sit at one end, with old John Gale in his customary Captain's chair at the other, Elliot and Suzie to one side and Dylan and Albie to the other. Beside Cathy sits Nell's favourite chipped red chair, conspicuously empty. Garlanded around the fenced panels and up over the back door and window are strings of fairy lights Albie has fished out of the Christmas box, and it pains Cathy that the poor lad thinks this is some kind of celebration, rather than . . . well, rather than what, she doesn't really know.

They eat, they chat, they avoid the subject of Grandad's terminal illness, and all the while, Cathy can only think about the one person not here: Nell. It is as though Cathy has woken from a deep sleep, as far as her children are concerned, and her guilt and confusion claw away at her silently. She thinks of her daughter, out there in that clapped-out old car, God only knows where, and, more terrifyingly, with whom. 'I'm really sorry about Nell, Dad,' she says now, for the third or fourth time. 'I told her this was important, but, I don't know . . .'

'I'll text her,' Dylan says, as Cathy and Elliot rise to gather the dirty pudding plates, and Suzie argues with Dad that they should get on with the washing up.

'The dishes can wait,' Dad says, pressing Suzie's hand to the table, gently preventing her from getting up. 'Just top up the drinks, lad,' he tells Dylan, who quickly pushes his phone into his pocket. 'And, Kip, fetch me the box on the sideboard, will you? We'll fill Nell in later. Whatever it is that's keeping her, it must be important. Albie?' he says, with a meaningful jerk of his chin.

Moments later, they're all gathered again, Dad with his old box of papers on the table in front of him, Albie with the rolled-up family tree chart he's been dragging around these past couple of weeks. *What is this?* Cathy wants to ask, and for some unfathomable reason, she feels railroaded, excluded, tricked—

'Dad?' she says, without even realising she's spoken.

Dad raises a hand, the grey of his face given brief respite by the golden glow of the lowering sun, as it breaks through from the allotments beyond. 'OK, Cathy. Before I start, I want you all to swear to let me finish talking before you jump in? There are things I need to say, important things, and some of them are going to, well . . .' At this, he gazes down the table with Cathy in his sights. 'I want you to hold your emotions and ask questions only when I'm done.'

A nerve in Cathy's neck has begun twitching, and in the twilight of her father's garden, with Nell's empty chair beside her, she feels as though she is looking at her own empty seat, as

301

though she is the one out there, in imminent danger. 'Do you think Nell is OK?' she whispers to Kip.

He takes her hand and squeezes it. 'Just focus on this, Cath. It's important.' And in that moment she realises: Kip is in on this too. Kip and Albie and the whole damned lot of them.

She takes a breath. 'All right, Dad,' she nods. 'No interruptions. I promise.'

Overhead, a light aircraft buzzes through the dimming blue sky, and Cathy thinks of Jago Neill in her living room next door, reading his book or playing his guitar, and her heart slows its pace.

Dad takes a stack of papers from an envelope and lays them on the tabletop, pushing his reading glasses up his nose. 'First things first. This week, I met with Ned Garner and had him rewrite my will. I want you to hear about this now, save any arguments further down the line. When I'm gone, it's up to you what you do with the Golden Rabbit and the property and the rest, but these are my wishes, written here.' He brings his forefinger down on the paper and draws his gravest stare over each one of his family gathered.

Elliot casts a glance at Cathy, and quickly looks away.

'I've been doing a lot of thinking, about family, and inheritance, and position and pecking order, and it strikes me that in this family the usual order won't work. We've got Elliot and Suzie, who've been running the campsite all these years, come hell or high water – and, Suzie, well, you've been like another daughter to me, in many ways.'

Cathy can't bring herself to look at her sister-in-law, and she can't conceal the sting of her father's words.

'And,' Dad continues, raising his voice to catch her attention, 'we've got Cathy, who, through no fault of her own, has been excluded from that business. Yes, girl, it was wrong. I see now just how wrong we got it, and I want to put that right.' Now he looks to Albie and Dylan. 'Albie, you're one of us Gales, through and through, but Dylan, you should know that so are you, by birth or not. And, of course, there's our Nell.'

For a second, Kip looks uncomfortable, as though suddenly realising he has no real place there, and Cathy bites her tongue as her father has instructed, despite her mounting terror.

'Kip, son. I've wondered about you over the years, and you know what, I think we could've made it easier for you to stick around here with our Cathy. Like a normal couple. If we hadn't been so hard on your unconventional choices along the years, if I'd been more forthright with . . . with others—'

'You mean *Mum*,' Cathy blurts out, bitterly. 'She's the one who thought Kip wasn't good enough. She's the one who kept me out of the business. The one who couldn't forgive me for getting knocked up—'

Dad glares a warning, and she falls silent.

'With all this in mind,' he goes on, 'I've taken the decision to divide my estate – the business, the property, the money in the bank – five ways.' He picks up the document and runs his fingers down a bullet list attached to the front page. 'Elliot, Cathy, Nell, Dylan and Albie – each of you will receive a twenty per cent stake in the business, transferable only within the family. Albie, as you're under eighteen, your parents will manage your share for the time being. And, all of you, well, you'll need to sit down as a group and thrash out how this is going to work, in terms of the day-to-day running of the business.

'My suggestion would be, Suzie and Elliot, you two keep running the campsite, and Kip and Cath take on the grounds and develop the smallholding you've always talked about. Fresh produce for the farm shop, home-laid eggs and suchlike. If the youngsters, Dylan, Nell and Albie, decide to explore other avenues, they will retain their share until such time as they decide whether they want a place in the business or not.'

'But why five ways?' Dylan asks, looking perplexed. 'I mean, thank you. But isn't it convention to leave your estate to your direct offspring, to later pass on to the next generation as they see fit?' He sounds like a fifty-year-old accountant, not a teenage gamer with a wispy beard.

Dad's eyes crease with amusement. 'Dylan, you're not wrong. That is usual tradition. But the problem I face is that the generations in this family are somewhat – how can I put it – untraditional. Muddled.'

'*Muddled*? In what way are they muddled?' Cathy asks, and it occurs to her that she's the only one at the table asking this question.

Dad pushes the will document to one side and pulls across the old box he had Kip fetch from the living room. 'This week, Kip brought young Albie to me, with this family tree project he's been mithering on about all summer.' He ruffles his grandson's head, and Albie's face breaks out a shy smile. 'He asked if he could look through all the old family albums and whatnot, and, well, cut a long story short, he ended up turning over a bunch of other stuff. Papers I hadn't looked at, from way back.' He eyes his two grown children significantly. 'Stuff your mother wasn't so keen on sharing and there's the truth.'

He reaches into the box and lifts out an old certificate. 'This one here,' he says, handing it to Elliot to read and pass along the table, 'this is the death certificate of our second child, Lisa Anne. Taken from us when she was just five years old. Elliot's little sister.'

Dylan is the only one who appears surprised.

'Lisa Anne was no secret, but, fair to say, we didn't talk about her.' Dad pauses a moment, his rheumy eyes on some unseen memory. 'Too painful. For your mother, in particular. And for Elliot.'

Elliot is wiping his eyes, the pain of his misplaced guilt still surface-level, raw.

'And this one here,' John Gale says, lifting out the next document, 'is your birth certificate, Cathy. Your original birth certificate, from 1984.'

What does he mean, *original*?

Her father hesitates, holds her gaze. 'And this document here . . . this is your adoption papers.'

Kip's grip on Cathy's hand intensifies, and she snatches it away, all at once certain that he knew before her, that they all knew. She looks around the table, mute with shock. Elliot and Suzie are huddled together, heads hung; Dylan has the expression of one who knew but had just been waiting for confirmation; and Albie is gazing at her wide-eyed, unblinking. Guilty. They all know.

'So, I'm not a Gale?' she asks, her voice hushed, her eyes locked on Dad's at the end of the table.

'You are a Gale,' he replies.

'But *by birth*,' she spits. 'I'm not a Gale by birth?' All these years, all those casual remarks about her being the spit of her dad, with her mother's red hair, and her brother's blue eyes – all these years, and every word of it – a fiction. *A lie.*

'You *are* a Gale,' he repeats. 'Irene, your mum – she loved you, Cath, but she didn't carry you, not like she did Elliot, or Lisa Anne. Even so, that's Gale blood running through your veins all right.'

Cathy loses it. She throws her hands in the air, brushing Kip away as he tries to calm her. 'I'm either a Gale or I'm not! I'm either *adopted* or I'm not! How can I have Gale blood running through my veins if I'm not yours?'

Now it's Elliot's turn to raise his voice. 'For God's sake, Dad! Just give her the certificate, will you! Let her see for herself!'

305

'Let me see what?!'

Elliot snatches the document from Dad's hand and leans over the table to pass it to his sister, who grabs it, her eyes struggling to focus on the boxes and headings laid out on the decades-old certificate before her. 'Adoption Release Form – Confidential'. There's nothing here that makes sense, nothing that Cathy can relate to at all—

With a clatter of wood and metal, Jago rushes through the back gate, cradling Albie's puppy like a child. He casts a dark glance about the party table, eyes landing on Dad. 'John,' he says, breathlessly, striding over to drop Lump into Albie's lap. 'I need the truck. It's Nell. She's with DS Ali, and I don't know what's going on – but I think they need help.'

'It's in the repair shop, lad,' Dad says, planting his palms on the tabletop, steadying himself to rise. 'Cathy . . .?'

Cathy shakes her head robotically. 'Nell's taken mine.'

Jago, usually so serene, is pacing in the space between the gate and the dinner table, murmuring to himself, one hand thrust into his hairline, the other at his chest, and he looks to Cathy like a man trying to solve an impossible riddle. His fear, worn so plainly, almost paralyses her, like a contagion.

In a breath, Dylan is on his feet, snatching up the keys to Suzie's Land Rover and throwing them into the open hands of Jago Neill. 'Mum's had a drink – you'll have to drive.'

Already heading through the back gate with Jago, Dylan's focus is on his mobile phone, as he zooms in on the screen and ignores his mum's protests. 'I know where they are,' he says, turning back to look at Cathy and holding up his phone. 'I've got her on a tracker.'

Elliot picks up the nearest full wine glass and downs its contents in a single pale-eyed gulp, this new crisis setting him back in one fell swoop. On seeing this, Suzie pushes her chair back from the table, disappointment in her expression. 'Dylan, wait!' she calls after her son, and with urgency – with authority – she beckons for Cathy to follow.

There is no way to make any sense of this; it is as though the gods have pressed a remote control and randomly changed channels on Cathy's life. Without pause, she too is on her feet, the adoption certificate flung aside, irrelevant. *They need help*, Jago had said. *Nell needs her help.*

'Kip, you stay with Dad and Albie,' she says, not waiting for a reply. 'I'm going with Suzie.'

The two women race through the gate, into the dark lane beyond, where Jago is fumbling with Suzie's bunch of keys in the fading light, trying to get a grip on the right one. Suzie snatches it from his hands.

'But I don't understand, Dylan. Why is Nell with the detective?' Cathy demands, her hand already on the rear passenger door. 'Why are they out there together?'

Dylan frowns. 'Because they're trying to catch the man. From the dating app!'

'What man?' Cathy yells, frustration overspilling.

The car doors unlock with a clunk.

'The man who raped Nell, Auntie Cathy.'

Cathy's world shunts again, and without another word, she and Suzie bundle into the back seats of the Land Rover, as Jago, engine revving, speeds them off into the night.

34. Nell

Sunday

Nell's hand is on the door handle like a reflex, and she's out the vehicle, standing in the twilit car park of the Five Bells, gaping at the space where DS Ali had been just moments ago.

'Nell!' Casey hisses, still clinging to the passenger seat, sticking rigidly to DS Samson's instructions. 'We're not meant to—'

'Fuck!' Nell shrieks. *'They've got her, Casey* – they've taken her!' She spins, a full circle, trying to locate Ali's whereabouts. It's as though she's vanished into thin air. *Where the hell is Benny?*

Behind her, a car engine starts up with a roar, and a tatty white Audi, its headlights illuminating the side of the Five Bells, tears out of the car park with a spray of gravel. Adrenaline pumping, Nell breaks into a sprint, out into the side street beyond, keys already in hand as she jumps into her mum's old Citroën and races it back round the side of the pub.

Casey is already at the kerbside, ready to jump in, just as DC Benny emerges through the back entrance, suddenly alert at the sight of his undercover car abandoned, doors open.

'They've taken her!' Nell bellows through her open window. 'It's a white Audi! They've taken Ali!'

And with this, she puts her foot to the floor of the knackered old Citroën Dyane and speeds onto the high street, thankful for once for the town's one-way system, restricting the route the other car can take. Up ahead, the traffic lights are on green, and there's no sign of the Audi at all. Nell pushes her foot harder to the pedal, jumping the light as it turns amber, and causing Casey to scream behind the shield of her hands.

'Is your seat belt on?' Nell barks, slotting her own into place as an afterthought.

Casey nods mutely, and for what feels like an eternity of held breath they sail along Market Avenue, terrified that they've lost her. That DS Ali is gone for good. Both girls know exactly what is at stake here; both fear the worst is already unfolding – that their drive to protect another has fallen at the first hurdle.

'There!' Casey cries out, catching a flash of the white vehicle turning right at the mini-roundabout ahead.

With grim determination, Nell leans into the steering wheel, jaw set, the engine of her mum's forty-year-old car railing against the thrashing she's giving it. 'We can't let them hurt her,' she says, throwing a glance at Casey in the passenger seat beside her, feeling the vehicle teeter a little as she takes the roundabout in third gear, barely touching the brake as she turns.

Casey hardly makes a sound, but, when Nell's mobile goes off from the footwell where she dumped it, she retrieves the phone and relays the messages popping up on the screen.

'It's Dylan. He says they're on their way – he wants to know what's going on.'

Nell scowls, focusing on the Audi far ahead on the last road out of town. When they hit the roundabout that's coming up, there are three possible routes, and if she misses which way they go—

'Tell him I'm fine. Tell him DS Ali has been taken – we don't know where, but we're approaching the big Esso roundabout—' Up ahead, the Audi takes a left. 'We're on the Port Regis road, heading out towards the campsite. He'll know.'

Casey relays the message, as Nell flogs the old Citroën as hard as it'll go, cursing as she hovers at the roundabout, waiting for a slow-moving haulage truck to pass. As she turns onto the Port Regis road, her stomach drops: the Audi, with its big sodding engine and fast acceleration, is nowhere to be seen.

'Ask Dylan who "they" is?' she says.

Casey taps away furiously, every now and then glancing up at the windscreen, whispering tiny prayers under her breath. A few seconds later, a message returns. 'Dylan says, *Cathy, Suzie and the pilot*,' Casey quickly reports. '*And your mum knows about the attack*, he says. *Sorry, it kind of slipped out.*'

Nell shakes the thought away; it's not going to help her now if she starts thinking about the implications of having to explain this horror story to her mum.

Out of the darkness, the rear lights of the Audi suddenly rematerialise, the vehicle having got stuck behind a large motorhome on the hairpin bends leading to Mere Farm. To Nell's disbelief, as they approach the entrance to the Golden Rabbit holiday camp, the vehicle slows and swings in, its rear lights now disappearing altogether.

'What the hell are they doing?' she says out loud, and, desperate to keep sight of the car, she gives the accelerator every last bit of welly she's got, until 'pop!' – something goes, and the Citroën spins like a dodgem, and lands nose-first in the shallow ditch.

35. DS Ali Samson

Sunday

It's their laughter that rouses her, not fully bringing her up into consciousness, but rather teasing her into a glimpse of the things that are happening, to her, around her, over which she has no control.

The man calling himself Max has got her by the legs, while the other – the landlord's son, she can only assume – has his forearms hooked beneath her armpits, as they manhandle her from their car. *Andy*. That's his name, she recalls, anchoring herself to firm details. Andy Flowers.

Fleetingly, Ali thinks about her phone lying broken in the gravel outside the Five Bells, and she wonders how far away Benny is, following the Bluetooth tracker disc she'd slipped inside her wallet hours earlier.

'Man, this is genius!' Andy Flowers is saying, as they deposit her on the ground, propped up against cold metal, legs stuck out straight, like a rag doll. 'What made you think of this place?'

Max nudges Ali's thigh with the toe of his sneaker, testing her for fight. She lowers her lids, feigns full unconsciousness, which is no effort whatsoever. 'I was camping here,' he says. 'When that plane came down last month.'

'Seriously?'

'For real. The night we did that ginger one.'

'Ha, the Gale girl. *Ironic*.'

'Ironic?'

'Well, her family owns the place – the campsite.'

Max laughs. 'I love a bit of synchronicity.'

Andy gives a little grunt, clearly not knowing what the word means. '*Yeah*. But how come you were camping?'

'It's what I do, mate. I like to keep moving. No trail. In my line of business, it's not a great idea to stay still for too long. It's why I never keep the same phone number for more than a week at a time. Why I won't do social media.'

'Your line of business?' Andy asks, and as though in answer, Max stoops, casually slapping Ali's cheek with an open hand.

'*Adult entertainment*, let's call it. You don't think I do this just for the fun of it, do you?' He laughs at his own joke, and it is a cruel sound. 'Anyway, I guessed the place might still be empty – I'm just gutted I didn't think of it earlier.'

Ali breathes shallowly. So, they are at the campsite? At the Golden Rabbit? She tunes in to the drag and pull of the tide beyond the coastal path, to the sea-spray damp of the August night air. Andy, Ali notices, has fallen quiet, and despite her physical fatigue, she is slowly gathering her thoughts enough to recognise that he is just a bit player in this game. That it is Max who calls the shots, and others, perhaps more than just Andy, who do much of his bidding.

Ali risks a look, easing open her eyelids to take in the scene around her. Beneath her fingers, the ground is gritty and rough, and through the almost total darkness, she can see the shape of the fallen shower block, lit only by the feeble light of the moon against a hazy mackerel sky. Ahead of her, the campsite spreads out into darkness, and at once she recognises that the metal object behind her, smooth and vast, is what's left of the skate ramp. She's in the crash site, right at the heart of it, and she has no way of knowing what these men have got in store for her.

'So, where are we going to do this?' Max asks. 'We should get some light on her, since we don't have to worry about anyone coming along out here. Oh, and check if she's got any cash on her, will you?'

Andy's breath is suddenly on Ali's neck as he stoops in close. She feels his hands inside her light jacket, rummaging about in search of a wallet, and her heart feels as though it might stop. He pulls back, and the flashlight of a mobile phone passes over her as he goes through its contents. With great effort, Ali flexes her fingers, testing her body out for the prospect of self-defence. But her movements are insignificant, her muscles weak as a baby's.

'Fuck me – no!' Andy gasps, drawing Max's attention as he waves Ali's ID card in the night air. 'You're gonna wanna see this.' He slides her wallet into his back pocket and hands over the card.

Standing over her as though she's not even there, Max takes the ID and holds it under the light. 'Oh, man,' he laughs, leaning on his knees to peer into Ali's face. 'A fucking copper? You have to be kidding me?' And for a moment Ali thinks she is saved. That now, surely, they will simply turn on their heels and go.

'We should get out of here, mate,' Andy hisses. 'We should—'

But Max just laughs again. 'A copper,' he repeats, and he leans in to squeeze her cheek between his thumb and forefinger. 'Would you believe it? You know, I think we're going to have to give this one a different tag.'

Andy, slow on the uptake, gives a nervous little grunt. 'Not *Alley Dog*, then?'

Max slaps his lackey on the arm and flings the ID into Ali's lap. 'Not this one, mate. This one's special. This one's a Pig.'

36. Cathy

Sunday

As the Land Rover plunges on along the dark night road, Cathy sits silently beside her sister-in-law on the back seat, her mind struggling to form a coherent explanation for any of what she just heard at her father's dinner table. But from the moment Dylan had blurted out those words, her own thoughts had seemed to stutter to a halt as she stared into the face of that terrible revelation, the worst of them all. 'They're trying to catch the man who raped Nell.' *Who raped Nell.*

It is everything she has ever feared for her daughter, and everything she has tried to protect her from. Everything she herself has run from, her whole adult life. When she thinks of the sleepovers her young daughter missed out on, the school residential trips Cathy claimed they 'couldn't afford', the potential boyfriends she'd disapproved of on sight; all in the name of protecting her Nell from the predator lurking in the shadows, or, worse still, hiding in plain sight.

How could this happen? First to Cathy, and now to Nell? How is it that a girl can't just go out into the world and get by, without arming herself against the monster around every corner? Almost two decades ago, in the aftermath of her own attack, Cathy had wondered how it was possible for a person to endure such proximity of violence and hatred and not die from a shattered spirit. As she'd carried Kip's baby – her Nell – to full term in the months that followed, she'd questioned, again and again: how did her baby not die, as a result of its mother's trauma?

Through the darkness, she feels Jago's eyes on her, holding her in the rear-view mirror. 'Steady, Cathy, my maiden. Yes? We will find her. Stay strong.'

Suzie turns to look at her. Her half-shadowed expression is grave, and for what feels like the first time in many, many years, Cathy does not avert her gaze, seeing her, being seen. 'We *will* find her,' Suzie echoes.

Leaning in, Cathy pats Dylan's shoulder, in the passenger seat beside Jago. 'Can you still see where she is?' she asks, and her nephew holds up his mobile in response, to show the tracking movement of Nell's phone. They themselves are on the Port Regis road now, the location the girl travelling with Nell had told Dylan, but in the past few minutes there's been no pick-up from Nell's mobile at all.

'Do you think they're headed to the campsite?' Jago asks. His eyes flash at Cathy in the mirror, small glints of light. 'Is it likely?'

Nobody responds; nobody knows. Cathy wants to ask Dylan for more details – more about this man they're pursuing, more about the attack, the when, the where, the why-didn't-she-tell-me – but nothing in Cathy's mind is working properly. In her mind, she sees a picture of her own men left sitting at her father's hastily arranged dinner table, still there beneath the stars in his ex-council house garden: her dying father, her patient man, her beautiful boy, and her broken brother slowly getting smashed on Suzie's white wine. A sob catches in her chest and she wishes Kip were here to hold her.

With a heavy foot on the brakes, Jago brings the Land Rover to an emergency stop and flips the headlights to full beam. There, nose-down in the ditch, just yards from the turning to the Golden Rabbit holiday camp, is Cathy's orange Citroën Dyane. And Nell is nowhere to be seen.

37. Nell

By just the light of their phones, the girls push through the hedge to a shortcut along the back field, sticking to the edge for fear of detection. Any injuries sustained in the ditch crash are no more than bruises, and now Casey and Nell seem to be operating in some strange kind of unity, in pursuit of their target. They move swiftly, silently, alert for signs of light or life coming from the holiday camp now just a few hundred yards from their position.

Only minutes ago, the car holding DS Ali had turned into the Golden Rabbit's entrance, so Nell and Casey know the men have brought her here, and they don't even want to think about what happens next if they don't reach her quickly enough.

They arrive at the low fence to the demolished playground, the mound of the crumpled skate ramp hazily outlined against the mottled moonlit sky. To their left, the empty campsite rolls down towards the cliff edge and beach below; to the right is the shower block, folded in at the far end but appearing strangely intact in the milky darkness.

Just as Nell tunes in to the sound of car tyres over gravel, headlights pierce the playground area, an assault on their dark-adjusted eyes. The girls drop to their knees, grateful for the great hulk of the skate ramp, and cautiously edge closer to the scene, undetected.

Squinting, Nell can make out one figure, passing across the full-beam headlamps of the Audi now parked beside the shower block entrance. The beam is aimed, quite clearly, into the space where the plane came down. Where Albie lost his arm. Where Albie nearly died. In the far distance, the ancient mound of Highcap Hill watches over them, a silent observer.

'It's Andy,' Casey whispers, breathing shallowly beside Nell. 'What's he doing?'

From their concealed position, it is impossible to see what Andy can see – what the car headlights are shining on – but as he moves to one side it becomes clear to Nell that he has his phone in his hand, and he's filming.

'Move her to the right a bit, mate!' he shouts over, the sound of his voice lifting clearly on the still night air.

'Like this?' Max yells back, a grunt in the last word, as though he's lugging something heavy.

They're positioning her, Nell thinks. *They're setting up the best angle, before . . . before they—*

Casey yanks the waistband of Nell's jeans, bringing her staggering back to the ground. 'What are you doing?' she hisses. 'They'll see you!'

'So what? There are three of us – and only two of them!'

'DS Ali's gonna be no use! Shouldn't that other policeman be here by now?'

Nell feels around on the ground, discarding pieces of shattered playground and rubble, until her fingers land on a metal bar: perhaps a fractured handle or safety rail. She weighs it up in

318

her hands, imagines swinging it at the back of Max's head. She nudges Casey and gestures to the south end of the playground.

'When I say "go", you run round that side and start making a load of noise. To distract them.' Pointing her bar in the opposite direction, she indicates which way she intends to head.

Casey's eyes shine brightly, her fear close to the surface.

'Just shout "POLICE!" or something,' Nell urges her, and with a sharp intake of breath, she hisses, 'GO!' and breaks into a sprint, praying to God that Casey doesn't bottle out.

Seconds later, despite the glare of the Audi's headlamps, she has Max in her line of vision, as well as DS Ali, who she can now see propped up against the metal skate ramp. Max is tugging at the detective's shirt, making a show of it for the cameraman, Andy, the one person Nell cannot see, try as she might.

From the far side of playground, Casey's cry pierces the hush of the abandoned holiday camp. 'Hello! Yes, police? Yes!'

Max springs back at the unexpected disturbance, his stance rigid as he prepares to attack.

'They're here at the Golden Rabbit!' Casey continues, yelling her fake phone conversation at the top of her voice.

Nell makes a run for it, raising the metal bar above her head, poised to bring it down—

But she never quite makes it that far, because, from somewhere in the darkness, Andy is on her like a panther, knocking her from her feet and slamming the wind from her lungs as her back hits the baked earth with a thud.

For a moment, she is dazed, too disorientated and breathless to hit back. Aware that he has her wrists pinned, she twists her head towards the sound of Casey's screech, only just able to make out the blur of two figures steaking past, one in pursuit of the other. Momentarily, Andy loosens his hold, and in an instinctive rush, Nell hooks her fingers into his hair, yanking his face against hers, to snarl a warning through her gritted teeth. 'That woman – she's got a tracker in her pocket. Any minute now her back-up will be here, and I hope they give you the kicking of your life.'

A fresh memory assaults her senses: the smell of him. A memory of this man, Andy Flowers, of a struggle in that nightmare alleyway, moments after her rape, as in her doped-up state, she'd fought to push past the hooded cameraman who jostled before her, mocking her, prolonging her humiliation.

Yes, she'd really fought back, hadn't she? Just as her mother taught her to. She *hadn't* just let it happen to her, any more than she'd wanted it, or asked for it, and, God knows, if she'd not been drugged almost to the state of unconsciousness, she'd have killed the bastards, she's sure.

She thinks of herself that morning after, weeping by the stone marker on her long walk home, right before that plane came down. She'd checked her watch for the time and seen with horror the hairs caught in its strap, not her own hairs. And, while still her mind couldn't quite acknowledge what had really befallen her, she'd known it was a bad thing, that that watch had to go. It was Andy Flowers' hair, torn from his scalp in her fury and shame; now buried, with the watch, deep in the earth upon Highcap Hill.

Nell releases her grip.

At once, the crushing weight lifts, and Nell rolls onto her side, to watch the dark silhouette of Andy Flowers sprinting towards the car headlights, from where the sound of a car door opening and closing echoes across the open grassland.

'Nell?' DS Ali is now sitting upright against the ramp where Max had dumped her.

With great effort, Nell pushes herself to standing and rushes to the woman's side. 'Did you see where they went?' Nell asks in a whisper. '*Max* – he was going after Casey.'

DS Ali swallows hard, as though parched. 'The shower block,' she manages, and, as Andy reverses the Audi, revving like a learner on his first driving lesson, Nell tears towards the building, momentarily halted by the glare of overhead floodlights suddenly illuminating the area, bright as day. She glances in the direction of the office, way over beyond the main path, the office where the electrical boxes are situated, along with the back-up generator necessary to power these lights. Who, apart from the Gales, would have keys to get in there? No one.

Which means someone from her family is here; they've come for her.

With renewed conviction, she snatches up the metal bar and strides inside the shower block to locate her friend.

38. Cathy

Sunday

Once inside the gates of the holiday camp, Jago kills the head-lights and navigates the speed bumps at a snail's pace, alerted to the presence of life down by the playground, where a car is parked, its headlamps on full beam.

'We should leave the Landie here,' Dylan says, as they draw level with the giant rabbit mascot, now leaning sadly in the shadows of the maintenance shed. 'Take them by surprise.'

'This isn't the movies, Dylan,' Cathy snaps. 'We're not executing some sort of hijack.'

Jago stops the car at the junction to the office. 'No, Cathy, he's right. We don't know what we're going to find down there. We might well need to take them by surprise, whoever they are. And we can only do that on foot.'

But as they pile out, it becomes clear that Jago, with his still damaged body, is going to slow them down.

Beyond the playground, distant shouting rises into the air: a girl's voice, but not Nell's. Cathy releases a whimper. 'We've got to get down there.'

Suzie pushes the large set of keys into her son's hand. 'Dylan, you go with Jago and open up the office.' She tugs at a red-topped key. 'This one, right? When you're in there, I want you to turn on the electrics in the cupboard – and if the electricity doesn't come on, switch on the generator, OK? It's the floodlights we want – they were all set up last week, so the minute that electricity gets through, they should come on.'

Dylan scowls at her. 'I should come with you, Mum – help Nell.'

Suzie gives a firm shake of her head. 'No time to waste, Dylan. You know where everything is – and grab some blankets on your way out, in case anyone's hurt.'

Jago grasps Cathy by the shoulders and steadies her, his eyes just inches from hers. 'Go find your daughter, Cathy. *Go!*'

As the two men hurry towards the dark office, Cathy and Suzie break into a jog, heading down the landscaped entrance path towards the shower block and that lit-up car, no words between them, matching each other step for step as both try to interpret the scene ahead of them.

Reaching the demolished end of the large shower block, Cathy can suddenly make out the shape of her daughter in the distant playground, where those car headlights are trained on a long-haired woman, propped up by the skate ramp. Nell is clambering – no, *staggering* – to her feet, as a young lad runs from her to the car, which he starts up, jerkily reversing, revving, stalling and revving up again.

All at once, the overhead floodlights bleach out the darkness, and Cathy and Suzie come to a fleeting halt, shielding their eyes as they read the scene. Nell hasn't seen them, focused as she is on her objective, and, with horror, Cathy realises she's running straight for the shower block entrance, mindless of the 'Danger' ribbons flapping out their warning in the night breeze.

With still some several hundred yards to go before they reach Nell, the two women hasten into a sprint, Cathy sticking to the firm footing of the main drive, Suzie racing alongside her on the grass. In the distance, the Audi has now picked up pace, accelerating up the drive towards them, speeding faster, ever faster – too fast for Cathy to react or leap aside.

As the car bears down on her, the last thing Cathy hears is the sound of Suzie screaming her name, before she feels herself thrown from the path by a mighty thump to the chest. It is only when the car, tyres squealing, ploughs headlong into the front entrance of the shower block that Cathy realises it's not she who is hurt but Suzie, who now lies bleeding into the grass, her ankle bent at a stomach-turning angle.

From the driver side of the shunted Audi, the young lad tumbles out and breaks into a run, across the campsite towards the coastal path, where he's swallowed into the darkness.

Cathy scrabbles over the ground to Suzie's side, already grappling her phone from her back pocket. 'Oh, Jesus, Suzie – *Suzie*? Can you breathe OK?'

Suzie exhales, gives the merest indication that, yes, she's breathing. Within seconds, Cathy has the emergency services on the line, and an ambulance is on the way. Another ambulance attending Golden Rabbit holiday park, just five weeks since Jago's plane came down, rupturing life as the Gale family once knew it.

'How did he hit *you*? You were way over on the grass – you—' Cathy brings her hand to her own chest, now smarting from the impact, and it comes to her in a flash of understanding that it wasn't the car that had collided with her, but Suzie. 'You pushed me clear?'

Wincing in pain, Suzie blinks in acknowledgement.

'But – why? Look at you, your ankle? Why would you do something so stupid?'

In the distance, bathed in the strange daylight white of the floodlamps, two figures emerge from the shower block, calmly walking across the ruined playground, hand-in-hand. And just as it occurs to Cathy that in fact it *is* like a scene from some dystopian movie, the shower block gives out a low animal groan and the remainder of its roof caves in.

Now supporting the third figure – DS Ali, Cathy finally recognises – Nell and the other girl stagger from the playground and collapse onto the dried grass, where Dylan fusses around, making himself useful with blankets and water from his backpack.

'You haven't answered me,' Cathy says, turning her attention back to her sister-in-law. 'I thought you hated me.'

Through her weakness, Suzie almost smiles. 'I don't hate you, Cathy.'

'OK, but I'm "the bane of your life", apparently. Why would you risk yourself like that?'

Suzie's expression is strangely tender, and she seems to take an age to answer. 'I think maybe you know why,' she eventually murmurs. 'Deep down.'

For long seconds, Cathy stares into that face, only looking away to glance towards the distant silhouette of Jago Neill, limping across the campsite draped in a blanket, looking every bit the fallen angel.

'The adoption certificate,' Cathy whispers, as the fog of her mind lifts, and it all becomes clear. '*You* were the one who gave me up?'

Only now does Cathy recognise that Suzie's relationship with her over the years hasn't been so much cold, but distant. No matter how Cathy has tried to get close to her sister-in-law, even from the youngest age, Suzie has always kept her at arm's length.

Now, Suzie's eyes are on her, and a single tear escapes into her pale hair.

Fixing her gaze towards the distant mound of Highcap Hill, Cathy thinks of her brother, forever tortured by the murder of his little sister, on his watch. All these years, Cathy had suspected it was that child's death that was at the heart of the special bond she and Elliot shared, but perhaps that was just another fiction. Perhaps his kindness, and his unwavering loyalty towards her, was something else altogether. 'And Elliot?'

'He's your dad,' Suzie replies, a whisper.

Cathy turns her attention to her own daughter across the dark grassy plain, putting herself at risk for those other women, and her love rears up like the tide. Far off, the sound of sirens drifts on the sea air, drawing closer by the second.

'She's tough,' Cathy says, meeting Suzie's gaze again. 'Nell. I think she's probably a bit like you.'

Suzie's fingers brush against Cathy's hand, and she answers, a sob and a smile in her voice. 'And you. Poor cow.'

39. DS Ali Samson

Tuesday

In the thirty-six hours since DC Benny Garner picked up Andy Flowers on the coastal path to Highcap, it seems all the loose threads of the case have converged. Questions which seemed previously too tangled have been answered, and test results are in.

Of course, Trelawney is furious, and Ali knows the only reason the boss hasn't suspended her for her 'unconventional' methods is because she got a result, and a good one at that. She makes a mental note to claim that pint he'd waged her, with his 'must be a previous offender' certainty.

As she pulls up in the police parking bay of Dorset County Hospital, she finds Benny already waiting for her, leaning against his vehicle, brushing crumbs from his jacket. They walk together, heading for the orthopaedic department, where Suzie Gale is being treated for a compound fracture to her right ankle.

'You feeling OK?' Benny asks, handing her a takeaway coffee he picked up on the way through. 'I thought Trelawney told you to take the week off?'

'The medics gave me the all-clear – and I feel fine.' She glances at him as he holds the door for her, scowling at the concern she sees in his face. 'Since when have you known me to dip out of a case before it's done, Benny?'

He laughs and follows her into the lift, thoughtfully drinking his coffee as they head up to the third floor.

Much as Ali had expected, most of the Gale family are gathered in Suzie's private room, even old John Gale, who she understands to be seriously ill with no prospect of getting better. Suzie's husband, Elliot, sits close at her bedside, while, opposite, Cathy perches on the edge of Kip's armchair, Albie beside them, his arm draped around his mum's shoulder. Suzie, fully alert but with the hooded eyes of someone in discomfort, is reclined in the bed, her leg elevated and encased in a protective cage.

'No Nell?' Ali asks, after the greetings are made and she and Benny have dragged in chairs from the waiting room outside.

But at that moment Nell appears through the door, with her cousin Dylan in tow, each carrying a large box of Dunkin' Donuts, and chatting lightly.

'Oh!' Nell says, on seeing Ali. 'I didn't know you were coming – d'you want one?' She holds up the box and smiles, and Ali realises this is the lightest version of Nell she's seen. In spite of the nerve-racking events of the weekend, she's like a different girl.

Ali gestures for the pair to take a seat. 'I'll have one in a minute, Nell, thank you. But, first, I wanted to update you on the case. On the cases.'

'*Cases*?' Kip frowns.

'Jago,' Cathy explains. 'The plane crash.'

Ali nods. She's just come from him, at Allotment Row, where she found him packing up his few belongings, with Albie's little puppy watching his every move, anxious at the signs of his human preparing to leave.

'Yes, Jago. We've now heard from the gentleman whose plane Jago was flying, and we have concrete evidence that the crash was completely unintentional – and, in fact, was down to engine failure. Jago Neill was not responsible for the crash or his son's death – or Albie's accident – and now that we have a fixed address for him, he's been told he's free to leave. I expect the authorities will want to talk to him about his disappearance at some point, but as far as we're concerned, here in Highcap, there's nothing more to do. I think he's planning on setting off this afternoon.'

A tangible melancholy permeates the room, and for long moments, Ali waits for someone to say something.

'The fella doesn't have to rush off,' John Gale says. 'Maybe it'll do him good to stay a week or two longer?' He casts a glance over his gathered family. 'No skin off our noses, is it?'

The room breaks into a clamour of agreement, and even Suzie, in her weakened state, seems to be in favour of having 'the pilot' stay for a while. 'Dylan,' she says, her voice raspy after her operation, 'step out and give him a quick call, will you? Tell him not to go anywhere until Cathy gets back?'

Dylan gives his mum a dependable bob of the head and exits the room, mobile in hand, that ever-present rucksack still attached to his back.

Ali lowers her voice, knowing the next part requires some sensitivity. 'And then there's the bigger case – and the incident from Sunday night, down at the Golden Rabbit.'

She rests her gaze on Nell, who has already given her permission to speak frankly, the girl having now broken the worst of it to her family. Nell gives her a slow, steady nod.

'I'm going to try to keep this simple, and I'd like you to save any questions to the end, all right? By now, you'll know that Nell was a victim of a sexual assault – a rape – after her drink was spiked during a first date in the Five Bells pub. That assault was filmed and circulated, without her consent.'

Ali pauses, to allow the information to settle.

'She was not the only victim, and, since joining up the dots with some of our fellow south coast police agencies, we are confident that the perpetrators of Nell's crime are just two cogs in a much bigger wheel of online attacks and illegal film distribution. Benny?'

Benny opens his little notebook. 'Unfortunately, while the victims in these videos are identifiable, the assailant has taken steps to ensure that *he* is not. Without physical evidence or witnesses, it's extremely difficult to make a case. But the pair attacked again, and this time we have several witnesses – including Nell and myself. The would-be victim was DS Ali Samson here.'

Stilling the shocked expressions of the assembled Gale family, Ali holds up her hands. 'I'm fine. Thanks to your brave gal here, coming to my rescue.'

Benny continues. 'Yesterday we had some lab results back, tying the DNA from beneath one victim's fingernail with – well, with something else we found on the scene. The two come from the same source – so all we needed now was a person to match them to.'

'And?' Cathy asks, unable to hold back.

'And we found him – trapped under the rubble of the collapsed shower block at your holiday park, where DS Ali's attack took place. We've tested his DNA and it's a match.'

'Thank God for that,' Kip exhales. 'So, you've arrested him?'

Ali addresses her reply to Nell. 'No. We've taken him to the county mortuary. He won't be hurting anyone else again.'

What was it Benny had told her, after he'd attended the scene that night, as paramedics were still checking Ali over?

'His head was a mess – he must've died instantly. Who knew that an overhead beam could cause an injury like that?' Ali has chosen to feign ignorance, but the truth is, she will never forget the sight of Nell heading into that shower block, in pursuit of her attacker, in defence of her friend. A metal bar in her hand.

'It was an accident,' Ali says now, her eyes still fixed on Nell's. 'There were plenty of "Danger" signs everywhere, but for some reason, that young man chose to go into a condemned building. Nobody's fault but his own.'

'And the other guy?' Elliot asks. 'The one videoing?'

Benny taps a pen against his notepad. 'Well, the good news is that we arrested Andy Flowers, who we believe to be the cameraman in all three of the cases we've been investigating here in Highcap. We think he was the one spiking the drinks at the bar; the one disabling the CCTV cameras at the back of the pub. We can charge him with kidnapping and attacking a police officer – in fact, he was found with DS Samson's wallet and tracker in his pocket. But the bad news is that, for the three sexual assaults we're investigating, for Flowers, we don't have anything other than circumstantial evidence. We don't have anything physical.'

'Oh!' Nell says, her eyes lighting on her cousin as he returns to the room. 'Dylan, show them what we've got in your rucksack.'

Ali and the rest of the group watch on, as the lad carefully unzips his backpack, and takes out a clear food bag containing a large red wristwatch.

'Is that the watch I gave you for Christmas, Nell, girl?' John Gale asks.

She nods, taking the bag from her cousin and passing it to Ali. There, coiled around the strap joint, is a clump of dark brown hair, dusted with what looks like earth. 'I fought him,' Nell says. 'Andy Flowers. After the attack. I fought him, and

331

his hair got caught in my watch. Would hair give you good DNA?' she asks.

Benny's face breaks into a wide smile. 'Oh, yes. Hair would give us some excellent DNA, Nell.'

Nell Gale turns towards her mother, still perched on Kip's chairside next to Suzie. 'I fought him, Mum,' she says, and it seems to Ali that this is the most important thing Nell needs her mother to know.

'Good girl,' the two women at the far end of the room say, in unison. Cathy and Suzie, both studying Nell with pride. 'Good girl.'

EPILOGUE

Jago | Two weeks later

The wedding takes place on John Gale's allotment, on an early September morning as the mist lifts lazily from the pumpkin beds and the rising sun throws long bean-trellis shadows across the dewy grass.

The bride and groom wear matching outfits, embroidered kaftans picked out at the artisan market in town, and each wears a crown of late-summer flowers, fashioned by the other's hands. There are no bridesmaids, no pageboys and no ushers, but the family are there, a gathering of Gales to celebrate the union of Cathy and Kip, old lovers who have survived the endless push and pull of life to stay connected for two decades, tethered by their children, and by their love.

Jago witnesses their vows and he wishes them every happiness, now that their time apart is at an end; he wishes for them the love he himself once shared with his wife, Julianne. He knows something about the pain of separation, for they'd had to wait three long years after his disappearance before they could finally, all too briefly, be reunited. Only after his death was officially declared could Julianne afford to discreetly buy the quiet island estate that would become their home – and Sonny's. It was there that he returned to her, as Neil Jacobs, an ordinary man, to live together in the kind of peace he'd so yearned for during his years of fame. The kind of peace he wishes now, for Cathy and Kip.

As the couple are declared husband and wife, old John Gale watches on from his recliner chair, weaker now, but strong enough to offer up his hands, his blessing, and, as requested, there is no churchy reserve at the announcement but whoops of applause, a stomping of happy feet.

'You did it!' Albie swoops into his parents' arms, quickly followed by Nell, as the puppy circles them, releasing a volley of excitable yips and muddying their ankles with his paws.

Jago steps back to retrieve his guitar, and the sun climbs further into the expansive morning sky, lighting up the rooftops and sheds of Allotment Row.

Seated on an upturned crate, Jago plays his guitar without thought; it is like breathing. He watches these people, planets orbiting around their sun, John Gale, and he wonders what the future holds for each of them, in this wondrous life of pain and joy.

Cathy laughs and hugs her daughter in a crushing embrace, and Jago thinks of their moment on Highcap Hill, when she'd shared with him her demons and his own had come rushing in to claim him. It was there and then that he had first experienced his grief for his Sonny, a grief so profound and delayed that he knew not what to do with it, and so he tucked it away for a later date. For, in that moment, he was there for these people, these living people, and so his own truth, by necessity, remained just out of reach.

Now, Albie joins him, arranging his keyboard and stand, nodding like an old bandmate as he falls into step with his piano harmony.

'I once had a son,' Jago tells him, feeling his soul lifted by the scene before them, a gathering of Gales swaying in the quiet morning light, taking in the music, and gifting their old man the last hurrah he'd wished for.

Albie smiles gently back at him.

'I once had a son,' Jago repeats, 'and a wife.' And the memory of that love fills him, and it is enough.

ACKNOWLEDGEMENTS

I've been fortunate enough to work with some real professionals in the fifteen years since my first book was published, with my most recent six going through the hands of the same agent, editor and copyeditor. In each case, we have developed a mutual trust, a shorthand of sorts, which means that, together, we care as deeply for each new book as we did for the last. I cannot understate the value of such relationships, and, while I send thanks to the entire publishing team who helped with this, my tenth book, a mention must go to these three wise women in particular: Kate Shaw, Sam Eades and Linda McQueen.

As always, thanks to my beloved Colin, Alice and Samson, and to my wider family, friends and cheerleaders. A special mention to an old pal, Chris Spirit, who shared with me generous insights into the world of private flying, on a phone call I made while hiking along the very same Dorset coastal path my fictional Nell walks in this book. Despite Chris's exceptional knowledge, I will have taken liberties on this subject, I'm sure. If you're a pilot or air traffic controller, forgive me.

Finally, huge thanks to my loyal readers. Many of you have been with me since *Glasshopper*, and I value you more than you can know.

Isabel Ashdown, 2024

CREDITS

Isabel Ashdown and Orion Fiction would like to thank everyone at Orion who worked on the publication of *Weathering* in the UK.

Editorial
Sam Eades
Snigdha Koirala

Copyeditor
Linda McQueen

Proofreader
Jade Craddock

Audio
Paul Stark
Louise Richardson

Contracts
Dan Herron
Ellie Bowker
Ollie Chacón

Design
Tomás Almeida

Editorial Management
Charlie Panayiotou
Jane Hughes
Bartley Shaw

Finance
Jasdip Nandra
Nick Gibson
Sue Baker

Production
Ruth Sharvell

Publicity
Sharina Smith

Sales

Catherine Worsley
Esther Waters
Victoria Laws
Toluwalope Ayo-Ajala
Rachael Hum
Ellie Kyrke-Smith
Frances Doyle
Georgina Cutler

Operations

Jo Jacobs